Praise for the

"A Perfect Ten! ... Debut author Diana Dempsey soars with *Falling Star*, a powerful, moving, riveting tale of greed and betrayal, love and self-discovery ... Excellent characterization, great dialogue, and non-stop action make the book almost impossible to put down ... Fast-paced, engaging, witty, and fun to read, *Falling Star* will grab you on the first page and hold you enthralled until the last. I highly recommend this fabulous book!"
– Susan Lantz, *Romance Reviews Today*

"Dempsey has reinvented the glitz novel for a new generation. This is glitz with heart! Clever and glamorous."
– *New York Times* bestselling author Jayne Ann Krentz

"(In *To Catch the Moon*) Alicia Maldonado, Deputy D.A. of Monterey County, CA, may have landed the case that could make her career: the murder of golden boy Daniel Gaines, who recently announced his candidacy for governor. Tough and self-assured, Alicia is a likable protagonist who achieved success through grit and determination ... Dempsey's low-on-glamour depiction of the D.A.'s office is on the mark, lending much credibility to this suspenseful novel. The romantic sparring between Alicia and Milo sparkles with wit and adds sensuality to this sizzling, tension-filled mystery."
– *Romantic Times*

"Skillfully plotted and filled with realistic detail ... (*To Catch the Moon*) deftly interweaves romance, murder, and ambition with issues of social status and trust."
– Kristin Ramsdell, *Library Journal*

"Diana Dempsey creates realistic and memorable characters, complete with flaws, that you can really root for; then she puts them into trouble so terrible you can't figure out how they'll ever triumph ... This is an author to watch."
— *Books for a Buck*

"Spicy, sexy, and sultry: (in *Too Close to the Sun*) popular Dempsey has another hit on her hands."
— *Booklist*

"A complex story with several exciting threads, *Too Close to the Sun* is the romance of Gabby and Will ... Kept apart by their extreme differences, their road is rocky and sometimes seems an impossible journey, but one that comes to a wonderfully satisfying conclusion ... This is a book that will long live in my memory ... *Too Close to the Sun* is an absolute must-buy for everyone, and I highly recommend it."
— Diana Risso, *Romance Reviews Today*

"In each of her books, Dempsey features such strong heroines and pairs them with the perfect match, thus creating fabulous contemporary romances. She has a permanent place on my book shelves!"
— Tracy Marsac, *Romance Junkies*

"How can you not like a character named Happy Pennington, the daughter of a retired cop and the current reigning Ms. America? Well, I liked her! And her sidekicks in crime-solving, fellow beauty queens Shanelle and Trixie, and a hunk named Mario Suave (yes!) and you have a fast-paced, funny, roller coaster ride ... The Beauty Queen Mysteries are on my must-read list, and I can't wait for the next installment."
— Jacqueline Vick, *A Writer's Jumble*

Available from Diana Dempsey

Falling Star

To Catch the Moon

Too Close to the Sun

Chasing Venus

Ms America and the Offing on Oahu

Ms America and the Villainy in Vegas

Ms America and the Mayhem in Miami

Ms America and the Whoopsie in Winona

Ms America and the Brouhaha on Broadway

A Diva Wears the Ring (novella)

Ring of Truth (featuring the novella *A Diva Wears the Ring*)

Social Media

www.DianaDempsey.com

www.Facebook.com/DianaDempseyBooks

www.Twitter.com/Diana_Dempsey

TO CATCH THE MOON
Diana Dempsey

BRAMERTON
PRESS

This is a work of fiction. Names, characters, places, and incidents are either the product of the author's imagination or are used fictitiously, and any resemblance to actual persons, living or dead, business establishments, events, or locales is entirely coincidental.

To Catch the Moon
All Rights Reserved
Copyright © 2011 by Diana Dempsey
Cover design by Freshwater Design

This book may not be reproduced in whole or in part, by any means, without permission.

ISBN: 978-1480209916
First electronic edition May 2011

Dear Reader,

To Catch the Moon is special to me in part because it takes place on the Monterey Peninsula, a part of the world that I love. It's also where I married. My husband and I return every year and find it as enchanting as the year before.

I hope you enjoy the book, and my other work as well. I would love to hear from you! I can be contacted at my web site, **www.DianaDempsey.com**, on **Faceboook** at **Diana Dempsey Books**, and on **Twitter** at **Diana_Dempsey**.

All best to you! Keep reading.

Diana Dempsey

To Jed

CHAPTER ONE

Alicia Maldonado exited the Monterey County district attorney's office into the high-ceilinged, red-tiled entry hall of the courthouse, nearly empty on a Saturday afternoon. Her arms full of case documents, she let the D.A. office's heavy glass door slam shut behind her and strode toward the stairs that would carry her to the third floor and the superior courts, where prosecutors like her spun tales of true crime to persuade juries to render just punishment. Which worked most of the time, but as Alicia knew all too well, not always.

Three in the afternoon and outside the courthouse it was chilly and overcast, a December wind whipping down the streets carrying with it the unmistakable whiff of manure that indicated farm work was close at hand. To the east rose the Gabilan Mountains, the Santa Lucias to the west, two formidable ranges that stood sentry over California's Salinas Valley, trapping heat in summer and cold in winter and farm smells year-round. Sometimes the valley was a beautiful place, Alicia knew, especially in spring when the rich soil gave birth to endless fields of blue-white lupins and wildly cheerful orange and gold California poppies. But Salinas itself, the county's little capital seat, wasn't exactly a picture postcard. It was too dull, too dusty and flat, too much a throwback to the 1940s. And as a street-corner Salvation Army Santa tolled his bell trying in vain to improve his take, it was too poor to do much about it.

Inside the courthouse, Alicia mounted the last flight of stairs and hit the third-floor landing, where a Charlie Brown Christmas tree strung with multicolored lights held rather pathetic pride of place. She met the eyes of Lionel Watkins, a burly black janitor who was as much a courthouse fixture as she was and had been for so long he was nearing retirement. He paused in his mopping to shake his head when he saw her. "You at it again? And on a Saturday?"

"Will you let me in?"

"Honey, don't I always? Even against my better judgment." He leaned his mop handle against a lime-green wall, a discount color found only in county buildings and VA hospitals, and without further instruction made for Superior Court Three, Alicia's good-luck courtroom. "You always win," he said. "I don't get why you bother to practice."

"I win *because* I practice."

"You win because you's good." They arrived at the courtroom door. On the opposite wall hung a hand-lettered sign: ONLY FOUR MORE SHOPLIFTING DAYS UNTIL CHRISTMAS. Apparently the sign had been hung on Tuesday, since numbers eight through five were crossed out. Lionel selected a key from a massive ring and poked it at the lock. "At least Judge Perkins is long gone on his Christmas vacation." He swung the door open and gave her a quizzical look. "So when you gonna run for judge again? Third time's the charm, they say."

Annoyance flashed through her, cold and fast. "I have no idea," she snapped, and pushed past him into the darkened courtroom. He raised the overhead lights, chasing the shadows from the jury box, which even empty seemed strangely watchful. Alicia turned back around and forced her voice to soften. "Thanks, Lionel. What'll I do when you get your pension?"

He chuckled. "Find some other soft touch." Then he was gone, the tall oak door clicking softly shut behind him.

Alicia dumped the file for case number 02-F987 on the

prosecution table, then loosed her dark wavy hair from its plastic butterfly clip and gathered it up again atop her head, a neatening ritual she went through a dozen times a day, whenever she stopped one task and began another. She shed the black jacket she wore over her jeans and white turtleneck. The jacket was getting that telltale shiny veneer that came from too many dry cleanings. That was a worry. Clothes were expensive and her budget beyond shot.

She chuckled without humor. She could barely afford to maintain a decent wardrobe. How was she supposed to pay for a campaign? Especially now, when nobody would put up a dime for a woman considered damaged goods?

Oh, she'd had her golden-girl period, when some of the top people in her party thought she was the next great Latina hope. She knew how they spoke of her: well-spoken, beautiful, star prosecutor, pulled herself up by her bootstraps, determined to win political office and do a good turn for the forgotten many who, like her, came from the wrong side of the tracks. It was PC to the max and a great story, or at least it had been until she lost. Twice. Then the bloom was off the rose. And off her.

She threw back her head and gazed at the huge wall-mounted medallion of The Great State of California. It baffled her no end how she'd managed to go from promising to stalled in the blink of an eye. Now she was a thirty-five-year-old shopworn specimen with a dead-end career and no man in sight, at least none she wanted. That was sure a prescription for a merry Christmas and a happy New Year.

Enough already! Get over yourself and practice the opening statement. "You're right," she muttered. Before long it would be Monday, nine in the morning, and she'd have to go to work persuading the jury to convict. She dug into her pile of papers for the yellow legal pad on which she'd scrawled her notes. But it wasn't there.

Damn, she must've left it on her desk. She'd have to go back and get it. She made tracks out of the courtroom and back down to the D.A.'s office, where she punched in the numbers on the code-pad door to buzz herself in.

She was partway down the narrow cubicle-lined corridor to her office when she realized that the main phone line kept ringing. It would ring, get picked up by voice mail, and ring again. Over and over. Somebody wanted to reach somebody, badly.

She marched back to the receptionist's desk and picked up the line. "Monterey County District Attorney."

"It's Bucky Sheridan." One of Carmel PD's veteran beat cops but not the brightest bulb. "Who's this?"

"Alicia. What's up?"

"I gotta talk to Penrose."

She had to laugh. As if D.A. Kip Penrose were ever in the office on a Saturday. He was barely there on weekdays. "Bucky, you're not going to find Penrose here. Try his cell."

"I have. All I get is his voice mail."

"Well, he's probably got it turned off." That was standard procedure, too. "Anyway, what's so desperate? What do you need?"

Silence. Then, "We got a situation here, Alicia."

She frowned. It was at that moment she realized Bucky didn't sound like his usual potbellied, aw-shucks self. "What do you mean, a situation?"

"I'm at Daniel Gaines' house. On Scenic, in Carmel."

"*The* Daniel Gaines?" Something niggled uncomfortably in her gut. "The Daniel Gaines who just announced he's running for governor?"

"He's not running for anything anymore." By now Bucky was panting. "He's dead."

***

"A minute back from commercial."

From his perch at the anchor desk, Milo Pappas nodded at the warning from the floor manager, who stood half-hidden in the shadows in the cavernous Manhattan studio where the *WBS Evening News* was taped every evening at six-thirty. This being a Saturday, it was the flagship broadcast's less illustrious weekend edition. But it was *Evening* all the same, and hence a new feather appeared in Milo's journalistic cap every time he broke from his *Newsline* correspondent duties to fill in as anchor.

Milo skimmed the lead-in to the last piece, all he had left to read save the promo for the Sunday-morning interview show and the good-bye. He was proud of himself. Despite his initial nervousness he hadn't bobbled a single word, managing to project the approachable yet authoritative demeanor WBS sought in its anchors. Millions of Americans from Kennebunkport to San Diego were watching, but Milo was far more aware of the handful of top WBS management scrutinizing his performance from their weekend homes on Long Island and in the Hamptons.

Suddenly he heard the director yammer in his earpiece. "We got an urgent bulletin, Milo—we're killing the last piece. You need to ad-lib it. Ninety seconds max. We're getting hard copy out to you"—and indeed just as the stage manager gave the thirty-second warning, a young female production assistant ran into the studio bearing wire copy—"so go to the good-bye whenever you're ready and we'll close out with a bump shot. You know the Daniel Gaines story, right?"

Milo's heart thumped against his rib cage. He certainly did know it, though truth be told he was far more intimately acquainted with Daniel Gaines' wife than with the man himself.

"Fifteen," the stage manager announced.

Milo grabbed the wire copy and struggled to grasp what he couldn't believe he was reading. The "Dewey Beats Truman" headline notwithstanding, urgent bulletins seldom got anything this big completely wrong.

He raised his eyes to the lens, addressing *Evening*'s director in the control booth. "You've got confirmation?"

"From the police department in Carmel, California, where the guy lives." The director paused, then, "You're sure you can handle the ad-lib, Milo?"

He felt a stab of irritation. "Watch me."

Then, "Ten," the stage manager intoned, "four, three ... we're on the wide shot—"

Two seconds before the director shifted to him straight up on Camera One, Milo raised his gaze to the lens, willed himself to keep his composure, and began speaking.

"We have an urgent bulletin tonight out of Carmel, California. Police there have confirmed that Daniel Gaines, who just last month announced his bid for governor of California, today was found dead in his home, the victim of an apparent homicide."

Milo surprised himself with how calm he sounded, as if to him this were no more than just a shocking news event, as if he didn't have years of personal history with the people involved.

"Gaines was a newcomer to politics," he went on, "but he gained a national reputation as chief executive of Headwaters Resources, a timber company that's won praise for preserving the so-called old-growth forest. Political insiders say Gaines also profited from his tie with the California-based Hudson family. Two and a half years ago"—Milo would never forget the date; it was seared in his memory—"he married Joan

Hudson, the only child of late California governor and US senator Web Hudson."

And, Milo added silently, allowing himself one beat to look down from the lens and take a single sustaining breath, *the only woman who ever kissed me off and never looked back.*

***

Joan Hudson Gaines veered toward the stairs that would carry her to the second floor, away from the cops who had invaded her home, her slight body pitched forward as if that would get her there faster. Once inside the master bathroom she slammed shut the door and flipped on the light switch. Then she saw her face in the mirror. Mottled skin, too-shiny eyes, blond Medusa hair. She snapped the light off and collapsed onto the mausoleum-cold porcelain of the Jacuzzi tub, rubbing her temples, trying to make her head not spin.

She must control herself. It was a mistake to let the cops see her so upset. She did the right thing to escape upstairs, away from their prying eyes. She should have done it earlier.

What a horrific day! If her father were here, he'd fix it. He'd make those cops stop tromping through her house as if they owned it. But he was dead, too, he couldn't help. And her mother had chosen this exact weekend to go to Santa Barbara.

Why were the cops so slow to collect their evidence? A petrifying notion shot through her, a thought that wouldn't leave her alone. What if they considered her a suspect? All those questions they asked! Why had she been in Santa Cruz last night? Why had she gone without her husband, only a few days before Christmas? Had she called him? Why not?

She raised her chin defiantly, though her pouty lower lip trembled. She'd told them only what she wanted to and not a word more. Why in the world should she? She was a Hudson.

Joan's bravado fled as quickly as it had risen. She rocked back and forth, cold, so cold, her body a foreign thing that trembled uncontrollably. There was so much blood! How could one man have so much blood? It seemed big as a lake on the library's hardwood floor, Daniel lying in the middle of it like a marooned ship. She wished she'd never seen it in the clear light of day, because now that she had, she would never forget it. That was how she would remember Daniel.

Daniel, her husband. Her husband, Daniel. Dead.

Snippets of memory careened unbidden into her frazzled brain. Meeting him at the Cafe d'Orsay in New York, stunned into silence by the tall, blond Adonis across the proverbial crowded room. Falling into a canopied bed at the Hotel Pierre the first time they made love, a bed over which he had strewn the petals of a dozen red roses. Their June wedding on the lawn of her parents' Pebble Beach estate, five hundred people bearing witness, the Pacific surf a crashing counterpoint to their vows. Back then he had made her feel like his entire world revolved around her. Before it all changed, before the cosmos tipped on its side and he started expecting her to revolve around him.

That was over. Now he was dead. Gone. Daniel was dead.

A widow, Daniel made me a widow. Joan shuddered. That made her feel ancient. Ancient and used up. But she was young, only thirty, and had all of life ahead of her. That was one thing Daniel couldn't take away.

Her back stiffened. In fact, Daniel couldn't take anything away from her anymore. That whole mess with Headwaters and her father's living trust? That would clear up now.

There was another good thing, too. The campaign was over. She wouldn't have to play the adoring political wife for the next eight years. And it would have been eight years, because Daniel would've won this election and then he would've won the next.

And you know why? she asked her dead husband silently. *Because of Daddy. And me.*

Maybe now with Daniel gone, *she'd* get credit for all she'd accomplished. People would seek *her* out, ask for *her* advice. Maybe at long last *she'd* be a dinner party's star attraction.

She certainly deserved to be, far more than Daniel had. He only basked in the Hudson family light. She cast it.

CHAPTER TWO

It was just five in the afternoon, but what little sun the Monterey Peninsula had enjoyed that winter solstice day was long gone from the sky. A drizzle was falling, a mist really, just enough to dampen the pavement, blur the view, and chill your bones.

Alicia shivered, staring out the floor-to-ceiling windows of the enormous steel-and-glass structure that Daniel Gaines had called home. They overlooked Carmel Bay and the Point, one of the most exquisite vistas money could buy, a sweep of sea and sand that all day had been overhung with gloom as if to reflect the horror that had transpired.

What Bucky had told her—she couldn't get it out of her mind. What a horrible way for a man to die. How grotesque; how primitive. She knew she shouldn't leap to conclusions, yet one was so very obvious. Still, she had to wait and see what the totality of evidence revealed.

She glanced down at the checklist in her hand, scrawled on the yellow legal pad that also held her notes for Monday's opening statement, whose importance was now dwindling into near nothingness. The top page had no heading, but she might as well have written: *How to wrest control of the Gaines case and jump-start your life,* by Alicia Maldonado.

In a small-time D.A.'s office like Monterey County's, there was a kind of finder's-keeper's rule regarding the best cases. When something high-profile happened, which almost never did, a prosecutor who got to the scene first could lay claim. It was ambulance chasing, county-style, about the only way a prosecutor could advance her career.

Well, she got there first. She could lay claim. Besides, she'd won more cases than any other prosecutor. *Penrose has to assign me this case. I'm the best he's got.*

And the bottom line was, this was big-time. Murders didn't happen in Carmel-by-the-Sea. But now one had, and of a gubernatorial candidate, no less. It could make or break the prosecutor who argued the case, depending on whether or not she screwed up. That explained the sick feeling in Alicia's stomach.

She forced her attention back to her list, the only thing that afternoon anchoring her to a sane reality. Item one: *Get the DOJ criminalists.* Done. They were in the house collecting evidence. *Get Niebaum.* Done. The pathologist was bent over what they had all begun to call "the body." *Get Penrose.* Done, unfortunately, because she had to. He was on his way. *Call the Gaines campaign.* Done, with a promise to call again when she had more info.

Her cell rang. She flipped it open. "Maldonado."

"Alicia, it's Rocco."

Great. Rocco Messina, the second-winningest prosecutor in the Monterey County district attorney's office, clearly calling to sniff out the situation and see if it was possible for him to sneak in.

Sorry, pal.

She made herself sound harried. "I apologize, Rocco, but I don't have time to fill you in right now." She thought fast. "Kip and I'll put together a briefing for the office Monday. See you then."

She nearly hung up but he kept talking. "Kip assigned you the case?"

"Yes," she lied, and this time did hang up. Another sin on

her Saturday scorecard, and this four days before Christmas. Some Catholic she made.

Well, she told herself, she needed advancement more than Rocco Messina did, and it looked like she was going to get it on the back of a dead man. A famous dead man. So there you go. Sometimes a woman had to do what a woman had to do.

She looked around, tentatively venturing farther away from the front windows, wary of disturbing evidence. The house amazed her, and not in a positive way. It was named *Dorado del Mar* since houses in Carmel didn't have addresses but names, a cute-ism that meant people had to trot to the post office every day to get their mail. But what a pretentious choice! Golden Treasure by the Sea? It irked her that white-bread Joan and Daniel Gaines had picked a Spanish name. Somehow it seemed they had no right. And the place looked more like a modern-art museum than a home. Alicia half expected to find a souvenir shop around one of its angular corners. It didn't have much in it, and what it did have was glass or metal, nothing plump or soft or squishy. It was impossible to find anything you actually wanted to touch.

Though of course it was tremendously valuable. People said the cheapest properties on Scenic near the Point went for five million bucks, and those were the tiny board-and-batten cottages. From the mid-nineties, Carmel-by-the-Sea had become an odd place. Few of the founding writers, artists, and poets who had given Carmel its bohemian flavor were left. Now most of the properties were second homes. There were almost no kids, because nobody who had kids could afford to live there. Prices had been driven up by the rich Texans and dot-commers who snapped up the beachfront, then tore down the classic chalkstone bungalows to put up monstrosities like the one she was standing in now. She remembered reading how Joan and Daniel Gaines had railroaded the planning commission into granting them the permits to build, even though they were going to obstruct lots of people's views.

Nice. But then again they didn't have to be. The Hudson family was American aristocracy, like West Coast Kennedys. They could do pretty much whatever they wanted.

She returned to the window and peered outside. The Carmel police, with the aid of the county sheriff's department, had cordoned off the property with sawhorses and yellow crime tape, keeping the huge number of reporters and TV crews thirty yards at bay. They huddled in the chilly air and except for the equipment looked like spectators for a late-season football game. But the only kickoff here would be of a media circus.

A commotion at the crowd's edge caught her eye. A tall man, mid-fifties, good-looking in an aging Ivy League way, moved importantly along the sawhorses, greeting the reporters, shaking hands, no doubt remembering names like the politician Alicia knew he lived to be. His face wore a grave look, as if to convey that he was the man who would distill this tragedy to its essence when the right moment came. She shook her head in disgust. Now it would really start. One of the clowns had arrived.

Monterey County District Attorney Kip Penrose made a noisy show of promising to return soon with a statement, then let himself past the crime tape and in through the home's front door, reeking of pomposity and sea air.

"Alicia." His voice was clipped. He took off his trench coat, as usual avoiding her eyes. She knew Kip Penrose wanted as little as possible to do with his rebel prosecutor, even visually.

"Hello, Kip."

"Where are we here?"

"Everything's in order. Shikegawa and Johnson are

making progress. Niebaum is going to be a while."

Andy Shikegawa and Lucy Johnson were the two Department of Justice criminalists she'd called to the scene; Dr. Ben Niebaum was the pathologist. Bucky Sheridan, the veteran Carmel PD beat cop who'd answered the initial call, had rapidly been sidelined as higher authority arrived. Alicia thought he seemed grateful to be relegated to crime-tape duty.

They were nervous, all of them. The shadow of botched high-profile cases hung in the air like smoke from a distant fire. O. J. Simpson stood in one corner; Claus von Bulow in the other. *Just do everything by the book*, Alicia told herself, which was easier said than done when she wasn't entirely sure what the book said. She'd successfully prosecuted two homicides but had never actually been at a "fresh" crime scene. Or seen a "body."

Penrose folded his overcoat and laid it on the floor. Rule one: Don't touch anything. "Who found him?" he asked.

"Gaines' wife. She told Bucky she got home this morning about eleven from Santa Cruz, from some overnight party she always has the weekend before Christmas with old friends from Stanford." Alicia paused. The next bit was weird. "She says she didn't find him till the afternoon."

Penrose skated right past that. "So it was Joan who called 911?"

Joan. On such familiar terms with her, wasn't he, old Kip. "At two-thirty." Alicia consulted her notes. "When Bucky got here ten minutes later she was standing in the street, pacing. He said she was kind of wild-eyed, kept messing with her hair, couldn't talk straight. Hyperventilating."

He frowned. "And Bucky calmed her down?"

That was hard to fathom. "Well, he talked to her for a few minutes, until she ran upstairs to the master bathroom."

"Where is she now?"

"Still there."

Penrose's face took on a horrified expression. "Still?"

"Chill out, Kip." She couldn't hide her irritation. "She's fine. I go up every once in a while to check on her through the door. She just wants to be left alone."

He seemed mildly placated. "Daniel Gaines was a great man," he declared quietly, then turned away, and Alicia was overcome by a wave of disgust, as un-PC as that might be while the man in question lay murdered in the next room.

Did no one else see Daniel Gaines for what he was? She'd read the newspaper articles; she'd seen the TV stories. And it seemed pretty clear to her that he was an opportunistic carpetbagger who married the daughter of a former governor and used the millions he'd raked in from his timber business to launch a gubernatorial campaign. Did any of that make him a great man? Hard to see how.

"Kip." She decided to broach the hot topic right away. Take the bull by the horns, seize the moment, just do it. "We need to talk about who's going to handle—"

His cell phone rang, cutting her off. He turned away and put on his official voice. "Penrose," he announced, then his tone slid from cocksure to sycophantic. "Libby, I am so sorry. So very sorry ..."

Damn. Now he'd never get off the phone. Elizabeth "Libby" Storrow Hudson, Gaines' mother-in-law and the widow of former governor Web Hudson, was one of Penrose's biggest campaign donors, hence an enormous blip on his political radar screen. She was one of those aristocratic types: richer than God, white-haired, thin-lipped, permanently wearing a disapproving expression. A Boston Brahmin, people called her, though Alicia wasn't sure what that meant. Quite a character, though. Alicia remembered reading that she'd even competed in the Olympic trials in her youth.

"You're in Santa Barbara?" she heard Penrose say. "Ah, at the San Ysidro Ranch."

A major destination for the rich and famous, Alicia knew, where JFK and Jackie had honeymooned in the fifties.

Penrose fell silent. Then, "One of my aides told me Joan is holding up all right and I was just about to confirm that for myself."

One of my aides. Alicia rolled her eyes.

"Yes," he went on, "let me put you through to her ..." and Penrose headed upstairs, cell phone in hand, his deputy D.A. forgotten, clearly caught up in his critical role of connecting mother and daughter at this tragic hour.

Alicia and Kip Penrose had a robust mutual dislike. She was a holdover from the prior D.A., and when Penrose had ridden in on his horse he'd promptly demoted every prosecutor who wasn't a stalwart in his own party. She'd been among the first to fall, losing her post as a department head.

Matters hadn't improved when he'd gotten a taste of how combative she could be. Penrose was big on plea bargaining—he was big on everything that meant less work—but Alicia was not. Sure, four out of five cases you did have to plea-bargain, but some just stuck in your craw: You knew the guy was guilty, you knew you'd be committing a sin against God and country to let him off. So she wouldn't, even though Penrose badgered her to, even though he told her she was "clogging up the system." To Penrose, the "justice" in "justice system" got lost somewhere in his postelection high.

"Penrose get here?" Andy Shikegawa, a mid-forties Japanese-American and, in Alicia's opinion, wildly competent criminalist, entered the room from the rear. Where the library—and Gaines' body—were located. "I thought I heard his voice."

"He just went upstairs."

Shikegawa regarded her through small wire-framed glasses. "You can probably go, Alicia. We're pretty much under control here."

"No," she said. "I'll stay."

"I don't want you to ..." He paused. "I don't know, get your hopes up."

She was silent. Was it so obvious?

"Penrose won't let this one get away," Shikegawa went on. "Especially not to you."

"But I'm here. I got you, and everybody else, in here." She couldn't help but protest. "Plus he hasn't handled a case in years. And he has a conflict of interest."

"Because he knew Gaines? That's hardly a conflict."

"Because the Hudson family is one of his biggest donors." But that wasn't necessarily a conflict either, though she didn't like to admit it. And it sure would be Penrose-like to lay claim to a case, for the first time in years, because it was high-profile.

Damn him. The ball of worry in her stomach churned as she felt herself careen from nervous to angry. She'd really be pissed if Penrose grabbed this case out from underneath her.

Shikegawa cocked his chin at the ceiling. "You know, maybe we should get the missus out of here before we move the body."

Alicia's heart rate ramped back up. "Are we at that point?"

"Niebaum says probably another hour."

They regarded each other silently. Then, "Should we widen the cordon around the property?" she asked.

"The cameras would still get the shot. I think the best thing is to tent the gurney."

"That'll raise a lot of questions."

"What choice do we have?"

She hesitated. "So it's still..."

"It's still in him." Shikegawa pinched the bridge of his nose, pushing up his glasses. "It's not coming out till the autopsy."

That shut them both up. Through the huge front windows they could see the glare of TV camera lights as reporters lined up in front of the property to do live shots for the local 5:30 PM news shows. She couldn't even imagine the commotion that would ensue when they rolled Gaines' body out, tented in a gurney.

"So"—she couldn't help it; she was damn curious—"what kind of evidence have you been able to get?"

"I have to say, a lot." Shikegawa started ticking off on his fingers. "The murder weapon, of course, with prints on it. Very clear bloody handprint on the wall, plus most of a footprint. More fingerprints all over the place."

"So if you can match the prints ..."

"Which I'm betting we can..."

They looked at each other. She waited until Shikegawa finished his thought. "Then this could be a slam-dunk."

***

Milo bided time in a cubicle in WBS's newsroom, the backdrop for *Evening*'s anchor set but decidedly unglamorous at 9:07 on a Saturday night. He wouldn't be sprung till ten, by which time the *WBS Evening News* would have aired in all continental US television markets and there would be no more opportunity to update the Gaines story. He'd already updated twice, for the feeds at seven and eight, despite how little fresh information had come in on the Reuters, UPI, and

AP wires. WBS execs clearly were going to milk this story for all it was worth. After all, how often did a telegenic young candidate who married into one of the country's highest-profile families get murdered in his home?

Milo was still stunned. Still, on some level, disbelieving.

And profoundly exhausted, as if Daniel Gaines' death had drained the lifeblood out of him.

He sank back in his chair, sipping lukewarm water from a Styrofoam cup and suffering one of those painful moments when he wondered what the hell he was doing with his life. Nothing like another man's death to beg that question. Sure, it was a glamorous gig being one of TV's most popular newsmen. But Milo was sufficiently self-aware to know it wasn't ability alone that had vaulted him to that position. He knew his movie-star looks not only worked wonders on female viewers but also cowed the often short, pale, brainy news management. On top of that Milo benefited from the exotic allure of being the youngest son of Greece's longtime ambassador to the United States.

He had learned, though, that there was a flip side to being blessed from birth with both looks and money. "Pretty-boy Pappas," *Newsline* executive producer Robert O'Malley called him, branding Milo from the get-go with the lightweight stigma. O'Malley was head of the anti-Milo Pappas faction at WBS and damn proud of it. He missed no opportunity to remind anyone who would listen that Milo hadn't exactly had to work his way up and so didn't deserve the fame and status he enjoyed.

The phone at Milo's elbow trilled, one blinking red light demanding attention. "Pappas," he answered.

"It's Robert," the caller said, and Milo's heart sank further. *Think of the devil.* "So much for the profile, I'd say," O'Malley went on.

Milo was silent. He'd never liked the idea of a *Newsline* profile on Daniel Gaines, entirely because he knew he'd be sucked into doing it. What a ratings grabber! Milo Pappas reporting on the very man who'd replaced him in Joan's affections. And even without the love-triangle aspect, Milo knew viewers would lap up the story of a dashing come-from-nowhere politician with national potential and a famous wife. Forty years later, Americans were still searching for another JFK. Briefly Milo shut his eyes. Looked like they found one, tragedy and all...

"Change in plans," O'Malley declared, and the note of triumph in his voice put Milo on alert. "The consensus is that we need you to get out to the Monterey Peninsula. Tomorrow morning. To cover the investigation and the—"

"Wait a minute." Like hell. He could smell O'Malley's machinations through the phone line. "Consensus? Among whom?"

"Lovegrove, Giordano, Cohen."

Damn. Milo could practically hear O'Malley's smirk and knew how the detestable sot had spent his Saturday night: working the phones, getting the news division's president, vice president, and domestic news producer all to agree that one man and one man only could do justice to the Gaines story. And this was a double win for O'Malley. Not only would he pump the ratings for *Newsline,* he could enjoy reminding Milo of the humiliation of getting dumped by Joan.

What a horrific time that had been. Milo didn't think he'd ever forget the tabloid headline: "Newsman Hunk Ditched by Politico's Daughter." He'd become a news story himself, of the most sordid kind, his indignity featured on everything from the *National Enquirer* to *Entertainment Tonight.*

"Sorry," Milo declared, though even as he said it he knew he couldn't refuse the assignment outright. O'Malley could really make hay out of that. "No can do. I'm anchoring *Evening* tomorrow night."

"I'm sorry, too." O'Malley even chuckled. "But don't worry about it. I've arranged for Jane Lerner to take over for you." Then he made his voice sound concerned. "I hope this doesn't upset your plans for Christmas."

A muscle began to work in Milo's jaw. "No," he lied, "not in the least."

"Good." O'Malley's voice was smooth. "You're booked on a flight out of Kennedy at seven in the morning. And even though these are tragic circumstances, this will give you a chance to renew your acquaintance with the Gaines family."

Softly, Milo hung up. *To hell with you, O'Malley*. He'd been checkmated. This time.

***

At quarter to eight in the evening, pathologist Ben Niebaum, MD, entered the Gaines' living room to declare that the body could be moved.

Alicia retreated from the window out of which she'd been staring for the last long, painful hour. Again her heart began racing. This must be like war, she thought, endless waiting punctuated by unexpected nerve-racking moments.

"The gurney is tented." Niebaum was nearing sixty and had the look of a seaman: bearded and weathered and wise. "Of course, given the situation we're not able to use a body bag. So beneath the tenting, the body is largely exposed."

Alicia and Penrose, now joined by Shikegawa, all nodded in silence.

"Is everybody out of the house but us?" Shikegawa asked.

"No." Penrose shook his head. "Mrs. Gaines is still upstairs. Her mother will come and get her, but that will still be some time. She's chartering a plane out of Santa Barbara."

"And the ambulance . . . "

"Is here," Alicia said. "We just need to get the gurney down the driveway." Again she went to peer out the window. It was pitch-dark, windy and rainy. The red and yellow lights of the waiting ambulance throbbed like a strobe, illuminating in pulsating beats the face of a reporter here, a sheriff's deputy there. "There are even more press now. And people who don't look like media at all, just gawkers." She turned to face the group, her heart thumping with a strange foreboding. "Time to tell Bucky we're coming out?"

"Let's roll," Shikegawa said, and the poor choice of words hung awkwardly in the air.

Alicia used her walkie-talkie to alert Bucky and the half dozen sheriff's deputies deployed outside to restrain the crowd. Then the paramedics entered the living room, rolling the gurney, its wheels noisy on the hardwood floor.

It was a weird-looking contraption, especially in the middle of that starkly elegant room. A yellow tarp hung like a shower curtain from metal bars that had been rigged three feet above the gurney to conceal the body on all sides.

They all stared. It was impossible not to. The body of the man who most likely would have been the next governor of California, and might well have made it all the way to the White House, lay strapped inside, lifeless. What a tale it could tell.

The paramedics rolled the gurney closer to the front door, where Alicia positioned herself at the ready. She took a deep breath.

"Count of three," Niebaum said. "One, two, three ..." and Alicia pulled open the front door, letting in a blast of cold, rainy air and triggering a commotion among the reporters, TV crews, and just plain curious pushing against the sawhorses and crime tape. Camera lights flared, reporters and photographers jostled, Alicia stepped aside, and the paramedics rolled past, one on each side of the gurney, Penrose strutting like a peacock just behind.

Alicia followed. The distance down the driveway to the waiting ambulance wasn't far, maybe thirty feet, but it was sloped and rain-slick. Wet wind lashed at her face and neck and quickly dampened her jeans, turtleneck, and jacket. The reporters were in full frenzy now, each struggling for a better position, shouting at one another to "Move!" and "Get left!" and "Hey, you! Down with that camera!"

The gurney had nearly reached the ambulance's open rear doors when someone shouted, "Watch it—you're in my shot!" Suddenly the mass of humanity surged forward like a rogue wave, sawhorses shoved aside like toy wagons.

The crowd pitched toward the ambulance, one pulsing uncontrollable mass, and Alicia watched with horror as one of the cameramen lost his balance and was shoved forcefully into the paramedics. The gurney, its makeshift tarpaulin tent whipped by the wind and the violent motion, rocked on its wheels while the paramedics struggled frantically to keep it righted. Alicia herself was stampeded by the mob and shoved back closer to the house, nearly to the front door.

Then it happened, another surge of jostling crews and reporters, and this time the paramedics couldn't hold on to the gurney. Alicia's hands rose to her mouth—*No!*—as it pitched violently to one side. Daniel Gaines' stiff, cadaver-white, half-naked corpse toppled onto the pavement and skidded a few feet until it came to rest. With, for one and all to see, a primitive homemade arrow piercing his blood-soaked chest.

CHAPTER THREE

God, her head pounded. Joan stared out the closed French doors of her ocean-view suite at the Lodge at Pebble Beach. It was an exclusive hotel, but still it was highly inconvenient to have to move out of her own home. Of course, after what had happened, she could hardly stay there.

Everything was so depressing. She sighed heavily, feeling very put-upon. Even by the weather. Beyond the French doors, Stillwater Cove was as steely gray as the late afternoon sky. Further across the water was Carmel Point, where somewhere in the mist her home stood cordoned off by crime tape. Far away she could hear sea lions bark, and close to her suite on the eighteenth green of the golf links a group of golfers bravoed each other every time one of them sank a putt.

Pound. Pound. The surf and her head. She dropped her chin and massaged her temples, round and round, increasing the pressure. No one understood how her headaches were worse than everyone else's. They were migraines, even if Dr. Finch couldn't diagnose them.

What a mess Daniel had left! Just twenty-four hours he'd been dead, and already her life was in chaos. She abandoned the windows to pace the pink-and-gray rectangle of Aubusson carpet next to the baby grand. Not only was the press hounding her, but Daniel's campaign aides, particularly that bitch Molly Bracewell, were circling constantly, wanting to know this, wanting to know that. That asinine D.A. Kip

Penrose kept calling her cell phone, six times just that day, to "keep her abreast" of developments.

The only consolation was that she had a plan. *Change creates opportunity*, her father always said, and for once she agreed with him. This was her chance, if she played it right.

The suite's buzzer sounded, a jackhammer on her brain. It had to be Henry Gossett, her father's attorney, whom she'd phoned the instant she got out of bed. Before letting him in, she paused at the foyer mirror. She plucked a speck of lint from her black wool trousers, teamed on this supposed day of mourning with a black cashmere turtleneck, and plumped her short blond hair. As often happened, she found herself slightly irritated with her reflection. She was so damn petite and pixieish, even in black it was a struggle not to look like Tinkerbell.

Finally she pulled open the suite's door. "Hello, Henry."

The attorney regarded her solemnly from the corridor. "Hello, Joan."

It was back in the seventies, when her father was serving his second term as mayor of San Francisco, that he had retained Henry Gossett as his personal counsel. Joan thought Gossett looked the same now as he had when she was five years old. Whatever the day, whatever the weather, he wore a suit and bow tie, with old-man's wire spectacles and, weirdest of all, a felt fedora. Henry Gossett was unbelievably staid and boring but he had one hugely redeeming characteristic: he would be loyal to the Hudsons to the end.

He entered the suite and set his fedora on the narrow foyer table below the mirror. "I am so very sorry, Joan." His expression was dour, though she couldn't remember ever seeing it otherwise. "This is an enormous tragedy."

"It's been unbelievably awful," she told him.

He nodded and spread his hands. "Whatever I can do..."

Joan nodded, then led Gossett into the suite. She knew full well that though he made all the right noises, Henry Gossett deeply disapproved of her late husband. *Sizzle but no steak*, she'd once overheard him say of Daniel in a rare, champagne-induced lapse. She might have been insulted, but by that point she agreed with the assessment.

She took a seat on the pale gray silk sofa in the main room and Gossett chose a matching wing chair. "Henry," she said, "I asked you here today because I have a few questions about my father's living trust. Now that I'll be trustee."

Gossett frowned and shifted, his gaze sliding away from her face. He looked damned uncomfortable. Joan suspected that like most people he expected a new widow to be so undone she couldn't think past her own grief. Well, that didn't describe this new widow.

He cleared his throat. "Joan, there is something you should know. Now that Daniel has passed away, your mother is the new trustee."

"What?" She could not have heard right. "My mother?"

"That is correct."

"But it should be me!" She was flabbergasted. "Why isn't it me?"

Gossett's frown deepened. "You know I'm not in a position to answer that question, Joan."

"Then who the hell is?" She rose to her feet and made her way to the French doors to stare out of them again, though nothing in the vista had changed. Stillwater Cove was as gray and choppy as ever. Maybe choppier. Angrier.

Unbelievable! She couldn't stop shaking her head. Again she'd been passed over, and again by her own father. She'd been livid when he'd picked Daniel over her as trustee in the first place, though it was all part and parcel of his blind eye where Daniel was concerned. But to heap insult over injury by passing over her again ...

And what did her mother know about managing money? Nothing. When had she ever gone to business school? Never. Joan was stunned. She'd assumed that after Daniel was gone it would be her in control for a change. But apparently not.

Would she always be underestimated? First by her father, then by her husband. Sometimes she felt as if people even thought more highly of her mother than they did of her. But what had Libby Storrow Hudson ever accomplished?

She turned from the view to face Henry Gossett. "What is the value of the trust's assets today?"

He hesitated. "I'm afraid I can't say, Joan. I don't have an exact figure."

"You mean you can't say because I'm not the trustee or you can't say because you don't know?"

He put on his patient voice, which irritated her further. "As a major beneficiary, Joan, you're certainly entitled to that information. I simply don't have an exact figure."

"It doesn't have to be exact. Ballpark."

Again he hesitated. "I truly can't say," he repeated. "The value fluctuates."

"Don't be such a lawyer, Henry!" she snapped. "What is it, give or take?"

He stared into the middle distance, as if calculating from rows of numbers. Then, finally, "Thirty million dollars."

She frowned. That was considerably less than she'd expected. "What about my father's stake in Headwaters?"

"Daniel purchased your father's stake, Joan." He spoke slowly, as if she wouldn't understand otherwise. "You and your mother received notification of that earlier this month."

She was impatient. "Yes, I am aware of that. But I thought the stake would revert back to the trust now that Daniel is dead."

"No, that transaction is complete. It won't revert back. It—"

"Then where is that stake now?"

"It's part of Daniel's estate. So—"

"Ah." She turned away from Gossett, her mind working. That was fine, then. She knew Daniel had a simple will, one that left everything to her. If he ever had plans to change it, he never got around to acting on them. She knew that for a fact.

She returned to the sofa and sat down. "I'll want to see the trust assets listed on a spreadsheet, Henry. I'd like you to come back the day after Christmas with it."

Gossett hesitated. "Joan, Dodie and I were planning to spend Christmas with our daughter in Boston. We have a new grandchild."

She was astounded. How could Gossett possibly be so self-absorbed as to consider taking a trip now, when she was in such a crisis? "Well," she said tightly, "I'm sure you'll find a way to do the right thing." Then she rose and walked to the foyer. This highly unsatisfactory meeting was over.

Gossett rose and followed her, returning his fedora to the top of his head. "Again, Joan, I am so very sorry."

"Yes. Good-bye," and she opened the door to let him out.

These damn men! She rested her forehead against the door after Gossett left and shut her eyes. A pain, surprisingly raw after all this time, shot through her. Again her father had passed her over, underestimated her, thought her capable of so little. How ironic that the one time she earned his approval was when she married Daniel. That turned out to be the biggest mistake of her life.

She needed a drink. She headed for the suite's wet bar. And what was this about the trust being worth only thirty million dollars? The only comforting possibility was that Gossett was being conservative in his estimate. That would be just like him.

She poured herself a scotch, then sipped at the crystal tumbler, its contents warm down her throat. The ache in her temples worsened, throbbing like dull blades against her skull. She decided to pop a few aspirin as well, resisting the impulse to take the Xanax Dr. Finch had prescribed her. She should be careful with those. Minutes later, listless, she wandered into the bedroom and switched on the TV.

She watched for a long time, propped up against the pillows, getting drowsy from the combination of aspirin and alcohol. Aimlessly she channel-surfed, until suddenly a familiar face appeared on the screen. She started, then stared at the flickering image. Tall, curly dark hair, broad shoulders, features that might have been stolen from a Greek god.

Milo. Milo Pappas. In Carmel.

Her heart pounded. The remote slipped from her hand onto the floor, where the plush carpet dulled the sound of its fall.

Milo. She narrowed her eyes, assessing how he'd changed in the years since they'd been together. Physically, very little. But professionally, quite a bit. She knew he'd risen through the ranks at WBS, even become a household name. Funny. Back when they'd dated, she thought he wouldn't amount to much. But apparently he'd become quite the network-news star.

She smiled, overcome by a surge of affection. Milo had always been so nice to her. He had always appreciated her. Unlike some people.

Mesmerized, she smiled at his image on the screen. And now Milo Pappas was back in Carmel. Imagine that.

***

Alicia raised bloodshot eyes from her dog-eared copy of

the California Penal Code, a navy volume with the size and heft of a big-city phone book, and considered the wisdom of making a third pot of coffee. The red numbers on her digital clock read 2:36 PM, and already she was terrifyingly close to caffeine-wired. She'd been in her office since dawn, after allowing herself four hours of sleep. The fact that it was a Sunday, and three days before Christmas, was irrelevant. She didn't want anything to happen in the Gaines case that she didn't know about. And the best way to make sure of that, in these early days when the situation was highly fluid, was to remain at Case Central, otherwise known as the D.A.'s office.

Penrose hadn't assigned the case to her yet. She wasn't surprised, but it worried her. After the chaos of Daniel Gaines's corpse pitching off the gurney in full view of the media, with the footage then being broadcast nonstop around the globe, she hadn't been able to get a word in edgewise with him. Nor had he shown up yet in the office. On a normal weekend Kip would never appear at work, but in these circumstances she expected that even he would put himself out.

Nothing could move slowly in this case: it was too high-profile. Everyone in the state, in the *country*, was watching. The pressure to name a suspect grew more intense by the hour; the speculation in the media more fevered. Everything else got shoved aside. The autopsy was already done. They could get a match on the fingerprints at any time. Soon, very soon, they might have enough to issue an arrest warrant. And once they did, Penrose would be forced to name a prosecutor.

She shivered, out of both fear and anticipation. In the last twelve hours she'd grown even more desperate for Penrose to assign her the case. Most prosecutors went through their entire careers without even getting near a case like this one. She couldn't let it slip away. She would stay till midnight if she had to, and beyond. She would sleep here. She would eat here. She would make Penrose give her the case, and she would win it.

Her phone rang and she almost jumped out of her chair. She grabbed the receiver before the second ring. "Maldonado."

"*Hola,*" said a man's voice.

She let out a sigh. "Hi, Jorge."

He laughed. "Think you can sound a little more enthusiastic?"

She raised her eyes to the ceiling. "Sorry. It's just—"

"I know, I know, you're working." He paused and his voice softened. "*Es que me haces falta.*"

She sighed. Not only did he miss her; he told her so. The damn thing was that most women would die to have Jorge Ramon in love with them. Her mother thought she was certifiable. Maybe she was. What Jorge had going for him, especially compared to what passed for an eligible bachelor in Salinas, was unbelievable.

He was Mexican. He was Catholic. He was thirty-nine and never married. He owned his own home. He didn't have any kids. He didn't have an ex-wife. He didn't do drugs or screw around. He didn't have a temper. He'd never been arrested. Not only did he accept her work, he even claimed to admire it. He was cute, or at least cute-ish. And to top it all off, he was a doctor. With, as her mother constantly reminded her, *su propria consulta privada.*

It was yet another way Alicia baffled Modesta Maldonado and the dozens of other Maldonados she called family. *Well, join the club.* She baffled herself.

"I miss you, too, Jorge," she lied.

"We never got to decorate the tree yesterday."

"No, we didn't." Her tree, he meant, because he'd

decorated his own a good two weeks back, being wildly efficient in every way. She'd worked that night, and winced remembering how she'd lied to him then, too. Oh, yes, she remembered saying, she would have loved stringing popcorn and drinking egg nog and listening to Frank Sinatra Christmas albums. That did sound fun, actually. She just dreamed of doing it with a man other than Jorge Ramon.

"Any new developments?" he asked.

"Nothing yet. But I'm expecting something soon..." she added hastily, to head off the very suggestion that next tripped off Jorge's lips.

"How about dinner? Especially since we missed last night."

She made herself sound regretful. "I can't, Jorge. I just can't. I have to stick around. Something could come down at any—"

"Okay, I understand. I just miss you."

"I miss you, too." Oops, she did it again.

"*Te amo.*"

" 'Bye." Softly, very softly, she replaced the receiver, as if to lessen the hurt of not responding in kind.

She had the same guilty feeling she often did about Jorge, the same worry that she was screwing him indirectly, like a sin of omission. A venial sin, she told herself, not the kind that'll land you in hell for all eternity. But she gave herself leeway, as she always did. She didn't know she wasn't going to end up with Jorge. It would only be bad if she knew, because then she'd be leading him on, giving him false hope.

The raw truth was that Jorge served a cynical purpose in her romantic life. He allowed her to be dating someone truly worthy, someone other people, even she sometimes, thought was a keeper, while still secretly keeping her options open. She had a companion whenever she wanted one. She had someone to watch videos with on Saturday night. She had a bedmate. More than anything else she had an answer for those pesky questions about her love life. "How's Jorge?" someone would ask. "Oh, he's great," she'd say, and she'd smile, like she was the most satisfied woman in the world and Jorge Ramon was a bedroom stallion and everything was on course for the diamond solitaire, the picket fence, and the Baby Bjorn carryall.

The truest, innermost secret was her sneaking suspicion that if she did say yes to Jorge, she'd lose part of her soul, some essential bit that made her Alicia. It would fly away, never to be found again, and its loss would leave her dried out and disappointed.

Did all this make her terrible? she wondered. Or did it just make her like a man?

Alicia rubbed her eyes, deeply tired. She would make more coffee, she decided. And she'd forage in Joyce Ching's desk for a chocolate bar. Maybe the double dose of caffeine would keep her going till dinner. Joyce was the best kind of fellow D.A., since she always had food and never locked her desk. A very handy habit for Alicia, since the second-floor snack bar was open only on weekdays and its concession machines were invariably empty by this late in the weekend. Unfortunately, Joyce's desk was on the exact opposite end of the office.

She clambered to her feet. Her own office was nothing to write home about, but she was proud of it anyway. It was hard won. Like every other county civil servant's office, it was small, fluorescent-lit, and generally depressing. Behind her desk was a single grimy window over which the shade was usually pulled, unless she wanted pedestrians on Alisal Street to peer in at eye level. She was convinced that if the prosecutorial workload didn't kill her, the asbestos lurking in the ceiling would. The ill-assorted furniture might well have come from Goodwill. Her desk was scratched-up oak, her file cabinets beige metal. What desk space wasn't occupied by phone and computer was taken up by canary-yellow felony case files and bulky black binders for those rare cases that actually made it to trial. The only decorative items were her beloved photographs.

There were three, hung on the wall directly opposite her desk for maximum inspiration. Alicia figured in all of them, standing alongside Congresswoman Loretta Sanchez in one; next to Congresswoman Nydia Margarita Velazquez in another; and with Congresswoman Grace Napolitano in the third. Sanchez was the most daunting: she got elected to Congress at age thirty-seven, leaving Alicia only two years to catch up. Velazquez made it at forty. Napolitano was sixty-three. Thank God, Alicia always thought, for small favors.

These women were her heroes. All her life, from as early as she could remember, she dreamed of going as far as they had. Thoughts of them got her through those exhausting years of college and law school, when she was working full-time to pay her way. Some mornings even now they inspired her to get out of bed. She figured they must have had times when they felt stalled, too. Maybe they still did. She hoped so. She hoped they were like her in lots of ways.

On those rare occasions during her childhood when her father was home—when he wasn't hauling produce along the nation's highways—he told her there was nothing those proud Latin women had achieved that his Alicia couldn't. She believed him then; she tried to believe him still. Yet it was no easy trick balancing her father's ambitions on her shoulders. Though he never said a word, she knew he'd had his days when he wished she was a boy. She'd had her days when she wished she wasn't the oldest, or the smartest, and that it was

Carla or Isela who was earmarked to get the good grades and be the first Maldonado to make it through high school. And beyond.

How her father fastened on law for her she never understood. Lawyers must have seemed the most powerful people to him; they must have seemed to understand how the world worked in a way he never did. *Law, law, law* was his constant refrain, and by the time she was ten she was singing the same tune. Now it was the only song she knew.

On her way out of her office she lightly, ritualistically, touched each of the three photo frames, then headed out the door. Getting to Joyce Ching's desk required her to navigate the narrow perimeter corridor past small D.A. offices on the exterior side and chin-high cubicle walls along the interior. The Monterey County district attorney's office took up the first floor of the courthouse's west wing and was full to bursting with about three dozen prosecutors. Most were two to an office; only senior D.A.s like herself got their own space. Alicia rounded the final corner, approaching Penrose's office down the long hall, and then saw, through his open door, signs of life.

Finally. Something must have happened. She quickened her step. Shikegawa was standing inside, with Niebaum and Bucky. Penrose suddenly came into view, bending to turn on a corner table lamp. Sunday or no Sunday, he was wearing a suit and tie. Knowing him, he probably wanted to be ready to go on camera.

Also there, she saw now, was Louella Wilkes. Big, blond, curvaceous Louella, transplanted ten years earlier from her native Georgia. Alicia always thought Louella looked like Marilyn Monroe back in her Norma Jean days, before Hollywood buffed and polished her. Even after fifteen or so years in the business, Louella was about the most unlikely

D.A. investigator you'd ever meet. And, Alicia thought, about the best.

Alicia felt a stab of anger, directed entirely at Penrose. He hadn't included her in this meeting, though he'd summoned all the other principals who had gathered the prior afternoon at the crime scene.

Worry rapidly displaced anger. This was not a good sign. If Penrose intended for her to prosecute this case, she would have been the first person he called.

He glanced over then, saw her in the corridor, and at least had the good grace to look embarrassed. She stepped inside his office without waiting for an invitation and immediately claimed one of the two upholstered chairs in front of his desk. It was no surprise that Penrose had the nicest furniture— genuine antiques—and the best wood paneling, oil paintings, and Oriental carpets taxpayer money could buy. The other decorations were photos of him shaking hands with every important person he'd ever been able to get on celluloid. It irked Alicia that they had that much in common.

Louella plopped down in the other chair and grinned, cheery as ever. "Hey, Alicia. Glad you're here." She looked at Penrose, her blue eyes mischievous. "Wanna kick it off, Kipper?"

Alicia knew he hated that but had long ago given up reprimanding Louella, who was a force of nature. "Right," he said, then sat down behind his desk, which unlike every other horizontal space in the D.A.'s office was bereft of paperwork. Not surprising, since Penrose spent most of his time sucking up to higher-placed elected officials, which didn't require much written documentation. He leaned forward, steepled his fingers, and looked over them at Niebaum, who was wearing a hole in the fancy carpet. "Let's start with you, Ben."

The autopsy had been completed with remarkable speed,

entirely because the victim was prominent and his murder a major news event. In death as in life, Daniel Gaines was getting VIP treatment.

The pathologist continued pacing as he spoke, and kept his eyes trained on the carpet. "The arrow's entry point was the left anterior sixth intercostal space. It lacerated the left main pulmonary artery and apparently caused a tension pneumothorax." He paused and looked up at his listeners. "This wound was fatal in two respects. There's no question that massive blood loss into the left thoracic cavity would have proved fatal within twenty minutes. But as it is, the victim died of asphyxiation in, I'd say, eight to ten minutes. Perhaps slightly less."

Alicia frowned. "Asphyxiation? Doesn't that mean he suffocated?"

Niebaum nodded. "That's correct. The arrow created a vacuum hole that allowed the victim's chest to fill with air, preventing him from taking a breath. The experience would have been like a slow drowning." He shook his head. "With every breath he struggled to take, he sucked more air into his chest. His lungs collapsed more and more each time, driving him closer to death."

Shikegawa winced. "What a way to go."

Niebaum's bearded face was thoughtful. "Indeed, if the killer wanted the victim to suffer, he, or she, succeeded brilliantly. Any arrow to the chest would cause massive damage, but this pinpoint placement, precipitating a tension pneumothorax, caused a particularly unpleasant demise."

Everyone was silent for a time before Louella spoke up. "When would you put time of death, Ben?"

"Given that the body remained in a stable environment with regard to temperature, we can narrow the time frame to two hours. I would put death at between ten PM and midnight."

"Thank you, Ben," Penrose said. "Andy?"

The criminalist, in his uniform of beige corduroys and plaid flannel shirt, cleared his throat. "What we have here is an extraordinary compilation of evidence." He spoke in his formal style, trotted out for momentous occasions like naming suspects and testifying in court. "All of which points in one direction."

You could have heard a pin drop. Alicia's heart beat so hard against her rib cage she thought it might burst out and land on Penrose's snazzy carpet.

"There is no sign of forced entry," Shikegawa went on. "The home is equipped with a state-of-the-art security system, which was not activated during the span of time in which Gaines was killed.

"In the house, we have four distinct sets of prints belonging to someone other than the victim, his wife, and their housekeeper, an Elvia Hidalgo. Mrs. Hidalgo left the house Friday around six PM and had the weekend off." He consulted his notes, printed neatly in a small, crimson leather-bound journal. "As for the prints, they were found on the exterior of the front door, on the arrow with which the victim was killed, on the hardwood floor next to the victim's feet, and on the wall of the room in which the body was found."

Shikegawa then looked at each of them in turn. "All those prints belong to the same person." He paused. "They match the prints of Treebeard."

"So it was Treebeard," Penrose said immediately. Alicia let out a shaky breath. It was what she had thought, too, what for sure they had all thought, for how could they not, given how Gaines had died and the well-documented history between the men?

"What about the arrow?" Louella asked. "You're sure it's

Treebeard's?"

"It appears to be exactly like the arrows that Treebeard uses, and let me explain that," Shikegawa went on hastily, as Penrose immediately objected to the word *appears*. He hoisted a silver metal briefcase onto Penrose's desk and opened it, taking out a videotape. "May I?" he asked Penrose, then opened a tall cabinet to switch on the TV and VCR stored inside.

Alicia thought this was yet another way Penrose was a jerk: he was in love with seeing himself on camera. Whenever he scored an interview with a reporter, he recorded the news to catch his performance. He went so far as to save the tapes and file them by case and date.

Shikegawa punched a few buttons on the VCR remote. On the television screen rose images from the local Channel 8 newscast. Shikegawa fast-forwarded, then began to play on the thirty-something blond female anchor. "The environmental activist who calls himself Treebeard is back in the news tonight in yet another public confrontation with local timber executive Daniel Gaines. Sherry Li reports."

Alicia knew the story's gist, mostly because she'd heard it so often. Treebeard's band of activists was constantly trying to derail the felling operations of Headwaters Resources, Daniel Gaines' timber company. At the tree-felling operations north of San Francisco in Humboldt County, Treebeard and his people would chain themselves to trees, throw animal blood on lumbermen, or lie across forest roads to keep the logged cargo from moving. Alicia sympathized with them to some extent. It bothered her, too, to hear that ninety-five percent of the virgin forest in the United States was gone, or that deforestation in the Northwest was worse than in the Amazon rain forest. But how could you not dismiss Treebeard as a kook?

His name, first of all, ripped off from a character in J. R. R. Tolkien's *Lord of the Rings*, who both looked like a tree and claimed to speak for the trees. His extremism, which was of a whole different ilk than that of Julia Butterfly, who herself had gained national notoriety for living for two years in a giant redwood to call attention to their eradication in California. His always dressing in fringed rawhide skins and a coonskin cap, camping in the woods, and, most chilling now, hunting his own game with bow and arrow.

Shikegawa spoke. "Look at this." And there on the tape was Treebeard, a man whose fifty-plus years rode hard on his face. His hair dark and stringy, his skin hardened by wind and sun, he stood in front of Headwaters' Monterey headquarters in his usual animal-skin getup. On a posterboard next to him was a hideous depiction of a wolf caught in a trap, and across it in jagged red letters, as if scrawled in blood, were the words *Timber Companies Kill*. And slung over Treebeard's left shoulder was a quiver of handmade arrows.

Alicia squinted at the image, as did everyone else. The arrows sure did look like the one that killed Daniel Gaines: roughly carved and with a distinctive treelike symbol cut into the wood near the rear feathers.

On the videotape Treebeard screamed at the headquarters, though clearly he was performing for the cameras. "Will you destroy California the way you've destroyed our forests?" He was shrill and melodramatic, almost a caricature of an activist. "Will you kill habitat to enrich yourself and your pampered friends?"

"Do we know where Treebeard is now?" she asked.

Bucky spoke up. "He abandoned his campsite. Soon's I saw the arrow I had the sheriff go check out where he was."

"They checked yesterday afternoon?" Louella asked. "But he was gone?"

"He was gone," Bucky repeated. "Campsite was cleared out. And who knows where he went?"

The question hung in the air. Treebeard was famous for having no address, no phone. Unless he was incarcerated, which he was fairly often, no one knew where he was.

"That's it," Penrose declared. "We've got more than enough to arrest him."

Alicia watched Penrose rise from his chair and puff out his chest. *Slam-dunk*, Shikegawa had said the prior afternoon. *This could be a slam-dunk*. In fact, most homicides were. Mystery fiction aside, clues in a homicide were usually obvious, the culprit most often sloppy. Yet still this bothered her. Treebeard might as well have left a calling card as kill Daniel Gaines with his own homemade arrow and leave bloody prints all over the scene.

"I'll place a personal call to the governor to tell him Treebeard is our man," Penrose announced, "and that we will issue a nationwide APB."

Alicia said nothing, unable to shake a vague discomfort.

***

"Another one down, only one more live shot to go," Milo heard the director say in his earpiece. "You're doin' great, buddy!"

Milo clutched at his chest and performed a fake stagger for the camera, knowing everyone in the control booth back east was watching. Then he stepped away from the shot, pulled out his earpiece and mike cord, and bent to retrieve the foam cup of cooling coffee he had set on the asphalt.

How the mighty had fallen. A mere twenty-four hours before he'd been fill-in anchoring the *WBS Evening News*, one of the network's plummiest assignments. Now he was freezing his butt off in California and suffering the personal humiliation of standing in front of Joan's property as if he didn't know her from Adam, grinding out live shots for WBS's sister cable network, which did news nonstop and on the cheap.

At least he had the lead story. What with the macabre video of Gaines' skewered corpse tumbling onto the pavement, aired over and over, usually in slo-mo, on every news outlet in the nation, this saga was far and away the airwaves' hottest ticket.

"I'm gonna go get some wide shots of the property," Mac told him.

"Great."

Mac McCutcheon, broadcast camera perched on his right shoulder, moved away trailing sound operator Tran Nguyen. The two made an incongruous pair, Mac blond and forty-five years old and built like Arnold Schwarzenegger; Tran a short, wiry fifty-seven, lifted by WBS out of Saigon thirty years before and employed in DC ever since. But they were killer, which was why they worked with Milo, and for *Newsline*.

Milo rubbed his eyelids in a futile attempt to de-gum his contact lenses. It'd been stupid to put them in when he had left New York, nearly twelve hours before. Under his black overcoat he was still in the wool trousers and open-collared dress shirt he'd flown in, though he'd been able to sneak in a dry shave before the first live shot, sitting in the rented Ford Explorer they'd picked up at San Francisco airport.

It would be grueling even without the emotional baggage Milo had brought on the trip. But this was downright embarrassing, him making hay out of Joan's tragedy. His only consolation was his complete certainty that she was long gone. Even if her husband hadn't died in the house, Joan would never linger in the eye of a media hurricane. She wouldn't tolerate it. So there was zero chance she'd look out her front windows and see him among the horde of grasping, opportunistic newspeople, with their live shots and telephoto lenses and satellite trucks.

His deepest desire was that he be able to leave the Monterey Peninsula without seeing her. He did not want to "renew their acquaintance," as O'Malley so euphemistically put it. He did not want a fresh reminder of his humiliation at being dumped. He did not want to be a shoulder to cry on. And he did not want to be compared to Daniel Gaines, god among men, of whom forevermore no unkind word could be spoken.

Mac and Tran returned. Milo stomped on the ground, trying to warm up, the wind off the bay biting. During the winter months coastal Northern California could be as damp and bone-chilling as the shores of the Potomac.

"Mac," he asked, "when's the last time we had to do back-to-back live shots?"

Mac shook his head. Tran just laughed.

Once a WBS correspondent and crew got to work for *Newsline*, which aired Tuesdays at the highly civilized hour of 9 PM, that kind of grunt TV labor was a thing of the past. Problem was that, thanks to O'Malley, Milo was now assigned to a breaking news story, and so was forced to feed run-of-the-mill news shows, even those on cable. And he had to do it cheerfully, despite his ego's insistence that such work was beneath him.

Mac spoke up. "After *Evening*, though, we should be clear."

"Should be." Milo chuckled without humor. "Unless there's a new development." Which could happen at any time and, according to a perverse truth of the news business, was likely to happen at a bad time, like when they were sitting down to a meal or finally about to get some shut-eye. "You have an idea where you want to go to dinner, Mac?"

He asked, though he knew. Like many network cameramen, Mac was a human Zagat guide. He obeyed his breed's cardinal rules: Be fast, fast, fast. Always have your camera with you, loaded with videotape and ready to roll. When you're not working, play. And know where to find pleasure, of both the food and female variety, in every corner of the planet.

Mac crossed his flannel-covered arms and narrowed his eyes, as if that would aid his decision. "For tonight, I was thinking of a little Italian place in Pacific Grove."

"It better be good," Tran said. "Remember that one we went to in Kansas City? With the white sauce that had those chunks in it? When we did that piece on roll-over tractors."

"That wasn't Kansas City," Mac said. "It was Des Moines."

"It was Lincoln," Milo said, then thought better of it. "No, you're right, Mac, it was Des Moines. But it wasn't the tractor piece—it was the quintuplets." It was a muddle, these stories, one after the next, blurring into each other in an amorphous chain that carried him from year to year. *Feed the beast*, one of the WBS bureau chiefs said about network life, and the beast was always famished. Milo calculated that the prior year he'd slept seventy-nine nights in his own bed. Sometimes it seemed pointless even to own a bed, though he loved the brownstone in which it stood waiting for him, just off Embassy Row, only a few blocks from the house he considered home even though his family had never owned it. It was the official residence of the Greek ambassador to the United States, and while the Pappas clan had been able to lay claim for fourteen years, they'd had to give it up eventually. Just another part of Milo's life stamped with impermanence.

"Let's wait it out in the truck." Mac hoisted the camera from the tripod. "It's too goddamn cold out here."

All three made for the white Ford Explorer, whose rear compartment was packed full of the bulky aluminum stowage containers loaded with broadcast gear that they hauled from site to site. They were using two vehicles: the rental Explorer plus an ENG—or electronic news gathering—truck on loan from the local WBS affiliate, which gave them live-broadcast capability. Milo claimed the Explorer's front passenger seat—shotgun being the standard correspondent position—while Mac got in behind the wheel and Tran crammed his smaller body onto the collapsible seat. Milo cranked the all-news radio station.

They'd settled in to wait the twenty-odd minutes until the final live shot, when the cell phone in Milo's inside jacket pocket vibrated. He pulled it out. "Pappas."

"Milo?" A breathy female voice, whispery, clearly half asleep.

He sat up straighter, his heart beginning to thump.

"Milo?" the woman repeated.

Instinctively he turned away from Mac toward the passenger window. "Yes?" He didn't want to say—or to assume—Joan?

"I saw you on TV. You're here."

It had to be Joan. And she'd seen him. But she didn't sound angry so much as out of it. How had she gotten his cell number? Apparently she was as resourceful as ever. "How are you doing?" he asked carefully.

"I'm fine." He heard a rustle—sheets?—and then she let out a long, soft breath. Milo remembered that breath. "You're very good, you know," she said. "Even better than you used to be. You're just"—another sigh—"amazing."

"No ..." Automatically he began to demur.

"Oh, yes. Amazing."

She said nothing more. Had she fallen asleep? He was unnerved. He gazed out the Explorer window at the gloaming sky. It seemed darker now than it had five minutes before.

"Why don't you come over?" she asked suddenly.

"What?" He was shocked. "Come over?"

"I'm at the Lodge. You know where that is?"

"I don't think that's a good idea. I mean ..." He stopped. *Your husband's been dead twenty-four hours and you want an old boyfriend to visit you in your hotel room?*

"Are you thinking about Daniel? Oh"—and she sounded dismissive, at the same instant she read his mind—"don't worry about Daniel. It doesn't matter about him anymore, anyway."

Soft click. She'd hung up.

***

Alicia lingered in the corridor outside Penrose's office while he made his phone calls. He even shut the door when he phoned the governor, as if her overhearing him would somehow be disruptive. Afterward he pulled the door open and ushered her back in. She felt like a kid being summoned into the principal's office.

He reclaimed the throne behind his desk. "Let's get a few things straight here and now," he said the instant she crossed his threshold.

That immediately got her back up. "Like what?"

"Don't think I haven't seen how you're trying to inject yourself into this case." His eyes were cold. "It's unseemly, this naked ambition of yours."

"You're going to sing that old tune?" She sat back down in the chair out of which she'd been hoisted twenty minutes before. "If Rocco Messina behaved the way I did, you'd be trying to think of a way to promote him. I've got news for you, Kip. The old-boys' club is officially illegal."

He looked affronted. "This has nothing to do with gender favoritism."

Right. "You also seem to forget *I* was the one who picked up Bucky's initial call."

"That's irrelevant."

"Is it also irrelevant that it was me who called Niebaum and Shikegawa to the scene?" She heard her voice get louder but couldn't seem to rein it in. "And me who got the Sheriff's department deployed to handle the press?" *All while you were AWOL, which didn't surprise anybody around here.*

"I don't like that tone of voice," he said. Then he slapped his desk and abruptly rose to his feet, causing his rolling chair to bang into the wall behind him. He leaned toward her over his desk and pointed a finger in her face. "And insubordination won't do you a damn bit of good."

She met his gaze steadily, refusing to blink. Finally he backed off and reclaimed his chair. "I'm not assigning you the case," he said, and her heart plummeted.

"Why not?"

"Because you don't have sufficient experience prosecuting homicide."

"That's a crock and you know it!" *Damn him.* She abandoned her chair to pace his office. This was exactly what she'd been afraid he would do, though it made no sense at all. It was so Kip-like! Thickheaded and counterproductive.

And no doubt inspired by sheer malice.

She decided to try to reason with him, though Kip Penrose was rarely moved by logic. She returned to her chair and leaned toward him. "I have done homicides," she said. "I've won them. I've been handling serious felonies for seven years. And I have the highest conviction rate in this office."

"I don't dispute that. But this is a special case."

"I don't dispute *that*. But you and I both know that when it comes right down to it, a case is a case is a case. You do the prep work, you pay attention to the details, you get a working knowledge of the record." She locked onto his eyes, blank as ever. "Kip, I'm the best you've got. I win more than anybody around here. And," she added as inspiration struck her, "it's a must that you win this case. Not only because of how high-profile it is, but because of your special tie to the Hudson family."

He stared at her, appearing to consider that. Nothing like a reference to campaign money to get Kip's attention. Finally he nodded, his gaze skidding away. "That's true," he said.

She was surprised, and pushed on. "Appointing me will make you look good. To the voters." She let that sink in. "You put a woman, a Latina, front and center? That makes you inclusive. It makes you forward-thinking. You can use it in November."

"True," he said again. He smiled, or at least his mouth did. His eyes, now back on her face, remained cold. "All right, Alicia. You'll be involved."

She frowned. Something about that phrasing made her wary. For all that he wasn't that smart, Penrose was a master of parsed language. "What exactly do you mean?"

"You'll work up the case." He leaned back in his chair and linked his hands behind his head, his eyes triumphant. "But *I* will argue it in court."

She felt like she'd been stomach-punched. "*You'll* argue it in court? When's the last time you did that?"

"It's like riding a bike, Alicia." His tone was offhand. "You don't forget."

Yes, you do! she wanted to scream at him, staring at his

stubborn, stupid, self-satisfied face. *You get rusty, you get nervous, your mind doesn't work as fast as it should. It's like the first time you run after not exercising for months.* But these were all things Kip Penrose didn't know. Why? Because he was never in court. And hadn't been since he was a prosecutor himself, years before in Massachusetts.

What a slap in her face. She stood up again, shaking, stunned, though she realized she shouldn't be, knowing what she did about Penrose. She walked away from his desk and stared sightlessly at the swinging pendulum of his grandfather clock. *Tick, tock. Tick, tock.* Beating away the precious minutes and hours of her career. She'd be behind the scenes, doing all the work and getting none of the glory. While Kip Penrose—*Kip Penrose!*—used her heavy lifting to score points with the voters.

"If you don't like it," he said to her back, "you're free to go elsewhere."

"You'd love that, wouldn't you." It wasn't a question.

The damnable truth was, they needed each other. They were like codependents, or spouses in a bad, inescapable marriage. She needed him because there was no other prosecutor's job in town, and moving out of Salinas, tempting though that idea often was, would leave her family high and dry. He needed her because she was his best deputy D.A., which was why she was standing in his office at that very moment.

And while she was sure that Penrose had his moments when he would love to get rid of her, he could never fire her and they both knew it. Ditch his star prosecutor, conviction rate 90.3 percent and Latina to boot? NOW and the Mexican Bar Association would be all over him. The press would have a field day.

"Of course, I'll handle the media," he continued.

"Another enormous surprise." Somehow she couldn't make herself turn and face him. Anger had gotten the better of her and she could barely speak for it. Times like these she understood how murderers could commit the crimes they did. Sometimes her own rage felt like a beast throwing its body against the bars of a cage.

Part of her wanted to tell Penrose to go straight to hell. Work up his own case. Fall on his own face. But another, more rational part—that later she would be glad was still functioning—thought better of it.

Penrose was a lightweight. He personified the term. What was to say that when the trial date arrived Alicia Maldonado wouldn't be front and center? Penrose cracked under real pressure, and the pressure of this trial would be enormous. If she worked up the case, she'd be ready to step in and argue it.

"I'm calling a press conference for tomorrow morning." He rose. She was dismissed. "I expect you to be there, but I don't expect to hear a peep out of you unless I ask you a direct question."

"Forget it. I've got a trial starting tomorrow morning."

"Get a continuance."

She shook her head, her heart pounding. He was so damn cavalier. "Why, Kip? Why should I?" Her voice rose. "Doesn't this tell you something? That you're already scared shitless you can't answer questions about the case without me there to tell you what to say?"

"I'm not worried about a damn thing." His voice was harsh. He pointed his finger at her face again. "But you just be there. For support only. No other reason."

That comment lifted the entire enterprise from infuriating to ludicrous. She put her hands on her hips and laughed. "Kip Penrose, you picked the wrong D.A. for that assignment."

CHAPTER FOUR

At nine the next morning, Kip Penrose was bending low over the sink in the D.A. office men's room. His right hand cupped water, which he then sucked into his mouth; his left carefully held back his faux Hermes tie so its tip wouldn't get wet accidentally in the sink.

Damn! Why had he left his mouthwash in his desk drawer? He'd never get rid of the vomit taste this way and his press conference was due to start this very minute.

Kip raised his head and imagined all those reporters and camera crews massed on the courthouse steps waiting for him. For him! This was only the second time in his three years as D.A. that he'd been able to justify calling a press conference. And for all he knew he could be holding press conferences every day this week. A thrill ran through him, followed by yet another wave of nausea. This was the most exposure he'd ever had. What if he screwed up? Then *whoosh!* All his hopes and dreams would get flushed down the toilet.

He grimaced. At the moment he could picture that all too clearly.

Kip backed away from the sink and grabbed from the hook on the stall the red-and-green-striped scarf he'd brought from home special for the press conference. A cheery holiday touch, plus it gave his face some much needed color. He draped it just so around his neck, then pulled on his Burberry-knockoff trench coat, bought at an outlet mall in the wine country. Apparently it had some defect, but for the life of him he couldn't find it. As the final step in his routine, as detailed as a pilot's preflight checklist, he smoothed the newly clipped hair at his temples and tamped down an unruly cowlick.

His ministrations complete, Kip stood back from the mirror to take in a wider view. As always, his reflection buoyed him. Even under the harsh fluorescent lights, he thought he looked pretty damn good for a fifty-three-year-old man. He puffed with satisfaction. Not one of those reporters would guess that he'd just upchucked. And every voter at home would think he had the look of a man destined for bigger and better things.

Privately, Kip wasn't sure what those things were. Most often he ricocheted between wanting to be state attorney general and thinking himself better suited to state comptroller, but sometimes he got so ambitious he thought, *Why not governor?* In his mind rose a vision of patriotic red-white-and-blue signs with PENROSE FOR GOVERNOR! in convincing block letters, plastered on trees and billboards and rear bumpers throughout the Great State of California.

Of course, Kip had a marriage problem. Two too many marriages, to be exact, and voters didn't always understand that sort of thing. His third wife was shaping up pretty well, but One and Two were driving him nuts, coming to him with their hands out like he was Midas himself. They both spent money like there was no tomorrow, and neither one could hold a serious job. One was an interior decorator and the other a caterer. Those were hobbies, not jobs!

Kip felt himself getting upset, as always happened when he thought about One and Two, but he forced himself to calm down. First things first. The press conference. He stood still and visualized a spectacular performance, reporters having so many pithy sound bites to choose from that they'd all be forced to use more than one. *You can do it,* he assured his reflection. Finally, when he could delay it no longer, he exited the men's room to find Rocco Messina outside in the corridor cooling his heels.

He didn't like Rocco Messina. Rocco Messina wanted his job. He didn't like anybody who wanted his job.

Kip gave Rocco a hearty slap on the back and made his voice boisterous. "How you doing, Rocco?"

"Fine, how are you? Ready for the circus?"

"Ready to rock 'n' roll!" he crowed. That couldn't be further from the truth, but Kip never let facts stand in the way of a good story. He headed back toward his office but saw Rocco's face kind of pucker as he walked into the men's room.

Uh-oh. Must still smell in there. Well, maybe Rocco would think somebody else did it.

Kip took long, confident strides down the corridor, as he knew a man of his position should. "Colleen," he boomed to his secretary as he passed her desk, not stopping as if he were very, very busy, "is Alicia in my office?"

"No," she called, which he could plainly see a second later when he arrived there. He paused at the threshold, his purged stomach roiling. Where in the world was she?

He would never tell her this but he would not, not, go out to that press conference without Alicia. The chance of one of those reporters asking him something he couldn't answer was extremely high. For all that she was an exceedingly annoying, full-of-herself women's libber, she was good on her feet.

And was she smart or what? It scared him sometimes. Good-looking, too. Thank God she was a woman, and Hispanic. Otherwise she could be a real rival. Fortunately, what with the agricultural and Italian communities, Monterey County was conservative enough that it was nearly impossible for a candidate like her. Both times she'd run for a judgeship, she'd lost. Of course, part of her problem was that she was so combative and opinionated. But now she'd never get the backing to run again, at least not for his job.

"You finally ready?"

It was Alicia, standing just outside his office. *Thank God.* "You're late," he informed her, making his voice stern, but she just rolled her eyes and headed for the exit, not even checking to see that he followed.

Which forced Kip to scramble to get out in front of her. *Most unseemly*, he thought, his stomach clutched in yet another knot. Thank God no one who counted had seen.

***

Milo hadn't covered a press conference in a long, long time. Unless it was happening at the White House, State, or Defense, a presser was a low-prestige event passed over by network news stars of his caliber.

He sipped the low-fat latte he'd procured at Starbucks and wondered when this show would get on the road. No sign of the D.A. and it was already twenty after nine. Milo was one of several dozen reporters, TV camera crews, and print photographers massed in front of the Monterey County Courthouse, a three-story structure built of oatmeal-colored sandblasted concrete that looked like a mix of New Deal construction and neoclassical pretensions. Carved heroic heads paid tribute to the Spanish, Mexicans, and Native Americans who'd once claimed California as their own. The building took up most of a city block in downtown Salinas, downtown being distinguished by two traffic lanes in each direction. Curb lanes on both Alisal and Church Streets were jam-packed with news vans and ENG trucks, their masts high in the air.

It was sunny, unlike the prior afternoon, but hardly

warm. Salinas was twenty miles inland and got a lot less fog. On a day like this, though, Milo still needed his overcoat.

"Milo Pappas?" A thirty-something guy in a tie and trench coat held out his hand. He had to be TV. He was too well dressed to be print. "Jerry Rosenblum, Channel 8." The local WBS affiliate.

"Good to meet you, Jerry." Milo took his hand. "You guys are being terrific hosts, as always. We really appreciate it."

Network people always felt compelled to be nice to the local affiliate folks, who often were tremendously helpful when a net crew blew into town. They provided local knowledge, editing bays at the station, and in this case an ENG truck. The locals usually felt both one up and one down to the network. They knew the terrain backward and forward but aired their reports only in that market, whereas the net reported to the nation.

Rosenblum nodded. "It's our pleasure. You might not have to be around for long, though."

Milo's ears perked up. "Why do you say that?"

"Well"—the reporter looked pleased to know something Milo Pappas didn't—"once the D.A. names the suspect today and we get past the funeral, there won't be much to cover till the trial."

"So Penrose will name the suspect today?"

"So I hear."

"And it'll be Treebeard?"

Rosenblum nodded. No news flash there. The only surprise was that it had taken this long to become official.

Milo was pleased. Maybe the gods would grant him his wish to get off the Monterey Peninsula sooner rather than later. He truly didn't want to see Joan. It hadn't been too difficult to resist her out-of-it invitation from the prior afternoon, though he couldn't quite forget it, either. It lingered at the edge of his brain like the proverbial apple dangling from Eden's tree.

It still embarrassed him how snookered he'd been by Joan back when they'd dated. Of course, he'd been a lot younger then, and though he wasn't exactly wise now he was no longer quite so impressionable.

It wasn't as if she were exceptionally beautiful or fascinating. Sure, she was good-looking, but in the way women with money were good-looking. They were so pampered, so cared for, so thin and well dressed. They did the most that could possibly be done with what they were given and ended up looking pretty damn good.

No, the bottom line was that it was a damn sexy thing dating American royalty. Certainly his own background, as the son of a diplomat, imbued him with a certain glamour. But dating Joan was a stamp of approval from the highest of the high, from a Rockefeller or a Bush or a Kennedy: a family with money, fame, power. His acceptance into their magic circle boosted him in the network-news world as well.

Once he'd been dumped, though, he'd realized that Joan had little going for her but money and fame and power, none of which she'd earned and all of which she lorded over him and everybody else who came into her orbit. There was little of substance in the woman herself. At long last he figured out that he had confused where she came from with what she was. It was a mistake he vowed he wouldn't repeat.

Milo was jolted back to the present by a commotion among the reporters. *Finally.* A tall, graying man Milo took to be the D.A. emerged from between the tall striated columns that adorned the main Alisal Street side of the courthouse, then moved swiftly down the few wide steps to the forest of microphone stands the TV crews had long since set up.

Milo assessed Kip Penrose. He had the look of an aging

Ivy League oarsman, together with the swagger even smalltime elected officials assumed. Milo couldn't help but notice that his coterie included a stunningly attractive brunette. He nudged Rosenblum's elbow. "Who's that?"

He didn't need to provide greater clarification for his fellow reporter to know exactly who he meant. "Alicia Maldonado. Really has her shit in gear."

"You don't say." Milo watched as she halted just behind Penrose's right shoulder, her lovely face impassive.

"She won this wild murder case a few years back." Rosenblum lowered his voice confidentially. "Guy's wife dies hanging on a clothesline and it gets ruled a suicide. But something makes Maldonado think the husband did it. First trial she gets a hung jury. But the second one she brings in this hotshot medical expert and nails him." Rosenblum looked impressed. "It was a huge story out here. The guy confessed later from prison, in his own suicide note."

Rosenblum gave him a look like *Hot shit, huh?* then moved off to join his cameraman. Milo positioned himself beside Mac, watching the prosecutor called Alicia Maldonado.

She was gorgeous, in a Mediterranean way he didn't usually go for. His standard female of choice was blond and rail-thin, more ethereal than earthy. But this woman had something Sophia Loren-esque about her, a hot-blooded, pent-up quality. What with the long dark hair, sultry eyes, and full lips, she was a fantasy made flesh. Milo had a devil of a time not staring.

Penrose began to speak. "I am Kip Penrose," he declared, then spelled out his name, a savvy aside for the benefit of the reporters. Penrose had done this before, apparently. "I am the district attorney here in Monterey County. To my right is Deputy District Attorney Alicia Maldonado, to my left Department of Justice criminalist Andrew Shikegawa, and to

Andy's left our pathologist, Dr. Ben Niebaum. I will give a brief statement, then be available, as will my colleagues, for your questions."

Penrose read a statement that said what they'd all expected to hear, since they'd all seen the arrow, or the video of the arrow, on Saturday night: that based on the physical evidence, a warrant had been issued for the arrest of John David Stennis, who called himself Treebeard, for the murder of Daniel Gaines, blah blah blah. Then it got more interesting.

" 'Late yesterday afternoon,'" Penrose read, " 'a nationwide APB was issued for Treebeard. Law enforcement officials have not yet located him so have been unable to serve the warrant.'" He paused and looked directly into one of the TV camera lenses, unfortunately not Mac's. "We ask the public to contact local law enforcement if they see anyone fitting Treebeard's description. And we warn the public that he is considered armed and dangerous."

Milo chuckled softly. Evidently Kip Penrose thought those arrows might go shooting off in any direction at any time.

"Questions?" Penrose invited, and the shouting began.

"What physical evidence do you have that links Treebeard to the murder?"

"Do you believe Treebeard is still in California?"

"What motive would Treebeard have for killing Daniel Gaines?"

It went on for a while, and there was only one notable thing about it, in Milo's opinion. More than once, Penrose did a subtle check with Alicia Maldonado before he answered a question. She would give a barely perceptible nod or shake of the head, and he would proceed accordingly. Once she even corrected him, on a bit of minutiae regarding special circumstances, or death penalty, cases, of which this was one.

Milo hadn't yet asked a question, but after all the back-and-forth between the D.A. and his deputy, one occurred to him. He raised his index finger and Penrose looked in his direction.

"Milo Pappas," he said by way of standard ID, "WBS News." He consulted his spiral-bound reporter's notebook, then again raised his eyes, his deliberate pause drawing everyone's attention. "Should this case come to trial," he asked, "who will be the prosecuting attorney?"

He saw a glimmer of amusement flicker in Alicia Maldonado's lovely dark eyes, and a shadow cross the patrician features of District Attorney Kip Penrose.

"I will, Mr. Pappas," the D.A. declared with some heat, but Milo couldn't care less about the answer. He might have asked several follow-up questions, plumbing the same obviously rich vein, but he didn't. No point getting the lead prosecuting attorney on the story he was covering all riled up.

Besides, Milo's instincts told him he'd already gotten what he wanted. He'd made progress toward winning himself an intelligent, not to mention highly attractive, inside source.

***

He's a slick one, Alicia thought. *No man with those looks could be anything but.*

She'd known who he was, of course, before he'd said a word. She wasn't a big TV watcher but hadn't been living under a rock, either. He certainly hadn't needed to say his name before he asked his question. It was kind of like Brian Williams introducing himself. But it was endearing, too, Milo Pappas acting like Joe Reporter.

Penrose was driving her nuts, so it was highly satisfying to see somebody else get a rise out of him. Not only had he made her postpone her trial, he'd also insisted she accompany him that night to update Joan Gaines on the case.

As if she could care less whether Joan Gaines was "apprised," as Kip put it. Let him do the fifty miles round-trip to Pebble Beach. It was his campaign her family was funding.

Then she thought better of letting Kip have a clear field where the widow Gaines was concerned. It might be valuable to get another close-up look at her, see if she'd started showing any regret that her husband had gotten skewered by an arrow.

A few interminable minutes later, Penrose ended the press conference. He always let them go on forever, seeming to think that would get him more face time on the evening news. "We'll hold a follow-up press conference when events warrant," he was saying now. Right, like when he broke a nail. "Thank you all for coming."

Alicia was up the stairs and almost at the courthouse door when she felt a tap on her left arm. She stopped and couldn't believe who had waylaid her.

"Milo Pappas." He held out his hand and smiled. No wonder mythology came out of Greece. Apparently gods were born there.

"Alicia Maldonado." She took his hand. His fingers were warm and his grasp just firm enough. She made herself let go.

"Seems to me you're the real expert in this case," he said. "I noticed that the D.A. kept looking to you for guidance."

"He values my judgment," she lied.

"Apparently he's not the only one. I'm told people around here hold you in high regard."

What a flatterer this guy was. She arched an eyebrow. "You've been around here long enough to pick that up?"

He chuckled, then met her eyes and held them. It struck her that he'd be a hard man to fool, which made her both wary and admiring at the same time.

"Do you have time for a coffee?" he asked. "Or perhaps a drink later?" And then he smiled again.

Hot damn. Professional ethics required that she keep reporters covering the Gaines case at a distance. She knew that and so did he. Milo Pappas was making one bold proposition by requesting private schmooze time.

Of course, he also knew that most red-blooded American women would mow down their ethics with an automatic weapon to get a one-on-one with him. But clearly that was no problem. This was not a man who had any compunction about using his charm to get what he wanted—in this case, inside information.

She crossed her arms over her chest. "If you had more questions about the case, why didn't you ask them at the press conference?"

He didn't miss a beat. "Because at the press conference Kip Penrose was doing all the talking. I wanted to get my answers from you."

"You could call the D.A. office's press person. She'd be able to answer all your questions."

"I'm sure she could." He smiled again. "But she's still not you."

Smooth talker. Alicia eyed this Milo Pappas, with his perfectly symmetrical features, curly dark hair, and bedroom eyes. Of course, she could play it safe, like she always did. She could keep her late-night date with her faithful but boring doctor boyfriend, who in the past few minutes had flown out of her mind so completely it was as if he'd been carried off by a tornado. Or she could entertain herself by getting together with this drop-dead-gorgeous network news star who would pass through her life but once. And throw a kink in his plans by staying tight-lipped about the case.

"Mr. ... Pappas, is it?"

He smiled again. This time at her. That old hard-to-fool thing again. *Damn.*

She kept her voice cool. "I'm in trial at the moment." It was only a white lie: she would be if Penrose hadn't made her postpone. "So I can't take time for a coffee. But if you'd care to meet for a drink later I could probably swing that."

He smiled. Something in his grin told her she wasn't coming off quite as offhand as she might hope. "Terrific," he said. "Where's convenient for you?"

She thought fast. Her meeting with Penrose and Joan Gaines would be in Pebble Beach and would probably be over around eight o'clock. "How about eight-thirty at the bar at the Mission Ranch in Carmel? Do you know where that is?"

"I'll find it."

She nodded and walked away. She could feel his eyes on her back as she walked toward the courthouse doors. Right before she disappeared through them, he spoke again.

"I'm looking forward to it," he called.

She hated her immediate gut reaction. Which was that she wasn't only looking forward to it. She could hardly wait.

CHAPTER FIVE

By ten o'clock Monday morning, a hired limousine was speeding Joan north through Silicon Valley on Highway 101. Pebble Beach was an hour behind her; San Francisco lay another hour of four-lane freeway ahead. She rode in the rear nursing a fizzy water with lime, on her lap a forgotten yellow legal pad.

This was a must-do trip. She absolutely had to have a new suit for Daniel's funeral: she certainly couldn't wear the same one she'd worn to her father's service. That had been televised, too. Serious shopping meant San Francisco, yet she knew a buying spree two days after her husband had been murdered could be badly misconstrued.

She sipped and recrossed her legs, impressed with her own problem solving. She'd simply made this a stealth mission. Even though she wouldn't be staying overnight, she'd booked a suite at the Ritz-Carlton, and arranged for Neiman Marcus to assemble some selections and bring them over. Joan would be closeted in the suite, so no one would be the wiser. And while she was at it, she'd have her hair and nails done, too.

Joan stared out the limo's tinted windows as it rocketed past 101's University Avenue exit, which led to Palo Alto and Stanford, an off-ramp she knew well from her undergraduate and business-school years. Noise-abatement walls along this stretch of freeway prevented any view, though the adjacent commercial strip was hardly scenic. The campus was a few miles west, red tile-roofed mission-style buildings grouped in quadrangles, set among sweeping lawns and groves of eucalyptus.

Even now, it angered her to think of those years. So what if she hadn't actually graduated from business school? Her parents made so much of that. She'd gotten most of the way through, hadn't she? She still couldn't believe her father had made a huge donation to the university right before she applied, as if she wouldn't get in otherwise. She remembered walking through the Quad, looking up at the Venetian mosaic on Memorial Church and imagining a time when people would no longer think of her as Web Hudson's daughter but as Joan Hudson in her own right. But all she'd done since was become Daniel Gaines' wife.

God, she'd been such an idiot to be so easily taken in by Daniel! Handsome, charismatic Daniel Gaines, who went from star quarterback at U Penn to megasuccessful Manhattan financier.

It embarrassed her to remember how she'd been bowled over. She accepted Daniel's very first proposal. And though she secretly found it easy to say good-bye to her investment-banking job, she hadn't liked leaving Manhattan. But Daniel said Headwaters was such an opportunity, and wouldn't it be wonderful to be close to her parents, and she'd bought into every last word. She imagined children, at least three in rapid succession, a big, boisterous family, the polar opposite of her own.

Tears stung her eyes. If only Daniel had been different. If only he'd been the man he seemed to be, instead of the egocentric, using bastard he was. Now she was forced to pretend to grieve a husband she could barely make herself miss.

Joan made herself calm down and focus on the yellow

legal pad on her lap. On it she'd jotted notes for a statement to the press, her top to-do item for the day. She would order Daniel's campaign to release it the following morning and was sure it would dominate the Christmas Eve news shows. She would then get another round of coverage with Daniel's funeral on Friday. She wanted to create an impression of dignified sorrow, like a modern-day Jackie Kennedy. Joan believed that appearance would serve her well down the road.

Carmel-by-the-Sea, California. Christmas Eve. At this hour of profound grief for my family, and for the family of my beloved husband, I wish to offer my sincerest gratitude to those many Americans who have offered their prayers and sympathy.

She bit her lip. For this next section, she'd have to lay it on thick if it killed her. She thought for a minute, then resumed writing.

My husband was a man of extraordinary judgment, intelligence, and commitment. I am sure that had he lived to continue my father's tradition of selfless political service, not only California, but all America, would have benefited from his efforts. A brilliant light has been cruelly dimmed, and I shall never rest until I understand why. To that end, I am offering a hundred-thousand-dollar reward for information leading to the arrest of the man who calls himself Treebeard, whom law-enforcement authorities have charged with my husband's brutal murder.

She reread it and smiled. *Very good!* Now all she needed was a closing line, preferably something upbeat. Ronald Reagan proved that voters liked a positive note even on the saddest occasion. Minutes later, she again put pen to paper.

I am reminded in this Christmas season that hope shines like a star in the night sky, even in our darkest hour. I seek that light for my family and for all Californians as we cope with this loss and move forward into the promise of the new year.

She capped her pen and took another sip of her fizzy water. She would make people see that everything Daniel had done, she could do better. She could run Headwaters, and she could run for office. And when she did, she'd be out from the shadows and into the light, getting the respect she deserved.

Invigorated, Joan pulled out her cell phone and punched in the numbers she needed. She steeled herself for the call, as she always did before any interaction with Molly Bracewell.

M.B., Daniel's pet name for her, had had so much plastic surgery and intensive help from personal stylists, she'd been remade from a pathetic frump to a mildly attractive woman. People seemed to think she was brilliant. Joan thought she was a low-born climber who'd gotten where she was on her back. But it was undeniable that she'd become one of the most sought-after press officers in the country. Joan couldn't stand her, partly because she knew Molly dismissed her as a pampered know-nothing political wife whose only asset was her family name. Wouldn't Miss Molly be surprised at just how much the wife of the candidate did know?

Finally the call was answered. "Molly Bracewell."

"It's Joan Gaines. I've drafted the statement and I'll e-mail it to you tonight."

Silence. Then, "Joan, I really do not think you need to—"

"I don't care to go over this again. Just get it on the wires."

Heavy, pained sigh. "Fine," Molly said, her tone grudging.

Joan jabbed at her cell's end button without uttering

another word.

Damn that woman. Damn her and everybody else who underestimates Joan Hudson Gaines.

***

Late the afternoon of the press conference, Alicia pulled the lever on the concession machine in the courthouse's second-floor snack bar. Down dropped a Snickers bar. *Plunk.* Healthy snack.

Back downstairs, across the west wing's high-ceilinged tiled foyer, through the security door. She unwrapped the chocolate while walking along the narrow perimeter corridor back to her office, then halted outside Penrose's open door. He wasn't inside but his grandfather clock was, ringing out six chimes. Didn't the network news shows come on at six in the evening?

She couldn't stop herself. She went into Penrose's office and switched on his television and tuned it to WBS, even though she almost never watched TV, and when she did she watched NBC. But somehow her finger insisted on pushing the up arrow on the remote until she hit Channel 8, and then it just stopped moving. She tried to be casual about it, just standing around in front of the set, not admitting to herself what she was watching for.

The newscast started, the *WBS Evening News with Jack Evans*, a serious-looking man with salt-and-pepper hair. To her surprise, right after he said, "Good evening," he started talking about Daniel Gaines' murder, then said, "We go live now to Milo Pappas in Salinas, California," and there he was.

He was still in the white dress shirt, red paisley tie, and black overcoat he'd worn at the press conference, and was as amazing-looking on air as he had been in person. He spoke for a while, then his story started, first showing video of Treebeard in front of the Headwaters building in Monterey. Superimposed on the screen's top right corner were the words *File footage*. Then Daniel Gaines appeared, which gave Alicia a chill. The file footage stayed on while Gaines talked about how frustrated he was that Treebeard never understood that Headwaters preserved the so-called "ancient" trees, the old-growth forest. He sounded pretty convincing and looked good, too: tall and blond and like a star college quarterback, even twenty years after he'd given up the gridiron.

Then there was a sound bite from Penrose, about how a nationwide APB had been issued for Treebeard. She was startled to see herself in that shot, standing behind Penrose's right shoulder. She looked whipped, her skin pale, and purple shadows under her eyes.

Great, now on top of everything else she had to worry about looking good for the cameras. She wouldn't exactly improve her electoral chances down the road, if she ever had any, by looking like something the cat dragged in.

Back to Milo Pappas. She watched as he talked about how Treebeard had fled his campsite within hours of Daniel Gaines' murder. Then Evans asked a question about when the trial might start and he gave a quick answer.

Then it was over. Alicia punched the remote's power button, her mind racing. So Milo Pappas might cover the trial, she realized. He might be on the Monterey Peninsula for some time. The notion was oddly exciting.

Her phone was ringing when she got back to her desk. It was Penrose, summoning her from his car phone. Time for the big powwow with Joan Hudson Gaines.

She got to the Alisal Street side of the courthouse just as Penrose pulled curbside in his sleek white Mercedes. She opened the door—he wasn't the kind to lean over the gearshift and do it for her; he wasn't the kind even to think of it—and escaped Salinas's chill evening air for the sedan's perfect warm comfort. Penrose rocketed away from the curb so fast his tires screeched.

She couldn't keep the sarcasm out of her voice. "Are we in a drag race I don't know about?"

He let that pass. So she would get the silent treatment for suggesting he didn't want to keep his A-1 donor waiting. Fine.

He turned on the radio. Bing Crosby crooned that holiday perennial "White Christmas." Alicia watched Salinas whip past in the dark, run-down houses with plastic Santas set up on browning squares of lawn, stores blaring holiday sales, cars with pine trees roped onto roofs.

As they hurtled toward the coast, the terrain shifted from golden brown to green, from pines to cypresses, from farmland to soft forested hills. She'd been amazed once to see hundred-year-old photos in which the whole coast was barren and windswept. Some places still were, like Seaside and Sand City. But most of it was like the Garden of Eden. Then again, the coastal areas were rich, and money bought gardeners, and gardeners planted whatever they could think of: eucalyptus trees and California live oaks, rock roses, Mexican sage, and lavender. All of it seemed to grow like wild once it got started.

Penrose got to the Highway 1 gate to Pebble Beach in twenty-eight minutes flat. He flashed his county ID at the guard and drove into one of the wealthiest neighborhoods on the planet. The "Circle of Enchantment," people used to call it. Alicia knew what she wasn't seeing, here in the dark: a paradise of palatial homes, many modeled after villas on the French and Italian Rivieras. In the old days people like Andrew Carnegie, William Vanderbilt, and Joseph Pulitzer owned them. Today, Clint Eastwood, Charles Schwab, and

Libby Hudson did.

Here Penrose slowed down. 17 Mile Drive twisted through the Del Monte Forest, dense with eucalyptus, Monterey pines, and jagged cypresses. During the day, the views out toward Carmel Bay were spectacular: amazing beaches, half-hidden coves, and the clifftop fairways that drew hordes of well-heeled tourists to the very place Joan Gaines was now staying.

They passed through yet another entry gate and along a curving drive, cutting a swath through the perfectly manicured fairways of the Pebble Beach golf links. Past a beach club, then a tennis club, then a spa, to the main building itself.

The Lodge at Pebble Beach was the snazziest hotel Alicia had ever seen, though she knew she didn't have much to compare it with. To her it seemed like more of a campus than a hotel. There were lots of understated white stucco structures with dark green awnings and fabulous landscaping. But once Penrose valeted the Mercedes and they walked inside the main building, the entire place reeked of money and luxury.

Alicia had been inside only once before, when Louella had persuaded her to celebrate a trial win by having a drink at a bar that was really more of a pub, with dark wood paneling and golf memorabilia from the annual AT&T Pro-Am. This time, Alicia was all at once painfully aware of how she looked. That is, how she looked compared to everybody else. She cringed at her slightly ragged cuticles and split ends, the scuffs on her navy pumps, and how much polyester had gone into her pin-striped suit. It wasn't as if she were poorly dressed or badly groomed, but she didn't look like she'd just stepped out of a salon, either.

No tremendous surprise that Joan Hudson Gaines was staying in a prime oceanside suite. Penrose halted outside her door. "I'll do the talking," he told Alicia, then jabbed at the buzzer. A moment later the young widow let them in.

Alicia's first reaction was that she looked incredibly better than she had two days before. Now everything about her was perfect, from her hair to her nails to her makeup to her clothes. She wore a white knit suit with black trim and gold buttons—a ladies-who-lunch suit—and lots of gold jewelry.

For a newly minted widow, she looked positively stunning.

"Thank you for coming," she said to Penrose, then turned cool blue eyes on Alicia.

"This is Alicia Maldonado," Penrose said, "one of the prosecutors assisting me in the case," and Alicia held out her hand. Joan Gaines shook it mutely, with no show of interest, then turned and led them inside.

The suite was gorgeous. Alicia had never seen anything like it, except maybe in old movies starring Grace Kelly or Audrey Hepburn as society women. She halted in the main room, heels sinking into the thick, cream-colored carpet. Every piece of the dark, elegant furniture was polished to a high sheen. Oil paintings hung on the walls, each illuminated by an individual light. A fire with real logs blazed in the marble-fronted fireplace, giving off a wonderful piney smell. Most of the side tables had crystal vases full of fresh-cut flowers, and a baby grand piano stood in one corner. Silk-shaded lamps gave the room a soft, golden glow.

Alicia took it all in. Something about the easy luxury angered her. She couldn't afford a single night in a place like this. Her father hadn't been near such a suite in his entire life; her mother and sisters never would be. Joan Gaines' stay had already cost as much as Alicia's car.

Well, I can't be expected to stay at that house, Alicia had heard her tell Kip Penrose. So she'd checked in here. The bill?

Thousands a night. She was so offhand, so casual about it.

There were two worlds on the Monterey Peninsula; Alicia had known that forever. There was her world, back in Salinas, the world of run-down bungalows and manure-smelling air and drive-by shootings, where you were lucky if you ever got to do what you wanted. Then there was this world, on the coast, the Carmel and Pebble Beach world, where houses were pleasure domes and people could do whatever the hell they pleased. Never in a million years would she be part of the latter, Alicia knew, and both that truth and her frustrated reaction to it irked her.

Penrose seemed out of sorts, too, but Alicia knew he was petrified of doing something to alienate his benefactress. The only person who appeared completely at ease was Joan Gaines.

They sat at a grouping of love seat and chairs beside the baby grand. On the coffee table in front of them was a tray with a delicate-looking tea set, one cup smeared with lipstick stains. A linen napkin had been tossed on top of an untouched tray of tiny sandwiches and cookies. Their host made no move to get rid of it or to order anything fresh for them.

Penrose cleared his throat. "How are you, Joan?"

She looked down at her lap. "As well as can be expected."

"Again," Penrose went on, "I am so very sorry about all of this. Your husband was a great man."

She said nothing, and Penrose launched into his spiel. About the evidence that had been collected from the house. The autopsy results. The nationwide search for Treebeard. Not once did Joan Gaines say a word. All she did was cross and recross her legs, and occasionally finger her hair, as if all she wanted was to get this over with.

Alicia watched. As a prosecutor she was constantly assessing people: defendants, witnesses, potential jurors.

After ten years in the business, she prided herself on her instincts.

Yet those instincts were in a muddle when it came to Joan Gaines. There was something false about her, though Alicia thought that was true of most rich people. She was about the coldest fish Alicia had ever run across. What kind of woman didn't ask a single question about how her husband had been killed? What kind of wife didn't care to know the details? It was so far from the typical spousal reaction that Alicia didn't know what to make of it.

Finally Penrose was finished. Silence fell.

"How did you meet your husband?" Alicia heard herself ask, and was rewarded with an affronted look from Joan Gaines and a scowl from Penrose. She was curious, she realized, not just to hear the answer to that question but to hear Joan Gaines talk about her murdered spouse.

"We met in New York," she said eventually.

"You were living there at the time?"

Her tone was curt. "I was working in investment banking."

"Was this before Mr. Gaines bought Headwaters Resources?"

"Yes, he was still in private equity."

Penrose cut in, with another pointed glare at Alicia. "Joan, I drafted a potential time line for the trial, assuming that Treebeard is picked up within the next few days, as we expect him to be. I know you need to plan your time." He reached down into the leather briefcase at his feet and pulled out a manila file. He was about to spread it open on the coffee table when he stopped. The dirty tea tray was in the way.

Slowly Joan turned her head from Penrose toward Alicia. "I'm so sorry," she said, though there was no apology in her smooth voice. Her blue eyes shone with a curious light. "Will you clear that, please?"

Alicia froze. Maybe she hadn't heard right, or had misunderstood. "Excuse me?"

"Will you clear that?"

She'd heard right. She'd understood.

Nobody moved. It felt to Alicia as if time stopped. Even Penrose seemed to be in a kind of suspended animation.

Something inside her seethed. The small, dark crypt in her soul where she'd buried the frustrations of thirty-five years. Always having to do without, her and her sisters. Her father never home because he was driving that damn eighteen-wheeler. The drawn, worried face of her mother, her beauty stolen at a young age by poverty and childbirth. Her own burden, knowing she was the only one who could pull the family out of the mire. And worst of all, that horrible night when she learned that her father had fallen asleep at the wheel, and knew from then on that what he had done, she would have to do. She would have to support her mother and sisters. Then and always.

Most times Alicia was resigned to her history. Sometimes it grated. And sometimes, as on this night, it fueled a cold anger that could barely contain itself within her skin.

"No," she heard herself say into the silent room, "I will not clear it. If you want it cleared, either do it yourself or call room service."

The other woman's eyes narrowed. Alicia forced herself to hold Joan Gaines' stare, though her heart pounded fiercely inside her chest. Penrose was oddly forgotten; it was as if the two women were alone in the room. Abruptly Joan Gaines stood up. "We're finished here."

Alicia had a feeling of having won a point in a contest that had not yet been declared. She remained seated and smiled, her heart still thumping. "Actually, I have a few more questions. I was curious what time you returned home last Saturday and what you were so busy doing that you didn't notice your husband lying with an arrow in his chest on the floor of the library."

"That's enough, Alicia," Penrose barked, his face flushed, but Joan Gaines said nothing at all. She didn't even acknowledge the question. Instead she strode to the door of her suite, Penrose scrambling to collect his briefcase and manila file. Alicia knew he'd read her the riot act but she couldn't say she cared.

After a moment, Alicia rose as well and made for the suite's main door, which Joan Gaines was already holding open. Penrose was clearly apologizing to her, putting his limited persuasive powers to the test. To Alicia it didn't look like he was having much success.

They had just entered the corridor when a young man in a chauffeur's uniform ran up, laden with shopping bags sporting the Neiman Marcus logo. Surprised, Alicia halted to watch.

"Sorry to be so slow getting your packages up, Mrs. Gaines." Nearly out of breath, he dropped the bags just inside the suite. "Let me know if you'll need me again tomorrow." He hurried away.

Alicia stood still, watching the young widow's fine features set into stone. *What woman*, she wondered, *goes on a shopping spree two days after her husband is murdered?*

The Latina prosecutor and the society wife regarded each other wordlessly, until Joan Gaines retreated a step and quietly shut her suite's door.

Alicia joined Kip Penrose at the elevator bank, her mind filling with unanswered questions. Even Penrose was silent as they exited the hotel into Pebble Beach's chilly December air.

***

Milo arrived early for his eight-thirty rendezvous with Prosecutor Maldonado but had plenty to survey at Carmel's Mission Ranch to keep him occupied before her arrival. In a small parking lot between some unassuming white clapboard buildings, he parked the rental Explorer next to an old-style green Ford pickup bearing, in small gold block letters, the words *Robert Kincaid Photography*.

He chuckled. It was the truck Clint Eastwood drove when he starred in *The Bridges of Madison County*, apparently being stored at the hotel the actor now owned. Milo had heard tell of Eastwood's long-standing attachment to the peninsula, his stint as mayor of Carmel, and his mid-1980s purchase of the ranch, which otherwise would have been demolished to make way for a condo development. That would have been a sorry fate for such a historic property, which in past incarnations had been not only a dairy but a World War II officers' club, and which boasted an enviable Carmel River Valley location. In daylight hours it provided a panoramic view of the Carmel Highlands and Point Lobos across a picket-fenced meadow dotted with grazing sheep.

Milo found the bar and set himself up at a small table. It was a cozy room with a country feel, warmed by a fire blazing in a stone hearth. In the far corner a television blared *Monday Night Football* to a group of avid male watchers, all nursing beers and flushed faces. "Dos Equis with lime," Milo told the waitress.

He had his strategy for the evening mapped out, mostly because he'd employed it before, on other players in other stories. He'd ask his lovely companion a few token questions about the Gaines murder case, less to get her answers than to pave the way for future disclosures. He'd gain her trust. He'd seduce her, not physically but psychologically, so that when he really needed inside info down the road, she'd give it to him.

Some might call it cynical. Milo called it good reporting. And who did it hurt? His viewers got better stories and his sources enjoyed his assiduous protection. Win-win, as far as he was concerned.

Minutes later, when Alicia Maldonado walked into the bar and brought to a halt every last murmur of conversation, Milo realized it was a good thing she was his companion for the evening. For if he had been with any other woman, he would have had trouble keeping his eyes from straying to the dark-haired, olive-skinned beauty who now stood before him.

She could not be described as glamorous. Or fashionable. Her navy-blue suit clearly had seen better days, and the same could be said for the wheat-colored overcoat topping it. Yet something about her confident stride, the intelligent light in her brown eyes, the careless toss of that long wavy hair over her shoulder, made her arresting, vibrant. As he'd found at the press conference it was hard not to stare at her, hard not to become mesmerized by the thoughts rapidly playing out on the expressive planes of her face.

"You didn't have any trouble finding the place?" she asked.

He rose, both out of politeness and to help her shed her coat. "None at all. Actually, my hotel's not far away."

"Oh?" They both sat, setting off a clatter of wooden chair legs on the hardwood floor. "Where are you staying?"

"The Cypress Inn."

"Doris Day's place? I'm surprised." Again the offhand toss of the hair. "It's a great little hotel, but I would think reporters would stay with everybody else who's here on business. Like at the Monterey Plaza Hotel."

"I just like the Cypress Inn." He paused, slightly chagrined. He felt odd making this admission. "There's always a dog or two in the lobby." The actress was famous for her love of animals, particularly of the canine variety, and ran one of the few hostelries that catered to travelers and their pets.

Alicia smiled. "You like dogs?"

"Love 'em. Grew up with Labs, big golden Labs who drooled all over and knocked things off low tables when they swished their tails. Paris and Helen." He shook his head, remembering those sloppy, adorable members of the family. "I wish I could own a dog now, but my travel schedule doesn't permit it. So I have to get my fix other ways."

She nodded, with a wise look in her eyes that said she understood a crazy work life. The waitress sidled over. Alicia glanced at Milo's Dos Equis. "I'll have the same, please," she said, which made Milo smile.

"What's so funny?"

"I can't remember the last time I was with a woman who ordered a beer. It's either wine or whatever is the cocktail of the moment. Usually something in a martini glass, with grenadine in it to make it pink. To mask the fact that it's made with three kinds of vodka."

She laughed, a pretty sound. "Where do you live that you meet all these vodka-drinking women?"

"D.C. Though—"

"You're hardly ever there."

"Right."

Alicia's Dos Equis arrived. They were silent while the waitress filled Alicia's chilled glass, took Milo's order for a second, and glided away.

"So," Milo said. Time to get the ball rolling. "I know it's not politically correct to say so, but you must be enjoying the

Gaines case. A high-profile murder prosecution is the sort of thing careers are built on."

"You're right." Her tone was light. "It's not politically correct to say so."

"How did you come to be involved?"

She hesitated. He had the idea she was deciding whether to tell him the truth or make something up. Then, "I was the first D.A. at the scene."

"Really? How did that happen?"

"Good luck, I guess."

He doubted that. "More likely good timing." He thought for a moment. "I know you've prosecuted homicides before. That must make you a rarity in the Monterey County D.A.'s office."

She shrugged. "There are a few of us."

"But still, you got selected to be the D.A.'s number two on the big case."

"As I say, I got there first."

"Penrose must have a lot of faith in you."

She said nothing.

"Have you worked with him for a long time?"

"Since he became D.A. Three years ago."

"Not before?"

She shook her head.

"Still, you must be one of his favorites."

Again she smiled that enigmatic smile, but was silent. It was a bit like having a drink with Mona Lisa. "So." He thought back to what he knew of the murder. "Daniel Gaines was killed on Saturday. How—"

"His body was *discovered* on Saturday," she cut in, then abruptly stopped.

"Aha!" Jokingly Milo pointed a finger at her. "Finally I learn something! So you have evidence it actually happened on Friday?"

She sipped her beer, her eyes averted. Milo waited. Still nothing. "It must have been difficult to be at the scene," he offered several seconds later. "Such a violent killing."

"There's no such thing as a nonviolent killing."

"Hm. Guess not." Closed-mouthed little minx, wasn't she? It was clear he wasn't going to get a damn thing out of her. Admirable, actually. "So," he said, "why did you decide to become a prosecutor?"

That line of questioning she didn't seem to mind. "Sometimes I'm surprised I did." She squinted, as though casting her mind back in time. "I don't remember what I thought I'd do when I was in law school. I had vague notions of practicing law for a while, then running for office. Then a friend of mine suggested I interview with the Monterey County D.A."

"Which went well, apparently."

"I remember going into it thinking they would all be a bunch of Nazis. They sort of were. In my first round of interviews I had three older white guys, all with buzz cuts, like they'd all been in the military. Not that I have anything against the military, but you know what I mean."

He nodded.

"But we actually had a conversation. A real give and take. I couldn't believe it for a while, but eventually I realized that I agreed with them about a lot of things. Then they invited me back for round two, then round three, then..." She stopped.

"The rest is history."

"As they say." She sipped her beer. He sensed she'd had enough of talking about herself, so wasn't surprised when she turned the tables. "Where did you grow up?"

"I was born in Bogota but then we moved to Germany. Then Paris, then Washington when I was ten, Washington all through prep school." He paused. He should have said "high" rather than "prep" school. Suddenly he found himself reluctant to provide copious details on his background.

She cocked her head, her eyes curious. "Pappas is a Greek name, right?"

"That's right. I have dual Greek and US citizenship."

"What did your father do that you moved around so much?"

He hesitated. Then, "He was in the diplomatic corps."

"What did he do in Washington?"

No way around it. "He was ambassador."

She fell silent and looked down at her lap. Milo shifted in his chair. *She thinks her background's so different from mine. And she's embarrassed about it, though she needn't be.* For a moment he saw a vulnerability in the hard-boiled prosecutor and found himself touched. How surprised she would be to learn the truth about his family history. Alicia Maldonado had more in common with Milo Pappas than she realized. "What did your father do?" he asked, suddenly curious.

She raised her eyes. "He was a long-haul trucker."

"So he was away from home a lot?"

"Yes."

"Just like mine."

She gave him a look that said, *No, different from yours.* "Did you grow up in California?" he asked.

"Yes. Not far from here."

"Have you lived here all your life?"

Again she dropped her eyes. "Sure have."

He watched a flush rise on her cheeks. "You're lucky," he said, then added, "It's a beautiful part of the world."

"Well, I guess I have to take your word for that. You've seen a lot of the world, so you would know." Then she raised her head again, and it pained him to see both the sadness and the hint of defiance in those lovely dark eyes.

He leaned closer to her across the table. "You'll travel, Alicia. You'll see the world."

"Don't patronize me."

"I'm not. I'm just stating a fact."

"You can see into the future?"

"Yes." Then he laughed, and that got her to smile. "Yes, I can."

They stared at each other. At that moment Milo could actually imagine showing this woman his favorite places. Bangkok, where crossing the street without getting hit by a three-wheeled *tuk-tuk* taxi was a daredevil exercise. Maui, for the sunset, where the sky glowed pink and purple and you could swear you'd glimpsed heaven. Even his favorite Upper West Side cafe with the endless Sunday brunch lines, where snow or sun you'd stand outside waiting for a table because the prospect of buttermilk pancakes and the *New York Times* was just too good to pass up.

Some of the football watchers let out a cheer, dragging Alicia's eyes away from his. "Game's over, apparently," she said.

"Judging from the reaction, I guess the good guys won."

"I wish it was always that easy."

"Come on." He smiled at her. "Is that Alicia Maldonado talking? Or the cynical prosecutor?"

"They're one and the same."

"Somehow I don't believe that."

She rolled her eyes. Milo realized he was enjoying himself more than he'd expected to. He didn't know quite what to make of this woman. She didn't fit into any of the usual categories. "I'm glad," he said, idly trailing a finger through the condensation on his beer bottle, "that you've realized I'm not the enemy."

She arched an eyebrow. "You thought you were?"

"Well, you gave me kind of a hard time at the press conference."

"No, I didn't. I just treated you like any other reporter. That's what you didn't like."

He laughed so loudly some of the football watchers looked over. "You're right! You're absolutely right." He lowered his voice. "I was hoping you might give me special treatment."

"You flatter yourself."

"That's a lot easier than waiting for somebody else to do it."

Then it was her turn to laugh, and he watched, pleased to have been the cause. They were silent for a while, sipping their beers, then he spoke up. "Well, I suppose I should ask you at least a few probing questions about Daniel Gaines' murder."

"Aren't you done with that yet?"

"Not yet." He shook his head. "I have to stick to my game plan even though I don't much feel like it. I'm having too good a time."

"Well, that's too bad. For you, anyway. Because I could tell you a thing or two."

He was surprised. Apparently he had succeeded in warming her up a bit. He forced himself to climb out of the pleasant stupor created by beer, repartee with a beautiful woman, and a roaring fire. He decided to ask a stupid, leading question, which occasionally elicited a valuable, explanatory response. "So isn't this about the most boring case in the world? I mean, apart from the fact that the victim was a candidate for governor of California, isn't it just so obvious who did it?"

She sighed. "You know the first people the police look to

in a murder?"

"Tell me."

"Spouse. Family. Friends. Almost always it's somebody close to the victim."

He'd known that. "But that's not true here."

She frowned. "Why do you say that?"

"Well..." He laughed. "*Spouse?* You think Joan Gaines would shoot her husband with an arrow?"

"Why not? Is she somehow less likely than other spouses?"

"Well, frankly, yes." He hesitated, then, "People like Joan Gaines don't go around murdering their husbands."

He watched Alicia narrow her eyes at him. The fire in the grate roared as fiercely as ever, yet all at once the air seemed to chill. "You mean because she's from a wealthy family? Because she's the daughter of a governor?"

That was pretty much what he'd meant, but he hesitated to spell it out. While he was debating what to say, Alicia resumed speaking.

"You know, murderers come from all walks of life. It's not just the poor who kill."

"I'm not suggesting it is. I'm merely pointing out that Joan Gaines is a good woman from a good family and she would never—"

"How do you know she's a good woman?"

Damn. This was the last thing he wanted to get into.

"Do you know her?" she demanded. Milo had a sudden understanding of what it would be like to be cross-examined by Deputy D.A. Maldonado.

He thought fast. He didn't want to lie. Nor was it advisable, since his history with Joan was hardly secret. "I know her," he allowed. "More to the point, I know the family. And when I compare Joan Gaines to Treebeard it looks to me to be pretty cut and dried who's the more likely suspect."

Silence. When Alicia finally spoke, her voice was cold. "It surprises me that you're not even willing to consider the possibility that this case might not be all sewn up. I thought reporters were supposed to keep an open mind. Naive of me. But then again, what do I know? I've never been off the peninsula."

She glanced at her watch then abruptly stood up, reached into her purse, and threw a twenty-dollar bill on the table. "I have to go. Good night." She grabbed her overcoat and headed for the door.

Damn. "Alicia ..."

But she was already gone. He grabbed his own overcoat and pulled out his billfold, extracting a twenty. The cold air when he exited the bar hit him like a slap.

He followed her across the parking lot at a half run, then reached for her arm when she stopped at a car. She shook him off, digging into her purse, apparently for her key. Her breath rose like a soft white cloud in the chill air.

"I'm sorry if I offended you. I certainly didn't mean to. And let me pay for our drinks. Here ..." and he tried to hand her the twenty.

"Forget it." She ignored the outstretched bill. "And you didn't offend me. I'm just surprised you have such a rosy view of the rich and famous." She found her key and poked it into the lock. "Though I shouldn't be, since you're one of them."

"Hey, now, wait a minute." He stepped between her and her car, its door still closed. "That's not fair. You talk about me having a closed mind?" He reached out and made a brushing motion on her right shoulder, as if he were trying to get something off.

They were standing so close together, her breath puffed in

his face. "What are you doing?"

"I'm trying to knock that chip off your shoulder."

She pushed back hard against his chest, her eyes angry. "You've got a lot of nerve!"

There was no thought on the path from impulse to action. He grabbed her shoulders and pulled her body toward his own, swiftly capturing her mouth. Her lips resisted at first, then parted, and he felt her body meld into his own. Not soften; it was far too passionate a motion for that. Vaguely he wondered what had possessed him to do what he was now doing, and with such enjoyment. Admiration, attraction, sheer curiosity had pooled to form a crazy, mixed-up brew that had gotten the better of his common sense, yet he couldn't say he was sorry. His hands were in her hair, he realized, as he twisted her head this way and that to get his fill of her. He had the fleeting idea that would not happen soon.

All at once she pulled back and stared at him, her eyes flaring and her mouth almost swollen from the ferocity of their kiss. She held up a warning finger and opened that delicious mouth as if about to say something, but then abruptly shut it again. Words failed her, apparently. They failed him, too.

He stepped back to allow her room to get into her car. She turned the ignition and revved the engine, backing out soon and driving away just as fast. He watched her, unable to look away until at long last her taillights disappeared into the fog.

CHAPTER SIX

"This is a hell of a way to spend Christmas Eve, Alicia." Louella Wilkes sat in the passenger seat of Alicia's silver VW bug, staring out the window and complaining. "This is pointless. Carmel PD already did this interview. What do you expect to get that they didn't?"

"It'll only take a few hours. I'll get you back to the office by three."

"Does Penrose know about this?"

"Of course not." Penrose would have a cow if he thought Alicia was spending one second on ground already covered, particularly such sacred ground as Joan Gaines' alibi for the night her husband was murdered. Alicia pushed her foot down hard on the accelerator and the VW surged forward. "Anyway, I completely disagree that it's a bad idea. Carmel PD isn't exactly experienced when it comes to homicide investigations. Besides, don't you think it's weird that Joan Gaines went shopping two days after her husband died?"

"She needed something for the funeral."

"And got her hair dyed? And her nails done? In San Francisco, no less, because that's the nearest Neiman Marcus? It's not her wedding day coming up, Louella—it's her husband's funeral."

The scenery whizzed past. Their destination of Santa Cruz lay about forty-five miles north of Carmel on Highway 1, the Pacific Coast Highway, a narrow thoroughfare that twisted along California's shoreline. Much of the scenery was gorgeous. Twenty miles south, around Big Sur, it was spectacular. But this stretch of PCH wound inland toward Watsonville, known as the strawberry capital of the world. As an agricultural outpost, it was less than scenic and less than fragrant. Kind of like Salinas.

"So maybe she didn't love him," Louella said. "Did you ever think of that? Maybe she didn't feel so bad he got offed. So she still wanted to go shopping, kind of show him up by looking fabulous at his funeral."

Alicia chuckled. "It's not like he'll be there to appreciate it, Louella."

"No, but she can still get the satisfaction." Louella toyed with her bleached-blond hair, again staring out the passenger window. "How's Jorge, by the way?"

"Oh, he's great." Alicia didn't bother with the smile, since Louella wasn't looking.

"What are you guys doing tomorrow? Or do you do Christmas tonight?"

"We'll go to midnight Mass tonight but get together at my mom's tomorrow. Then at Jorge's mom's later."

Yet even as Alicia talked about Jorge, she knew the man most on her mind was Milo Pappas. What was it about that guy? First she broke her "Keep reporters at arm's length" rule by agreeing to meet him. Then she laughed in the rule's face by kissing him. And why? He'd dazzled her. It was so humiliating. Despite the fact that he was full of himself, and had pissed her off by saying she had a chip on her shoulder, he'd dazzled her. He was gorgeous and exciting and moved in a big, wide, important world she was dying to know more about. And dying to enter, though she'd have an easier time catching the moon.

That morning over cereal she did what she never did. She watched TV. She'd turned on her rinky-dink set in the kitchen, set it to the WBS station, and watched its morning show for almost an hour. She didn't even flip to other channels during commercials for fear she'd miss him. She'd seen him twice, though only on taped stories. The fact that he wasn't doing live reports like before upset her. Maybe he'd already gone? Though he'd be back, right?

Then again, what did it matter? As her mother would say, he wanted her for one thing and one thing only. Well, two things in this case, but that was no less an insult. She raised her chin in defiance, though Milo Pappas was nowhere in the vicinity to witness her resolve. She would refuse to provide either inside info or a roll in the hay, despite how tempting the latter prospect might be. She had her pride. She would not be some jet-setting newsman's Salinas squeeze, then be tossed away like yesterday's newspaper when he was done with her.

"What about you, Louella?" she asked. "What are you doing for Christmas?" They were back to hugging the coast now, a sodden and deserted Seacliff State Beach to their left. It was a dreary afternoon, intermittently drizzling and dumping serious rain.

"Same old, same old." Louella sounded bored and a little depressed. "My folks are here visiting. We'll exchange gifts tomorrow, and my mom and I'll cook. Maybe a movie tonight."

Louella was an only child and stated loud and often that she wanted to get married and have a pack of kids. The pack got smaller every year she couldn't pull off the first half of the equation. It made Alicia feel especially ungrateful about Jorge.

Louella had confided once that men were put off by her being a D.A. investigator. It wasn't feminine, apparently, to chase down bad guys and put them behind bars. But Louella stuck to her guns. She loved her work, period. Alicia admired that.

She looked away from the road at Louella. "Thanks for coming with me, by the way."

"Ah, no problem." Louella made a dismissive wave of the hand. "It's nice to be needed."

"Well, you are." No question about it. Alicia couldn't risk doing investigative work without a D.A. investigator. If this jaunt did turn up evidence, Alicia would need someone other than herself to testify. She couldn't be both a prosecuting attorney and a witness in the same case.

"You know," Louella said, "a woman like Joan Gaines wouldn't kill her husband anyway. She'd divorce him. Or at worst she'd get somebody else to kill him."

"But if she got somebody else to kill him, that somebody else would know. It's too risky." Alicia shook her head. "Louella, I'm not saying she killed him, necessarily. I'm just saying her behavior is odd. Supposedly finding the body hours after she got home, the lack of emotion, the shopping—it just doesn't add up."

"So you want to check out her alibi."

"Right."

"You want to figure out if she really was in Santa Cruz, like she told Bucky."

"Oh, I believe she was. I can't imagine she would have lied about that. It's too easy to check out." Alicia maneuvered past a slow-moving crimson-colored SUV that was hogging the fast lane for no apparent reason. "No, I want to find out if she could have gone back and forth to Carmel while she was supposedly overnight in Santa Cruz."

Louella said nothing for a while, twisting her body to face Alicia by leaning back against the passenger door. She just watched. Alicia found it unsettling. Then, finally, Louella broke the silence. "Can I ask you a question?"

"Sure."

"I don't want to piss you off."

"You're not going to piss me off."

Louella didn't seem convinced. She took a deep breath, as if she were gearing up. "I have never known you to be illogical, Alicia. It's a big part of what makes you such a good prosecutor. But in this case..."

"You think I'm being illogical?"

"Aren't you clutching at straws? I mean ..." She paused. "Isn't it possible you just hate women like Joan Gaines? Because they have everything handed to them on a silver platter? Could that be the reason we're doing this?"

Alicia was a little pissed off. Again the chip-on-her-shoulder accusation? "Why would I hate her just because she's rich? Why?"

"Hell, *I* kind of hate her just because she's rich. And she didn't try to make me clean up her dirty dishes after her."

Alicia had told Louella about that. Now she regretted it. "That would make me pretty small-minded, wouldn't it?"

"I don't think so. It's understandable."

Alicia said nothing. She had had enough of being a case study in how the have-nots vented their frustration toward the haves. She exited Highway 1 and turned right on a cloverleaf that eventually dropped them on Santa Cruz city streets.

Santa Cruz was an attractive beach town but not nearly as wealthy as Carmel. It had real working people and children and everything. Alicia stopped at a red light. Two corners were taken up with off-brand gasoline stations. The others had competing shops selling wet suits and surfing gear.

"All I'm saying," Louella said, "is that she can be a royal bitch and still not have killed her husband."

"I understand that."

The light changed. Alicia drove forward. *But she can be a*

royal bitch and could have killed her husband, too.

"We're here," she announced a few turns later, slowing to a halt on a wide tree-lined street in front of the gorgeously restored Victorian owned by Courtney Holt, Stanford Class of '94 and apparently one of Joan Hudson Gaines' best gal pals. Both women remained in the VW, staring at the house through the raindrops gathering on the windshield.

"I half expect Anne of Green Gables to come waltzing out of there," Louella said.

"It's beautiful, isn't it?"

"It's amazing. I guess that's what they mean by gingerbread."

The house stood on the corner, and unlike every other property on the block appeared to take up several lots. Its facade sported an incredible amount of Victorian-style ornamentation. It was painted yellow, but the trim was white with both light and dark green accents, and shiny gold designs everywhere. It even had a stained-glass window, and an actual turret.

Louella got out of the VW and opened her red plaid umbrella over her head. "They don't build 'em like this anymore, not even in the South."

Alicia, who'd forgotten an umbrella, raced up the narrow flagged walk, then hopped the stairs to a small porch. On the door hung a huge eucalyptus wreath with a red velvet bow. She paused to look at Louella before ringing the doorbell. "Ready?" Her own heart was thumping, and not just from the exercise.

Louella sighed. "Let's get it over with."

***

Joan paced the drawing room of her mother's 17 Mile

Drive estate, rain cascading down the large, paned windows. Every so often she'd sip from her white wine, trying not to down it before her mother finished dressing and came downstairs for lunch. This was about the last place in the world she wanted to be, but it was Christmas Eve and duty called. She would much rather have been in her suite watching the news to see what kind of play her statement to the press was getting. But midday TV watching was one of the many things upon which Libby Storrow Hudson frowned.

Joan knew all about her mother's disapproval. She threw back the last of her wine. It was damn hard for anybody to come up to Libby Hudson's highly placed snuff. Born into Boston North Shore money, she was a puritan of the old style, the sort of woman who swam every day in frigid ocean water because she believed it was good for her. She rose at dawn, got a million things done, went to bed early, and repeated the process the next day. Now that she was no longer campaigning for her husband, she spent all her time raising money for charity, and invariably was elected president of this and chairwoman of that. If Web Hudson had won elective office because he could connect with the common man, Libby Hudson ruled in philanthropic circles because of the very opposite trait: her pure elitism. She made unrepentant blue bloods completely comfortable.

Joan suspected that was why her mother had never liked Daniel. As far as Libby Hudson was concerned, he was a social-climbing upstart unworthy of Joan's hand. That attitude hadn't done much to improve mother-daughter relations.

"I apologize for keeping you waiting, dear." Libby Hudson swept into the room. She might be lunching alone with her daughter but she was dressed to dine at the White House. She wore a severely elegant black Armani suit and enormous pearls at her ears and throat. Her short white hair was set in the soft curls she'd long favored. She was impeccably made up, though her skin was still flushed from her recent exertions. She'd kept her daughter waiting because she was late finishing her daily two-mile run.

At age sixty-five. On a cold, drenched Christmas Eve.

Joan flushed at her own self-indulgent morning. She tried to set down her empty wineglass without being obvious but saw her mother's mouth pucker with disapproval. It was hopeless. Even though she was going through a nightmare her mother would still find a way to condemn her. She sank onto the yellow cushion of a satinwood Louis XVI chair. "So tell me about your trip to Santa Barbara."

"There's very little to tell." Her mother settled on a white damask sofa, crossing her thin legs at the ankles. "I saw some old friends. It's a beautiful part of the state."

"Do you ever think of moving back to Massachusetts now that Father's gone?" Joan wondered what had possessed her to ask that question, though now that it had occurred to her it didn't seem a half-bad idea.

"I considered it, but never seriously. After all these years, California is my home."

Web and Libby Hudson hadn't debated long where to retire. They'd lived almost all their adult lives in Northern California, with the exception of the six years her father served in the US Senate. The obvious choices were San Francisco; Woodside, the most exclusive community in Silicon Valley; and Pebble Beach. The ocean, the golf, the natural beauty, not to mention the guard gates, decided them on Pebble Beach. And, of course, 17 Mile Drive.

Joan remembered her mother telling her that this particular estate was inspired by the Chateau de Clavary, built in the south of France in the early nineteenth century. As chateaux went, it wasn't large, but it was very beautiful. The landscaping was superb, formal on the side that faced 17 Mile Drive but running more to nature where it fronted the Pacific. One of her father's favorite features was the duplication in the entrance hall of the Picasso mosaic laid in the original French chateau.

"Thank you for arranging Daniel's service, Mother," Joan said a few seconds later into the silence.

It was to be held Friday, a public memorial service followed by a private burial. She and her mother both wanted to get it over with before the New Year. And when her mother offered to make the arrangements, Joan agreed instantly. She had zero interest in handling it.

"When will Daniel's family arrive?" her mother asked.

"Thursday."

"Shall I host them here?"

Joan was surprised. Daniel's parents were not exactly her mother's kind of people. She always referred to Jack Gaines, who owned car dealerships in the Philadelphia area, as a "merchant," and didn't bother to describe Diane, a society wife so lowly placed she didn't even register on Libby Hudson's social ladder.

"There's no need, though that's very kind of you," Joan said. "I've arranged for them to stay at the Lodge."

Her mother nodded. Then, "You know, my dear..." She stopped, seeming to choose her words carefully. "I am sorry about Daniel."

Joan looked down at her lap, saying nothing. She didn't think her mother was sorry at all.

"I hope you're not terribly aggrieved," her mother went on.

"I'll survive," she said.

Her mother frowned. "I hope you'll do more than that.

Have you made any plans?"

"Well..." Joan arched her brows, surprised that her mother of all people was the first to recognize that she had more going on in her life than widowhood. "I've done some thinking," she offered.

"Good. And what have you concluded?"

"Well..." There was one thing she could tell her mother at this point. "That as soon as possible I want to take over as CEO of Headwaters."

"What?" Her mother narrowed her eyes in the disapproving squint Joan knew so well. "Why in the world would you want to do that?"

This wasn't what Joan had expected to hear. "Excuse me?"

"Why would you want to have anything to do with that awful business?" Her mother waved a dismissive hand. "There are people already there who can run it. I speak to them every day. You—"

"You speak to them?" Joan was indignant. "You're not even a shareholder since Daniel bought out Father's stake! Isn't it my role to deal with Headwaters?"

"I hardly think so, no." Her mother laughed, that imperious, North Shore laugh that said, *I understand things far better than you ever will. Accept it.* "You shouldn't be thinking about Headwaters, Joan. You should be thinking about traveling, renewing your soul, perhaps getting involved in charity work. In time, meeting a new—"

"You think that's all I'm good for? Wasting my time doing charity work and getting married again?" Joan was on her feet, she realized, and her voice was raised. Her mother's thin, parchmenty skin was flushed, and this time not from her run. "You don't think I can run Headwaters. You don't think I can run the trust, either. You're thrilled Father made you trustee."

"I spent my entire adult life being a good wife to your father and doing charity work." Her mother's tone was glacial. "I hardly consider either pursuit a waste. Now sit down."

"I am not going to—"

"Sit ... down."

Silence fell. Rain battered the windows and made the fire in the grate hiss. Joan retreated to her chair, though she felt like a fractious child being sentenced to a time-out.

Finally her mother spoke. "There is no need for you to involve yourself in the trust, Joan. It is my concern."

"I guess so, since you're now trustee." She knew she sounded snippy.

"It's not a job I relish, I assure you."

What a lie! "I still think Father should have made me trustee. I'm the one with the master's in business."

Her mother stared at her. Then, "You studied *toward* a master's in business. As I recall you did not actually earn it."

Joan clenched her jaw. "We're back to that again?"

"There is very little you've begun that you've finished, Joan."

"For example, business school. And of course you would consider my investment banking job a failure, too."

"I would hardly consider it a success. My recollection is that you lasted only six months."

Joan bit back the impulse to correct her mother. *Eight months!* she wanted to scream, but there was no point. No one understood that when she was finished with a project, she was simply finished with it. Why stay at Stanford Business School just to get the degree? Why stay with Humphrey Stanton when she'd lost her interest in I-banking? No one gave her credit for knowing when to move on. Well, she knew it right now.

She rose from her chair. "I have realized that I cannot stay for lunch," she declared stiffly. "Good-bye, Mother."

Joan walked out, holding her head high. She told herself she'd won that argument, though she wasn't entirely sure she had. She felt her mother's eyes on her back the entire time she exited the enormous drawing room of the 17 Mile Drive estate.

She pulled open the chateau's front door and walked out into the rain. She was alone. Her father was gone. Her husband was gone. And her mother might as well be.

***

Christmas Eve found Milo seated at his older brother Andreas's Park Avenue dining table, participating in one of the few family events in which he engaged per year. He'd flown cross-country for the dinner gathering, but Milo flew halfway around the world to shoot a few stand-ups. Newspeople flew like commuters rode the bus.

At the table's head, Andreas carved a massive turkey, bestowing on it the same intense concentration he gave the documents that crossed his desk as a managing partner of the Wall Street law firm Fenwick, Reid & Patcher. Directly opposite Milo sat Ari, Andreas's twin in every way but two: he had chosen investment banking over law and London over Manhattan. At the moment the wives were doing mysterious things in the kitchen, and the five offspring were raising a ruckus kicking each other under the table. Milo's parents were absent, because neither Mana nor Baba would undertake international travel over the holiday season. They preferred the gorgeous serenity of their retirement home in Thessaloniki, and Milo could hardly blame them.

"So, Milo," Andreas asked over the din, "what stories have you been working on lately?"

Brothers they might be, but intimates they were not. With Mac and Tran, Milo could spend hours dissecting the meaning of life. Or even better, saying nothing at all. But with his brothers, exchanging pleasantries and professional data was the deepest their conversation ever got.

"Oh, the usual." Milo straightened the oyster-white napkin on his lap. "New revelations about terrorist-linked overseas bank accounts. Scandal at a nuclear power plant near San Diego. And of course the Daniel Gaines murder."

"That is so shocking!" Andreas's wife Helen swept in, bearing platters of yams and carrots. Blond and snooty and rarely out of Upper East Side air, Helen handled serving dishes only on major holidays, and then only when forced. "When are they going to arrest that Treebeard man?"

"When they find him."

"Poor Joan." Helen's face assumed an expression of dismay, but Milo could see the naked curiosity behind the false concern. Clearly she wanted inside dirt to pass along to her fellow society doyennes. "I feel so terrible for her. How is she doing, do you know?"

"I don't know."

"But haven't you—"

"We need a serving platter here, Helen." Andreas looked up from the turkey and shot his wife a pointed look that said, *Shut up about Joan*. Helen scowled but said nothing, flouncing off to the kitchen. For once, Milo was grateful to his brother.

Joan and Milo's sordid romantic history was a family non-secret. Everyone knew that Joan had thrown Milo for a loop when she'd cut him loose. Or, as Helen liked to put it, when she'd "dumped him from a dizzy height." Given that the man Joan eventually married had gained national prominence as a timber executive and followed that up with a promising gubernatorial run, Milo knew his siblings thought Joan had made the smart choice. Even with Daniel Gaines dead, in this crowd Milo suffered by comparison.

Milo watched Andreas systematically dismantle the twenty-eight-pound turkey and, with no effort at all, slid back into the role of Pappas family black sheep. However high his star rose, however brightly it shone in the network-news firmament, in his family circle he would forever be Milo, the lackadaisical student. Milo, the career hopper. Milo, the incorrigible womanizer, who at age thirty-eight was still unmarried and had sired no sons to carry on the Pappas name. Milo knew his father and brothers secretly believed his TV-news success to be a fluke, one that would eventually be righted.

Milo never ceased being proud that what he had achieved in broadcast news, he had achieved on his own. In late 1990, while the Gulf War loomed and he dithered over his dissertation, he heard from a Georgetown friend that WBS was looking for people with overseas experience to base in London. He applied, and after several rounds of interviews got hired as an entry-level producer. When he abandoned his Ph.D. for the job, his family howled in protest, warning that Milo would regret the decision for the rest of his days.

They shut up when Milo parlayed that first job into a much more visible on-air correspondent's position. They let out not a peep when years later he did such stellar work covering the war on terrorism that he was promoted to a plum correspondent role on *Newsline*.

"Children, keep it down!" Marissa, Ari's wife and a red-haired upper-class Dubliner, bustled in. She put her hands on her hips, which, unlike her sister-in-law's, were spreading. "Or does all this noise mean none of you wants dessert?"

Outraged yells answered that question. Order was restored and finally every Pappas was seated. Ari, older than Andreas by three minutes and hence the patriarch when Baba was absent, had the honor of making the toast. After several rambling sentences about the great joy that possessed him whenever his family was gathered, he raised his wineglass. "*Kali oreksi!*"

"*Kali oreksi,*" they all duly repeated, Greek for *Bon appetit.*

The white Bordeaux slid down Milo's throat, chilled and delicious. The feasting began, no simple matter when it required the passing of a dozen serving dishes to five adults and an equal number of rambunctious children.

It both amused and irritated Milo to see his brothers act like WASPs, reproducing the Pilgrims' feast on Christmas Eve because they couldn't get enough of it just once a year. The only concession to their heritage was the *arni stofourno,* a baked lamb dish that Marissa made and that Helen, with her horror of all things high fat, wouldn't touch.

Once they'd dispensed of the latest in every Pappas male's professional life, Helen turned her eagle eyes in Milo's direction. "So," she said, her tone coy, "are you dating anyone interesting?"

The face of Alicia Maldonado flashed before his eyes. "Not lately," he replied. He realized, with some surprise, that for once he had no romantic exploits to polish off and display. What a rarity.

Milo learned soon after his network star began to rise that his fame was a powerful erotic magnet, even to exceedingly attractive females. Moreover, life on the road invited sexual escapades. Tantalizing offers were frequently made. How was a man to resist? More to the point, why should he? Even many of his colleagues with wives in the home port routinely indulged. Why shouldn't the unencumbered, uncommitted

Milo Pappas?

Yet it was Milo who was tarred by these episodes, in the gossipy mouths of his network brethren; Milo who overindulged, laid waste to young hearts, ran roughshod over vulnerable women. All thanks to his reputation as Pretty-boy Pappas, O'Malley's favorite moniker for the newsman he would forever dismiss as a jet-setting playboy.

As his brothers and their families chattered on around him, Milo let his mind drift to Alicia. She was different, toughened by life in a way he didn't usually encounter. True, network newswomen were a hard-nosed bunch, but they enjoyed big-time money and big-time attention. They envied no one, except perhaps their counterparts who occupied higher rungs on the network-news ladder than they did.

The fact of it was, Alicia intrigued him, and not just as a source. She was proud. She was scrappy. A little touchy, but that was understandable given where she came from. And while for whatever reason most women kowtowed to him, this one didn't. He actually felt one down to her, which oddly enough was invigorating. And that kiss of hers ... There was a lot of juice in that woman, a lot of life. He didn't know quite what to expect from her and discovered he was eager to see her again just to find out what she'd do next.

Milo's cell phone rang, jolting him back to the reality of his brother's dining table. He excused himself and repaired to the hallway to take the call.

It was O'Malley, unfortunately. "We're going to need you in San Diego Saturday," O'Malley told him. "Turns out our deep throat will give us an interview."

The nuclear power plant story. "Let me guess," Milo said. "He's agreed to go on camera so long as we hide his face, alter his voice, and don't use his name."

"That's about the size of it."

It would still be powerful. Former operator disclosing details of close calls, pressure to hit targets, and safety lines crossed. Milo had an unrelated thought. "What are you doing working, O'Malley? Aren't you in Florida with your son's family?"

He sounded impatient. "Yes, I'm in Florida."

Typical. Christmas Eve, on holiday with his family, and O'Malley was working the phones. That was why he was a network producer star. He painted his personal life into as small a corner as possible, then stepped on it when he needed to and figured somebody else would repaint.

"How's the lovely widow?" O'Malley's tone was snide. "Crying on her old friend's shoulder?"

"Wouldn't know," Milo replied. "Sorry, gotta go." Then he jabbed the end button on his cell.

Damn O'Malley. Milo snapped the phone shut, then returned it to his trouser pocket. From down the hall he could hear his brothers and their wives engaged in a lively debate about the relative merits of vacation homes in the Caribbean versus the Mediterranean.

So San Diego Saturday. After the Monterey Peninsula Friday to cover Daniel Gaines' funeral, at which no doubt he'd see Joan. Milo began to walk toward his family's voices. The woman he'd much rather run into was Alicia Maldonado.

***

Alicia listened as the doorbell at Courtney Holt's Victorian home set off an impressive resounding chime. A moment later an older Latina answered the door.

Alicia flashed her ID. "*Yo soy* Alicia Maldonado, *de la Oficina del Fiscal de Distrito.*"

"*Si,*" the woman said, and waved them into an elegant

foyer, then a high-ceilinged front parlor. They claimed two armchairs by a fireplace, its ornate carved mantel covered with Christmas cards. Deep in the recesses of the house they could hear children battling over a toy, and the scolding voices of a few women younger than the housekeeper, also speaking Spanish.

"I guess the nannies don't get Christmas Eve off," Louella muttered under her breath.

"It sounds like there's one nanny per kid. Have you ever heard of that?"

"I think that's standard for this crowd." Louella made a face like *Who knows?* and Alicia continued her inspection of the Holt front parlor.

It was a beautiful room with elaborate white molding. The furniture was dark and traditional, and the hardwood floor was partially covered by a thick Oriental carpet in rust, green, and gold. Above a white-on-white striped sofa was a stunning oil painting of a young girl. The room was dominated by an enormous Christmas tree, as tall as the ceiling, its white lights twinkling. Beneath it was quite a collection of presents waiting to be unwrapped.

"Not too shabby," Alicia heard Louella murmur, and she had to agree. Joan Gaines' friend might not be as rich as Joan but she was doing just fine.

Then Courtney Holt appeared in the flesh to reinforce that opinion. She was thin and good-looking with short blond hair, and was decked out in cream-colored trousers and a matching cashmere sweater. Alicia doubted she'd dressed up for them; more likely this was a typical weekday getup. She had the look of somebody who might show up on the cover of Town and Country.

"Would you like coffee? Or tea?" she asked. Her offer sounded halfhearted and her green eyes were cold. That didn't surprise Alicia. Most people weren't thrilled to find a prosecutor and her sidekick investigator in their front room.

Alicia declined. "I appreciate your taking the time to see us on Christmas Eve."

"I must say, I find it odd." Courtney Holt perched on the sofa and crossed her legs at the ankles. Her tone was accusing. "I already had a lengthy discussion with several officers from the Carmel Police Department. Don't you think the district attorney's office should be focusing on finding that Treebeard man?"

"Many resources are being deployed in that direction."

"Then what do you need with me?"

"We'd just like to go over some things again. Louella?" Alicia looked pointedly at Louella, who they'd agreed on the drive up would do most of the questioning.

Louella picked up the ball. "I understand that Joan Gaines stayed overnight here at your home last Friday?"

"That's correct."

"What was the occasion?"

"It's a tradition. The Friday before Christmas our group of Suitemates gets together for dinner and .. . well, we call it a sleepover, even though that's rather a girlish term." Courtney Holt smoothed a nonexistent crease on her trousers. "Sometimes it's the only night all year we see each other."

"Your 'Suitemates'?"

"We lived together in the Suites at Stanford."

"Do you always meet in Santa Cruz?" Alicia asked.

"No, it varies. Last year we stayed at Joan's, actually. The year before we did the Ventana Inn, down in Big Sur."

"Where did you have dinner this time?" Louella asked.

"At Pasatiempo. The restaurant at the golf club."

"At what time?"

"Five o'clock."

Louella paused, then laughed, which seemed to surprise Courtney Holt. "You ate dinner at five o'clock? For me it has to be seven at least, even in winter when it gets dark so early."

Alicia watched their hostess carefully. For the first time since they arrived, she seemed ill at ease. Abruptly she rose from the sofa and walked to the fireplace. Alicia could see her furrowed brow in the huge gold-edged mirror above the mantel.

Finally she spoke. "Joan was very tired." Her tone was defiant. She spun around. "Campaigning is exhausting. She was exhausted and wanted to eat early."

"So it was Mrs. Gaines who wanted the early reservation." Louella looked down at the spiral notebook open on her lap. "And what time did you get back?"

"As I told the officers, I'm not quite sure. Probably a little after six."

"That was a quick meal."

"We wanted to have dessert and coffee here."

"And did you?" Louella asked.

She hesitated, then, "Yes."

Silence. Louella glanced first at Alicia, then back at Courtney Holt. "May we see the guest room where Mrs. Gaines stayed?" Her face creased in a smile. "We'd appreciate it."

For a second Courtney Holt didn't say a thing. Then, "If you must. Joan stayed in the guesthouse. It's this way ..." and she led them down the narrow corridor that split the first floor in two, then pushed open a rear door that opened onto a garden. She halted and they all looked beyond the door frame. A flagged walkway led thirty yards to a white shingled cottage that reminded Alicia of a gingerbread house in a children's book. She half expected to see a dwarf peeking out from the curtained windows.

Courtney Holt crossed her arms over her chest. "That's it."

"It's charming," Louella said. "Why did Mrs. Gaines stay there rather than in the main house?"

"It made the most sense since she wanted to get to bed early." Courtney Holt made it sound painfully obvious. "She was far less likely to be disturbed there than she would have been upstairs in a guest room."

"So she asked to stay there?"

"Yes."

"May we see it, please?"

Courtney Holt heaved a deep put-upon sigh, but preceded them outside into the drizzle, up the path and to the cottage.

Alicia was not particularly interested in the cottage's decor. What caught her attention was a second brick path, visible through a window, that curved from the side door to an alley, perhaps thirty feet away. On whose muddy surface, she noted, were unmistakable tire tracks. "Did Joan park there?" she asked Courtney Holt, indicating the alley.

"Yes." She could not have been more curt.

A few minutes later they made their way back to the main house. "Did all of you have an early night?" Louella asked when they'd gotten back to the foyer.

"Yes." Without warning Courtney Holt opened her front door and stood in front of it to prop it open, letting raindrops blow in onto her gleaming hardwood floor. She couldn't have made it more clear that she wanted them to leave if she'd forcibly ejected them. "Are we finished here?"

"Not quite," Alicia said. "When you got back to the house from the restaurant, did all four of you have dessert and coffee?"

Courtney Holt said nothing for a long time. Then, finally,

"I don't remember."

Silence. *That is very odd*, Alicia thought. "You don't remember if Joan had dessert and coffee with the rest of you?"

"She may have." By now Courtney Holt sounded openly hostile. "Or maybe she didn't. I told you I don't remember."

"What time did everyone go to bed?" Louella asked.

Alicia watched Courtney Holt's Stanford-educated mind work through credible answers. Finally she spoke. "Around nine."

No one moved. Rain pelted the Holt foyer. "Are we finally finished here?" Courtney Holt repeated.

"One more question," Alicia said. "Did you see Mrs. Gaines for breakfast?"

Courtney Holt shook her head as if she couldn't believe Alicia's audacity. "Yes. Around seven-thirty. And since I'm sure you'll need to know, she had one soft-boiled egg, one slice of toast, and two cups of coffee. The toast was lightly buttered and she took her coffee black."

Alicia had dealt with unfriendly witnesses before. She refused to be fazed. "What time did she leave?"

"Around ten. When everybody else left."

"Thank you for your time," Louella said.

They'd barely cleared the threshold when Courtney Holt slammed the front door shut behind them. A whoosh of air hit Alicia's back, and behind her the eucalyptus wreath nearly launched down the front steps.

"She's a charmer," Louella remarked when they were back in the VW. "Too bad I can't arrest people for being a pain in the ass."

Alicia was silent, strangely exhilarated. She turned the ignition, did a three-point turn, and started them home.

"I know what you're thinking," Louella said a moment later.

"So you agree with me?" Alicia couldn't keep a note of triumph from creeping into her voice. "That Courtney Holt was very uncomfortable answering a lot of our questions? That they ate dinner weirdly early at Joan's request? That she claimed not to remember whether Joan was with the rest of them for dessert? That Joan made a point of staying in the guesthouse, the one place where she could come and go with no one seeing her?"

"So she stayed in the guesthouse. So what? The fact remains that you need a hell of a lot more than that to start thinking the woman offed her husband. Like actual evidence." Louella's cell phone rang. "Hold on a sec," she said, then flipped open her cell. "Louella Wilkes."

Alicia made the right turn that got the VW back on Highway 1, heading south. Despite Louella's skepticism, for the first time Alicia felt she was making real inroads on the widow Gaines.

"No shit," she heard Louella say a second later. She turned her head to see Louella's face assume a peculiar excited expression. "What is it?" Alicia mouthed.

Louella laid a hand over the receiver. "Pedal to the metal," she whispered. "They've picked up Treebeard."

CHAPTER SEVEN

Late afternoon on Christmas Eve, with early darkness falling, Kip Penrose stood on the wide courthouse steps flanked by Alicia Maldonado and a few other D.A. office lackeys. He felt himself master of the moment. This was *his* press conference. *He* had enormous news to impart. If all the world was a stage, then *he* was the star player.

He stared down at the reporters massed below him, their faces raised toward him expectantly. "Thanks to the tireless efforts of my office," he began, "three days ago law-enforcement agencies not only in the state of California but throughout the nation launched an extensive manhunt for the environmental extremist known as Treebeard."

It didn't faze Kip that, behind his left shoulder, Alicia Maldonado gave a little snort when he delivered his "tireless efforts" line. So what if his office hadn't really led the manhunt effort? That was splitting hairs. What she didn't know was that if you could take credit for something big, Just Do It.

"As I apprised the media forty-eight hours ago," he continued, "John David Stennis, who calls himself Treebeard, is the prime suspect in the murder of gubernatorial candidate Daniel Gaines. Physical evidence collected at the crime scene points conclusively to him. And hours after Mr. Gaines was brutally killed, Treebeard fled his longtime campsite, in haste," he added, index finger in the air to emphasize the point.

Kip raised his chin a notch. He was much more comfortable than he had been at his newscon a few days earlier. *Newscon* was an insider term he'd picked up from one of the reporters, and he intended to sprinkle it liberally into his conversation. Insider terms showed how savvy he was, how much he understood, how totally he was in the loop of the movers and the shakers.

He paused. He'd arrived at his most important line. In its honor, he assumed his most portentous tone. "I am pleased to announce that the fugitive known as Treebeard has been apprehended."

Videotape rolled. Bulbs flashed. Reporters scribbled. Again Kip paused, partly to allow the import of his words to sink in, partly to bask in the knowledge that all eyes were on him. These reporters might sometimes have their way with him, skewering him in their newspapers and on their radio call-in shows. But not here. Not now.

"Where was Treebeard picked up?" a male reporter called, which annoyed Kip. He hadn't finished his prepared statement yet. But he had to respond.

"In Mendocino County, near the town of Laytonville."

"Where's that?" the same reporter yelled.

Kip had no idea. Didn't these people have maps? Then he heard Alicia's voice in his left ear.

"It's a hundred and eighty-five miles north of Salinas off Highway 101. He was on Branscomb Road, we believe heading for the south fork of the Eel River and the Admiral William Standley State Recreation Area."

That woman's ability to retain detail was amazing. Of course, it also proved her limitations. She might be good at seeing the trees, but it was Kip Penrose who understood the forest.

Feeling magnanimous—and also aware that he'd already

forgotten most of what Alicia had whispered to him—he let her tell the reporters where Treebeard was captured. Then the questions kept popping up and it was impossible not to answer them. How did Treebeard get all the way north to Mendocino County? Did he resist arrest? Who gave law enforcement the tip-off that Treebeard was in the area?

The ins and outs of the surveillance detail and of Treebeard's hitchhiking weren't all that interesting to Kip, mostly because he'd had nothing to do with them. Finally, though, the questions circled back to his territory. "Where's Treebeard now?" a woman TV reporter asked.

"He is currently being held in the Monterey County Adult Detention Center. And a decision has been made that he be held without bail," he added.

The woman reporter frowned. She was middle-aged and frowzy, Kip thought, surprised she still had a TV job. "What decision had to be made?" she said. "Of course he's being held without bail. Isn't this a capital case?"

Kip was momentarily flummoxed. Then, "She's right," Alicia whispered into his ear. "You should know that, Kip."

How irritating! He did know it! He'd just had to think about it for a second. He felt his cool slip away, like the top scoop of ice cream on a jumbo cone.

But the questions kept coming, so he had no time to collect himself. Had Treebeard admitted to the murder? No, he'd refused to say a word about anything. Would he hire his own legal counsel or be appointed a public defender? Too soon to tell, but a public defender was likely. Since the local jury pool might already be tainted by the press coverage, would there be a change of venue?

At that last question, Kip was horrified. "Change of venue?" he heard himself repeat. Meaning he might not be able to prosecute the case? Meaning he might lose all that exposure in front of the voters? Kip heard the shock in his own voice and realized the reporters must have heard it, too, because some of them were giving him strange looks. "No, there is no possibility of a change in venue," he declared, then took one more question so it wouldn't look too odd and ended the press conference.

"What is the chance of a change in venue?" he whispered to Alicia the moment they were out of earshot.

"Don't worry about it, Kip. It won't happen. And even if it did, you'd still get to prosecute the case."

He glanced at her, surprised. She actually sounded gentle. She seemed preoccupied, too, staring at the ground as they walked, her brow furrowed. He felt a surge of gratitude. She hadn't made fun of him or yelled at him, both of which were par for the course for her.

Then, "Not all the network people were there today," she said. "Don't you think that's weird?"

She was actually asking for his opinion! "Yes, it is," he immediately agreed. "Why wouldn't they all be there?" Then he started to worry. Didn't a press conference he called carry enough weight? Were the national media already getting bored with the story?

Alicia punched the code in the keypad door, then seemed to brighten. "Maybe they just didn't have enough notice." The buzzer sounded and she held the door open for him. Kip, amazed at this first-ever show of politeness, walked through ahead of her. "What was the notice, about two hours?" she asked. He nodded. "The network people aren't hanging around here—they're off doing other stories. They were the last ones to show up when Gaines got killed, remember? But I bet they'll come back now that Treebeard's in custody."

The things that woman knew. It amazed him. She had a lot figured out, even about things she had no business knowing.

Kip headed for his office, liking Alicia Maldonado more than he usually did. It saddened him that she wasn't in this mood more often. It was nice behaving like real colleagues, instead of people thrust together by work who hated each other.

***

The next day was Christmas. Alicia spent the morning in the D.A.'s office, which she had entirely to herself. She had a few hours to get some work done before starting the so-called festivities, round one at her mother's house with her sisters and nieces and nephews, and round two with Jorge at his mom's. She should be happy, she knew; she had family who loved her, a man who loved her, all her life ahead of her. Well, all her life past age thirty-five. Yet the only thing she could think was, *Another year down. Another one bites the dust. And what do you want to bet I'll be sitting here just like this next year, too?*

After another twelve months of slaving away for Penrose.

Her stomach knotted at the thought of him. So pompous, so self-satisfied, so damn lazy. His idea of a rough day at the office was a few hours schmoozing on the phone, then entertaining fellow politicos at a boozy lunch and sticking taxpayers with the bill. He was a master of sucking up, though that skill vied with his other great talent of getting other people to do his work.

Yet ...

It galled her, but to herself she had to admit it. Who'd won elective office, him or her? He'd won on his first try. She'd lost on her first two. And why? Because he did all the things she didn't. He networked like a maniac, and played the name game, and never ruffled anyone's feathers. Except of those unimportant birds perched below him on the pecking order.

Like her.

She sighed, exceedingly tired, and not just from midnight Mass. She was pulling the plastic wrap off a broken mini candy cane, hoping a sugar rush would lift her mood, when her desk phone rang. "Maldonado," she answered.

"Merry Christmas."

Her heart quickened. It was a male voice. A male voice that sounded exactly like—

"Aren't you going to wish me Merry Christmas, too?" The voice was teasing.

She lolled back in her chair, a smile on her face. All anger at Milo Pappas receded into the unlit, unprobed corners of her memory. "I would wish you Merry Christmas but I didn't think you big news types celebrated the holidays."

"We deign to celebrate the major ones."

"Where are you?"

"Driving south on 101. We just got into SFO."

"Oh!" San Francisco airport. "So you were out of town."

"Yes, in New York and D.C. But now I'm back, in your beautiful neck of the woods." She felt oddly pleased at his phrasing. "You know," he went on, "you're the first person I've called since I got in."

"I'm flattered. As clearly you want me to be."

"Actually, I lied. You're not the first person I called." Small commotion in the car, then he continued. "The first was my executive producer, whom I detest but to whom I am contractually obligated to report my every move."

"What a pain in the ass."

He laughed. "You don't know the half of it." More commotion. "So, Alicia Maldonado, why in the world am I reaching you in your office on Christmas morning?"

She felt a crashing embarrassment. What a huge smoke signal that she had no life. "Well"—she tried to keep her voice light—"you're working, aren't you?"

"I am, indeed." He sighed, and to her surprise she sensed that Milo Pappas—big network-news star Milo Pappas—might be a little frustrated himself. "That's why I'm calling, actually," he went on, and her heart sagged. Despite their friendly sparring, their easy familiarity of not even exchanging names—especially despite that single kiss she was having such difficulty forgetting—she should know that Milo Pappas was calling Alicia Maldonado strictly for business reasons. "I was hoping you could bring me up to speed on the Gaines case. I understand Treebeard was arrested yesterday, but I have a few questions. For example—"

"I'm sorry," she cut in, "but I don't have time to brief you."

"So I'm getting the official brush-off again, am I?" He chuckled. "What'd I do this time, Alicia?"

He was so personal, so intimate, as if they were fast friends, or so much more than friends. Using her name so often, too, which unlike most people he pronounced the way she did: *A-lee-see-uh*. It was part of his charm, she knew, which apparently he could spin like a web whenever the need arose. Like when he wanted something. Her back stiffened.

"You can guess from the fact that I'm in my office on Christmas Day that I've got a lot of work to do," she told him. "If you have any questions you'll have to ask our press—"

"I know, I know, your press officer. But I'll bet she's not working today." He sighed, then laughed again. "You know, Alicia, you're a tough one. But that's why I like you. Anyway, Merry Christmas." Then he hung up.

Slowly she replaced the receiver. Damn that man. Damn

how she always felt when she thought about that man. Damn how those three simple words *I like you* would bounce happily in her memory for the rest of the day, then resurface that night when she crawled between the sheets and stared at the ceiling in the dark. How could someone she barely knew get such a rise out of her?

She bit off the curvy end of her candy cane. She didn't like a single one of the possibilities.

***

Two days later Milo huddled with Mac and Tran in the chilly vestibule of a Carmel Valley Episcopal church whose name he couldn't for the life of him remember. Episcopal churches ran together in his mind: all of them massive and dusty and brooding, like English castles on rainy days. In minutes Daniel Gaines' funeral service would begin, and renowned industrialists and politicians would be forced to speak well of their dearly departed rival for the first and last time in their lives. And Milo would be forced not only to listen, but to take notes.

He sighed, cold even in his wool overcoat, reluctant to take his place among the reporters and photographers and camera crews in the rear pews reserved for the press. His body ached from lack of sleep and too many live reports filed from windblown street corners, and his mind felt unsettled and distracted. He was loath to admit it, but knew full well the cause of his disquiet. Today, for the first time since she'd left him, he would see Joan in the flesh. No more grainy newspaper photos or slick magazine images; no more videotape; just the woman herself. True, she would be at a distance, and he would be the last thing on her mind, but the mere prospect of her physical proximity unnerved him.

Slowly the media pews filled, their occupants raucous in comparison to the studied solemnity of the mourners. *No wonder Alicia Maldonado doesn't like reporters,* he thought, then corrected himself. It wasn't that she disliked reporters; it was that she distrusted them. That was probably smart, though it didn't exactly aid his cause.

The question he'd been mulling resurfaced in his mind. Why not ask Alicia to dinner? Why not pursue the attraction? Milo had finely tuned antennae when it came to women. He knew when a woman found him attractive, and he knew that Alicia Maldonado did. His antennae were fairly vibrating in her case.

So he was reporting on a case she was prosecuting. So what? Why couldn't they separate their personal and professional lives? Of course they'd be treading a fine line, but he believed them both up to the task. And it would be too late to get to know her once the case was over. He'd have to move on to other assignments, and the window of opportunity would close forever.

Mac, who stood beside Milo in the vestibule, shuffled his feet. He was loaded with gear, and Milo knew he wanted to get inside to claim a camera position before all the good ones were taken. Yet both Mac and Tran seemed to know what it cost Milo to be there. They'd been oddly solicitous all morning, not razzing him, not rushing him, not saying much at all. Respectfully quiet, as if he were grieving.

Mac met his eyes, then cocked his chin toward the nave. Milo sighed. "Okay, let's go in," he said, and all three made their way deeper into the church.

Milo no longer caused a flurry among his fellow reporters. He was old hat now. They were used to the star correspondent being among their ragtag number. He unceremoniously pushed a few people aside to claim an aisle seat for himself while Mac staked out a prime position among the jostling camera crews, though it was really Mac's height that would give him a superior vantage point. Milo whipped his reporter's notebook from the inside pocket of his overcoat, intending to take a stab at writing a lead-in to his piece for the *WBS Evening News*. But two reporters in the pew behind him were whispering so loudly he found himself listening to every word they unleashed.

"What's to say she can't do it?" A woman's voice, hissy.

"What's she ever done except be born a Hudson?" A man, cocky and dismissive.

"What's she ever done?" The woman sounded affronted at the very question. "How about get an MBA at Stanford? And work on Wall Street? Those are both tougher than anything you've ever done, buddy."

"Nothing's tough when you're born into the right family." The man chuckled. "Besides, she didn't actually get an MBA, remember? And she worked on Wall Street for about ten minutes, thanks to Daddy lining up a job for her. My nine-year-old could do better."

"But if she has even half her father's ability, she could be a fantastic—"

"*If* is the operative word, especially now that her father's not around to make things happen. 'Daddy, daddy, help me …' " The man assumed a whiny falsetto, and the woman collapsed in giggles, conversation ended.

Milo jabbed his pen through the spirals of his notebook. Speculation about a political future for Joan had begun, and not just among the press. The prior night at a restaurant he'd overheard a conversation among people clearly jazzed at the idea that Web Hudson's only child might step up to the political plate now that both her father and husband were gone. It was the way Americans looked to every Kennedy, or every Bush, to see where they might find the next star. The statement Joan had released on Christmas Eve had something to do with it, and he wondered if it was a calculated move.

Politics and Joan didn't strike Milo as a good mix. She possessed some fine qualities, but a thick skin and an appetite for hard work weren't among them. Not to mention that she didn't exactly exhibit a lot of staying power. Unless she'd undergone a radical metamorphosis, he thought she was far better suited to enjoying the fruits of other people's labors than to working in the fields herself.

Milo watched as familiar faces in business and government filled the pews to capacity. There were a few hundred mourners already and still more pushing their way into the church. An organist played something dirgelike, a gloomy accompaniment to the rain pelting the stained-glass windows. He recrossed his legs, eager to get the service over with but reluctant to see it start.

There was a commotion behind him. The organ music slid into a different, equally funereal melody. As if they were one, all heads pivoted toward the rear of the church.

Milo turned to see a phalanx of black-clad men and women slowly move up the central aisle. Pallbearers bore on their shoulders a dark, gleaming casket on which rested an enormous spray of white lilies. And there, behind them, was Joan.

She was smaller than he remembered. Slighter. Paler. She walked beside her mother, who cut the same aristocratic figure she always had. Both women wore black from head to toe. Joan sported no jewelry and only the subtlest trace of makeup. To Milo's eyes she looked frail and tragic, as though she might shatter at any moment.

She was a few feet away. For some reason he stood up. The motion must have caught her attention, because her gaze traveled in his direction, and her eyes met his. There was a flicker of recognition, then a small smile. She held his gaze for so long, with such intensity, that Milo knew his fellow journalists noticed. He sensed their surprise, then their envy, and was overcome with discomfort and a strange foreboding.

He hadn't wanted to see Joan, and now he had. Or more to the point, she had seen him.

**

It was shortly after noon on Friday, unrelievedly blustery and rainy. Alicia was working her way through both a ham and cheese sandwich and a crime-scene report when her desk phone rang. "Maldonado," she answered.

"Pappas."

His calling was both good and bad. Good because she loved hearing from him; bad because she loved hearing from him. "What can I do for you?" she asked, her standard opening gambit for business calls.

His voice was cheery. "You can give me a sound bite!"

She frowned. Outside her window two older women she recognized from the Public Works Department trudged up Alisal Street in bright raincoats, their arms linked, their heads bent, their umbrellas held low to fend off the wind. *That'll be me and Louella in a few years*, she thought. *Hell, that's pretty much us now.*

"Alicia? Aren't you familiar with the term?"

"Sorry." She'd forgotten to say something. "Of course I am. But why aren't you calling Penrose?"

"Anticipating that you'd ask that very question, I already did. But your boss apparently keeps banker's hours, because he's gone for the day. The press officer put me on to you."

That was true. Alicia clicked on a new e-mail telling her to expect a call from one Milo Pappas, WBS News, New York. She was cleared to talk to him on camera. That was both good and bad. Much as career advancement required exposure, TV cameras made her nervous. And she didn't care to probe too deeply into her nervous system's reaction to certain male television correspondents.

She cleared her throat. "When do you want to do this?"

"ASAP. I need to file the piece in two hours."

"What's it about?"

"Daniel Gaines' funeral. Your job is to say something pithy about the murder investigation."

"Where do you want to do it?"

"We could do it quick and dirty on the courthouse steps."

She arched a brow. Quick and dirty was certainly one way to do it with Milo Pappas. She could think of others. "I'll meet you downstairs in ten minutes," she told him.

The interview was over in a heartbeat, and thanks to the downpour was conducted not on the courthouse steps but in its entry hall. The cameraman and sound guy wired her up, Milo asked a few questions, she answered them, then the cameraman and sound guy unwired her.

Milo drew her aside while his crew packed up their equipment. "You know"—and he gave her that smile that lit up both his mouth and his eyes—"I'm glad your boss takes such a lackadaisical approach to his work. Otherwise I would have had to interview him and would've missed seeing you."

She stared at him. He could say anything and any woman in the world would believe him. That was probably what he'd built his career on. "You're certainly full of compliments."

"I can't help myself when I'm around you."

"Will you stop laying it on, Milo?" She couldn't help it. This guy was too smooth for words. She crossed her arms over her chest. "What do you want from me?"

He looked taken aback. "I was hoping you'd join me for dinner."

He could not possibly be asking me out. "You're still trying to pump me for inside information?"

He raised his hands, all innocence. "I won't ask a single question about the case."

Fat chance. She could see the scenario play out in her head as though it had already happened. Mr. Slick would do what he'd done at Mission Ranch, start out by being all warmhearted attentiveness. Then after a few glasses of wine he'd bring the conversation around to the investigation. If the last time was any indication, before long she'd cave. It humiliated her to admit it, but he'd dazzle her and she'd cave. *I can't do it.*

The simple fact of the matter was that she was at too much of a disadvantage when it came to Milo Pappas. He had everything—money, celebrity, and, as a result, power. She was a county employee slaving away for a fool D.A. and barely making it from one paycheck to the next. She desperately wanted what Milo had but she didn't have it. And by the looks of things she never would.

And it pissed her off that he would use everything in his arsenal to get what he wanted from her. He'd use his looks, his fame, his charm, and now dinner at a snazzy restaurant she could never afford on her own. He probably did that with all women. Well, she wasn't all women, and if he didn't know that already he was about to find out.

"Look, Alicia." He edged closer to her then, probably because she hadn't said yes yet, and his voice got softer. He was inches away, breathtakingly near. "I like you. I'd like to get to know you. If we don't discuss the case it's not verboten, is it?"

Even as she tested the words *I like you* to see if they

carried the ring of truth, "There's an issue of appearances," she heard herself say. When did she ever talk like that? For once in her life she actually sounded like a lawyer.

He frowned. "Somehow you don't strike me as somebody who worries too much about what other people think."

Oh, but she did. She had to. She was a woman and she was Latina. So far she'd been smart enough not to do anything to jeopardize her professional reputation. Why should she start now? For a man who would soon be long gone? While she was working on the very case that could propel her career to a whole new level?

But she couldn't expect him to understand that. Not the ambassador's son.

"Sorry." She kept her voice light. "It doesn't work for me."

Then she edged closer to the D.A. office's glass entryway and watched while he weighed whether to ask her again. There was a very good chance that if he did, she'd say yes this time.

But he didn't. She could see from the veil dropping over those dark, dark eyes that he decided not to. "I'm sorry, too," was all he said, then he rejoined his crew and was gone.

CHAPTER EIGHT

8:15 Friday night. Alicia lay on the couch in the pitch-black living room of her yellow bungalow of a house, watching television and nursing a second glass of cheap red wine. By now she was sick of watching news shows, or more to the point, sick of watching Daniel Gaines' funeral service covered on news shows. Somehow—she had no idea how, given how long she'd been watching—she'd missed Milo Pappas's version of the story.

On the street a few yards from her front window, a car sped past, rap music blaring. Next door the Lopezes were fighting, though it didn't sound like the kind of knock-down, drag-out that would land *senora* in the ER.

Another Friday night and here she was alone on her couch, though she had only herself to blame. In the end she'd begged off seeing Jorge, claiming fatigue and a headache, and not having to lie about either.

It's punishment, she told herself, *punishment for lying to Jorge, punishment for not caring about him as much as he cares about you, and punishment for thinking twice about Milo Pappas.*

Then a chuckle, more like a snort, escaped her. *Right.* Even after countless years of Mass-less Sunday mornings, apparently she was still loaded with enough Catholic guilt to concoct an idea like that one. As if God meted out punishment whenever it was called for. Neither He nor Earth's more slapdash justice system could manage that trick.

She hoisted her left arm in the air and watched as the

tennis bracelet Jorge had given her for Christmas slipped down her wrist to settle at the cuff of her gray sweatshirt, its tiny diamonds winking incongruously against the frayed cotton. It was beautiful. She'd never been given anything like it. She'd thanked him profusely, verbally and otherwise, and he'd flushed and mumbled something about other diamonds in her future.

And what had she given him? A book and a sweater. Granted, she made a lot less money than Dr. Jorge Ramon, but in her heart of hearts she knew lack of funds wasn't the real reason for her uninspired gift giving.

She let her arm drop back to the couch with a thud, drowned in another thick wash of guilt. Nights like these she believed she mucked everything up. Love life: fake. Career: stalled. Finances: shot. She even judged herself deficient in home decor.

She'd bought this house a year ago, over frantic objections from her mother. *Loca!* her mother had yelled, *loca* for a single woman to buy a house! As far as Modesta Maldonado was concerned, a single woman should just bide time until she got married. Didn't matter if she was sixty years old when her "big day" came. Buying real estate was way too permanent. It was as though—horror of horrors—Alicia was admitting she might never marry.

Then, to make matters worse, Alicia bought on Capitol Street right near the courthouse, so she could walk to work. *Loca!* her mother screamed again. The neighborhood, to put it nicely, was transitional. The mix of ugly 1960s apartment architecture and run-down California bungalows, with the occasional garbage-strewn, fenced-in lot thrown in, wasn't exactly pretty. Not to mention there were more shops selling bail bonds than groceries.

But it was the best she could afford. Anybody who

thought all lawyers made scads of money didn't consider those who worked for local government, let alone those who had to support an aging mother and a can't-hold-a-job sister with two kids by different men. Alicia had scrimped for the down payment and finally been forced to buy mortgage insurance because she couldn't manage the bank's usual minimum. Initially she'd had visions of repainting each room in soft pastels. Replanting the garden. Sewing filmy curtains for the windows, which would have been a good way to hide the iron bars. But work intruded, sucking up the hours, and one desperate Saturday, after months of living in empty rooms, she'd raided IKEA and run her credit card up to the limit buying sale castoffs. All she was really proud of were her Navajo throw rugs in desert shades of rust and ocher, and the Frida Kahlo posters plastered to the walls in every room.

Her admiration for the painter approached reverence. Both were of Mexican ancestry and had had tough early years. Yet Kahlo triumphed, despite both childhood polio and a bus accident in which she got impaled by a metal bar. All Kahlo's short life she suffered by comparison to her husband and fellow painter Diego Rivera, yet was an object lesson in persistence, Alicia thought, radical, strong, and passionate.

What Kahlo went through in the 1930s and '40s didn't seem to Alicia all that different from her own experience. When she started as a D.A., how many times had she gone into court only to have the judge ask if she was a Spanish interpreter? Or a secretary? Or to hear some cop mutter "wetback" when she walked past? It didn't help that she'd been so very green. She prosecuted the very first jury trial she ever saw. She hadn't even known which table to claim. She'd stood around till the defense sat down, then meandered to the table they'd left empty. Assumptions of her incompetence hadn't felt so misplaced back then, and sometimes didn't even now.

In one swift motion she rose from the couch. Enough wound licking. It was exactly one week ago that Daniel Gaines had been murdered. After the Courtney Holt interview, Alicia had badgered Louella into knocking on a few doors in the neighborhood to try to uncover something new about that night, but as Louella had predicted, it proved fruitless. Nothing, nothing, nothing.

But what if Alicia gave it a go? Not to talk to neighbors but to watch, listen, observe. And not during the day, as Louella had done, but at night, when the murder had actually happened.

Alicia felt adrenaline kick into her veins, battling the wine for dominance. Action was always good, she told herself, far better than sitting alone in the dark.

She ran to get her parka.

***

Everything in Joan's suite was in order, ready for Milo Pappas to arrive.

Joan smiled to herself. And arrive he would, though it had taken some arm-twisting.

She'd tracked him down on his cell phone when she got back from the cemetery. *It was so good to see you today. It gave me such comfort to see a friend.* He'd sounded cautious, so she started crying. *Will you have dinner with me? Tonight of all nights I don't want to be alone.* She'd heard the hesitation in his voice, she'd sat through the litany of excuses, but she hadn't let any of it dissuade her. *Come after you file your story,* she'd urged him. *We'll keep it simple, eat here in my suite.* Of course, eventually he'd agreed. Who could refuse a woman in mourning?

She was very pleased with herself. Tonight she didn't even miss being in her own home; she knew there was nothing like a hotel suite for entertaining a man. It was more immediately suggestive than a home, somehow; more mischievous. Maybe it was because the bedroom was never more than a few steps away.

Not that she and Milo would end up in the bedroom, not that night anyway. She was in a testing stage with him. Was he worth her while? He'd always been wonderfully considerate, but would he still be? And while in the past he'd seemed to understand their relative social levels, would he be confused by his network-news success and presume to think he was her equal?

Even if she weren't just testing him, Joan strongly believed in making a man wait for sex, usually until he was nearly beside himself with desire. Three dates at a minimum; personally she was much keener on six, just to prove how much value she put on herself and give the man in question a standard to shoot for. But though she had no intention of sleeping with Milo that night, she wanted him to want to sleep with her. She wanted that badly.

It was so delicious to be desired, and she hadn't been for ages. Daniel had gotten bored so fast and so thoroughly that she'd been both shocked and humiliated. By now she'd had all she could take of chastity. She was primed for a real man — particularly a successful, handsome, prominent man, whose devotion she could flash like a badge of honor. It was yet another way, perhaps the most important way, for a woman to exhibit her superiority among women. She Who Nabs The Best Man Must Be The Best Woman.

Yet it wasn't clear that Milo was The Best Man. The name Pappas didn't exactly show up in the social register. It really was such a shame he wasn't the British ambassador's son. Still

... Joan closed her eyes and ran a hand down her naked throat, her mind traveling back to their time together. She shivered. In some ways, Milo Pappas could not be bested.

She forced herself to gather her wits and perform another check of the suite. The staff had done a superior job getting it in order, sparing no detail on the dinner for two set on a small linen-draped table in front of the fireplace. She only hoped their professionalism would extend to keeping their mouths shut about Joan Hudson Gaines requesting such arrangements on the very night her husband had been buried.

She'd made sure she was turned out as carefully as her surroundings. She fingered her floor-length black crepe Gaultier, which could safely be described as a cross between lingerie and evening wear. It swirled dreamily around her naked legs and was cut low on her small breasts. In an effort to banish Daniel from memory—both hers and Milo's—she'd stashed her wedding and engagement rings in the safe. And remembering that Milo disliked a heavy hand when it came to makeup, she wore only mascara and lip gloss. What with the fire's glow and her own excitement, she hardly needed more.

She gazed at her reflection in the French doors that overlooked the surging black sea. The shining glass mirrored the tiny pinpricks of candlelight behind her that flashed like fireflies. They reminded her of summer, summer on the East Coast, where the air was hotter and heavier than it ever was in California. It was in that swollen atmosphere that she'd known Milo the first time.

The suite's buzzer sounded. *Remember*, she told herself, *you're soft and sweet and vulnerable*. She strode to the door, then pulled it open and stepped back to allow Milo to enter. Seeing him in the flesh she felt such a jolt she nearly forgot her game plan. In many ways he was just as he had ever been: a tall, commanding figure with intense dark eyes, hair curling lightly over the back of his collar, five o'clock shadow darkening his jaw like a cocky show of testosterone. Yet so much time had passed, he was also new to her, just the tiniest bit mysterious. He shed his overcoat and tossed it over the back of the sofa, as she'd seen him do in other rooms a dozen times before. Yet he was a different man than he had been all those other times, and she was a different woman.

"Thank you for coming," she told him.

He turned to face her. Six feet separated them, the air between dancing with an electric charge she was almost surprised she couldn't see. "I'm sorry about Daniel," he said.

She cocked her head. *I'm not.* "May I ask you a favor?"

"Of course."

"I'd rather not talk about Daniel. It's so horrible, so..."

His brow furrowed. "I understand."

"It's just that I'm so wrapped up in it all the time. If it's not on the news I'm getting calls from the campaign. Or from Daniel's family. Or from Headwaters. Or from the lawyers or the D.A. It's ..." She shook heir head. He stepped closer and she raised her eyes to his, feeling his breath on her face, taking in the manly scent of him. She had always reveled in the difference in their height, that he could make her feel so small, so feminine. Daniel was tall, too, but not so powerfully built.

The room was hushed except for the crackle of the fire in the grate, where one log broke and tumbled into another. "I understand," he said. "You don't need to say more, Joan."

She looked up into his dark eyes. "You always did understand me, didn't you, Milo?"

She watched him frown and step away. *Mistake. Too much, too soon.* His voice took on a businesslike tone. "I should warn you, I'll have to make it an early night. I have a plane in the morning—"

"Of course."

"—down to San Diego, and I still need to prep for the interview I'm conducting and—"

"Of course," she repeated, then put what he had said out of her mind. She led him to the small table that had been laid for two and lifted the bottle of California Syrah that had been breathing for the last hour. "Will you have some wine?"

He looked hesitant but then said, "I'll have a glass."

She bent her head to hide a smile, then poured the wine and handed him a glass. They toasted wordlessly. "Remember the trip we made out to the wine country?" she asked.

He chuckled. "How you wanted to get massages, even though it was past six on a Saturday night ..."

"Of course, it was too late for Auberge to arrange anything."

"I must've called a dozen spas before I finally found one that would take us." He grinned. "I tipped them like you wouldn't believe. Where was it? St. Helena?"

"Calistoga, wasn't it?"

He crinkled his eyes, then shook his head. "I don't remember. It was fun, though. That dinner was wonderful, too."

"At Tra Vigne. Yes, it was." She sipped her wine, which wound a pleasantly warm path down her throat. "But lots of times were wonderful with you, Milo."

Again he frowned. "Well, that's all in the past, Joan." Then he walked away from her, toward the French doors that faced the sea.

She stared at his strong, sure back, forcing herself not to cross the room to lay her head against its comforting breadth. *Slowly, slowly.* "I want to tell you something, but I probably shouldn't, tonight of all nights."

He turned his head slightly, so she could see his profile.

"Tell me what?"

"I have regrets, Milo."

Silence. Then, "About what?"

"I regret that I left you," she told him, and watched his brows arch with surprise. And pleasure, too, didn't she see pleasure there? "My marriage wasn't happy." He began to protest but she quieted him. "I know I shouldn't say it, especially tonight, but I can't stop myself. Can't I be honest with anyone?" She began to cry. "I'm putting up a front with everybody. Can't I tell anybody the truth? Can't I tell you?"

He turned to face her, and through her false tears she saw what looked like genuine concern on his face. "Don't you have anyone to talk to, Joan?"

"No, I don't," she lied, and threw in a sob for good measure. "There's no one I can really trust."

He set down his wineglass and came toward her. He didn't quite bundle her into his arms like she hoped he would, but he did stand very close and make little consoling noises. "You can talk to me, Joan," he said, and she wanted just to collapse against his chest.

Why had she left him? The truth was, she didn't think he'd give her what she wanted. Much as the demands grated sometimes, she knew she liked a big, public life. She liked what came with celebrity: the envy, the surreptitious glances, the being in the center of things. She knew from the beginning that Daniel wanted to run for governor, and she knew that with her father's backing he would win. Just as she had been a governor's daughter, she would be a governor's wife. That was a life she understood, and could have thrived in, if Daniel had given her her due, as her father had given her mother.

But Milo? Back when they were dating he was a low-level TV newsman. He wasn't a public figure in the same way. Who would know who his wife was? Who would care?

"Daniel's dying reminds me of losing my father," she told Milo. "You know how much I loved Daddy."

This time she felt Milo's arms come around her. *Finally.* She sank against him, sobbing softly, losing herself in the constant *beat, beat, beat* of his sure heart. Only after a long time did she pull away, and when she did Milo held out a handkerchief so she could mop her face. "Feel better?" he asked.

She sniffled, the handkerchief wadded around her nose, and nodded her head.

"Better enough to eat?"

She laughed, then had to cough, choked by her own sobs. "But it's probably cold by now."

"I'll call down and have them send up something hot. And meanwhile ..."

He found their wineglasses and refreshed them, then raised his in a second toast. "To happier times," he said, and she clinked her glass to his.

"Happier times," she repeated, and added silently, *I'm happier already.*

***

On the narrow curving street called Scenic that bordered the bluff above Carmel Beach, Alicia stood in the shadows of the Gaineses' sleek, contemporary home, its perimeter ringed by fraying yellow crime tape. Her parka provided slim comfort against the sea wind that slapped her face and whipped her long dark hair.

She'd been there about an hour. Watching. Waiting. Wondering. And seeing absolutely nothing.

She decided to do one more pass along Scenic, north toward Ocean Avenue, then back again. That would be it. If she saw nothing, she would hightail it back to Salinas. Ocean Avenue was seven blocks away and usually a gorgeous stroll, but at ten o'clock on a Friday night, when she knew a murderer had recently lurked in these very shadows, it was far from pleasurable.

Alicia raised her hood over her wind-tossed hair and set off at a rapid pace, fists balled in her parka pockets, running shoes crunching on the small stones that littered the asphalt. None of the residential streets in Carmel-by-the-Sea had sidewalks or streetlights, in an attempt to maintain the quaintness both the tourists and the locals loved. Most of the homes that lined Scenic were dark, though in a few she saw the odd purple-blue flicker cast by a television set. Some people still hadn't turned off their Christmas lights, strings of pretty white bulbs coiled around trees or dripping from shrubbery. To the left, Carmel Beach was deserted, and the ocean a heaving mass of silver, heavy as lead. Occasionally a car whizzed past, always in the middle of the road, as if the driver was a local and knew he wouldn't encounter another vehicle at this late hour. An older man in blue sweats who smelled of cigars walked past with his dog, a frisky white terrier that seemed to think every bush and tree needed his own particular brand of watering.

Ten minutes later Alicia arrived at Ocean Avenue, Carmel-by-the-Sea's cute-as-can-be main commercial strip. Boutiques and bistros lined both sides of the avenue, bisected by an island densely planted with shrubs and flowers. The avenue climbed steadily as it traveled inland away from the bay, forcing eastbound pedestrians into a breathless uphill hike. Save for the wind, which clawed at Alicia's face, all was quiet and still. Carmel rolled up its sidewalks early even on a Friday night.

Alicia shivered, feeling conspicuously alone, then turned

around to retrace her steps. Over, finished, done. As Louella had proved, it was pointless.

About a third of the way along Scenic back to her car, she again ran into the older man and his dog. "You still out here, young lady?" He clucked disapprovingly.

"You're out." She pointed at the terrier, energetically lifting a leg over some ice plant. "And excuse me for saying so, but that doesn't exactly look like a guard dog."

"Different thing," he announced. The terrier strained at his leash in Alicia's direction and the man walked closer. "And don't you know we had a murder here just last week?" Another disapproving shake of the head, a *What in the world have we come to?* scowl.

"Oh, that's right." Alicia tried to sound encouraging. "I did hear something about that."

"Mrs. Gaines was out walking that night, too," he went on. "Didn't listen to my advice, either, and look what happened to her. Or to her husband, I should say."

What? "Mrs. Gaines? You saw her that night?"

"Sure did. Saw her when I was out taking McDuff here on his evening constitutional. She was out on the street, just like you. Though"—he motioned back over his shoulder, toward the Gaines residence—"she was back there, closer to her house."

I can't believe this. "Are you completely sure it was Mrs. Gaines? And that it was last Friday night? Exactly one week ago?"

"Of course I'm sure it was Joan Gaines! We all know who she is," he snapped. Then he stepped back and his eyes narrowed. "Who are you?"

"My name is Alicia Maldonado," she told him, and held out her hand. "I live sort of around here. And you are?"

"Harry McEvoy. Live over on Twelfth." He shook her

hand, his suspicion of her seeming to fall away as quickly as it had risen. "It's a tragedy," he added.

"Yes, yes, it is." She was almost breathless. *Harry McEvoy. An eyewitness. This'll be enough to get me a search warrant.* "It's ironic that you saw Mrs. Gaines that particular night and that she was just walking around."

"Yup. Seemed to be waiting for something. Couldn't believe when I heard on the radio the next day what'd happened."

"I can imagine."

The terrier pulled furiously at his leash and Harry McEvoy followed. "You go straight home now, young lady," he called back over his shoulder.

"Yes, yes, I will." She was trying to process this new information when her cell phone rang. She pulled it from her parka pocket and flipped it open. "Maldonado."

"Sorry to call so late, Alicia. It's Jerome."

"Jerome! This is a surprise." Jerome Brown was a thirty-something star in the public defender's office. Somber and well-spoken and earnest, he was like a black James Stewart in *Mr. Smith Goes to Washington*. He single-handedly put paid to the notion of public defenders as lousy attorneys. Alicia had long thought that all their trial experience, plus the fact that they had to take on every case that walked through the door, made many public defenders very good lawyers indeed. "So what's up?"

"I've been assigned to Treebeard."

"Are you kidding?" This was not good news for Penrose. It hadn't even started yet and it was already crystal clear who the bright light in this courtroom drama was going to be. "Have you told Penrose yet?"

"Come on, Alicia." Jerome laughed in a way that said, *Why would I bother telling Penrose anything?* "Anyway, I spent the last few hours with Treebeard and he finally started talking."

"That's good news, right?"

"Turns out it's very good news." He paused. "That's why I'm calling, Alicia."

She frowned. "What are you telling me, Jerome?"

"I'm telling you that you have got to hear what Treebeard has to say."

CHAPTER NINE

From a hundred yards away, the Monterey County Adult Detention Center made Alicia think of a public high school in a down-at-the-heels municipality. A single-story, solidly built concrete structure rimmed by a sad-looking lawn, its parking lot was filled with the kind of seen-better-days cars owned by people who barely made it from paycheck to paycheck. People like teachers and, apparently, prison employees. When Alicia's own silver VW got closer and the compound's tall barbed-wire fence and windowless expanses came more clearly into view, she could no longer have any doubt that this was no educational institution.

At least not in the traditional sense.

She met Jerome Brown in the anteroom. He was decked out in the loafers and tweed jacket he favored, though this being a Saturday his button-down blue dress shirt was open at the neck. His small-lensed tortoiseshell glasses gave him the look of a fashion-conscious black professor well on his way to tenure. Alicia wore a turtleneck, boots, and a black skirt, forgoing the jeans she preferred on the weekend. No denim was the rule for prison visitors. Otherwise the civilians would look too much like the inmates and could find themselves getting shot at in the event of a jailbreak.

"Hey, Alicia." Jerome held out his hand. "Thanks for coming. Especially on a Saturday."

As if she wouldn't, weekend or not. She was dying to hear what Treebeard had to say. "Sure," she said mildly.

"Have you spoken with your client today?"

"Not since last night."

"You still think he'll talk to me?"

Jerome shrugged. "What's he got to lose?"

What, indeed? No doubt Jerome had told Treebeard that the D.A. practically had him drawn and quartered. But still, it was hardly standard procedure for defendants to get chatty with the prosecutors maneuvering to convict them. It happened only in highly unusual circumstances, for example when defense counsel thought such a conversation might blow a case wide open.

Both attorneys stood at the anteroom's reinforced security glass to go through the ID-approval rigmarole, then after being tagged with bright orange badges were buzzed into the sanctum sanctorum. Alicia had the willies, as usual. It didn't matter how often she visited jails. It didn't matter how in her prosecutor's heart she completely believed that the vast majority of people who found themselves serving time deserved exactly what they got. She still hated them. The misery that seemed to pervade the very walls, as if they held the silent screams of a thousand men. The unnatural quiet and stale, poorly ventilated air; the jarring, unexpected clang of buzzers and bells; the unbreachable chasm between the two rotating populations of guards and inmates.

Down one long fluorescent-lit corridor, then down another. Alicia began to feel she was in a maze. Her boot heels clattered on the Crayola-green linoleum, buffed to such a high sheen that it gave back her own reflection. Her nostrils picked up the competing odors of heavy-duty cleaning chemicals and the sweat of unhappy men living in far too close proximity.

Finally they arrived at an interview room, as cheerless as everything else. A metal table surrounded by a few folding chairs was centered beneath a bare hundred-watt bulb dangling from a cord. The room was equipped with a two-way mirror they would not use that day.

Alicia had gotten up at dawn to prep. She'd given Penrose a heads-up, knowing he would neither object to the interview nor want to conduct it himself. What? On a Saturday? Interrupt his massage or his tee time or whatever other round of pleasure he'd scheduled for himself? Not a chance. Though he hadn't come up with a single question to add to her list—she doubted he'd even read it—he did insist she e-mail him a full report by five o'clock that day. Chances were excellent, though, that he wouldn't read it till Monday.

Finally Treebeard appeared, accompanied by a guard. Alicia took one look at him and thought, *slam-dunk*, all over again.

Some people were just easier to convict than others. Alicia knew that virtually all you had to do to put some people behind bars was to get them in front of a jury. It sure looked like Treebeard fell into that luckless category. Nobody cut a good figure in prison orange, or sporting manacles at their wrists and ankles, but few looked as scrofulous as Treebeard did. His beard was scraggly and uneven, and it seemed like his chin-length dark hair hadn't had a run-in with shampoo since the turn of the millennium. As the guard shuffled him toward a chair and he collapsed noisily into it, his entire demeanor screamed *surly*.

Alicia had done her homework. She'd read up on Treebeard's history. John David Stennis was a sixties radical who never adjusted to the end of the decade of love. While the college friends who'd once protested at his side eventually laid down their signs and morphed into leaders of government and industry, he retreated into California's forests and made their preservation his cause. That was admirable in many respects, but somewhere along the way

Treebeard became his own worst enemy. He traded argument for histrionics. He grew to hate the system so much, he could no longer figure out how to fight it. As his hair lengthened, so did his rap sheet: a motley assortment of minor drug infractions and illegal protests. And as his ineffectiveness grew, so did his cynicism. People came to dismiss Treebeard either as a kook or a lost soul, and Alicia couldn't say she disagreed with either analysis.

"Good morning," Jerome said, which elicited a grunt. Treebeard trained his eyes on the floor. "This is Deputy D.A. Alicia Maldonado," Jerome went on, "who I told you about. I'm hoping she can help us."

The guard removed the manacles and left the room, indicating he'd stand by in the corridor. Treebeard began a fast gyration of his right leg, his knee bobbing rhythmically at nanosecond intervals. He had a barrier of resistance around him that was almost palpable.

"Are you willing to talk to Ms. Maldonado?" Jerome asked. "Tell her what you told me?"

Treebeard still said nothing, still refused to look at either of them. He kept up the knee bob, a motion Alicia found remarkably irritating.

"You know, I am here to help you," she told him.

At that he raised his dark eyes to hers. "Bullshit."

"You don't believe me?"

"You want me to believe a D.A.? How stupid do you think I am?"

Alicia leaned forward to rest her elbows on the table. "Let me tell you something about prosecutors. We're out to get at the truth more than we're out to get convictions. Personally, I have zero desire to put an innocent man behind bars."

Again his eyes dropped. He shook his head as though not one word she said could possibly be believed. His leg continued to gyrate. "Bullshit," he repeated.

"I consider Jerome a good judge of character," she went on. "When he calls me late on a Friday night and says his client's got something I gotta hear, I believe him. You know how many people in this facility have told Jerome they're innocent? Probably every last one of them. But when you said it, he thought it might actually be true. You want to tell me about that?"

Treebeard just shook his head. Silence. Then, finally, "It's all bullshit," he said again.

"Fine, that's it." She clattered out of her chair and grabbed her purse from the floor. Out of the corner of her eye, she saw Jerome shut his eyes and rub his forehead. "You know what's bullshit, Treebeard? Spending my Saturday doing this. I could be out shopping or getting in a workout. I'm outta here."

Treebeard waited till she had the door open and was nearly outside in the corridor.

"I am innocent," he said, "and I saw who did it."

That stopped her. She halted with her left hand holding the door ajar. "What did you say?"

He looked at her, and this time she saw something new in his dark eyes. A flicker of something genuine. "I said I saw who did it."

She waited a moment, then slowly walked back into the room, letting the door ease shut behind her. She pulled her thick spiral-bound notebook out of her purse and sat down, pointing her pen at his still gyrating knee. "All right, I'll listen. But stop that goddamn thing with your leg because it's driving me crazy."

A few gyrations later he stilled. She opened her notebook to a clean page. "Take me back to the night of the twentieth."

***

Milo felt as if he were floating in a cotton cloud. He was perfectly, deliriously comfortable. Somewhere far away a bird sang, trilled really, a high-voiced little bird that went on for a time and then stopped. Sing, sing, sing, stop. Sing, sing, sing ...

Slowly, with great reluctance, he climbed out of semiconsciousness. He flipped onto his back and linked his hands behind his head. The bedroom's blackout drapes were pulled shut, though in the center where they met he glimpsed a thin vertical line of white light. *What time must it be?* he wondered. Not late. He never slept late. And here in California he would wake even earlier, because he was still running on East Coast time.

It occurred to him that Joan must still be asleep. The suite was silent, her bedroom a few yards beyond his closed door. Briefly he shut his eyes, relieved he'd had the presence of mind to resist her charms the night before and opt for the second bedroom.

Just hold me, she had said, after dinner and conversation, when it really had been time for him to go. *Can you understand I don't want to be alone tonight?*

He had half understood, half been wary. Even if her marriage had been less than perfect he could only imagine how bereft she must feel on the night she buried her husband. Yet he knew from experience that it was unwise to take anything Joan said at face value. Invariably she operated with some kind of agenda. What was it with him?

Seduction, at least partly. She'd gone off to change into a peach-colored negligee that left little to the imagination. At her urging he'd sat next to her on the sofa, watching the fire die in the hearth. There was no denying she was an attractive woman, especially when she was nearly undressed. Naturally she had relaxed into the crook of his arm, and naturally he had toyed with the notion of taking her where clearly she wanted to go.

But he'd restrained himself. The fact was, Joan was not the woman he wanted to be with. He might have his ignoble moments, but he was not such a cad he'd use her as a substitute.

He sighed. *Alicia, Alicia, Alicia.* She was an enigma, wrapped in a delectable shell.

He wasn't giving up on her yet. He had little experience pursuing women—usually they fell at his feet—but he had to admit there was a certain thrill to the chase. If she wanted to make him work for it, fine. It wasn't exactly hard labor.

What time must it be? Milo forced himself out of bed, then pulled on the trousers and shirt he'd heaped on the floor. He tiptoed out into the hall and paused to allow his eyes to adjust to the blindingly strong light flooding in through the south-facing French doors. This was the first time since he'd been on the Monterey Peninsula that it was genuinely sunny.

His mind began to work faster, with more agility. What time was it? His gaze raked the room, settling on an ornate clock resting on the fireplace's white marble mantel. He strode toward it, only to look at its devilish gold hands, then have to look again, to convince himself what they revealed.

It was just past 7:30. His flight for San Diego left San Jose at nine. San Jose was an hour's drive north in the best of conditions, and these were hardly those: he needed to shower, shave, dress, and check out of his hotel before he hit the road. A different hotel from the one in which he was currently standing.

Shit and double shit. He could not miss an interview because of a woman, particularly one with whom he had a tortured past and who just so happened to be the widow of his current story subject. He would never live down that kind of mistake again. O'Malley would climb to the roof of WBS's thirty-story headquarters and shout, *Pretty-boy Pappas!* to the Manhattan sky.

Milo stood in Joan's gorgeous suite, rendered considerably less glamorous by the detritus of dinner congealing on the small linen-draped table, and wondered what to tackle first. Then the damnable trilling started up again and this time he recognized it for what it was. Not a bird but his cell phone, nearly suffocated between the plump pillows of the love seat. Milo fished it out, then he punched TALK. "Pappas," he answered firmly.

Long, relieved breath, which Milo recognized as belonging to Mac. "Whew, man, I'm glad you picked up. I was really starting to worry. Look, we had to go on without you. I must've tried your cell a dozen times." Mac paused for an explanation.

Which Milo had no intention of providing. "Where are you now?" he asked instead.

"About fifteen minutes south of San Jose airport. We're running a little late, have to return the rental car and check the gear."

"Do you know anything about later flights?"

"There's another one just before eleven."

Milo could make that. His mind began to tick off the practicalities. "Okay, how about this. I'll book a driver to San Jose. When you and Tran get down to San Diego, shoot all the B-roll, then set up for the interview in the guy's office. I'll cab it from the airport and get there as fast as I can."

Brief silence, then, "That'll work."

It would. Setup alone for a *Newsline* interview, with its high production values, could easily take a half hour. What with the other shooting Mac and Tran would be able to do minus their correspondent, Milo would barely be missed.

Barely. No doubt the interview subject wanted his share of the *Newsline* star's time and would be more than a little peeved not to get it. This interview would be touchy enough without that dynamic. "Listen, Mac, do me a favor? Make my excuses for me?"

There was another brief, grudging silence before Mac said, "All right."

Mac didn't need instruction on the "excuses" score, and both men knew it. Mac and Tran would do a song and dance about another piece that was taking up Milo's time, make it sound like an expose of the highest order, national security and all that, and before long the stood-up interview subject would feel like he had the inside scoop on the biggest story of the day.

"Thanks, buddy," Milo said.

Mac grunted something in response and hung up. Mac was angry at him, Milo knew, both for missing their departure time and for skipping out on some of the work. Call times were sacrosanct in TV news, as deadlines were tight and constant. But as a cameraman Mac was too low on the network food chain to ream a star talent, at least to his face.

Milo did a quick check of how many cell messages he'd missed. Nine. Seven from Mac, one from his brother Ari, and one from O'Malley. He slapped the phone shut and stowed it in his trouser pocket. He'd listen to them later.

Again he was immobilized in the lovely suite, this time by indecision. Should he wake Joan?

It didn't take long to settle on no. If memory served, she wasn't good about leave-takings. No, he'd just write a note. He found a sheet of hotel stationery and began scribbling.

7:30 AM Saturday. Joan, I'm off to catch my flight. It was good to see you last night ....

He chewed the end of the pen. What else could he say? He hadn't the slightest idea. And zero time to think it through. Again he put pen to paper.

Take care. M.

It was lame but it would have to do. Now to hightail it out of there.

Back on tiptoe, back past Joan's closed door, back into his room. He made quick work of dressing, then tiptoed once more into the hall, the note to Joan clutched in his hand. He knelt by her door and slipped it underneath, grimacing when his knee cracked. Carefully he stood up. Done. He could go.

"Milo?" Soft female voice behind the door. He halted. "Milo? Are you leaving?" The door opened to reveal Joan, still in her peach negligee, her face pink and confused and dazed with sleep.

"I have to catch my flight," he told her.

She held out her arms. "Say good-bye."

For a small woman, she had a powerful grip. "When are you coming back?" she whispered.

"I'm not sure."

"Tonight?"

"No, not tonight."

Small sigh of disappointment. "Call me."

Damn. He said nothing and tried to pull away.

"Call me later."

"Okay." What else could he say? This time he succeeded in extricating himself, but she caught him by the right wrist. She pouted—"I'll miss you"—and held on to his wrist.

"Really, I have to ..."

With seeming reluctance she released him. Then she cocked her head and smiled again. "Call me."

He nodded, then turned and walked out of her suite. Once outside, he lucked into a cab dropping off a golfer and began to hope his luck might hold. If he made the later flight to San Diego, no one at WBS headquarters in New York would be the wiser. His close call would disappear like fog in the morning sun.

He found himself relieved to be out in the brisk but gorgeous day, Pebble Beach in late December doing a brilliant imitation of spring.

***

Alicia did not find Treebeard a good storyteller. He stopped, he started, he forgot details—or he changed them—and just to make things even more entertaining, he occasionally retreated to surliness and went for a while without talking at all. If he didn't have such an amazing tale to tell, or if she didn't have her own doubts about whether he'd murdered Daniel Gaines, Alicia probably would have abandoned the entire exercise. But as it was, she was enthralled.

They were about an hour into the interview. Alicia and Jerome were nursing bad jailhouse coffee in foam cups. Treebeard had a glass of water. Alicia glanced down at her notes. "So you said that it was on Thursday, December nineteenth, that you received a letter on Gaines campaign letterhead."

"Right."

"And what did it say?"

"It said to meet Gaines at his house at nine the next night."

"It specified to come at nine on Friday night?"

"That's right."

"You must have thought getting an invitation to Daniel Gaines' house was pretty odd. You two weren't exactly on social terms."

"I thought it was weird, yeah."

"But you went anyway."

"Why not? Like the letter said, the guy wants to talk."

"Tell me about that." She dropped her pen and leaned back, her arms crossed over her chest. "What exactly did the letter say about him wanting to talk?"

"I don't remember exactly what it said." Another surly silence ensued. Finally Treebeard squinted into the middle distance, as if that would help him reproduce the letter in his mind's eye. "It basically said he thought it was time to clear up our differences."

"And that made sense to you?"

Another shrug. "I figured he thought I might really muck things up for him, now that he was running for governor. So I saw it as an opportunity."

"An opportunity?"

"To hammer out a deal. He'd agree to stop logging old growth and I'd agree to lay off him."

"He always said his company didn't do that."

Treebeard glared at her. "Well, he was lying. They did. I saw it with my own eyes."

Alicia tapped her pen against her notebook. "What does the Gaines campaign letterhead look like?"

"I don't know." He waved a dismissive hand. "It's red, white, and blue."

"You still have the letter?"

"No."

"That doesn't exactly help your case."

His tone got belligerent. "What do you want me to do about that now?"

She shook her head. "So what does the stationery look like, Treebeard?"

"I don't know! It said 'Gaines for Governor' on top."

She raised her voice. "You gotta give me more than that."

In a heartbeat he was standing up and leaning over her chair, yelling, his face twisted. "You don't believe I got it, do you? I shoulda known you wouldn't believe me!"

"Sit down." Jerome rose from his chair and pushed on Treebeard's shoulder, knocking him back a step. "Sit down and calm down."

"She doesn't believe me," Treebeard muttered under his breath, but he collapsed back onto his chair.

"She needs details, you know that. Now think."

Long silence, during which Treebeard did a lot of shaking his head and muttering. Finally, "Okay, there's something I remember. It was like the flag, you know? White stars on a blue background, with red and white stripes. And it was like the flag was underneath and the words 'Gaines for Governor' were cut out from it. Like all the stars stuff was on the left. And on the right, where it said 'Governor,' it was just the stripes."

"Okay, good." Alicia scribbled hastily in her notebook. "I can picture that. Now was it handwritten or typed?"

"Typed."

"And who signed it?"

Long silence. Then: "I don't remember. But it wasn't Gaines. I'm pretty sure it was one of his campaign people." Finally he threw his hands up. "I don't know. Some woman. I can't remember."

There was a lot about that letter Treebeard couldn't remember. But still, there was something about it that had the ring of truth. Alicia consulted her notes. "How did you even get the letter, since you don't have an address?" That was yet another of Treebeard's eccentricities. He refused to live indoors. He camped year-round.

"When I got back to my campsite that day, the letter was stuck to a tree."

"What do you mean?"

"I mean stuck to a tree. Pinned. Like all my other mail."

Alicia arched an eyebrow. "You had a bunch of mail pinned to a tree?"

"You got a problem with that?"

"Is that a standard way of communicating with you?"

"People know where I camp. They want to say something to me when I'm not around, they write a note and pin it to a tree. So it doesn't blow away."

Again she tapped her pen against her notebook. "When you got back to your campsite that Thursday, did you notice anything out of the ordinary?"

"You mean messed up? No."

"Nothing taken?" Alicia felt Jerome's eyes fix on her with a new intensity.

"You mean did I have arrows there and were any missing?"

"Yes."

"I had arrows there." His expression grew more hangdog. "But if any were gone, I didn't notice."

But one might have been taken. It was possible.

"Let's take a break," she said. "Fifteen minutes." Alicia called for the guard. Treebeard was warmed up but she wanted him to be fresh when she questioned him about the actual night of the murder. He shuffled out, the guard guiding him by the elbow.

"You're thinking what I'm thinking," Jerome said once Treebeard was gone.

"That this was a setup?"

Jerome nodded.

Yes, she was.

CHAPTER TEN

Joan had to struggle not to look happy. It wasn't seemly for a new widow to look happy, especially when she'd just buried her murdered husband the day before. But neither the weather nor Joan's mood made that easy.

As was her habit, Joan drove her navy blue Jag convertible at breakneck speed along the narrow roads that twined through wooded Pebble Beach. Her destination was Henry Gossett's home, at which she hoped he had both coffee and the living-trust spreadsheets waiting. In a nod to Grace Kelly, she had tied a silk scarf over her blond hair and donned big black sunglasses. In a dismissal of her role as New Widow, she'd put the car's top down. This was one of those taunting winter days California's gods occasionally bestowed, so spectacular that residents jettisoned caution along with their overcoats. It looked like April and smelled like April but would not last like April; chances were excellent that the very next day the temperature would drop thirty degrees and the skies would open. So, in homage to the moment's fleeting beauty, Joan had let decorum be damned.

She was in such a good mood she wasn't even angry at Gossett anymore. She'd been livid at him the day after Christmas, when he'd failed to show up at her suite with the spreadsheets, as she had told him to do. Of course, he'd called with some cockamamie excuse, but she'd seen right through him. She suspected immediately that her mother had interceded to keep Gossett from sharing the trust details with her, so she confronted her mother over the phone. Of course, she'd been right.

Well, Joan thought, mimicking a favorite expression of her father's, *that will not stand!* She had informed Gossett in no uncertain terms that she would see the spreadsheets, if not that day, then at his home on Saturday morning. His discomfort at being caught between mother and daughter had been evident, but she could not have cared less.

Joan arrived at Henry Gossett's Tudor pile, a structure she considered both dull and perfectly suited to the attorney and his stout wife. Interesting how people paired off, she thought as she abandoned the Jag on the curving sweep of driveway that led to the house, blithely blocking both of the Gossetts' Mercedes sedans in the garage. Sometimes men and women who were almost carbon copies of each other came together, like her parents and the Gossetts. Sometimes total opposites attracted.

She wondered what she and Daniel had been. Similar in some respects. They both liked to be out and about, at restaurants or parties or concerts. At some point early in their marriage, she had noticed they weren't at their best alone. And very often Daniel fell into sullen moods she hadn't understood. It happened when things weren't going his way, either with Headwaters or the campaign. Then nothing would make him happy but work, work, work, which was very trying.

The far more fascinating question was, How compatible were she and Milo? Joan tripped lightly up the few steps to the Gossetts' entry and rang the bell. She had concluded the prior night that Milo was as charming as ever, and as handsome. Perhaps even more so, because now his aura of success was so much more powerful. He was kind to her, very considerate, though his refusal to share her bed was a worry.

Didn't he find her attractive anymore? No, she decided, that wasn't possible. Could he be seeing someone? She frowned, then smiled, her concern fading fast. It wouldn't take Joan Hudson Gaines long to beat out any competition. One other thing she hadn't liked, she remembered: that he'd left so early to catch his plane. That didn't show what she considered sufficient regard. Still, she would allow him that lapse if he phoned her early enough in the day. Before eleven in the morning would be best; between eleven and three was acceptable; she deemed anything after three to be rude. So what if he had an interview to tape? She tapped the toe of her high-heeled pump impatiently as she waited for someone at the Gossett residence to let her in. Well, this would be a good test of whether Milo Pappas had his priorities straight.

Finally Henry Gossett himself pulled open his front door. He wore his suit jacket and bow tie, though in the privacy of his own home he'd forgone his felt fedora. At least that. "Good morning," he said, lugubrious as ever.

"Good morning, Henry." She pushed past him into the foyer, a dark, cheerless space that did justice to the owner's personality. He directed her toward a library that was all wood paneling, mahogany furniture, and crimson leather. Oil paintings depicted mallards paddling across murky ponds or horses waiting patiently to be saddled for the hunt. An antique uniformed housekeeper crept in with a bone-china coffee service.

"How are you, Joan?" Henry settled himself behind his desk.

"I'm managing, Henry. Thank you for asking."

They sipped their coffee and exchanged pleasantries, both maintaining the fiction that this little get-together wasn't occurring under duress. Joan ached to delve into the spreadsheets she'd already spied atop Gossett's desk. Finally she felt able to move the attorney past the preliminaries into the business at hand.

"I imagine that in the last several days you've been able to generate a more trustworthy estimate of the current value of my father's living trust," she began.

Gossett cleared his throat. His eyes, behind their wire spectacles as dull a gray as the mallards' wet feathers, dropped to the spreadsheets. "It appears," he said, "that my prior estimate was fairly accurate."

Joan stilled. "Excuse me?"

"Yes. I believe I estimated the value at thirty million dollars—"

"It is thirty million dollars?" she cut in.

Gossett moved his index finger across the spreadsheet's lined, pale green surface. "Twenty-eight point four million." He raised his eyes to hers. "And change."

Sunshine poured in through the diamond-shaped panes of the casement windows behind Gossett's head. A car sped past, the engine producing the sort of guttural roar only German automaking could achieve. And somewhere outside she heard men, presumably gardeners, speaking Spanish in loud voices. Laughing occasionally. It seemed inappropriate, somehow.

It took her a minute or so to be able to talk again. Then, "Henry, correct me if I'm wrong, but my recollection is that at the time of his death, my father's trust was valued at something like a hundred million dollars."

"Your recollection is correct."

She took a deep breath. "If that is correct, then how in the world could the value now be less than thirty million?"

Gossett said nothing. For a few seconds his gray gaze didn't waver, then it dropped again to the spreadsheets.

"Are you telling me that the trust lost seventy million

dollars under Daniel's stewardship?" She heard her voice rise. "He was trustee for only a year and a half but he lost seventy million dollars? Is that what you're telling me, Henry?"

"It's not accurate to say that it *lost* seventy million dollars."

"What is it accurate to say, then?"

"Forty million dollars went into Headwaters."

She did a quick calculation. "But that still leaves us thirty million shy. Where did that go?"

Gossett's brow furrowed. "Your husband made some investments which, I would say, didn't quite pan out."

"What kind of investments?"

"In the technology area."

No. She dreaded asking the question. "When you say 'the technology area,' do you mean Internet investments?"

Gossett nodded. "Primarily, yes."

She had a terrible sinking feeling then, like the one that came from the steepest daredevil plunge in a roller-coaster ride. Daniel had fancied himself Internet savvy. He had fancied himself one of the great minds of Silicon Valley, though he had never lived or worked there. The closest Daniel ever got was tee times with venture capitalists or Web business CEOs, after which he'd come home spouting off about IPOs and valuations and lockup periods. She hadn't been convinced he knew what he was talking about but hadn't imagined it really mattered.

Suddenly she feared that it had.

She tried to form a coherent line of questioning, though her mind whirled with terrible ideas that repeatedly spun around and crashed into each other, like bumper cars driven by drunken teenagers. "Henry, isn't it true that my father made considerable money in Internet investments?"

"Your father did, yes." Gossett paused. "In fact, those

investments contributed nicely to the value of the trust. But, Joan, remember that your father was making those investments in the early and mid-nineties."

"So?"

"So he was able to cash out of many of them by the late nineties. When Daniel took over as trustee, he poured a good fraction of those proceeds back into Internet companies."

"But then those companies began failing." She shook her head, remembering the shocking stories she heard people gossip about, or read about in the newspaper. High-flying Web companies, once valued at millions of dollars, suddenly worth zero. The people who invested in them going overnight from paper millionaires to paupers. "A lot of those companies went bankrupt, Henry—they shut down."

"Yes." The attorney nodded somberly. "Yes, Joan, they did."

She erupted suddenly from her chair. "But that was an incredibly stupid thing for Daniel to do!"

"It was a mistake many people made, Joan."

"But not with my money!" She glared at Gossett, whose expression hadn't changed one iota. She thought that if he told her the trust was worth a billion dollars or a thousand, his expression would stay the same. "Why didn't you stop him, Henry?"

Gossett said nothing for some time. Then, "Your husband had a mind of his own."

"But you were the attorney! You could have stopped him!" Yet even as she said it, she knew it wasn't true. She hadn't been able to stop Daniel from doing anything and she was his wife. Daniel would do what Daniel would do. That was another thing she had learned about her husband. After she married him.

Something in her fizzled then. She felt as though she lost

her will somehow, as though it drained out of her onto the navy-and-crimson Oriental carpet. Perhaps her mother had been right after all. Perhaps she would have been better off not knowing any of this. Perhaps now she'd be better off just doing what her mother had suggested. Traveling. Shopping.

Maybe even—oh, God, she couldn't abide the thought—doing charity work. She collapsed back into her chair. Gossett poured her more coffee.

"This is a blow, Joan," he said, "but it is not as dire as you might think. Your mother and I have some ideas about conservative yet rewarding investments that over time will produce substantial returns for the trust."

"Over time?" She shook her head. "I don't have time."

She saw Gossett hide a smile and she wanted to smack him. Old people always thought young people had all the time in the world. Well, they didn't. She had things she wanted to do now, and they cost money.

"I would make one recommendation," he said then, in an especially careful tone that immediately arrested her attention. "It is based on the fact that the trust's remaining assets are not highly liquid. Much of the value is tied up in your mother's estate on 17 Mile Drive and in your property on Scenic. So therefore—"

"Are you telling me I'm house rich and cash poor? Do I have a cash-flow problem?"

"Perhaps it's more accurate to call it a cash-flow *concern*." That reassured her, but only momentarily. "I would recommend that you embrace, shall we say, a prudent lifestyle in the short to medium term."

She narrowed her eyes. "What do you mean, prudent?"

"Simply"—he spread his hands—"a lifestyle which, while very comfortable, is more thoughtful about major expenditures."

"Henry, I have no intention of buying another house or a jet or a yacht or anything! What are you talking about?"

"Well, for example, perhaps you might consider moving back into your home from the Lodge. Or, if that is uncomfortable for you," he added, as she was about to launch again from her chair, "as well it might be under the circumstances, perhaps you would consider moving into your mother's home for a time?"

Are you insane? she was thinking. *What a hellacious idea!* And impossible for a variety of reasons, not the least of which was the reappearance of Milo Pappas on the horizon. Who, she suddenly realized, hadn't called yet. She glanced at her watch: 11:08.

Abruptly she stood up. She had had quite enough. "Henry, I find it impossible to believe that a few thousand dollars a night will make any difference whatsoever. I will remain at the Lodge for the foreseeable future, and that is the end of that discussion." She made it to the library door before she forced herself to turn around. "I'm sorry, Henry. I apologize for being abrupt. As you might imagine, you did not bring me the happiest news today. But thank you again for all your efforts, and I will be in touch. No"—she raised a hand to stop him from rising from his chair—"I will show myself out."

Once she was back in the Jag, her cell rang. It had to be Milo, she thought—finally. But she mustn't let on she wasn't in a fabulous mood; glumness was not something men found attractive, even in new widows. She prepared to be cheery as she pushed the talk button. "Hello!"

"I am so glad I finally caught you."

Damn. Courtney Holt, who had left numerous messages over the past few days. "I'm so sorry I didn't call you back, Courtney, I've just been so—"

"It doesn't matter—don't worry about it. But you must hear who came by my house Christmas Eve."

***

"I kind of remember now who signed the letter," Treebeard offered.

They were back at it, round two of Treebeard's interview. Alicia's behind was numb from hours sitting on the unforgiving metal folding chair, her breath sour from overheated, Cremora-ed coffee. Jerome apparently wasn't feeling all that spry, either, as he'd downed a few aspirin during the break. As for Treebeard, he seemed one degree less suspicious, which made him that much easier to deal with, but his grasp of detail had not improved.

"What do you mean, you kind of remember?" Alicia asked.

"It was a woman. Mary something. Something like Mary Baker. Mary Bakewell, maybe."

Mary Bakewell? Alicia didn't remember anyone of that name from Gaines' campaign staff, not that she'd cared before now. She jotted it down. *Mary Bakewell.*

"You know," Treebeard went on, "I had the letter with me when I went to the house."

"When did you realize you'd lost it?"

That question seemed to deflate him. "Not till a lot later." He shook his head. "I was already way up north."

So much for the letter. "Let's move on. You arrived at Gaines' house. What time was it?"

"I don't know. Close to nine."

"You're not sure?"

He raised his right arm in the air. "I don't wear a watch."

Of course not. "What happened when you arrived?"

"I walked up to the front door. This was weird. The door was open."

Alicia frowned. "It was open?"

"Yeah, a little open. So I pushed it and leaned my head in and called hello. A few times. Heard nothing."

Treebeard paused to take a deep breath. Alicia eyed him. He seemed jittery, as if he were reliving those moments. If he wasn't telling the truth, he was a good liar. "So what did you do?"

"I walked inside. Man, it was quiet, like a tomb." He shivered. "I called out again. Still nothing."

"Were the lights on?"

He nodded. "There were lights on. Not many but it wasn't pitch-dark."

"Which room were you in at this point?"

"The living room." All of a sudden Treebeard heaved himself to his feet. "Man, I should've left! I knew something was shit-ass wrong—I should've left right then."

"How did you know something was wrong?" Jerome asked.

"Because it didn't feel right! Because it was so goddamn quiet! Because the front door to this ... mansion was frigging wide open!" Treebeard was panting and shaking his head. "Man, I was so stupid! I walked right into it!"

"Did you think about leaving?" Alicia asked.

"Sure, I thought about it! But I was curious, you know what I mean?" He looked at her. Yes, she knew what he meant. For a moment the two eyed each other, until Treebeard looked away. "So like an idiot I kept going into his house, still calling out Gaines' name. Then ..."

Alicia remained silent. In her own mind's eye she could picture Daniel Gaines' corpse, in all its skewered grotesquerie. But she'd seen it hours later, when it was no longer fresh, but had been sanitized by police procedure. When its horror had been diluted by time and process.

"I saw him. Lying on the floor. There was all this blood. And he was wearing, like, a white robe, but he had—" Treebeard motioned at his own chest, then began pacing. Back and forth. Back and forth. "I couldn't believe my eyes—I couldn't believe what was in him. I ran over to him and knelt down. I got blood all over me, my knees, my hands. I looked down at him and his eyes were open. But he wasn't looking at me. He was sort of looking beyond me. Man ..." Treebeard halted and put his hands over his face.

"Did you think he was dead?" Alicia asked.

Treebeard shook his head, mute for some time. Then, "I knew he was dead. And I think that's why I kinda freaked. Would you believe I tried to get the arrow out of him? I actually tried to pull it out." Treebeard's face pinched, as if the memory itself pained him. "The guy was dead and one of my frigging arrows was in him."

"Was it one of your arrows?"

"Oh, for sure it was one of mine."

"And you touched it?"

"Of course I touched it! I was pulling on it. I was trying to get it out."

No one said a thing. Alicia stared at her empty foam cup, its rim stained with the coral-colored lipstick she'd applied that morning, carefully outlining her lips then painting them in, as if getting it right were the most important thing in the world. For those thirty seconds, it had been.

Alicia knew it was easy to get screwed in life. It was easy to go from just fine to royally screwed, in minutes. Seconds, even. Get in the path of a drunk driver—bam. Board the wrong plane—over. Look like somebody else's perfect way out of a bad situation—that was possible, too. Was that what had happened to Treebeard?

He was speaking again. "Then, I don't know, I just thought, I gotta get out of here. I gotta go. But I sort of fell. I was standing up but it was wet all over, with the blood, and I sort of fell and grabbed the wall on the way down. I saw my own handprint on the wall—that freaked me out more—I just ran." Treebeard stared at the green linoleum floor, shaking his head. Eventually he raised his eyes to Alicia. "I just ran."

She stared at him. "You told me before that you know who did it."

Silence.

"What did you mean by that?"

Treebeard took a long time to answer. Finally, "I saw someone. Just when I got into the house, when I was standing by the front door trying to decide what to do, I saw someone."

"Where?"

"By the side of the house. The right side."

"You mean you were inside and you saw the person pass by on the outside?"

"Yes, through the window."

Alicia vaguely remembered a picture window overlooking a passage between the Gaines property and the house to the south. "How clearly could you see?"

He shook his head. "It was dark." He paused. "She was short. Slight. With light-colored hair."

"You're saying it was a woman."

"It was a woman."

The interview room seemed especially still suddenly. To her right, Alicia felt Jerome's concentration, so intense as to be almost a physical thing. The smell of sweat hung in the stale air—hers, Jerome's, Treebeard's, she had no idea. She cleared her throat. "Did you see this woman's face?"

Again Treebeard looked pained. "No."

She felt a rush of disappointment, and irritation. This man was not doing much to help her. He wasn't doing much to help himself. She heard her voice rise. "How can you be so sure it was a woman?"

He replied instantly. "By the build. And the way she moved."

"Could it have been Joan Gaines?"

He eyed her steadily. "It could've been."

"But you're not sure."

"No."

She shook her head, hearing the anger in her own voice. "Do you have any evidence that this person was ever inside the Gaines house? How do you know it wasn't the neighbor just walking down that passage?"

"I don't know."

Alicia threw her pen down. "And I'm guessing that you could not pick this supposed female out of a lineup."

Silence. Then, "No."

Treebeard went on to recite further details about that night, and Alicia dutifully took notes. She heard how he cleaned himself off and grabbed what he could from his campsite and fled, hitchhiking north, camping on the road like usual, but not like usual at all. She took notes, and asked questions, and wondered how much of what this man said was truth and how much was fiction. Whether he would ever get out of the pit into which he had fallen. Whether he deserved to get out of it. And who, if anyone, might have put him there.

CHAPTER ELEVEN

"I'm not used to getting out of bed this early, you know," Milo heard Joan whisper coyly in his ear.

She'd come up behind him. He'd been so taken with the view from the Lodge's ocean-facing restaurant terrace he hadn't even noticed. He followed her progress as a waiter seated her at their small table draped with a pale yellow linen cloth. "Good morning," he said.

"Good morning to you! I'm so glad you could join me for breakfast." She leaned close to him, smiling, elbows on the table. "Especially on such short notice."

Milo settled in his white wrought-iron chair and watched Joan chat and smile. It was Treebeard's arraignment that had brought him back to the Monterey Peninsula, but somehow Joan's antennae had picked up his imminent return to her domain. An hour after he got his e-mailed flight reservations from WBS's travel department she called to cajole another assignation out of him. He'd agreed because she was, after all, an important source. She gave him an inside track, and he would be a fool not to use it. Yet he felt himself being sucked back into her orbit, as if she were a solar force and he a mere small moon unable to resist her greater power.

The restaurant terrace on which they sat was a redbrick affair with California's obligatory ferns in terra-cotta pots and the neoclassical touch of Doric columns supporting an overhead arbor. It was rimmed by a low wall built of Carmel's native chalkstone, beyond which a velvety lawn stretched toward the golf link's eighteenth green and beyond that to Stillwater Cove, where the surf broke in gentle tongues against the rocky shore. Again this Monday morning they were blessed by the weather. As if taunting the advent of January, the spectacular sun and warmth of the last few days had held.

The waiter sidled over. "Do you have any questions about the menu?"

Joan immediately spoke up. Milo was amused to hear her order in typical fashion, which was to request whatever she wanted whether it appeared on the menu or not. "I would like an egg-white frittata with a baked tomato on the side, please. No oil. And whole-wheat toast, no butter."

"For you, sir?"

Milo would not order the same. "The American breakfast," he said, and handed over his menu. He looked across the table at Joan, who was as perfectly turned out as Pebble Beach's famed fairways. Then again, she always looked assembled, he remembered, regardless of the circumstance or the hour. Always in the right clothes, always combed, always made-up. Models and actresses could get away with grunge, but not politicians' wives and daughters. Middle America wouldn't stand for it.

He found himself both irritated by her public perfection and admiring of it. His intimate acquaintance with those of the female persuasion had taught him that it was hard work to look that put-together at all times. Then again, it was the only work Joan did. "What are your plans for today?" he asked.

Her gaze slid away from him. "I'm going into Headwaters."

"Really?" That piqued his interest. "Is everything all right over there?"

She frowned. "I'm not sure." Then her face brightened and she looked back at him. "I take that back—I'm sure it's fine. But I feel I should put in an appearance, talk to people, boost the morale a bit. You understand. They must be worried about the company's future now that Daniel's gone."

Something in her tone stopped Milo from asking what she thought that future might be. The consequences of Daniel's death on the campaign were obvious; that wasn't the case with Headwaters. Since the company was privately held, there was little public information about it. Milo did remember a *Wall Street Journal* piece on how Daniel and Joan's father had pooled resources to acquire Headwaters from the Idaho family that had founded it years before. It had been a controversial transaction, particularly for the conservative former governor, since it involved a highly leveraged takeover scheme.

"And what do you have on your agenda?" Joan refreshed his coffee from the bone-china service.

He hesitated, then, "I'll be covering Treebeard's arraignment this afternoon." He watched the radiance retreat from her face. "I'm sorry to have to bring it up."

"It's all right."

"You must be relieved he was picked up."

She shrugged, a casual reaction that surprised him. "I knew they'd catch him. A man like that can't dodge the authorities for long."

"Are you convinced he's guilty?"

She looked at him sharply. "Isn't it fairly obvious that he is? Why would you even ask that?"

Alicia Maldonado's face flashed through Milo's memory. *It surprises me that you're not even willing to consider the possibility that this case might not be all sewn up ...*

He shrugged. "It all seems a little, I don't know, cut and

dried."

"Aren't most murders?"

"Beats me." The conversation had taken an odd turn. Fortunately they were interrupted by the waiter, who came bearing one healthy breakfast and one monstrosity of cholesterol and calories. Milo accepted the latter and watched Joan cut into her frittata.

"I must say," she went on a moment later, "I'm not too keen on the woman the D.A. has helping him with the case."

"You mean Alicia Maldonado?"

Joan's head snapped up. "You know her?"

Milo thought for a moment. "She's been at all the press conferences. She seems more on top of things than Penrose is. I'd say he's lucky to have her."

"Well, I sincerely doubt she's as good as you seem to believe. You would not—" Joan made a dismissive wave with her hand. "Oh, forget it."

"What?"

"I don't care to go into it."

"Come on, now you've got me curious."

Joan shook her head, her jaw set. She had the look of her mother at that moment, he thought. Abruptly she set down her fork. "All right, I'll tell you. She drove all the way to Santa Cruz to talk to Courtney Holt. Even though the police had already interviewed her. You remember Courtney, one of my Suitemates from Stanford?"

He remembered. Attractive woman. Nose a little high in the air, but that described most of Joan's friends. "Weren't you at Courtney's house overnight when Daniel was killed?"

"Yes, I was. And of course that's what I told the police. But apparently that wasn't good enough for that prosecutor woman. She put Courtney through the mill, all to find out exactly what the police had already found out. It was very rude," Joan added, "and completely unnecessary."

Milo found himself reluctant to point out that it didn't fall into the category of "rude" for the D.A.'s office to reconfirm Joan's whereabouts the night her husband was murdered. But her reaction didn't surprise him. One of Joan's less attractive characteristics was her unwavering conviction that society's usual rules didn't apply to her, and her subsequent indignation when she was informed that they did. Then again, that point of view was a direct result of growing up a Hudson.

He spoke carefully. "It does surprise me that she went out to Courtney's house herself. Seems to me that even for a return visit, that's police work."

"Apparently she had some investigator with her. But Milo, that's beside the point. I just don't like her. She's very full of herself, very arrogant."

He downed the last of his eggs, scrambled hard just the way he liked them. "It sounds as if you've met her."

"I have. She came here to the Lodge once, with Penrose."

He would love to have witnessed that meeting. Again he thought carefully before speaking. "You know, Joan, the best thing in the world is for you to have the strongest possible prosecutorial team. Penrose doesn't strike me as a brain trust, but Alicia, she's a different story. Apparently—"

"You call her Alicia?"

Milo looked up to see that Joan's eyes were as cold as her tone. "When I cover a story, especially one that will carry on for some time, it's to my benefit to be on good terms with the major players. Of course I call her Alicia. Do you expect me to call her Ms. Maldonado?"

That seemed to mollify her. "Still, I think she should have a better idea of her place."

"Apparently her place is at the head of the class in the

D.A.'s office," he heard himself say.

Joan flounced back in her seat and crossed her arms over her chest, as if about to launch into a full-out tantrum. Her tone was pouty. "You're certainly very high on her."

"She is impressive." He kept his voice mild. "And attractive as well," he added, knowing even as he said it that crowing to one woman about the good looks of another was neither a smart move nor the done thing. But somehow he felt goaded.

"You think she's attractive?" Joan's face took on an appalled expression. "Well, I suppose she might be," she allowed, "in an ethnic sort of way."

Classic Joan, he thought, then had the impulse to goad her right back. "Just like me," he said.

"Oh, honestly, Milo! The things you say sometimes." Then Joan frowned, and her cheeks flushed a light pink. She lowered her voice and leaned across the table. "I certainly don't mean to say anything derogatory about Hispanic people, but she is very common-looking. Have you seen how she dresses? She's not like you at all. And despite what you say," she went on as he was about to protest again, "I still would rather she wasn't on the case." Joan leaned back and smoothed the linen napkin on her lap. "I don't think she creates the right impression. And I may talk to Penrose about it."

This conversation was pointless, he realized. It also reminded him of something else about Joan. She won all arguments. She won because she refused to consider any point of view other than her own. She had the conviction born of lack of analysis. It was frustrating, he remembered. Then he was returned to the present by the sound of muffled sniffling. He raised his eyes to see Joan's head bent over her open handbag, her face now suffused with color, her cheeks damp.

"Joan ..."

She waved a *Not now* hand, then pressed a tissue to her nose. Milo waited out the display, mildly irritated. Maybe he'd gone on too long about the case, but it was Joan who'd brought most of it up. "Are you all right?" he murmured a few seconds later.

She put down the tissue, recovered except for some residual puffiness around her eyes. "I'm sorry for being snappish," she said. "It's just that everything about this situation upsets me."

Well, that had to be true. "I'm sorry," he said.

She raised her eyes to his. "You are so sweet, Milo." Then she reached across the table and grasped his hand. Her fingers were unbelievably fragile and soft. Her whole body was like that, he remembered, a malleable, tender thing he used to worry he might crush.

She tilted her head to one side, the hint of a smile on her lips. "Thank you for forgiving me."

"There's nothing to forgive."

"I'm just so emotional these days. It's all ... it's all of this. Sometimes it's very hard."

He nodded, saying nothing. Should he pull his hand away? She showed no sign of letting it go.

Again she spoke. "May I ask you a question?"

"Shoot."

"I'd like to have a few friends over to the suite tomorrow evening. Would you join us?"

He frowned. Wasn't tomorrow ...

"I know it's New Year's Eve," she went on hastily, "and it's short notice, but ..." Again the tilt of the head. Again the big eyes. "You don't already have plans, do you?"

He didn't, unfortunately. He had a vague notion of flying back east for the holiday but didn't relish the prospect of another get-together with his brothers and their families. Obviously there was no hope of seeing Alicia.

Joan was waiting. He was being rude. His choices were either Joan or solitude, and Joan was an old friend, an inside source, and newly bereaved. Besides, her friends might be interesting. "It would be my pleasure," he heard himself say.

"Wonderful." She squeezed his hand once more before she let go.

***

Alicia plucked a cellophane-wrapped banana-nut muffin from the overflowing basket of baked goods in the courthouse's second-floor snack bar. It was a sign of how early she'd gotten to work that it was still warm. She laid it on her orange plastic tray next to her apple and coffee and turned to Louella, behind her in the cash-register line. "I don't know what else to tell you," she said, "but I can't just drop it."

Louella shook her head, dubiousness written all over her features. Squeezed into a white turtleneck with her blond hair less rigorously straightened than usual, Louella looked more Norma Jean than ever. "I bet you want me to go to a judge and get you a subpoena."

"Can you do it this morning?"

Louella just shook her head again. "What do you want to see?"

"Credit-card bills and cell-phone records."

At that, Louella rolled her eyes. "A dollar forty-five," the cashier announced in a bored voice, tapping her fingernail on her metal register as Alicia painstakingly counted out the dimes and nickel. Louella paid for her coffee and muffin and grabbed a handful of paper napkins. "It's so nice today, why don't we eat outside?" she suggested.

The women arranged themselves on a park bench in the courtyard between the courthouse's east and west wings. Boxwood hedges edged the expansive planters, all of them spilling over with petunias, agapanthus, and birds-of-paradise. It would be a floral splurge for the county budget were this not Northern California, where all flora and fauna thrived. They sat with their backs to Alisal Street, which on this semi-holiday thirtieth day of December was much quieter than usual.

After a few muffin bites, Louella spoke up. "What time's the arraignment?"

"Three."

"You expecting a lot of media?"

Expecting? No. Hoping for, in one particular case? "Some," she said. "Not a full house."

Arraignments were the least exciting of all courtroom dramas because they yielded so few surprises. The defendant and his lawyer went before the judge; the clerk read the charges; the defendant entered a plea. Most times everybody knew in advance what that would be.

This afternoon at the appropriate moment, Jerome Brown would nod at his client, and Treebeard, if he was talking, would say, "Not guilty." Then the judge would set the date for the preliminary hearing, in roughly ten days. If this weren't such a high-profile case, the arraignment would be thoroughly boring. But as it was, a fair number of media would be in attendance, if only to photograph a manacled Treebeard in prison orange.

Alicia sipped her coffee. "Jerome called yesterday to say Treebeard passed a lie-detector test."

"Wow!" Louella's tone was fake impressed. "It's a wonder they don't just drop the charges and let him out this morning."

"You made your point."

"Those tests are meaningless. You know that, Alicia."

Alicia said nothing. While the public seemed to think a lie-detector test was a good barometer of guilt or innocence, the judicial system had never been convinced. Because a polygraph could be fooled by an accomplished liar—which described many an accomplished felon—most often the results were inadmissible in court.

Still, Alicia was unwilling to dismiss these particular test results as meaningless. Not definitive, certainly, but perhaps indicative?

"So let me see if I've got this straight." Louella half rose from the bench to swipe the last of the muffin crumbs off her trousered lap, then sat down again. "Basically, there are three things you want me to do. First, interview this Harry McEvoy who lives on Twelfth, find out if he's a kook or really did see the widow Gaines in front of her house the night of the murder. Despite the fact that she told us she was in Santa Cruz and that we've got eyewitnesses who put her in Santa Cruz for dinner that night."

"Right."

"Then, assuming McEvoy has all his marbles, you want me to go to a judge and get a subpoena for Joan Gaines' credit-card bills and cell-phone records."

"Right."

"And last but not least, you want me to check out who lives just south of the Gaines house. See if by some chance one of the residents happens to be a height-impaired female who gets her kicks out of trotting up and down the passage between the two properties in the dark. Have I got it so far?"

Alicia turned to regard Louella. "Do you have to be so sarcastic?"

"Let's just say I feel it's my duty as your colleague and

friend to remind you that given the evidence it is crazy to think that somebody other than Treebeard murdered Daniel Gaines. 'I've been framed,' he says? Honestly, Alicia, how many times have we both heard that?"

"And it's never true," she murmured.

"No, it's never true. Or one time in a million it's true. And do you understand that it's especially crazy to think that the person who framed Treebeard is Joan Gaines?"

A trio of sheriff's deputies walked past in their olive-green uniforms, guns in their holsters and walkie-talkies in their belts. They would agree wholeheartedly with Louella. They would think she was crazy, too.

Yet she couldn't get past it. Treebeard's story was plausible. It had the heft of truth. She could visualize it happening the way he described, picture him pushing open the Gaines' front door, imagine him stilled by the house's eerie quiet. Sure, he didn't have the letter, and couldn't identify the phantom woman, but both those lapses could be explained. And it still didn't feel right that Treebeard would have murdered Gaines with his own arrow, left an array of physical evidence at the scene, then fled the county believing he wouldn't be caught. Now, *that* was crazy.

"Do you understand," Alicia said, "that my gut just bothers me on this one? Do you understand that?"

"Yes. I also understand that your gut has been pretty accurate in the past." Louella leaned closer and lowered her voice. "But as I said before, Alicia, the problem is that this time your gut bothers you for the wrong reason. You're trying to pin this on the wife for the wrong reason."

"The old 'Alicia resents rich women' thing, is that it? 'Alicia thinks they have it so easy and she has it so hard.' "

"Well, is that so far off?"

The question hung in the sunny, warming air, though it

required no answer. Louella was right on the money, Alicia thought, smiling grimly at her own pun. Women like Joan Gaines did have it a hell of a lot easier and Alicia did resent it. They didn't have to worry about the progress of their careers, for the simple reason that they didn't really have to work. They didn't have to watch every dime, or pack every spare dime off to family members to keep them in rent and groceries. They didn't have to grow old living from paycheck to paycheck, every passing year amazed to discover that despite all their efforts, they were still in the same pit they were in the year before.

So she did have a chip on her shoulder. Fine. That damn Milo Pappas was right. But what the ambassador's son didn't realize was that anybody else in her position would have one, too.

"I know you're looking for a big hit, Alicia," Louella murmured. "I know you need one to run for judge again. And you'll get it, eventually. But I've got to tell you, it's not this. It is not this."

It has to be this. I need it to be this. I'm running out of time. But instead she said, "Can you believe tomorrow's New Year's Eve?"

Louella drooped against the back of the bench. "Don't remind me. I'll ring in another New Year sitting with my parents drinking Asti Spumanti and watching *Rockin' New Year's Eve* on TV. It makes me feel as old as Dick Clark." She sighed heavily. "I did turn down a date, actually."

"Really? With who?"

"You know Tom in the Water Resources Agency?"

"The one with the beard? He's kind of cute."

"Kind of." Louella grimaced. "But I don't know, I just couldn't say yes. It'd be like setting the bar for New Year's Eve too low, like I'd never get it up again afterward. At least now I can maintain the fantasy of having a fabulous date. You know what I mean?"

"Unfortunately, I do."

"How's Jorge, by the way?"

"Fine." Alicia poked the last of her muffin segments into her mouth. Was she imagining it or was there something odd in Louella's voice when she asked that question? Like she was trying a little too hard to be offhand? But she had no time to think about it because of what Louella asked her next.

"You're not that excited about him, are you?"

It was pointless lying to Louella. "There's just no fireworks."

"You want *fireworks*?" Louella just shook her head. "Geez, at this point I'd settle for a flare." She glanced at her watch. "I should get back."

They collected their cellophane wrappers and foam coffee cups and tossed them in a garbage bin near the bench. "So will you do something else for me?" Alicia asked.

Louella halted. "You have got to be kidding."

"Will you get me a list of the Gaines campaign staff? And a sample of their letterhead stationery?"

Louella just shook her head. "You're crazy, you know that, Alicia? You're crazy when it comes to Jorge and you're crazy about this."

"But you'll do it?"

Louella just threw up her hands.

"Thanks. I owe you one."

"You owe me about *ten*."

***

For a variety of reasons she rarely cared to probe, Joan hated going into Headwaters' Monterey headquarters. This morning her aversion was even stronger than usual, a palpable thing that threatened to wrest control of the Jag's steering wheel and return her forthwith to the Lodge. She forced herself to exit Highway 1 at Munras Avenue and head due north into the heart of the city, less glitzy but more historical than Pebble Beach or Carmel.

Monterey was to the West Coast what Gettysburg was to the East. It was founded in 1770 by Spanish sea captain Sebastian Vizcaino, who promptly erected the first of California's four presidios on the bay, then teamed up with Father Junipero Serra to convert the heathen natives to Catholicism. It was California's first capital under Spanish, Mexican, and American rule, and where the state's constitution was ratified.

When Daniel and Joan's father acquired Headwaters from its Idaho founders, Daniel relocated most of the company's executive operations to Monterey, leaving only a skeleton staff in Boise. Later, for both convenience and symbolic value, he chose Monterey as the site of his campaign headquarters.

Headwaters was housed not far from the Presidio in an enlarged adobe whose original foundation dated back to 1817. In the heady early days of her marriage, Joan threw herself into its renovation. At a certain point, though, she gave up, sick to death of placating the History and Art Association. Daniel hired a preservationist to finish the job but never let Joan forget that she "dropped the ball," as he put it. Headwaters soon took its place on the list of what her family considered Joan's incomplete projects.

She turned onto Pacific. In front of her was the marina; the blocks ahead were jam-packed with tourists heading for Cannery Row and the aquarium. The unseasonably warm air was heavy with the smell of fish, an aroma Joan detested.

She closed the window and cranked the Jag's air

conditioner, hating life. What in the world would she find in Headwaters' books? Daniel had wreaked absolute havoc with her father's living trust. What might he have done with Headwaters, which now represented a huge chunk of her wealth?

The only potential saving grace was that unlike her father's trust, Daniel hadn't been running Headwaters alone. Far from it, in fact. The primary day-to-day manager was a man named Craig Barlowe, the chief operating officer. Barlowe was one of Daniel's Wharton cronies—a boring one, Joan always thought, one of those cookie-cutter business-school types—but Daniel always seemed high on him. Then there was the board of directors, though Joan knew it was packed full of Daniel's sidekicks from private-equity days and not really much of a watchdog.

A good part of Joan didn't care to deal with any of it, but she had to. Not only to wipe the smugness off her mother's face but to investigate taking over Daniel's job as CEO. Somehow that whole idea felt different now, though. When she'd thought of it originally, it had seemed bold and sexy: take over as chief executive, showcase her talents, lay the groundwork for her entree into politics. In other words, prove that what Daniel had done, she could do. But now, after that dreadful conversation with Gossett, she felt she had to take over as CEO to keep getting Daniel's salary and deal with the unbelievable cash-flow problem.

Having to work for money? Joan clutched the steering wheel. It was extremely distasteful. She just prayed Gossett was right and cash flow would be only a short-term difficulty.

No one could know about it. Not Milo, not anyone. Thank God no one outside the family knew how Daniel had acquired the company in the first place. He'd even tried for a while to keep the facts from her, but he'd spilled them eventually.

She'd been enraged, of course. He never appreciated how much her father had done for him, never.

Well, that was over. It was all over.

One traffic light later, Joan made a series of zigzag turns to escape the tourist logjam. Finally she arrived at Headwaters, only to be stunned into immobility by what she saw through the windshield.

Parked on the street out front was a small moving truck, its ramp deployed. Men in orange shirts bearing the words *Fine Art Capital* were walking between the adobe office building and the truck carrying what were obviously oil paintings wrapped in brown paper.

Carrying them *away*.

She abandoned the Jag by a fire hydrant and raced inside, where several employees were emptying the contents of their desks into cardboard boxes.

"What on earth is going on?" she demanded of the woman closest to the front door, a hefty middle-aged creature with red-rimmed eyes and the most hideous floral-print dress Joan had ever seen. Immediately the woman burst into tears, ran right up to Joan, and grabbed her arms with such ferocity Joan couldn't shake her off.

"Mrs. Gaines! Mrs. Gaines!" she kept shrieking. "I am so glad to see you! Maybe you can stop this from happening!"

"Stop what from happening? And where is Mr. Barlowe?"

"He's firing people! He's in his office firing people." That seemed to deflate the creature. She let go of Joan to extract a wadded-up tissue from up her short tight sleeve, a place Joan was most surprised to see it. The woman blew her nose noisily, the flesh on her upper arms shaking with the effort.

"I'm one of the first he fired," she went on. "Today's my last day. 'Have to rein in expenses,' he said—that's why the art's going, too. Three weeks' severance I got, that's it. The economy the way it is, I don't know what I'm going to do." She sniffled and rubbed the tissue against her reddened nose, then before Joan could step away again grabbed Joan's arm. "I'm so sorry for going on like this, telling you my troubles." Her watery blue eyes again filled with tears, making Joan think of the pools in the aquarium a few blocks away. "After what you've been through, losing Mr. Gaines the way you did, you shouldn't have to hear about my problems. But I wonder if you couldn't just"—she stepped closer and Joan cringed at the nearness of the woman's wet, mottled, flabby cheeks—"just talk to Mr. Barlowe and see if maybe he doesn't really have to let me go?"

The woman's eyes were importuning, but all Joan wanted to do was shake her hands loose and escape outside. How her father had spent all his adult life—as mayor, governor, then senator—not only listening to people's sob stories but actually doing something about them, amazed her. *Maybe*, she thought fleetingly, *politics wasn't her game* ...

"What's your name?" she asked the woman.

"Dolores Hartnett, ma'am."

The way she said it, Joan thought she might bob a curtsy. "All right, Dolores." Joan pulled her arm free but tried to put a comforting look on her face. "I intend to speak with Mr. Barlowe right now. Will you remind me where his office is?"

"I'll do better than that. I'll take you there." The woman wedged her body between the packing boxes and led Joan to a closed oak door at the rear of the adobe's main level, on which Craig Barlowe's name was spelled out in gleaming brass letters.

Joan made her voice dismissive. "Thank you. I appreciate your help, Dolores."

The woman nodded and backed away, with such a naked plea in her eyes that Joan wished she'd just go, already.

Finally she did. Joan leaned her ear against Barlowe's door, through which she could hear the murmur of male voices.

It didn't take her long to decide that it was just too damn bad that he had somebody in there with him. Now that Daniel was dead, she was the lone shareholder of this company. This company that was losing money. *Her* money.

Joan felt an icy nervousness wash through her. Daniel screwed this up, too. He got too aggressive and screwed up, first the trust and then Headwaters. She had a sudden strong physical memory of her husband, as if he were standing right there in the hall with her. Watching. Waiting. Wondering what she would do next.

She shivered, then forced herself to get a grip. One thing she would not do was wait in this corridor until Barlowe freed himself up. She needed answers now.

She rapped sharply on the heavy oak door, then twisted the knob and pushed it open. Craig Barlowe half rose from behind his desk, the eyes behind his wire frames widening in obvious shock at the identity of this unexpected guest.

Quickly he masked his reaction and strode toward her. "Joan!" he said, his tone falsely hearty. He was a paunchy man Daniel's age who looked at least ten years older. He grasped her hand. "It's a pleasure to see you, as always, but you should have called first."

"Today isn't a bad day for my visit, I trust?" She glanced pointedly at the man still sitting in the chair facing Barlowe's desk, assuming him to be another employee getting the ax.

"Not at all." Barlowe included the man in that reply, then introduced him as a banker and swiftly got rid of him, with best wishes for a happy New Year. From the grim expression on the man's face, that didn't seem likely.

Barlowe waved Joan to the seat the banker had vacated, then returned behind his desk. "May I offer you coffee or tea,

Joan?"

"No, thank you." She set her handbag on his desk. "Craig, what in the world is going on here today?"

"Oh"—he made a dismissive gesture—"it's nothing to worry about. Just some minor cost cutting."

"Minor cost cutting? I see paintings going out the door and people losing their jobs."

Barlowe's face assumed a somber expression. *Did he learn that from Henry Gossett?* Joan wondered. Perhaps law and business provided essentially the same training. "It's always very, very difficult to let people go, Joan. But we have to keep the bottom line uppermost in our minds."

"I agree." She was a great fan of a healthy bottom line, particularly her own. "But is there some pressing difficulty at the moment?"

"Not pressing, no." Barlowe shook his head. "I simply judged it prudent to trim a few expenses before the end of the year. Which is tomorrow, of course."

"Of course." *He's feeding me the party line, as if I'm the stupid wife who doesn't deserve the true story.* She stiffened. "Craig, you realize, of course, that I am the sole shareholder of this company and as such am entitled to full disclosure of its financial state."

He looked startled. "Joan, I am providing full disclosure. I just don't want to worry you unduly."

"Let me decide how worried to get." Briefly she wondered if she should fire this Craig Barlowe when she took over. He annoyed her, but then again he did know how to run the place. Or did he only know how to run it into the ground?

She had a sudden thought. One thing she knew for sure was that Daniel and her father had acquired Headwaters in a leveraged buyout, meaning the company assumed a great deal of debt on which regular interest payments had to be made. "Does all this cost cutting have to do with servicing the debt?"

She felt a thrill of pleasure watching Barlowe's eyes once again widen with surprise. *No*, she told him silently across the expanse of his antique desk, *I am not the stupid wife. In fact, I know a great deal that even* you *don't.*

"The debt payments are substantial," he allowed. "The regulatory constraints on what we can harvest seem to be getting tougher all the time. And it doesn't help that lumber prices have dropped as the economy has slowed down."

Here we go again, she thought. "Is Headwaters experiencing a cash-flow problem?"

He hesitated, then, "A small one, yes."

Damn. That would mean she'd have trouble hiking the CEO's salary when she took over. Daniel had paid himself only half a million dollars a year. She'd been toying with the idea of doubling it. "How many people are you laying off?" she asked.

"Six. We were already fairly lean, so we'll really feel these cuts."

They might have to get leaner still if she was going to get her million a year. Too bad for Dolores Hartnett. But this was business. Tough decisions had to be made.

"Craig, I would like you to walk me through the profit-and-loss statements for the last year." She rose from her chair and walked toward his door. "First, though, I have a quick call to make. I'll take care of that in Daniel's office and return shortly. Please have the books ready when I come back."

She couldn't care less about the stunned, barely hidden animosity that suddenly appeared on Craig Barlowe's wide, square face. Instead she laughed quietly to herself, imagining his reaction when he found out she would be his new boss.

Joan had almost made it to the stairs on her way to

Daniel's second-floor corner suite when she got waylaid by Dolores Hartnett, who again halted all forward progress by attaching herself to Joan's left arm.

"Mrs. Gaines?" the woman asked.

Again Joan was vaguely repulsed. The woman's lower lip was actually trembling. Joan twisted her features into a regretful expression. "I am so sorry, Dolores," she murmured. "I did my best but I'm afraid I could not talk Mr. Barlowe into retaining your services. I am so sorry."

The woman nodded, looked again as if she might burst into tears, then released Joan's arm and backed away.

"I'm sure things will look much cheerier for you in the New Year," Joan called, then turned her back on Dolores Hartnett and ascended the stairs, her mind moving on to the next item on her agenda.

***

Nothing like a Rotary Club lunch, Kip thought with satisfaction, *to raise money.*

He looked up from his roasted chicken, mashed potatoes, and green beans to scan the crowded hall, a midsize banquet room in the local Embassy Suites hotel. There were about seventy-five Rotarians in attendance, grouped at ten round tables, and they were Kip Penrose's kind of folk—all male, all conservative, and all primed to write a check to plump up his campaign coffers. Not that they needed much plumping. He had about a hundred and sixty grand in the bank; another thirty or so would set him up just fine for November. Not to mention scare off Rocco Messina or any other potential challenger who might otherwise think he could match Kip Penrose's war chest. Not likely.

Kip tuned in to the conversation going on at his table.

They'd already rated the San Francisco 49ers' current crop of receivers, denounced the University of California's latest admissions criteria—which all agreed smacked of hidden affirmative action—and pondered the spotty record of the ongoing war on terrorism. Now they had moved on to the never-ending debate over whether part of San Francisco Bay should be filled in to expand runways at San Francisco's airport. Though Kip knew that in this crowd there really wasn't much to debate on that topic.

"Seems to me," he informed his rapt listeners, "this is an economic rather than an environmental issue. Forget terrorism. Business travelers will shun the city in ever greater numbers if we can't improve the on-time record at SFO."

Nods all around. Kip could almost see the donation checks getting bigger. Man, he loved these people. They were the kind he'd grown up with, outside Boston—small-business owners, subcontractors, or insurance salesmen, like his dad. The big dogs were dentists or owned car dealerships. He pretended Libby and Joan Hudson were his kind, but that was all an act. They made him nervous, truth be told. With these folks he could be himself, or at least a more relaxed form of himself.

A Hispanic waiter came by to bus his empty plate. Kip sipped from his coffee, which at Rotary lunches was a thin, diner-style brew served alongside the meal, and prepared to deliver his speech. It honed in on one topic and one topic only: how Kip Penrose's policies had single-handedly reduced serious crime on the Monterey Peninsula. He'd just double-checked the order of his index cards when his cell phone rang. He twisted his body away from the table to answer. "Penrose," he said.

"Kip, I am so pleased to have reached you. It's Joan Gaines."

Kip's heart rate ramped up, as if he'd just increased the speed on the cross-trainer he'd purchased for the renovated basement of his home. Immediately he rose from the table to head to a private corner of the banquet room, putting an expression on his face that might lead his tablemates to believe he'd just been phoned by the governor. "What can I do for you, Joan?"

"There's a small matter I thought I should bring to your attention."

There were no small matters where a Hudson was concerned. "Yes?" he prompted.

"The woman who is assisting you on my husband's case ... Alicia Maldonado, is it?"

"Yes?" By now Kip's tablemates would have noticed that he was frowning.

"Well, I understand, of course, that she's just doing her job, but she paid a visit to a friend of mine to confirm that I stayed overnight at her house the night Daniel was killed." She paused to sigh heavily. "Kip, the police had already spoken to my friend over the weekend and, I must say, taken up a great deal of her—"

Damn! Kip clenched his cell phone. Joan Gaines would never understand why her whereabouts had to be confirmed. But why the hell hadn't Maldonado warned him about this? Better yet, left it to him to handle it?

"—Courtney Holt? You know the name?" Joan was saying. "Her husband is Lawrence Holt, the attorney. Of course I explained to—"

Double damn! The Holts were donors, or at least they had been. Maybe he could have his secretary send them flowers to apologize? No, he realized instantly, that would look like favoritism, and he had to avoid that appearance at all costs.

This whole case was so damn complicated! He would've

been so much better off if Daniel Gaines hadn't been murdered. Then Gaines would have become governor, and who knew how he might have helped Kip then? It was so frustrating Kip could barely think straight.

He forced himself to sound calm. "Joan, I do apologize for the inconvenience to your friend. And you can rest assured that I'll talk to my aide about it this very afternoon."

Another sigh. "I would be so grateful, Kip. I would just hate if any of your supporters thought your office wasn't handling my husband's case properly. It would be such a shame."

Joan hung up shortly afterward. Kip watched, almost blind with fury, as the Hispanic waiters buzzed among the tables clearing plates and distributing the custardy dessert. He could have throttled Alicia Maldonado right then and there.

CHAPTER TWELVE

"All rise. The court is now in session."

Judge Timothy Pade banged his gavel. "Good afternoon" was exchanged all around, and the few dozen people—most of them press—in Superior Court Four reclaimed their seats.

Since Treebeard's arraignment happened to be the first item on the docket, Alicia was already in position at the people's table, Penrose at her side. At the defense table to their left sat Treebeard and Jerome Brown, a natty figure in a black-and-white houndstooth sport jacket and perfectly creased gabardine slacks. In front of Alicia hulked the black binder filled with three-hole-punched case notes. With the police report, Treebeard's DMV history and lengthy rap sheet, evidence form, and other paperwork that went into bringing a homicide case to trial, the binder was as big as a VCR. And twice as heavy.

Which meant, of course, that Alicia had hauled it up the six flights of stairs from the first-floor D.A.'s office, Penrose climbing unencumbered by her side. No courthouse staff ever used the elevator. It was a creaky, unreliable piece of equipment that moved at roughly the speed of the county bureaucracy. For some reason Penrose had seemed very keyed-up, his steps unusually jerky, his face flushed. She'd felt duty-bound to ask him whether something was wrong. He'd pushed out, "You're damn right something is," through clenched teeth, then twisted his features into a cheery smile as they passed the potential voters lined up on the second floor for jury duty. Alicia knew she'd hear what had him all riled up before the day was over.

Whatever was going on with Penrose, Louella had scored a victory just before lunch. She'd gotten a judge to allow her to subpoena Joan Gaines' cell-phone and credit-card records for December. So before long Louella would have her hot little hands on what might provide some interesting insights into Joan's activities the night of her husband's murder.

"I'd like to think I've become tremendously newsworthy," Judge Pade deadpanned. "Maybe you all heard that I finally broke par." Halfhearted chuckles broke out in the rear of the gallery, the area set aside for the media. A bearded, even-keeled veteran of the Monterey County justice system, Pade didn't look as if he expected a more rousing response to his tepid attempt at humor. "But I know better." He waved a hand at the gallery. "I imagine all of you are leaving after the first item of business?"

Another round of chuckles. A man called out "Yes, sir!" Alicia twisted in her chair, trying to be casual, trying to scan the occupants of the press rows without looking too obvious. She realized quickly she hadn't succeeded. There sat Milo Pappas, second to the last row on the left, looking straight at her and wearing an *I know who you're looking for and you just found him* grin.

Damn. She pivoted back around to face the bench. Momentarily she was catapulted back to third grade at Our Lady of Lourdes Elementary, where every morning Sister Gonzaga gave Alicia her only reprimand of the day for squirming in her seat trying to find Hermano Bautista, an eight-year-old bad boy of the best kind. Somehow Hermano had always seemed to know she was looking for him, too.

"Let us dispense, then," Pade said, "with the first item on this afternoon's agenda ..." and the bailiff piped up without missing a beat: "The People versus John David Stennis."

At the defense table, a jumpsuit-clad Treebeard rose to his feet, his ankle manacles clattering. As form required, Jerome also rose, as did Alicia and Penrose. Behind her, Alicia could hear the soft whir of camera equipment as the only still photographer and TV cameraman allowed inside the courtroom focused their lenses on the accused.

The attorneys stated their names for the record. The charges were read. Pade asked Treebeard if he understood them, and Treebeard said he did. Alicia thought Jerome looked relieved and guessed that he'd been worried his client would refuse to speak that day.

Pade stared at Treebeard. "On the count of murder in the first degree with special circumstances, how do you plead?"

It seemed to Alicia that everyone stilled. From her position on the right side of the people's table, she leaned forward to see around Penrose and get a better look at the defendant. Treebeard dropped his chin to his chest and shuffled his manacled feet. The thought flashed through her mind that maybe he was a fabulous actor playing out this moment for all its dramatic worth. Finally he raised his head and stared straight at the judge. "Not guilty, Your Honor."

As they'd all expected. She relaxed. But then Treebeard went on talking, which sent a palpable wave of surprise through the courtroom.

"I'm not just pleading not guilty." His voice took on the hostile edge Alicia knew so well. "I'm honestly not guilty, Your Honor. I didn't do it."

"That's enough, John," Alicia heard Jerome murmur, and watched him lay a hand on his client's left arm.

"No, I mean it." Treebeard's voice rose. He shook off Jerome's hand. "Somebody set me up. I didn't do it."

Judge Pade raised his voice, though he gave no other

indication the defendant was out of order. "The preliminary hearing will be held Monday, January thirteenth, nine a.m. Next case." He banged his gavel on its little wooden stand, which seemed to agitate Treebeard further.

"No!" he shouted, and shook Jerome off with such force the lawyer was knocked backward a few feet, crashing noisily into one of the chairs at the defense table. The still photographer and TV cameraman scooted up to the bar to get closer to the action. "Can't I get a word in edgewise here?" Treebeard yelled. "What the hell kind of justice is this?" Now two armed guards were on him, trying to manhandle Treebeard out the side door into the defendant holding area. But Treebeard squirmed and kicked and shouted, looking for all the world like the kind of crazed maniac who would shoot an arrow through Daniel Gaines.

Alicia watched the display with a sick heart. It gave her not one iota of satisfaction, though it would help her win the case. Treebeard had single-handedly turned his own arraignment from a nonevent into a top news story, one that would convince most Americans he was a guilty man.

Yet when she saw this angry, impotent side of Treebeard, she thought him less likely to be guilty of murder than of gross stupidity. If Treebeard had been framed, whoever picked him as the mark had made an inspired choice.

***

Milo stared at Alicia's profile and saw nothing in the play of expressions on her face that he would have expected. Instead of triumph, he read regret. Instead of vindication, sadness. *She's honestly not convinced Treebeard did it. She wasn't just feeding me a line when she said the case wasn't all sewn up.*

But if not Treebeard, who? He pictured Alicia's face as she

sat across from him at the Mission Ranch bar. *Almost always it's somebody close to the victim.* In his memory, her face was still, thoughtful. *Spouse, family, friends.*

Milo remained seated on the hard wooden bench, watching Treebeard get dragged through the courtroom's side door. Spouse? It simply wasn't possible. Joan wasn't capable of murder, literally wasn't capable of it. For good or ill, she was too much of a hothouse flower to be able to drive an arrow through a man's heart. At least any way other than metaphorically.

Again Alicia's voice reverberated in his memory, this time cold, resentful. *You mean because she's from a wealthy family? Because she's the daughter of a governor?* No. Because she'd never had to do anything difficult in her life. And killing your husband, even if you desperately wanted him dead, was difficult.

His fellow reporters were filing out. He stood to allow those in his row to exit, and came face-to-face with D.A. Kip Penrose, who was grinning at him broadly and holding out his hand. Milo took it and glanced at Alicia, grim-faced at her boss's side. "Milo, good to see you again," Penrose was saying. "I'm gratified to see that WBS has you covering this important story."

Milo didn't let himself say any of the things that sprang to his mind. Penrose was gratified? Because Milo was on *Newsline* and *Newsline* was the hottest prime-time magazine on the air and the D.A. would dearly love its national exposure? "Certainly," was all Milo could make himself say, but that was apparently enough for Penrose, who gave him a comradely slap on the back and preceded him out the courtroom door. Alicia, Milo noted with disappointment, was already gone.

The reporters were setting themselves up in the corridor

for an impromptu press conference. There was only one cameraman, serving as the pool, who would provide dubs of the day's video to the outlets requesting it. Milo joined the throng, spiral-bound reporter's notebook in hand. Penrose was faster than the defense attorney at stepping up to the lone mike. He bent his head and cleared his throat. The cameraman turned on his light, bathing the D.A. in a wash of illumination. "Rolling," the cameraman said, and immediately Penrose began talking.

"Kip Penrose, K-I-P-P-E-N-R-O-S-E, Monterey County district attorney. First let me make a statement." He paused to arrange his features into solemn lines. "The case against John David Stennis, who calls himself Treebeard, is extremely strong. This afternoon's arraignment is an important first step in bringing a barbarous murderer to justice, but much remains to be done. In the preliminary hearing in ten days' time ..."

Milo tuned out, already bored. Penrose would offer no interesting insights, even if he had any, which Milo doubted. Alicia hadn't even bothered to stay for the performance, a sure signal of just how dreary it promised to be. And if by some chance Penrose, or later the defense attorney, did let fly something notable, Milo would hear it on the pool tape.

He sidled away from the mob, stowing his reporter's notebook in his overcoat pocket. His feet led him down the red-tiled stairs to the first floor, where across the central hall was the unprepossessing glass-door entryway to room 101, the district attorney's office. He stared at it, then traversed the hall, pulled open the door, and gave his most winning smile to the twenty-something red-haired receptionist who sat behind the reinforced glass partition window. She—the gatekeeper who buzzed visitors through a locked door into the sanctum sanctorum—smiled back.

"I have a four o'clock appointment with Deputy D.A. Maldonado," he lied, and flashed his laminated, all-purpose press pass for effect. "My name is Milo Pappas."

"I know who you are." She smiled again.

Milo smiled again, too. "I'm a little early, but would you be kind enough to let me in? I'd like to make a swing past the men's room and would rather not use the facilities out here."

"I understand completely," she said, and buzzed him in. That was that. Milo saw no sign that she alerted Alicia to his imminent arrival, so he would maintain the advantage of surprise.

What did he want? he asked himself as he strode down the narrow corridor as if he knew where he was going, peering into each of the minuscule offices he passed. Well, he wanted to see Alicia. He wanted to talk to her. Give asking her out another whirl. Maybe this time he could convince her that dinner, just the two of them, wasn't so out of order. But she was nowhere in sight. Many of the offices were shut down for the night—lights out, desks cleared. Not surprising, given that it was late afternoon on the thirtieth of December. He did find a men's room, where he made the promised pit stop, then resumed his circumnavigation of the office.

The few people around took little notice of him. In fact, most were grouped in one office, devouring what appeared to be a New Year's sheet cake. As he walked past, he heard the pop of a champagne cork, followed by laughter and whistles.

He turned another corner and there in front of him, at the end of the corridor, was an office whose superior furnishings indicated that its owner had to be Kip Penrose. Just as he made that deduction Milo watched Alicia enter the office from the corridor perpendicular to his own and claim one of the two upholstered chairs in front of the sprawling desk. She crossed her legs, threw back her head, and stared at the ceiling, the picture of raw impatience.

Clearly she was waiting for Penrose. Milo retreated behind a cubicle wall and pondered what to do. This would not be a good time to interrupt her. He wanted her undivided attention and wouldn't get it while she was waiting for her boss. Nor did he want Penrose to interrupt them in what he hoped would be a personal conversation. But he couldn't lurk in these corridors forever. Maybe he could wait in the men's room?

He was considering that humbling option when he leaned forward and saw Penrose enter his office from the same corridor Alicia had used, then slam shut the door.

For a few seconds, Milo remained in place. No one was near him. The party continued a few offices away. Cautiously he inched forward. When he reached Penrose's door he saw that the office to its left was empty and dark. Its owner—R. Messina, judging from the nameplate just right of the doorjamb—was apparently gone for the day.

Milo gave another quick look around. Still all clear. On impulse he slipped inside the empty office, half closed the door, and stood in the shadows with his back against the wall adjacent to Penrose's office. Some instinct told him that Alicia and Penrose were about to discuss the Gaines case. The journalist in him was curious to know what they would say, and he soon realized he would be able to—for the voices next door were being piped loud and clear through the offices' shared heating duct. He stilled and listened.

"Why should I care if she called you?" Alicia's voice, indignant. "Is that what you've been upset about?"

Penrose. "You should have warned me you were going to interview Courtney Holt a second time."

"Why? So you could have forbidden me to do it? Or come along and fawned all over her the whole time?"

"It is highly questionable whether a second interview was even necessary. You're constantly telling me how busy you are." Penrose slammed something. "Maybe you'd clear off your desk faster if you didn't traipse off to Santa Cruz redoing what the police have already done."

"Maybe I wouldn't have to if the police were more competent."

"So now you've got a gripe against Carmel PD? What the hell's your problem with them?"

Milo could hear the rising anger in Penrose's voice. For once he couldn't blame him. He knew where Alicia was headed with this and it didn't make much sense to him, either.

She was talking again. "They don't even mention in the report of their interview that Joan Gaines didn't actually stay in the Holt house that night. She stayed in the guesthouse."

"So what?"

"So I'll tell you what. Given the separation of the guesthouse from the main house, and where she parked her car, she was able to come and go with no one being the wiser."

Penrose laughed out loud. "I repeat! So what?"

"So she *did* come and go."

Silence. Milo frowned.

A second later Penrose spoke again, sounding truculent. "What the hell are you talking about?"

"I have an eyewitness who puts Joan Gaines in front of her house at ten p.m. the night her husband was killed. When she was supposedly asleep in Santa Cruz."

Milo reared back from the wall. *What?*

"She lied, Kip," Alicia went on. "She lied about her whereabouts. What else do you think she might be lying about?"

There was a long silence. Then Milo heard a loud scoffing sound, presumably from the D.A. "That's absurd," he heard Penrose say.

"Louella is deposing the eyewitness right now."

Another few beats of silence. Then, "Who is this supposed eyewitness?"

"His name is Harry McEvoy. He lives on Twelfth, just a few blocks from the Gaines' house. He—"

Alicia went on talking but Milo missed it, too busy sliding his reporter's notebook from his overcoat pocket and jotting down what he had heard, though his hand trembled and he didn't really believe it. Either Alicia had something wrong or this McEvoy character did. Somebody was confused or lying or something.

"This is crazy!" Penrose, loud and angry. "You know how unreliable eyewitness accounts are!" Milo heard a slamming sound, as if the D.A. slapped his hand down hard on his desk. "We do not need to second-guess Joan Gaines' whereabouts the night her husband was murdered. She is not a suspect in this case."

"Well, maybe she should be. Let's see. Not only did she lie about her whereabouts, but an eyewitness places her at the scene of the murder at the time of the murder. She's shown no emotion. She's shown zero interest in the case. She went on a shopping spree two days after her husband was killed. She—"

Penrose interrupted. Perhaps it was because Milo's heart was thumping, or because crazy thoughts were thundering across his brain, or simply because Penrose had lowered his voice, but for a time Milo did not catch the conversation beyond the wall. When he could again focus, Alicia was speaking.

"Don't think for a minute that I'm going to back off. I don't give a damn if the Hudsons are huge donors to your campaigns. I don't give a damn if you and everybody else in this county is one hundred percent convinced Treebeard is guilty. I am not convinced. And I am not going to let it drop."

Shuffling noises, as though someone had risen out of their chair. Probably Alicia, getting ready to leave.

"I'll tell you another thing," she said, her voice suddenly much clearer. Milo held his breath. She must have moved closer to the duct. "As a prosecutor I feel a very strong duty to get at the truth. People's lives are at stake here, Kip."

Her voice grew fainter. She must have moved again. She would probably leave soon. Milo edged toward the door and pushed it slightly more closed, wincing as it groaned with the movement. Then he scooted back to his hiding place in the shadows.

Penrose's door opened. Milo watched a shaft of light spill across the corridor and into it step Alicia's shadow. Very clearly now, he heard her again speak. "And FYI, I am not doing this on my own. This morning Louella got a subpoena for Joan Gaines' cell-phone and credit-card records."

She stomped off. Milo stood motionless, reluctant to try to slip past Penrose's open door. Thirty seconds later the shaft of light in the corridor disappeared. *He's shutting off his lights*, Milo thought with relief. *He's going.* Then he watched Penrose leave, wearing his overcoat and striding rapidly down the corridor past R. Messina's office.

Milo waited a minute more, then cautiously approached the door. From down the corridor the noise from the party rolled toward him in waves.

He had just stepped into the corridor, planning to exit by slipping past the party, when he was halted by the voice of the last person on earth he wanted to see at that moment.

"Hey!" The voice was female. Commanding. Angry. "What the hell are you doing here?"

Milo turned his head to look into the flaring eyes of Alicia Maldonado.

***

He heard everything. He heard every word. Alicia didn't need to confirm it. She knew it in the marrow of her bones. The only question was what would he do with what he had learned?

Wrong—there was a second question, she realized. What did she want him to do with it?

"In here." She grabbed him by the elbow and pushed him back into Rocco's office, then shut the door behind them and flipped on the overhead fluorescent lights. She turned to face him. "How did you get in?" To her own ears her voice sounded shrill, demanding.

For a second he was silent. Then, "I slipped in while some of your coworkers were coming out."

She shook her head. "Don't lie to me, Milo Pappas. I could charge you with felony trespassing."

"It wouldn't stick." He half sat on the corner of Rocco's desk and crossed his arms over his chest.

He gave no sign of being flustered. She found herself both admiring of his self-possession and irritated by it. "You're pretty damn cocky for somebody who's just been sneaking around government buildings eavesdropping on privileged conversations."

"It's called reporting."

"Oh, really? Reporting is getting information any way you can, is that it? It doesn't matter under what false pretenses?" Something was starting to get away from her. She felt anger ignite in her chest like heartburn. "You don't follow a single ethical guideline, do you? You're completely comfortable trespassing and eavesdropping and, oh, let's add a third category! Trying to seduce the prosecutor so she'll give you inside dirt when you need it."

He slid off Rocco's desk and approached her across the small distance that separated them. His eyes bored into her own. "I did not try to seduce you for inside information. I merely asked you out and you refused me. If anyone should feel insulted here, it's me."

"That's ridiculous," she said, then turned away from him, his proximity making her thoughts leap in a direction she could neither predict nor control. If any insult existed it was to her own dignity, for that single kiss he had given her stuck in her memory like the heart a lovesick teenager carved into the bark of a tree. Images of this delicious, infuriating man wrapped around her, above her, within her, took delectable shape in her mind, making her heart thud and her skin flush. His kiss came back to her in excruciating detail. What more could that mouth of his do, if she allowed it freer rein?

Stop it. Stop it.

She forced herself to look at him again, and to keep her gaze cold. "What are you going to do with what you heard?"

He seemed to ponder that. He averted his gaze, and his brow furrowed. "I don't know."

"I warn you, Milo. This is an ongoing criminal investigation."

"I am well aware of that."

"You mess with it and you're in deep shit."

"I have no intention of messing with it."

"What intention do you have then?"

He raised his voice, still not looking at her. "I told you, Alicia, I don't know."

She watched him. A muscle twitched in his jaw, which was showing the trace of a five-o'clock shadow. It was puzzling. He wasn't excited or defiant from his journalistic coup, which she would have expected. Instead he seemed disturbed, profoundly so, as if what he'd learned—that Joan Gaines had lied about her whereabouts the night of the murder—bothered him in some fundamental way.

Then she remembered what he'd told her at the Mission Ranch. He knew Joan Gaines. He knew her family. He had a personal tie.

Not surprising he'd be upset then, though any intimacy between Milo and Joan chafed. He was an ambassador's son. She was a governor's daughter. No doubt they attended the same Ivy League schools, dined in the same five-star restaurants, flew to Europe in the same first-class cabin.

The chasm between Alicia and Milo Pappas yawned before her in all of its heartbreaking clarity, an unreachable divide built of money and class and education, all the things that equal-opportunity Americans weren't supposed to think mattered. But to Alicia they were as real as the nicks on Rocco's battle-scarred wooden desk, the streaks of dirt on his perennially unwashed windows, the nasty brown stains on his carpet left by the coffee spills of prosecutors past.

She raised a warning finger in his direction. "You listen to me, Milo Pappas. If I hear that you let a single word of this slip out, you can damn well be sure that I'll go after you for felony trespassing. And believe me, I'm one prosecutor who could make it stick."

She walked out then, tempted to flip off the fluorescent lights and leave him in Rocco's office in the dark. But she didn't, though part of her ached to lash out at this untouchable man in whatever small way she could manage.

CHAPTER THIRTEEN

Shortly before noon on an overcast New Year's Eve, Joan lay on her back on a massage table in a private treatment room of the Lodge's spa. Her naked body was draped by a sheet, her eyes were shielded by a hand towel, and her skin was warmed by a fire in a mosaic-fronted hearth a few yards to her right. At her instruction the masseuse was working her horribly tense trapezius muscles. The air was scented with pine, both from the Douglas fir strung with holiday lights in a corner of the room and from the fire; the lighting was dim; and the sound system piped forth a gentle medley of New Age favorites.

She had been wise, she decided, to choose the three-hour Stress Reliever package, though even that had been fraught with tension-creating decisions. Fine, she would begin with the Pebble Beach Water Experience, but which bath additive should she choose? Mineral sea salt, seaweed and aromatherapy, or rose petals? Then which scrub? The Sea-salt Body Scrub, Cypress Pine Exfoliation, or Huckleberry Herbal Body Wrap? Even the choice of massage was daunting. Therapeutic, lymphatic, or Shiatsu?

Joan considered whether she should take the therapist's recommendation and add the Cranio-Sacral Therapy Session as a fourth treatment. Surely no woman was in more desperate need of balancing her energy and relaxing her central nervous system. Not after the last few days.

It turned out that Headwaters needed serious work. Such

serious work that it buried beyond excavation any desire Joan ever had to be chief executive officer.

Going over the books with Craig Barlowe, she had wanted to weep. The debt payments? Enormous. The P&L for the year? Lots of L and not much P. The regulatory constraints on harvesting timber? Tightening constantly. Her compulsion to shuck it all? Growing. Oh, yes, growing.

It was just all so much trouble. It was probably possible to turn Headwaters around, but it didn't look easy. Being CEO was all well and good, but not of a company that was in such difficulty. What fun would that be? Very little, as far as Joan could tell. It didn't seem to her that Barlowe, in his capacity as acting CEO, was having such a grand time.

Plus, thanks to Daniel, too much of her money was tied up in that damn company. Thanks to him she was cash poor, which was nearly as bad as being actually poor.

The masseuse dug into a particularly tender area of her nape. Joan winced. "I'm sorry," the woman murmured, though her pulverization continued at no less pressure.

In a way the pain felt good, though, distracting. Joan freed her mind to roam over the solution she had begun crafting.

She had worked as an investment banker for about eight months after she'd left Stanford Business School. As far as she was concerned, she knew all there was to know about selling companies. So as soon as the holidays were over, she would call the San Francisco I-bankers Daniel and her father had used to acquire Headwaters and talk to them about selling it. Why not? It would free her up in so many ways. Good-bye, corporate headaches. Hello, cash flow.

And she judged this the perfect time. Who would question why Joan Gaines wanted to sell her murdered husband's company? He was no longer alive to run it. Who would doubt that it gave his widow too many painful memories? Most likely she would even enjoy a certain premium from selling it quickly. She was a new widow: wounded, bereaved, vulnerable. Even hard-nosed businesspeople would be reluctant to drive too tough a bargain. And if they did, she could retaliate by dropping a word or two to the press. Milo would help, wouldn't he?

Joan knew she could get a lot of mileage out of the young-widow bit. Losing your husband to a brutal murder at age thirty made you sympathetic even if you were from a prominent family. Look at Jackie Kennedy. She'd been able to ride that wave her entire adult life.

Joan fought a rising disappointment as she realized her massage was winding to a close. In the final moments the masseuse signaled the last act by lightly running her fingers in silky, smoothing motions over Joan's face and neck. Then, unfortunately, she stopped, and murmured some cooing phrases about how Joan should take her time and lie still for a while. She exited the room so quietly that all Joan heard of her departure was the soft click of the door closing behind her.

Joan resumed her contemplations, reluctant to disrupt the pleasant stupor in which she found herself. She imagined her life after she sold Headwaters for every last cent it was worth. Shedding the company would free her from having to live on the Monterey Peninsula. More and more she thought of it as a backwater. For one thing it had virtually no desirable men. Who was it who said that Carmel was for the newly wed and the nearly dead? It was so, so true. All the resident males were either aged or married, and usually both. The dregs were struggling poets or artists, and she'd lost interest in that category a decade before. No, Los Angeles and maybe San Francisco were much better bets.

Of course, she had to have a better idea what to do about

Milo. At the moment she had no idea, though the notion had traipsed across her mind that he might provide some useful ... shall we say, *release* that very evening. After all, it was New Year's Eve. What healthy thirty-year-old woman didn't have sex on New Year's Eve? Surely the holiday gave her leave to dispense with her usual "Make him wait" calendar.

She chuckled to herself, entranced by her own cleverness. What a brainstorm to tell him she was having friends over! She knew that would make him much more likely to accept her invitation. Obviously he was hesitant to be alone with her. But he'd get over that fast enough. She'd make sure of it.

He could be so delicious, she remembered. The things he did, with such gusto ...

She squirmed on the massage table, recalling one particular ministration in exquisite detail. Daniel hadn't done that to her in eons. Maybe it was the Greek thing again.

Joan smiled a private smile in anticipation of the evening ahead. Ethnicity might have its drawbacks when it came to the social register, but clearly it had its place in the bedroom.

***

7:30 on New Year's Eve. Alicia sat on her mother's living room couch—the plastic that usually covered it temporarily removed in honor of the holiday—and watched Modesta Maldonado, in her best Christmas housedress, bend down to hold a tray of deep-fried cheese-stuffed jalapeno peppers tantalizingly close to Jorge's nose.

"*Andale, Jorge, prueba otro,*" she said, her wide face positively beaming. Nothing Modesta Maldonado liked better than having a real live man in her living room eating her food, especially one who might marry her eldest daughter.

Jorge winked at her mother. "*Con mucho gusto.*" He

reached for the biggest, Cheez Whiziest popper, and her mother's smile widened even further. How her face had enough room to hold that big a grin, Alicia had no idea.

Well, she might not be in love with her boyfriend, but her mother sure was.

From her perch at Jorge's side, Alicia tried to think what in this house had changed in thirty-five years. Now she had nieces and nephews, that was different, and of course her father was gone, but the living room looked much as it had when she was a kid, and no doubt it would look the same still on the day Modesta Maldonado went to claim her heavenly reward.

Alicia both loved this house and hated it. It was where she had started, yet she often feared it would be where she'd end up, too. Certainly she was the one writing the checks to keep it going. Yet at the same time it gave her great satisfaction to know that her father would be proud of her. She hadn't let the family down.

Tonight it was a raucous scene, the living room full to bursting with people and noise and furniture. People because there were nine Maldonados plus Jorge: herself, her mom, her two sisters, the one husband, the four kids. Noise because no one ever seemed to shut up and both the TV and stereo were on. And furniture because the prior summer Alicia had bought her mother a living room set from IKEA, but her mother had refused to get rid of any of her old stuff, worn though it might be. Who knew if she might need it someday? she asked, and that was the end of that. To Alicia it was yet another mysterious working of her mother's mind.

Then there were the Christmas decorations, starting with the silver foil Christmas tree with the red and green balls hauled out every year from the garage to be stood next to the television. The plastic reindeer that most people would put on their lawn but which stayed inside because of the high likelihood that outside they would be stolen. The Nativity set too large to be contained beneath the tree, so that the myrrh-bearing wise man was forced to stand right next to a reindeer.

"Alicia made tonight's main dish," her mother informed Jorge.

"Think of it as Mexican lasagna," Alicia told him. "Instead of mozzarella it has picante sauce and refried beans."

Jorge grinned. "I can't wait to try it."

"It's not the healthiest thing in the world. Nor are the *hongos enchilados* Mom insisted on making."

Jorge chuckled. "Deep-fried mushrooms?"

"Deep-fried in *manteca*." She wouldn't actually use the word *lard*, though that was the shortening of choice in her mother's kitchen. Modesta Maldonado could not be torn from her old-world habit of not only using lard in her cooking but making her own by frying flabby chunks of pork in a thick-bottomed pot.

"*Esos parecen sabrosos tambien, Dona Modesta*," Jorge told her mother, who beamed so brightly at the compliment to her mushrooms that Alicia half expected her to blow a fuse.

Jorge was such a diplomat, he might have been the ambassador's son, she thought. He was on his best behavior that night—then again he always was—spruced up in a blue suit, starched white dress shirt, and festive holiday tie, for the benefit both of the Maldonado clan and the local bar the two of them would patronize later to greet midnight. His dark eyes shone with kindness and good humor; he listened intently to every word that dropped from her lips; he showered her family with luxuries they could never afford, like the pearl stud earrings her mother was how sporting.

I should love him. There's something so wrong with me that I don't. Why she should be vaguely bored by Jorge Ramon and hanker lustily after Milo Pappas made no sense in the world. Yet she sat next to one man and thought of another. When her mind wasn't wandering to the Gaines murder.

That reminded her. She rose from the couch. "I'll go check on the lasagna. It's been almost an hour in the oven." She picked her way around the reindeer, furniture, and children—most of whom were sprawled on the floor engrossed in the Game Boys Jorge had given them—toward the kitchen. The lasagna was an excuse for her to take yet another look at the contents of the manila envelope Louella had dropped off at her house just as she and Jorge were leaving for her mother's.

It was lying next to her purse on the white Formica counter. She opened it and pulled out the two sheets inside.

One was a sheet of Gaines campaign stationery. And sure enough, the logo was exactly as Treebeard had described. *It was like the flag, you know? White stars on a blue background, with red and white stripes. And it was like the flag was underneath and the words 'Gaines for Governor' were cut out from it ...*

Did it prove anything? No. But if Treebeard had gotten the logo wrong, his claim to have received a letter from the campaign inviting him to Gaines' house would have been seriously undermined.

On to the second document: a typed list of Gaines' top campaign staff.

Mark Donovan—CEO

Don Monaco—COO

Molly Bracewell—senior strategist

Marty Ziegler—pollster

Molly Bracewell. The name popped off the page. *I kind of remember now who signed the letter ... It was a woman. Mary something. Something like Mary Baker. Mary Bakewell maybe.*

Did that mean anything? Maybe. Maybe not.

Alicia leaned against the kitchen counter, the Formica

hard against the small of her back. Pretty soon Louella would get Joan Gaines' credit-card and cell-phone records. Both of them might be a bust, revealing nothing. But if so, she could take it further, try another tack.

Alicia stood alone in her mother's kitchen, in the house where she'd lived the first twenty-five years of her life. Everything around her was familiar: the smell of corn from her mother's nonstop tortilla making; the chipped, mismatched platters on which soon they would serve dinner; the mix of boisterous Spanish and English bouncing off the walls of the jam-packed living room. She should feel warm and happy, she knew. She should be eager to have Jorge wrap her in his arms at midnight. She should be able to forget the murder that had ended the life of a man too young to die. She should be strong enough to banish from her mind the lurking vision of a man's dark, intense eyes and warm, demanding lips. Yet not even the most festive night of the year could make those wishes come true.

***

Twenty miles yet a world away, Milo cut across the Lodge's small, elegant reception area. An overcoat shielded his tuxedo, and in his right arm, cradled like a gilded football, was a bottle of chilled vintage Perrier-Jouet. He veered right and continued down a dimly lit carpeted corridor whose left side was lined with glass cases full of golf trophies from the AT&T Pebble Beach Pro-Am held every January on the hotel's famed links.

He felt himself on a cloak-and-dagger mission, which was an odd sensation for what should be a purely celebratory evening. Yet after what he'd overheard in the D.A.'s office, how could he not be driven to question Joan about the night her husband met his maker? Penrose's voice reverberated in his memory. *We do not need to second-guess Joan Gaines' whereabouts the night her husband was murdered. She is not a suspect in this case.* Then Alicia's. *Maybe she should be.*

Even given how much Alicia resented Joan, Milo couldn't help but give weight to her prosecutor's instincts. And obviously an eyewitness placing Joan back in Carmel the night of the murder was highly problematic.

So his mission was clear. Somehow that evening he would get Joan away from the other guests to ask her a question or two. He would elicit what he needed to know. He would warm her up and then go in for the kill.

So to speak.

He had barely knocked on her suite's door when she threw it open. Despite himself he caught his breath.

"Hello," she murmured.

She was as far from widow's weeds as a woman could get, a vision in a glittering silver sheath held up by whisper-thin straps. The dress shimmered when she moved, like the scales on a fish, giving her a bit of the look of a mermaid.

Milo smiled to himself. This New Year's Eve at least, Joan indeed was a man-killer.

He shed his overcoat. "You look beautiful," he told her, then glanced around, surprised to find the suite empty. "Am I the first to arrive?"

She relieved him of the champagne and plunged it into a waiting ice bucket. "Actually, you're the only person coming."

Immediately he castigated himself. *I should have known.* It was bait-and-switch, a classic Joan maneuver. Yet he was out of practice where she was concerned and hadn't seen it coming. "You told me you were having several people over," he said.

"I hope you're not disappointed."

Nice dodge, he thought, and considered pressing the issue, before he realized that their solitude gave him the perfect opportunity to question her about the night Daniel was killed. He walked to the fire in the marble hearth to warm his hands. "There's something I should warn you about."

"Oh, no." She came up beside him. "What is it?"

"I might be called away tonight."

"Called away?" Her face twisted. "Don't tell me that! Why?"

"It's unlikely." He abandoned the fireside to extract the Perrier-Jouet from the ice bucket and hoist it, dripping, in her direction. "Shall I?" She nodded, her brow still furrowed, and he went to work tearing off the bottle's metallic casing. "There's been another terrorist threat, this time against a specific target."

"What target?"

"The Rose Bowl."

"You mean the parade and football game down in Pasadena?"

"Right. The annual New Year's Day festivities." He twisted off the cork's protective wire cap. "If anything happens I'm going to have to go down there."

Her face relaxed. "You had me worried for a second." She moved away and perched on the love seat, the slit in her gown widening to reveal a devastating view of her shapely legs. "You won't have to go to LA, Milo. Nothing will happen. Nothing ever has after any of these warnings."

True enough. But the domestic news producer had put him on notice. Milo was the news division's biggest star who also happened to be on the West Coast this New Year's Eve and hence would be called upon if a big story broke.

"I hope you're right. But I'm going to have to keep my

cell phone on, just in case." He wrapped a small towel around the champagne bottle, twisting it slowly while he maintained a death grip on the cork. Seconds later he was rewarded with a soft pop. "Voila."

He poured and they faced each other, champagne-filled flutes in hand. "What shall we toast to?" she asked.

He thought for a moment. "How about simply to the New Year?"

She smiled. "Perfect." Then she touched her flute to his.

"Come sit down." He led her to the love seat. Time to begin the mini-interrogation. "How are you feeling?" He kept his tone soft and concerned. "I'm sure part of you would rather be alone." He spoke the words though he didn't believe them. Joan was never a woman to seek solitude.

She bent her head. "I'm just sorry you have to spend your New Year's Eve cooped up here with me. After all, you could be out and about, having a grand time."

This wasn't the moment to remind her she'd gotten him there on false pretenses. "Who says I'm not having a grand time?" he replied mildly, and she flashed him a grateful look. He paused, then, "You must miss Daniel terribly."

Again she dropped her eyes. It was some time before she responded, as if she were choosing her words carefully. "I miss the good times."

"I'm sure there were a lot of those."

"There were. Early on."

"Tell me about them."

She shook her head. "Milo, I can't believe you really want to hear about my marriage."

"I'm curious. That is, if it's not too painful to talk about."

"No. In a way, it feels good." Her face was thoughtful. "Do you know we went to Italy on our honeymoon?"

That made him wince. "The trip you and I never took."

"See? This is a bad idea."

"No, no, really. Tell me. Where did you go?"

"The Amalfi coast. And Florence."

"Two very romantic spots."

She nodded, then smiled. "The funny thing is we were both so exhausted from the wedding we barely did any sightseeing at all. We'd sleep till noon, then have lunch and wander around. Then go back to the hotel ..." She hesitated.

"And go back to bed?" He chuckled. "That's what honeymoons are for, Joan."

Her smile faded. "It didn't stay that way, though."

Something changed in the air, a subtle intimation that truths were about to be revealed. "What happened?" he asked.

She was silent, then, "Daniel got bored. With me."

Milo was so surprised at the admission that for a moment he couldn't think what to say. At length he gathered himself. "Do you mean—"

"Yes." She raised her eyes to his. If Joan manufactured the pain in their blue depths, she did a masterful job. "He was unfaithful. We got married in June and by September ..." Her voice faltered. She looked away.

The wind whipped at the French doors and whistled down the chimney, making the fire in the grate sputter. This might be Joan, he thought, with all her Hudson arrogance and ego, but he couldn't help but hurt for her. "I'm sorry."

"Can I tell you something else?" Again she turned her eyes to his. "That night I was in Santa Cruz, the night Daniel was killed—" She stopped.

He held his breath. "What?"

"I feel so guilty about it." Her gaze skittered away. "The terrible thing is I wanted to be away from Daniel that night. I wanted time to think. Milo, I was actually considering leaving him. For good. Then the next day, when I found him ..." She shook her head, grimacing as if in pain. "You can imagine how I felt."

He frowned. "No, I honestly can't."

"It was horrible. And so painful when that prosecutor woman kept wanting to confirm that I was at Courtney's! It made me feel guilty all over again for being away from home that night. For wanting to be." Her eyes teared up. Abruptly she rose from the love seat.

"So you were at Courtney's the whole night?" He watched her.

She began pacing, quick little steps next to the baby grand. "Of course! But what if I had been home? Maybe I could have kept this whole thing from happening."

That was almost laughable. Joan staving off a murderer? "It's a very good thing you weren't. Who knows what might have happened if you'd gotten in the way?"

She put her hands over her face and began to tremble, so much that it was visible from across the room. "Oh, God."

Milo rose and approached her, rubbing his hands down her arms. Her skin was ice cold to his touch.

"Just hold me." She raised her eyes to his, a beautiful, demanding beggar. "Please."

He complied, and rubbed her naked back as she collapsed onto his chest. What she said was plausible. He could imagine the scenario unfolding as nightmarishly as she described. And that fellow who claimed he'd seen Joan back at her house? Well, eyewitness reports were notoriously unreliable. People had Elvis sightings, for Christ's sake! Penrose had pointed out as much to Alicia in the conversation Milo had overheard, but of course she'd have none of it. The sad truth was that for whatever mix of reasons, Alicia had it in for Joan.

Who cried for a long time, then finally pushed herself

away. "I'm all right now." Yet her face was streaked with tears, rivulets that cut across the powder on her skin like angel's tracks on newly fallen snow. "Milo, I've made so many mistakes. But I want you to know I'm different than I used to be. I've learned a lot. I've grown up a lot."

How to respond to that? "We all make mistakes," he said.

"No, I want you to understand." She forced him to meet her gaze, their faces only inches apart. He had the idea this was a prepared speech, yet something in him wanted to hear it delivered. "I made a mistake leaving you. I took you for granted. I know that now. I didn't appreciate you."

He shook his head. "We were both much younger then."

"Yes," she said instantly, "that's my point. We're older now, and wiser. I know what's important now."

What she wanted began to dawn on him. He frowned. "Are you saying—"

"I'm saying I want to try again. You and me. Do you think you could give me another chance?" Her eyes were huge blue pools, deep and endless. A man could drown in them. He used to, himself.

Could he again? These nights he dreamed of brown eyes, flashing and dark. But they belonged to a woman who kept pushing him away, time and again.

He was thirty-eight years old, and alone, and in his arms was a woman he'd once cared for deeply. She wasn't perfect, but then neither was he. She spoke of making mistakes; that was terrain he trod constantly. Didn't the mere fact that she could make that admission show what a different woman she had become?

"Tell me something, Joan." He pushed her slightly away. "Did you invite anyone else here tonight?"

"No." Her reply was instant. "But I knew you wouldn't come if you thought it would be just you and me."

Yet more evidence of the new, honest Joan in action. "Why wouldn't I have come?" he persisted.

"Because you don't trust me yet. And I can't say I blame you. But I believe you'll come to trust me again." She held his gaze as she stepped closer, so close he could see the fine texture of her skin, smell the sweet, fresh scent of her body. "Remember, there was a lot that was right between us, Milo. Remember that." And then she brushed the lightest of kisses on his lips before pulling away. "I'll be right back—I just want to go and freshen up." On her way out she plucked his overcoat from the sofa, where he'd tossed it.

Milo was still for a moment, then ambled toward the ice bucket and pulled out the champagne, ice-cold drips falling onto the creamy white carpet. What a surprising turn this night was taking. Yet, strangely, it was comfortable, like the best of the times he'd ever had with Joan.

***

Joan felt light-headed as she walked out of the suite's main room, as if the champagne bubbles had floated to her head and taken over her brain waves. She was being brilliant. So very brilliant. An Oscar-winning performance.

Just around the corner from the main room, so that Milo couldn't see, she pulled open the door of the small closet between the entry foyer and the half bath. She reached into the pocket of his overcoat and smiled, closing her fingers around the very thing she was looking for.

It was a metallic blue Nokia cell phone, so small yet capable of wreaking so much havoc. Though she didn't really believe Milo would be called away that night—why should a terrorist threat prove real that night?—she didn't care to take the chance.

She used her nail—painted for New Year's a light pearly pink—to push the phone's tiny power switch. It emitted a tinny little beep, then went dark. Pleased, Joan dropped it back into Milo's pocket, then continued down the hall to the en suite bathroom for the promised freshening of her makeup. But before picking up her powder puff she used the bathroom phone to call down to the hotel operator, requesting that all calls be held. "I'm having an early night," Joan informed the operator, who clucked with understanding. Of course. So tragic. The new widow must be so heartbroken on this New Year's Eve ...

Joan gazed at her reflection in the marble bathroom's mirror. Her cheeks were flushed and her blue eyes glinted. With her blond hair curled, she looked like a feverish china doll.

He's mine, she told herself—needlessly, because she'd known from the moment she set her trap that he would be. She knew exactly what to say to pull him in. He might be surprised but she wasn't. She'd always known she was not to be underestimated.

Milo was warming his hands at the hearth when she returned to him. She stopped halfway across the room. His eyes lit up when he saw her, and his lips curled in the lazy half smile she remembered so well. "Shall we call down for dinner?" he asked.

"No."

His brows rose in surprise. "You're not hungry yet?"

She stepped closer. "No."

Understanding seemed to dawn in those dark eyes of his. He stood completely still. When she got very close she ran her hands up the starched front of his tuxedo shirt. His ruby studs were cold and bloodred. The ornate clock on the mantel chimed the hour.

"Nine PM," he said into the stillness when the last note sounded. Joan noticed, her hands still resting lightly on his chest, that his heart was beating very quickly.

She smiled. "I'm not making you uncomfortable, am I?"

He shook his head in instant denial. "No, no."

No part of her believed him. She cocked her head. "Would it be so very wrong?"

He said nothing. His eyes were cautious but she could see desire too in their black depths. She rose on her toes to brush her lips against his. "Would it be so very wrong to make love?"

His face froze. "Joan—"

"I'm alone." She kissed him again. "You're alone." He began to protest anew but she silenced him with a soft finger on his mouth. "We could make each other happy."

"We could also regret it."

"How could I regret being with you?" So, so true. And she'd never been much for regrets as it was. They held you back. They kept you from doing what you wanted.

"But it hasn't been very long—" He stopped.

"Since Daniel died?" She didn't think that much mattered, but knew that Milo, like everyone else, thought it did. How strange. Daniel was dead. He wouldn't be more dead in a month. But she mustn't say that to Milo.

So instead she looked deeply into his eyes and said, "Daniel was lost to me long before he was killed, Milo. I've been alone for a long, long time. I don't want to be alone anymore. I don't want to be alone tonight."

And then she made her next kiss seal the bargain.

CHAPTER FOURTEEN

Alicia lay awake in bed with her eyes closed and her face buried in the pillow, debating whether to rise or remain cocooned beneath the duvet. At her back she heard Jorge's deep, even breathing. It was the first of January. *Happy New Year*, she told herself. She sighed and fluttered her eyelids open.

She realized it must still be quite early. No light snaked around the blinds, though this time of year the sun didn't rise till close to seven. Darkest before the dawn.

She slipped out of bed, the warped peg-and-groove floorboards she kept vowing to refinish cold on her bare feet. She and Jorge had come back to her house the night before. She hadn't packed an overnight bag for Jorge's and studiously avoided leaving much at his condo. A toothbrush, yes, her favorite face and hand lotions, but nothing by way of clothing. She did it partly in homage to her mother's Catholic fantasy that she and Jorge weren't sleeping together. In truth, though, the deception suited her just fine.

She pulled on a terrycloth robe, tiptoed out of the bedroom, and once in the kitchen made coffee. Then, in what of late had become a kind of guilty pleasure, like chocolate first thing in the morning, she flipped on the small television set that hunched on the white tiled counter next to the phone.

There was no need to change the channel. As ever it was tuned to WBS.

An anchorwoman appeared, Asian, not the usual blonde.

A substitute, Alicia knew, because in the last few weeks she'd become more than passingly familiar with the news staff. She turned away to set her mug beneath the stream of coffee issuing from the drip coffeemaker, only to have the anchorwoman's clear voice cut through the fog of her drowsiness. "We just received a wire report from AP that the number of fatalities from the bombing is up to six—"

Alicia jerked back around to face the television. Now, instead of the anchorwoman, a brunette reporter stood before a gargantuan pile of smoking debris, over which rescue personnel in yellow and orange gear swarmed like crabs on a beach. The images immediately took Alicia back to that horrendous September day no American would ever forget. But this time the words in bold red capitals on the bottom of the television screen read ROSE BOWL UNDER ATTACK. And in a blue-and-white ticker-tape scroll beneath that: EXPLOSION RIPS THROUGH PARADE GROUNDS . . . TERRORIST LINK SUSPECTED . . .

Alicia clutched at her throat. *Oh, my God. Not again.*

"We can confirm the number of fatalities," the reporter was saying, clearly struggling to keep her composure amid the chaos. One hand clutched a microphone; the other was clamped over her left ear as if she were at that moment getting information in her earpiece. "I'm hearing now that the injured number well over fifty, and that several of those people are in critical condition."

Alicia shook her head, disbelieving, despite the undeniability of the horror playing itself out before her.

"What is it?"

She heard rather than saw Jorge pad into the kitchen, as she couldn't stop watching the television. Out of the corner of her eye she could see that he wore his blue-and-white striped pajamas, like a Latino Ward Cleaver. He came to stand beside her with his back against the counter and wrapped his arm over her shoulders, hugging her close. "My God," he said, parroting the very words she kept hearing in her own head, as if her vocabulary had been reduced to two primal sounds that on that tragic New Year's morning said it all.

Shoulder-to-shoulder they watched. There was one piece of good news among the bad: the bomb had gone off around 3 AM, so the full complement of parade workers was not yet on hand. If it had been, the casualty count would have been much higher.

Soon the picture changed from the female reporter to an Asian male standing on the White House lawn, talking about how the president would soon speak to the nation. Next came video of various cabinet officials hurrying into the White House, their grim expressions an incongruous contrast to the casual clothing they wore for what should have been a relaxing holiday.

Vaguely she was aware of a sizzling sound behind her, then another. Jorge pulled away from her. "Alicia—"

Her mug had overflowed, the excess coffee sizzling against the coffeemaker's hot plate. As her hands began automatically to clean up the mess, her mind cranked into a higher gear.

I wonder if Milo is covering this story. He might well be. He'd been in Salinas on Monday and this was only Wednesday. And Pasadena was a short flight away. Then again, who knew where Milo Pappas might have jet-setted off to, to celebrate New Year's Eve? Images of him in Paris, with a stunning female creature on his arm, crashed across her brain, sickening in their clarity.

Jorge came back into the kitchen—though she realized she hadn't noticed him leave—bearing the *Salinas Californian* and a legal-sized manila envelope. He held it out to her.

"You got another one of these. Slipped under the door. Louella must've come back last night after we left for your mom's."

Alicia took one look at the envelope's label and knew it came from Louella. She ripped the package open. Inside were Joan Gaines' credit-card and cell-phone records for the last month, the records Alicia had sought in the subpoena.

She pulled out the phone records first, her eyes skipping down to December twentieth. Joan Gaines had made only a few calls from her cell that day, and none past 5:47 PM.

Alicia turned to the credit-card receipts. American Express, nothing interesting. On to MasterCard, which recorded a huge number of purchases, most in what were to Alicia astonishingly large amounts. Finally she reached December twentieth.

Her eyes stopped on an entry. She blinked and stared at it again: Dec. 20, Shell No. 27937563936, Carmel, Ca.

And next to it, in Louella's neat print, was the exact time the transaction had occurred: 9:46 PM.

At 9:46 PM. When Joan Gaines said she was asleep in Courtney Holt's guesthouse.

Alicia raised her head, staring unseeing across her small kitchen. Joan lied. She was in Carmel, gassing up her Jaguar. What else was Joan Gaines doing in Carmel that night?

Alicia looked at Jorge, who was making a ruckus holding the toaster over the sink shaking out the crumbs. "She lied," Alicia told Jorge's back. "She lied about her whereabouts the night her husband was murdered."

He pivoted to face her, toaster in his hands, frowning. "What are you talking about?"

"Joan Gaines. Daniel Gaines' wife." Alicia ran out of the kitchen. "I have proof she lied. And I'm going to call her on it."

***

Only after Milo had pulled open the door of Joan's suite to find Alicia Maldonado standing in the hallway did he vow that never—*never again!*—would he be so careless. He had thought for sure that it was room service. He had made just that one dangerous assumption as his bare feet padded across the soft ivory carpet, as the rapping repeated itself, louder the second time around; *Joan must have called for something to be sent up before she got into the shower*, he assumed, reaching for the knob as he heard the water in the adjacent bathroom pound. In fact, he even anticipated a delicious repast. A frittata, perhaps? Or eggs Benedict? On the first morning of the new year, maybe even Joan would indulge.

Oh, he saw the astonishment, the bewilderment, then the comprehension in the prosecutor's dark eyes. He saw himself as he must look to her, with his morning stubble and slept-in hair, wearing over his nakedness a fleecy white robe with The Lodge at Pebble Beach embroidered in a half moon over the heart. He might have been a gigolo, a married man, even a priest—the guilt that pierced him was so intense. Alicia's disapproval was writ large on her beautiful face, and reflected in the rough shoulder she gave him as she brushed past him to enter the suite.

She pivoted to face him. "You weren't kidding when you told me you knew Joan Gaines."

"It's not what you think," he heard himself say, but it was exactly what she thought, and they both knew it.

Alicia cocked her chin in the direction of the shower, where Joan, Milo was embarrassed to hear, was singing some cheery song whose lyrics and melody were both unrecognizable. "I take it that's the lady of the manor?" she asked.

He ignored the question. "Let me explain," he said instead, and found himself wanting to, though he knew he wasn't obliged. Alicia had turned him down, he reminded himself. He was a free man. Joan was a free woman. Yet somehow he felt as if he'd gone from one woman's bed to another's without missing a beat in between. "I can explain," he repeated, and felt even more of a fool.

"Don't bother." Her voice was both cold and dismissive. "I'm here to see Joan," she informed him. "I'll wait." Then she walked further into the suite and settled herself on the sofa near the baby grand.

He felt excruciatingly conscious of his nakedness. It put him at such a raw and obvious disadvantage. Yet what was he to do? Repair to the bedroom and put on his tuxedo, which he knew was heaped on the floor? Maybe call down to the pro shop and ask them to send up a pair of madras pants and a polo shirt? He walked to the phone. "I'll call down for coffee."

She remained silent. So did the elephant in the corner of the room.

The businesslike transaction of ordering from room service made him feel marginally less impotent. And slightly more contentious. Alicia was being self-righteous, he decided. Holier than thou. "How was your New Year's Eve?" he asked her. He heard the belligerent edge to his voice.

"Not as good as yours, apparently."

"Mine was delightful."

"I'm so glad to hear it."

"You brushed me off, remember?" He watched her shake her head, though she couldn't deny the truth of his words. "You have no right to sit in judgment on me."

"Were you conducting an affair with Joan Gaines while her husband was alive?"

"I am not conducting an affair with her now!" His voice

had risen, he noticed. He lowered it. "We are two single adults. Our being together is no sin. It is certainly no crime." Yet even as he said it, a cooler part of his brain wondered whom he was really trying to convince.

"If you were sleeping together while her husband was still alive, it would arguably be both."

He moved a step closer. "Oh, so you prosecute adultery?"

Her dark eyes were cool. "It would be adultery for her. Fornication for you."

Even through his anger, he was reminded yet again that Alicia Maldonado was a force to be reckoned with. "I see your Catholic upbringing is standing you in good stead."

"It has its uses."

"I'll tell you again. What Joan and I have done is no sin. Certainly not by the moral code I live by."

"Well, we've established how stringent *that* is."

He jabbed a finger in her direction. "What is your problem? Exactly what is it you've got against Joan? She is a widow—need I remind you of that? She lost her husband."

Milo was forced to wait while Alicia raked her eyes slowly up and down his body. Suddenly it was as though the fleece robe were made of gossamer silk. "I can see how deeply she's grieving."

Milo shook his head, yet again bested. *Damn that woman.* "Not that I owe you any explanation, but Joan and I have a long history. We've been friends for years."

"So I repeat. Were you sleeping together while her husband was alive?"

"Are you asking as a prosecutor? Or as a woman I made the mistake of pursuing?"

Silence. The flash of pain in her eyes gave him a shiver of ill-gotten satisfaction. "I asked you a yes-or-no question," she said finally. "It doesn't require context."

"Maybe I want a lawyer present to answer it."

She arched her brows, then, unexpectedly, she laughed, and looked down in her lap to finger something there. It was the first time he noticed that she was carrying a large manila envelope. "You're right about that. You may want a lawyer present."

That unnerved him. Once again his impulse was to lash out. "You would be so much better off preparing your case against Treebeard than engaging in this insane pretense that Joan should be a suspect in her husband's murder."

"Oh, really." Her tone was dry.

"That supposed eyewitness of yours has got it all wrong. Joan and I talked about the night Daniel was killed. She was in Santa Cruz the entire night, as she has told you more than once."

"Yes, that's certainly been her story. You may want to wait and see if she sticks to it today." Milo watched Alicia's gaze slide past him. "Good morning, Mrs. Gaines."

Milo turned to see Joan enter the room with her hair wrapped in a towel, dressed in the same exact robe he was sporting. He felt a new rush of humiliation, as if Alicia had caught them playing house.

Joan looked at him, her eyes bewildered, her right hand steadying the pyramid of towel on her small head. "What's she doing here?"

"I don't know." Milo moved closer to Joan. He was taking sides, he realized. So be it. "Apparently she wants to kick off the New Year by lobbing more crazy accusations."

Joan's skin paled. "Why did you let her in?"

"I thought she was room service."

Then Joan looked at Alicia. "Why didn't you call first?"

Alicia remained on the sofa, sleek and calm as a cat. "I tried. From the house phone. But the hotel operator told me you stopped all calls."

That surprised him. Then again, he could easily imagine how at some point during the prior night Joan might have decided she wanted no interruptions.

Joan looked up at him, a plea in her childlike blue eyes. "I don't want to deal with this right now, Milo," she murmured.

"You're completely right," he told her. "In fact, you shouldn't." He grasped Joan's elbow and was surprised to find that she was trembling. He turned toward Alicia. "I'm sure Joan will answer any questions you have, repetitive though they are bound to be, but only when she has a lawyer present. Call later to make an appointment."

He began to steer Joan toward the short corridor that led to the bedrooms. But in a heartbeat Alicia was standing right beside them and had Joan's other elbow in her grasp. "Joan is going to talk to me right now," she said.

Joan's lower lip trembled. "No."

Alicia's voice was low, cajoling. "You want to tell me the truth this time, Joan? You're better off telling me the truth."

"This is insane." Milo pulled on Joan, but Alicia didn't release her. Joan was like a rag doll being fought over by two warring children.

"I'm warning you." Alicia had raised her head and was talking to him now in that same low, commonsense tone. "In fact, I've already warned you. Do not interfere in a criminal investigation."

"Joan is not a suspect!" He shouted it rather than said it but no longer cared. "We are rapidly getting to the point where I will encourage her to file harassment charges against you and the entire district attorney's office. You back off or I swear she'll do it."

Alicia looked from him back to Joan, as if he were a pesky annoyance not worth bothering about. "Tell me the truth,

Joan. Because I have proof, incontrovertible proof, that you went back to Carmel the night your husband was murdered."

By now Joan was crying. Plump tears ran down her pale, pale cheeks, whipped into irregular trails by Joan's vehement shaking of her head. "No," she was saying, "no ..."

Something in Milo's mind registered that Joan's reaction wasn't quite right. She should be angry. Yet if anything she seemed petrified. Curious, he released her elbow, just as Alicia did the same. Then Alicia pulled a document out of her manila envelope and waved it in Joan's face. Milo had the disconcerting sensation of being the odd man out, as if the women before him were the only characters in this impromptu drama who had starring roles to play.

"I'm giving you one last chance," Alicia said. "Not only do I have an eyewitness who puts you back at your house the night Daniel was murdered, I also have proof in black and white. Proof any jury would believe. Now do the smart thing and tell me the truth."

Joan was mute and sniveling, the towel askew on her head, her hands clutching ineffectively at the air, unable to reach Milo because he'd backed away a step or two. "I have nothing to say," she got out finally, which was when Alicia shook her head, as though with profound regret.

Her voice was low and steady. "I have here the record of your MasterCard purchases for the month of December. On the twentieth, the night your husband was murdered, when you claim to have been at Courtney Holt's house in Santa Cruz, at 9:46 PM you purchased gasoline at a Shell station in Carmel, only a mile from your home." She paused. "Did you gas up your Jaguar before or after you killed your husband?"

"I didn't kill him! I didn't kill him!" Joan was shrieking now, her arms flailing, the towel off her head and toppled on the floor, her blond hair wet and straggly. "All right, all right, you really want to know? I drove back to Carmel and stood outside my own home and spied on him, because I was sure he was having an affair with that bitch of a campaign aide of his, Molly Bracewell! And I wanted to catch him in the act! I wanted to prove it!"

Alicia just watched. Milo watched, too, though he felt himself in a sort of daze, as though a movie he'd seen a dozen times suddenly took off in a new and unexpected direction. *She lied to me, she lied,* his mind kept repeating. *She went to such pains to tell me she stayed in Santa Cruz, that she needed "time to think." How much she regretted being away because she might have been able to stop the murder. And all the while she was lying.*

Again he'd been tricked. Again he'd been duped. And for what? For the woman before him, who had become a caricature of a hysterical female, a woman in a movie madhouse, unable to speak coherently for the sobs racking her body. Through the haze that enveloped him, Milo understood that the revulsion he felt for her was nothing compared to what he felt for himself.

"Are you happy now? Are you satisfied?" Her face was mottled several sickly shades of white and pink. "Have you embarrassed me enough?"

"A man has been murdered," Alicia said. To Milo's eyes she appeared completely unperturbed. "Seems to me your being embarrassed is beside the point."

Joan went on sobbing, as if in a world of her own. Alicia looked at him. "Someone's at the door. I heard knocking. It's probably the coffee you ordered."

"Should I get it?"

"I don't see why not. I'll move her"—Alicia indicated Joan with a cock of her chin—"into the other room."

Mito forced himself to the entryway, finding it a small relief to engage in this pointless task. This time he looked through the peephole, and this time indeed it was room service. A tall young man bore a silver coffee service on a tray hoisted high above his shoulder, as if he were weaving a path through a crowd of diners. Milo let him in.

"Sorry it took so long." The waiter swept into the suite and deposited the tray on the coffee table between the sofa and love seat. "Everyone in the kitchen is so preoccupied with the news this morning, orders are moving slower than usual." He looked up at Milo. "Should I pour?"

"No. Thank you." Milo was puzzled. "What do you mean, preoccupied with the news?"

The waiter's brows flew up. "The bombing. You haven't heard?"

A rush of cold shivered through Milo's body, as if the French doors had blown open to let in the chill off the sea. "No," he said slowly, "I haven't."

"Oh, it's terrible." The waiter edged away, shaking his head. "It looks like another terrorist attack. Down at the Rose Bowl. Something like six people dead and fifty injured. It's terrible," he repeated, before sprinting the few steps to the door. "Nobody can believe it. Sorry, gotta go."

Slam of the door. The waiter was gone. Milo was alone.

He stood motionless in the gorgeously appointed suite, sunshine spilling through the floor-to-ceiling French doors in the harbinger of yet another glorious California day. Where was his coat? Where was his cell phone?

It didn't take him long to find the foyer closet, to reach inside his overcoat pocket to extract the tiny blue Nokia cell phone, and to note that it was turned off. That last didn't come as a surprise. He knew before seeing it that it would be turned off, and he knew by whom.

Nor did it take Milo long to ascertain that he had received seventeen voice-mail messages in the last six hours, all of them from WBS personnel. They broke down neatly into calls from Stan Cohen, the domestic news producer, calls from Mac, one call from Tran, and the rest from Robert O'Malley. The final killer call, delivered precisely twenty minutes before, asked him to return as soon as it was convenient to WBS headquarters in New York. Not to bother flying south to Pasadena. *Don't bother*, was the exact phrase used with obvious gusto by Robert O'Malley.

Going AWOL was a mortal sin for a newsman. There were worse transgressions, perhaps—blowing up on live air, for example, or standing up in a production meeting to tell the president of the news division to fuck off—but being unreachable, when you had been expressly told to be reachable, when one of the biggest news stories of the year was happening a short flight away, was a career-killing misstep.

In the adjacent room, Milo could hear Joan sobbing, though by now it sounded one degree more restrained. He could also just make out Alicia's low tones. He considered whether she was getting a confession. It was possible, though by this point he would not even hazard a guess as to how many crimes Joan Hudson Gaines might have on her conscience.

CHAPTER FIFTEEN

Alicia pushed through the lunchtime crowd to grab a small Formica-topped table in Dudley's restaurant. She dumped her stack of canary yellow file folders at what would have been Louella's place if Louella had been able to break free of her "Happy New Year" workload. That was the crazy thing about the holidays if you were employed in a D.A.'s office. Your work didn't stop. It just piled up. Now it was Thursday, January second, and everything that hadn't gotten done in the last two weeks was standing up and screaming *Now! Now! Now!* Louella would be going nuts for the next month. So would Alicia.

The waitress came by, a mid-forties brunette and Dudley's veteran. She didn't bother giving a regular like Alicia one of the plasticized menus. "What'll it be, honey?"

"How about a BLT? And a Diet Coke."

"What dressing you want on the salad?"

"I'll take ranch."

The woman nodded and moved off, scooping up the handful of coins left on the two-top to Alicia's right. *What a way to make a living,* Alicia thought, before she remembered how slim her own wallet was.

No doubt most of Dudley's patrons were in Alicia's same leaky boat. Like the man to her left, who looked like retired military, many had seen their best days back in the fifties. That was probably when the mural on the wall opposite Alicia had been painted. It depicted an idealized Salinas

Valley, complete with a Norman Rockwell gray Victorian surrounded by a white picket fence, its backdrop rolling hills and purple mountains majesty.

She stared at it, finding it hard to believe that ghastly crimes could occur in such a pastoral setting. It was hard to believe that only twenty miles west, a rich wife might have offed her husband and framed a down-on-his-luck activist for the crime. It was even more difficult to fathom that a handsome, famous network correspondent might have been in on the deal.

The waitress came by with Alicia's Diet Coke, dispensed in the sort of tall, chunky glass that could survive an industrial-strength dishwasher. A sad-looking lemon wedge floated on the ice, and a thin white paper wrapping clung to the top half of the straw.

Alicia rolled up the paper, her fingertips reducing it to a tiny moist ball. It was one thing to suspect that Joan Gaines might have murdered her husband. It was quite another to think Milo Pappas might be in on it. But one truth Alicia couldn't ignore: the hollow in her gut when she thought of him in Joan Gaines' suite. The unshaven, tousle-haired, clearly just-spent-the-night Milo Pappas.

That same gut told her he wasn't a killer, but then again Alicia knew she should trust none of her body parts when it came to judging that man. He had too great an effect on far too many of them. All that still functioned with a degree of detachment was her brain, and yet that, too, had trouble pinning him with the crime. What would he get out of it? He would have to have been conducting a pretty torrid love affair with Joan Gaines to get mixed up in murdering her husband.

Despite the drama of the moment, Alicia had noted that Milo distanced himself from Joan PDQ when he heard Alicia outline the credit-card evidence. He had seemed positively stunned. He couldn't even speak. Not for a second did he dispute it.

Another idea had occurred to Alicia, which in a funny way was balm on her soul. Maybe Milo was using Joan Gaines the same way he'd initially tried to use her as a source of inside information. It was easy to imagine any red-blooded female succumbing. Briefly Alicia closed her eyes. Very easy.

The other possibility, of course, was that Joan and Milo had started seeing each other in the two weeks since Daniel Gaines had died. That would be quick work on both their parts, but Alicia wouldn't put it past either of them. And if Milo Pappas was falling in love with Joan Gaines, he could damn well have her. Alicia took a swig from her Diet Coke, then slammed it back down on the Formica tabletop, making the ice cubes jump and drawing a raised brow from the military retiree. If Milo Pappas thought a new widow who lied about her whereabouts the night her husband was murdered was a worthy conquest, he didn't deserve one iota more of Alicia's attention.

The fire began anew in Alicia's belly, the fire that demanded she pursue further evidence against Joan Gaines. If anything, now it burned brighter than ever. Clearly the woman was hiding something more than that cock-and-bull story about Molly Bracewell. Alicia's strategy of confronting her with the credit-card evidence had shocked her into that revelation, at least. Yet Alicia needed more, much more, and time was not on her side. Treebeard's preliminary hearing was fast approaching, and there was no question he would be bound over for trial. She would be working like a dog to prosecute him. How was she supposed to find time to go after her? Particularly when she had no idea what her next step should be.

Her BLT arrived, with its white-bread toast and iceberg

lettuce salad. "Refill on the Coke?" the waitress asked

"Please."

Dudley's might not be glamorous, but Alicia kept coming back because it was close to the courthouse, the price was right, and the food wasn't half-bad. She'd just bitten into one of the BLT's toasty squares when Kip Penrose strutted into Dudley's, shaking hands and slapping backs. Alicia shook her head, though part of her envied Kip his easy affability. Everybody was a voter to old Kip, and every outing a campaign stop.

He saw her and walked over. "May I join you?"

"Why not?"

He set his briefcase on Dudley's worn blue carpet, where Alicia relocated her pile of file folders. He flirted briefly with the waitress, then made fast business of ordering a burger. "Glad I ran into you," he said.

"Why's that?"

"Something's come up I need you to handle." He bent down to pull a folder out of his briefcase and hold it across the small table.

Just what she needed. "Kip, this is hardly a good time." But she wiped the mayo off her fingers and took the folder, flipping it open to scan the documents inside.

The police report made it look pretty simple. Twenty-nine-year-old Theodore Owens III, no priors from the look of it, brandished a small-caliber pistol at a bar on a Friday night. Apparently he got pissed off seeing a woman he'd dated a few times chatting up a new guy. People were freaked but nobody got hurt. Owens got arraigned in late December and was out on his own recognizance. The cops thought it was misdemeanor brandishing, though it was up to the D.A.'s office to decide. Everything looked pretty much in order until Alicia saw the next court date.

"Kip, the probable-cause hearing is next Wednesday! Why am I just seeing this today?"

"Well, what with the holidays and everything it kind of fell through the cracks." His burger showed up. "I just didn't get around to it till now." He slapped the bottom of the ketchup bottle and a big red blob sloshed onto his beef. "Sorry."

She shook her head. "Well, I'm sorry, too, but I don't have time to work this up. I'm going flat-out already, and what with the preliminary hearing for Treebeard so soon it's going to ramp up even more." She tossed the folder back at him, where it skidded across the Formica. Kip grabbed it just before it slid onto the carpet. "Give it to somebody else. Give it to Rocco."

"I am not giving it to Rocco. And don't throw things at me," he said, just as he tossed the folder back at her, as if they were playing a legal-file version of Hot Potato. "What's the big deal? It's a first offense. There's no reason to go balls-out on this one. You should just make an offer."

Kip and his plea bargains. It amazed her. He'd dispense of a case with a casual conversation and a swipe of pen across paper. True, she probably overanalyzed which cases to fight and which to settle. Louella accused her routinely of being idealistic about how the system should work. But she just couldn't wear lightly the incredible responsibility the D.A.'s office had in deciding which crimes to pursue and which not. She doubted Kip had even bothered to talk to victims when he'd been a prosecutor himself, before he sailed off into private practice.

"Even if I did decide to make an offer," she said, "I don't have time to get ready. I'd have to do it Monday."

"So today's Thursday."

"So that doesn't give me enough time to talk to

everybody."

"So talk to whoever you can and leave the rest."

She was about to object again when he threw down his burger and said, "Alicia, just do it! Cut a corner for a change, like everybody else. You're getting this case and that's the end of it."

Why the hell was he being so insistent about this? Usually he backed off when she put up a fight. It was weird, yet at the same time it was Kip-like for him to drop the ball and then expect her to run it for a touchdown.

She wiped her lips with the paper napkin, clattered out of her chair, and grabbed her file folders, Kip's included. "Fine," she told him. "But you're buying lunch."

***

Joan decided that all things considered, she had dodged a bullet New Year's Day.

She drew this conclusion as she sat at the antique writing desk in the suite's study, more of an alcove, really, adjacent to the bedroom. She had risen early that morning—it couldn't have been a second past eight-thirty—and immediately did her workout, had a little breakfast, and went to the spa for her manicure and pedicure. Then she'd pulled a suit out of the closet, because she intended to go into Headwaters that very day. It was all part of feeling efficient and businesslike, a woman very much in control of her life, and rather a stark contrast to how she'd felt twenty-four hours before.

Joan laid down the slim silver Tiffany pen the Lodge provided as a writing instrument and shuddered, remembering the petrifying stretch of New Year's Day when that Maldonado woman had appeared at the suite, entirely without warning. What a horrible time for her insidious accusations to be flying, what with Milo present to witness every millisecond of the exchange. But though Joan was deeply embarrassed at how overwrought she had become, the more she thought about it the more she believed that she had acted exactly right. She'd revealed just enough to explain away the one piece of supposed evidence that presumptuous creature thought she had. True, Joan was caught in a lie about returning to Carmel the night Daniel was murdered, but what wife in her predicament wouldn't have done exactly the same thing? What wife would freely admit that she suspected her husband of cheating? What wife would willingly lay herself open to the humiliation that entailed, especially with the husband dead and absolutely no good to come of the revelation?

No, any reasonable person would completely understand and accept what Joan had done; it was all in the name of protecting the reputation of a marriage; and it would be an outrageous leap to claim that Joan's lying about one thing meant she was lying about another, far more serious thing. No, as her father would have said, *that will not stand!*

Joan reveled in the intoxicating rush that followed of feeling competent and powerful. It was time for her to take care of Alicia Maldonado once and for all, and she had a good idea how to do it. She would take an extra precaution as well, just to be safe. She lifted the phone and punched in Henry Gossett's home number.

The antique housekeeper answered. "Gossett residence."

"This is Joan Gaines. May I speak to Henry, please?"

"Mrs. Gaines, he's at his office. Would you like that number?"

"I already have it." Joan managed a perfunctory "Thank you" and hung up, slightly peeved. She glanced at the Ebel watch circling her wrist, a platinum band with diamonds ringing the pearl face and winking on every hour except XII and VI. It was only quarter past noon on the very first working day of the year, and yet Gossett, that old moose, had beaten her into the office. She punched in his direct line there. "Henry," she said, after dispensing swiftly with the requisite New Year's greetings, "I need you to retain the services of a criminal defense attorney."

Silence. A heavy, clearly shocked silence. Then, "Joan," he said, his tone as lugubrious as ever, "are you in some difficulty you wish to discuss?"

"I am in no difficulty whatsoever," she told him. "I am simply requesting that you put a criminal defense attorney on retainer on the extremely slim chance that I should require his services. I have received a few visits from a prosecutor working on Daniel's case, a woman who clearly does not understand who she is dealing with. It might set her straight to see that I am taking steps for my own protection. I would rather err on the side of prudence," she told Gossett, knowing that phrasing would warm the cockles of his geriatric heart.

"And Henry," she added, "if you value your position as counsel for this family, as I know you do, I strongly recommend that you not breathe a word of this to my mother. I trust we understand one another. Thank you, and good day." She hung up. That, as they say, was that.

Now, should she call Milo? Joan sank back against the Queen Anne chair's unforgiving wooden spine. No, her every instinct told her she should wait for him to call her.

She thought back to the prior morning, whose misery had peaked when Milo abandoned her to fly to New York. He'd come into the bedroom after that prosecutor finally left, brandishing his little blue Nokia cell phone.

What do you have to say about this, Joan?

Oh, Milo, I'm sorry. She'd assumed a regretful expression, and knew she looked both pathetic and sexy huddled among the rumpled sheets where they'd shared so much pleasure the night before. *I just wanted to be with you. I couldn't abide the thought of you being called away.*

But Milo refused to be mollified. *That terrorist threat you were so sure wouldn't come to anything, Joan? Well, it's a damn good thing you're not in charge of Homeland Security, because a bomb went off at the Rose Bowl.*

What astonishingly bad luck. She couldn't have been more surprised if Milo had announced that aliens landed at Cypress Point. Then he'd ranted about how irresponsible she'd been, didn't she understand he had a job to do, did she even remember what a job was—it had gotten fairly insulting. She would have become quite angry if she hadn't realized that it was just Milo being Milo, passionate and melodramatic and Mediterranean. By the time he declared he was leaving for New York, in what he termed an attempt to save his reputation, if he still had one worth saving, she'd offered to go with him. Nothing like a few nights in Manhattan—wouldn't a stay at the Pierre be nice? With perhaps some shopping on Fifth Avenue and a show or two?—to get a man back on an even keel. But Milo wouldn't hear of it. In fact, he seemed shocked at the suggestion.

Didn't you hear a word I said, Joan? I'm fighting to keep my job! Then he'd scowled at her. *Or maybe you'd rather I didn't keep it, since you find it such a damned inconvenience?*

No, she wanted him to keep it—after all, a man without a job was hardly a catch, unless he was between jobs, sitting on his fortune and plotting where next to increase it—but she just wished Milo's job weren't so unpredictable. Frankly, yes, it was inconvenient that he was a hostage to news events. It was very difficult to plan dinners or parties or trips when something bad happening somewhere in the world would derail everything.

Joan sighed, feeling quite annoyed. Honestly, she didn't know how Meredith Brokaw put up with it.

***

Milo cooled his heels outside the office of the president of WBS's news division, his mind spinning doomsday scenarios for his professional future. He'd gotten quite good at that particular game in the last twenty-four hours. It was a macabre version of mental solitaire in which every deck was stacked against him.

He had played the game at the San Francisco airport, where his and every other flight was delayed thanks to beefed-up security, a direct result of the terrorist bombing story he'd failed to cover. He'd played it while flying east, every passing mountain range and heartland plain bringing him that much closer to the dreaded showdown with WBS brass. And he'd played it during those restless overnight hours, when his high-priced Manhattan hotel room failed to offer succor or relief.

The voice of the president's secretary, a well-preserved blonde who'd trailed Richard Lovegrove as he climbed the news division's executive ladder, sliced into Milo's thoughts. "Richard shouldn't be long now," she assured him, though she'd told Milo exactly the same thing a half hour before. "Are you sure I can't get you some coffee?"

"No, Rachel, thank you very much."

She nodded, wearing a rueful expression that Milo knew he wouldn't see on her boss's face when he was finally ushered into his office.

Milo found the fact that he was meeting with Lovegrove extremely worrying. He'd anticipated a severe dressing-down from Stanley Cohen, the domestic news producer, and knew O'Malley would be present for the sheer joy of personally delivering a few body blows. He'd half expected a pro forma wrist slap from Al Giordano, the division's senior VP and one of Milo's few longtime supporters. But the fact that his transgression had drawn face time with Lovegrove himself boded ill indeed.

Glumly, Milo resumed staring around him. It was ironic how often nondescript offices housed extraordinary power centers. Here he sat at WBS's Midtown headquarters, a glass-and-steel monolith in the red-hot vortex of network news, and the carpet was industrial, the furnishings ho-hum, and the artwork nonexistent. Instead, framed posters of network talent served as decor throughout much of the building. From the wall behind Rachel's desk, a photographic replica of Jack Evans, anchor of the *WBS Evening News* and the person Milo most wanted to replace, gazed at him with a half smile that oozed intelligence and sincerity. Next to Evans grinned the cheery duo who anchored the highly rated breakfast show. Just at the moment Milo was finding their multimillion-dollar, no-cut contracts particularly grating, Lovegrove's office door swung open. The man himself emerged, looking every suave inch the top-dollar management consultant he had been before he segued smoothly into the network management ranks. He waved Milo inside and shook his hand, but desisted from the comradely back slap he typically dispensed as part of their ritualistic greeting. Milo took the omission as a bad sign.

Everyone Milo had expected to see was present and accounted for and stood up in turn to shake his hand. In contrast to the elegant silver-haired Lovegrove, Stan Cohen looked like a poor man's newsman. Complete with paunch, receding hairline, and rolled-up shirtsleeves, he could have replaced Ed Asner as TV's Lou Grant. Then there was sleek, perfectly groomed Al Giordano—a man after Milo's own heart—sporting his usual three-thousand-dollar handmade Italian suit. Rounding out the lynch mob was the hangman himself, Robert O'Malley, indulging his affectation of dressing all in black, as if he were a TV-news producer by day but morphed into a theatrical director after hours. Milo suspected that even executive producing *Newsline*, prime time's most celebrated newsmagazine, wasn't sufficient gratification for O'Malley's enormous ego.

They all took seats on the upholstered chairs and small sofa in Lovegrove's corner office. The thought raced across Milo's mind that this must be what it felt like to be the defendant in a court trial, though here Lovegrove served as both judge and jury. Milo was his own defense counsel and no doubt O'Malley would play the role of prosecuting attorney. It made Milo think of Alicia Maldonado, whose opinion of him by now must be rock-bottom low. At the moment, he couldn't say he deserved otherwise.

Lovegrove kicked off the proceedings. "Milo, can you explain what happened yesterday?"

"I can explain it, Richard, but I won't try to excuse it." He glanced at Cohen. "Knowing I would be on the West Coast over New Year's, Stan alerted me to the latest round of terrorist warnings issued by the FBI and the Department of Homeland Security. I have to admit that, given the history, I didn't think they would amount to much. In fact, Stan didn't, either. He and I discussed that." Milo paused, and the older newsman nodded agreement. "But I certainly understood that it is only when the government takes a threat very seriously that it goes beyond warning law-enforcement agencies and actually alerts the public. And in this case, of course, the threat was directed not only at a specific target but during a specific time frame."

"The point is," Cohen interrupted, "that I told you I might need you. Who gives a shit how likely it was whether I would or not? You agreed to make yourself available, so I didn't line up a fallback. I shouldn't have needed one."

Milo watched Stan Cohen struggle to control his anger. Clearly he'd taken some heat for Milo's failure to show. *Great.* Milo had few allies at WBS to begin with, and now he'd turned the domestic news producer into an enemy.

"Again, Stan," he said, "I will not try to excuse my behavior—"

"You damn well better not."

"Stan." That warning came from Lovegrove, who then turned again to Milo. "What exactly is the reason Stan couldn't reach you?"

Milo had decided in advance that he would stick as close to the truth as possible but omit those details he could avoid divulging. He'd vowed he would not outright lie, a strategy born less of morality than pragmatism. He'd learned as a teenager that an invented story invariably had holes.

"The reason," he said, "is both simple and inexcusable. I turned off my cell phone."

"You turned off your cell phone." O'Malley repeated Milo's words with obvious derision. "How did you expect to be reached with your cell phone turned off?"

Milo could feel the back of his neck getting hot but said nothing, judging it best not to joust with O'Malley. If he started, he might not be able to stop. And if there was one thing he had to do during this inquisition, it was to keep his cool. If he could manage that, he might be able to keep his job.

Giordano jumped in. "I take it you had a social obligation New Year's Eve, Milo?"

"I did."

This was territory Giordano understood. His "social obligations" at any given time consisted of a minimum of two mistresses and his legal wife in the co-op on Park Avenue.

"And I imagine," Giordano went on, "you did not want to have the evening's festivities interrupted?"

"Heaven forbid," O'Malley cut in.

"I didn't, but let me repeat, that is no excuse." Milo focused on Lovegrove, the man who more than anyone else held Milo's fate in his hands. "I understand my obligation to make myself available whenever news events warrant. Particularly when I say I'll be available. I absolutely respect that obligation, Richard," he added, despite an audible snort from O'Malley's direction.

"As I see it," Cohen said, "the problem is that the entire system breaks down when correspondents aren't where I need them when I need them. This time I had to rely heavily on affiliate reporters, and Farley was forced to hire a Lear to get down to Pasadena from Sun Valley. That took time and it cost money."

For a moment, Milo remained silent. *I am so hosed*, he thought. He had the most pathetic excuse in the world. The only weaker excuse would be the unvarnished truth. *Well, guys, I don't know what to tell you, but the woman I slept with New Year's Eve, who happens to be the widow of the guy whose murder case I'm covering, turned off my cell phone because she wanted to make sure our sexual antics didn't get interrupted.*

What could he do but reiterate his apologies? "Again, Stan," he said, "I'm sorry. Believe me, I know it was a serious lapse of judgment to turn my cell phone off, but it happened only once and it won't happen again. You have my promise on that."

A ripple of discomfort ran through the room, though Milo noted O'Malley didn't seem to participate. Lovegrove crossed his arms over his chest and frowned, Giordano examined the ceiling, and Cohen noisily cleared his throat.

It was Lovegrove who broke the silence, with a comment that both confused and unnerved Milo. "If this were the first time I'm sure we'd all be looking at this differently." Then he pressed his intercom button. "Rachel, have McCutcheon and Nguyen arrived?"

Mac and Tran? Milo struggled not to show his shock. What were they doing here? Clearly they were surprise witnesses, summoned to court to blow the case wide open, but to what transgression could they testify? Then Milo remembered, and his heart sank.

The two walked in—Tran shuffled, really—and Milo felt a surge of guilt at being the sort of correspondent who forced his crew into playing snitch. He rose to greet them, shaking their hands in turn. Tran wouldn't meet his eyes. Mac shot him a look that reflected such a complex brew of emotions Milo couldn't immediately parse them, and wasn't sure he wanted to. Anger? Disappointment? Disdain?

Mac and Tran claimed the last two empty seats. The workmen of the news business, they were outfitted in LL Bean cords and flannel shirts. To Milo's eyes they looked strangely bereft without their gear.

Lovegrove cleared his throat. "I wanted Mac and Tran here today because Robert believes they can shed some light on the situation, given an incident last weekend." He shifted his eyes to O'Malley. "Robert?"

Here it comes, Milo thought. He felt as if he were on a jetliner that had gone into a death spiral. He was powerless to save himself. The only question was how painful the end would be.

O'Malley clearly was trying to look somber, but to Milo his glee was evident. "Last Saturday, Milo, you were scheduled for a nine a.m. flight out of San Jose down to San Diego. For a *Newsline* shoot." O'Malley turned to Mac. "Tell us what happened, Mac."

Mac shifted on the small sofa. He looked down at the carpet, where Tran, too, was staring. "Milo missed the flight," he said. "For a while we couldn't reach him."

"Did you know where he was?" O'Malley asked.

Mac hesitated, then, "We knew he wasn't in his hotel room."

Milo jumped in. "I did miss the flight, but I caught the next one and we finished our shoot with no problem."

"Yes." Tran looked up. "The interview went fine. We had no problems."

Milo shot Tran a grateful look but O'Malley went on as if Tran hadn't spoken. He pulled what Milo could see was a *Newsline* location log from a sheaf of papers and displayed it in Milo's direction. "After the shoot, you immediately flew back to the Monterey Peninsula, didn't you, Milo?"

"Of course I did. Because Treebeard was being arraigned."

"Oh, so that's the reason?" A malevolent light gleamed in O'Malley's dark eyes. "Where do you stay while you're in town, by the way?"

"I don't believe that's any of our concern—" Giordano began, but O'Malley cut him off.

"It sure as hell is if it affects whether or not he makes call times."

Lovegrove raised his hands. "All right, gentlemen."

But O'Malley wouldn't let up. This time he looked at Tran. "You knew where Milo was when he missed the San Jose flight, didn't you?"

Tran said not one word. The silence deepened, lengthened, like a stream of water strengthening into a creek.

Milo felt a fresh surge of hatred for O'Malley at that moment. O'Malley knew full well that Tran felt a profound loyalty to WBS, the network that had lifted him out of a ravaged Vietnam thirty years before. Tran would not willingly betray a correspondent, yet his deeper loyalty lay with the network.

"Tran?" Lovegrove asked, and Milo felt a looming dread.

Tran looked up, his features stony. "I didn't know where he was."

"But you suspected," O'Malley said.

"That's enough," Milo said. "Stop badgering him, Robert. I'll tell you where I was, since you're so all-fired interested in knowing. I was in Joan Gaines' suite in Pebble Beach."

For a second there was silence, though Milo could swear he heard the words *Pretty-boy Pappas!* ricochet off Lovegrove's creamy office walls. O'Malley looked around the room as if trying to assess the impact of this sordid revelation. To Milo he seemed almost grotesquely excited to see his pretty-boy characterization take such solid and irrefutable form. But little reaction was visible on any man's face, which worried Milo even more. Apparently he was past the point of surprising anyone with anything he did.

"You were with her New Year's Eve, too, weren't you, Milo?" O'Malley asked. "And you turned your cell phone off because you didn't want your little soiree to get cut short."

"Joan and I are old friends," Milo went on, though his words sounded hollow and pathetic even to his own ears. "We've known each other for a long time."

"Her husband was killed on December twentieth, isn't that right?" O'Malley said. "And you stayed overnight in her suite exactly one week later? You must be old friends."

"That's enough, Robert." Lovegrove's tone was sufficiently stern that O'Malley actually did shut up. Then Milo felt Lovegrove's gaze come to rest on him. He had the strange sense that the verdict—or was it the ax?—was about to come down.

Lovegrove seemed to weigh his words carefully. Through the double-glazed windows, Milo heard the wail of sirens. An emergency somewhere else in Manhattan. Milo wondered whether it, too, was self-induced.

Finally Lovegrove spoke. "I'm giving you one more chance," he said, and for several seconds Milo was so grateful he couldn't speak.

Stunning. Unbelievable. He wasn't getting fired. He would come out of this after all. Finally he found his voice. "Thank you, Richard. I very much appreciate it. Thank you."

"But make no mistake," Lovegrove went on, "this is your last chance. While I agree with Al that generally speaking it is not the network's business how our correspondents conduct their personal lives, you're on shaky ground here. Your focus should be covering the murder trial, yet your involvement with the victim's widow has caused you to go AWOL twice in one week." He paused. "Would you rather I removed you from the story?"

"No, Richard," he heard himself say, "I would rather stay on it," and he knew every executive in that office was relieved to hear that answer. They all craved the ratings draw of the love triangle.

Lovegrove nodded. "Fine. But until this story is wrapped, I want you to maintain an arm's-length relationship with Mrs. Gaines. After that, what you do is your business. But make no mistake, I don't want any behavior on your part to give even the appearance of a conflict of interest."

"I understand, sir."

"You should be adhering to a high standard of ethical behavior, Milo. You're one of the news division's most visible faces. I would even go so far as to say you're one of its most beloved personalities. You should be above reproach."

Milo nodded. He agreed. And thank God he was a "beloved personality," as Lovegrove put it, because that was the only thing that had kept his ass from getting canned. There was some value after all to being WBS's stud correspondent, beefcake disguised as a reporter, who brought in the female demographics *Newsline* needed to stay on top.

"Milo," Lovegrove said, "I mean it when I say this is your last warning. If there is one more mistake, of any kind, you will be out of this network. Do we understand one another?"

"We do, sir. Thank you." And with that Milo rose, shook Lovegrove's hand, nodded at everyone else, and walked out of the office. He was saved, but only just.

CHAPTER SIXTEEN

If ever there were a case where it made sense to do a plea bargain, Alicia thought, *this is it.*

The red numerals on her digital desk clock read 4:10 PM. It was Monday afternoon. Outside her office, January sun poked feebly through the overcast sky, a laughable antidote to the frigid air whistling down Alisal Street. Commuters tromped noisily past Alicia's window, bundled against the chill. No doubt they hoped their buses for once would be on time and not leave them exposed on the corner, where their foot stomping would be a staccato counterpoint to Alicia's thoughts.

Uppermost among those was Theodore Owens III, the likely plea bargain, and her immediate problem.

She squinted into the middle distance, her mind reviewing what she had learned in the twenty-five minutes she'd allotted his case so far. She was heavily reliant on the police report on this one, which she hated. Sure, most cops did a good job, but they were wildly overworked and tended to draw quick conclusions from sketchy evidence. Usually they got everything right but not always, which was why Alicia liked to do some of the footwork herself. But in this case what choice did she have? She was "balls-out," as Penrose liked to say, on Treebeard, leaving her almost no time or energy for anything else. Let alone a case that screamed both misdemeanor and deal.

It was true, sad but true, and hugely undermining to the

prosecution, that the woman Owens had gotten so angry at in the bar, the woman at whom he brandished his pistol, did not want to testify. She'd made that crystal-clear to Alicia over the phone.

How many times do I have to tell you? I dated the guy twice, I never want to see him again, and I sure as hell don't want to waste my time coming to court!

Alicia had been as persuasive as her own limited interest had allowed. *I understand that. But what he did was wrong. And dangerous. And illegal. Not to mention very threatening toward you.*

I don't care.

Don't you want to teach him a lesson?

Long pause, then, *You know what? I'm no teacher. He can learn his lessons from somebody else.*

The CLETS criminal history came up clean. No priors on Owens' record in California. His DMV record revealed numerous transgressions, including several speeding tickets, but nothing notable.

Fine. She'd be a good girl and do her due diligence and put in a call to the jail, a step harried prosecutors usually skipped in the interest of time-saving. It didn't take long to get an Adult Detention Center clerk on the phone. Late in the afternoon she sounded incredibly ready to call it a day.

"I'm calling about Owens, Theodore the Third," Alicia said. "Are there any holds on him?"

"Lemme check." Alicia heard rapid computer key clicking, then the clerk spoke again. "Nothing."

"You're sure?'

"I'm sure."

So Owens had no outstanding warrants in any other state. Alicia went round and round a few more times, trying to get witnesses on the phone. No success. What she was left with all pointed to the same conclusion: Owens, the son of a lawyer and himself an engineer, was a hotheaded jerk. It would be great if she could convict a guy for that—though California's prisons couldn't handle the load—but the bottom line was that the cops were right. The best she could get this guy for was misdemeanor brandishing. Minimum penalty ninety days in county jail; maximum one year. Chances were good that would make him think twice next time.

Fine. She'd make that her opening bid. She might have to come down from there, depending on what opposing counsel came back with.

Now the clock reported 4:24 PM. Better to call fast before Owens' attorneys quit for happy hour. Alicia had a low opinion of defense lawyers, particularly the slick, high-priced specimens that Theodore Owens III had hired.

Alicia was thankful to find Veronica Hodges still in her office, and still, apparently, in the mood for work. She delivered almost nothing by way of greeting or preamble before diving headlong into argument.

"I sincerely hope you're not making more of this than there is. I'll grant you that Teddy probably had a little too much to drink, but it was late on a Friday night, he was just coming off a long and difficult week, and the last thing he should have had to tolerate was such callous behavior from a woman he'd cared for deeply."

Alicia rolled her eyes. She didn't give a hoot about Owens' stress level or supposed self-esteem problems. But you had to hand it to defense lawyers. They were even better at spin than politicians.

"Be that as it may," she told Veronica Hodges, "your client behaved in a hotheaded, reckless manner that endangered the lives of everyone around him."

"I must dispute that characterization. He was upset, yes,

but understandably so, and I would hardly call his behavior reckless. As a matter of fact—"

Veronica Hodges launched into the sort of spirited defense "Teddy" was paying her so well for. Alicia half listened while poking her nose into the top folder on her caseload pile, a mini Tower of Pisa on the right front corner of her desk. After a minute or so of Veronica Hodges's spiel, Alicia cut in. "I'm prepared to make an offer. For misdemeanor brandishing."

Silence. Then, "Misdemeanor brandishing?"

"Right."

"Let me get my client on the phone. I'll call you right back."

"Fine." Alicia disconnected and pulled the next folder off her caseload pile. This one too looked like a prime candidate for settlement. That or she was getting lazy in her old age.

She'd just begun reading the next case's police report when Veronica Hodges called her back. "We'll take it," she said. "But we want the minimum ninety-day sentence."

The next case stared up at Alicia. The digital clock clicked to 4:31 PM. Her New Year workload would keep her in the office till nine that night, at least. And in by seven the next morning, at the latest.

"Fine," she said. "We've got a deal."

***

Joan sat in the San Francisco conference room of the investment banking firm Whipple Canaday and reviewed all the many reasons why she didn't care for investment bankers. Never had. It was one reason why her own tenure as an I-banker—immediately after her truncated stint at Stanford Business School—had been so short. The other, of course, was

Daniel's marriage proposal, which had offered a socially acceptable path out of long-houred, high-pressured high finance into the much more salubrious arenas of home and family.

And lunch, and tennis, and massages, and shopping.

Now investment bankers were making her wait, which irritated her Hudson sensibilities no end. Joan nursed a mug of double cappuccino and tapped the toe of her pump on the Tabriz rug, the rhythm quickening with each passing minute.

She hoped these damn bankers were more efficient at selling companies than they were at keeping appointments. Whipple Canaday was the same firm Daniel and her father had hired when they purchased Headwaters two and a half years before. Her deepest desire now was to extract as much money out of the company as possible and thereby solve her cash-flow problem. She had an idea how best to achieve that goal. And once she had, she would plan her next step, whatever that might be.

The looming question of her future made the mopes yet again descend on Joan's spirits. She rose from her chair and slunk toward the conference room's bank of floor-to-ceiling windows. The north-facing view from the forty-eighth floor of the Bank of America building gave on to a panorama of the Bay Area: from the East Bay and Berkeley hills to the prison island of Alcatraz to the Golden Gate Bridge and lush green contours of the Marin headlands. Directly in front of her, poking into the overcast winter sky, was the pyramidal apex of the Transamerica Building. Far below, the financial district huddled in checkerboard squares of white and brown and gray.

The problem with Joan's future was that she was discovering she had little enthusiasm for either of the paths she had initially imagined for herself. Becoming CEO of

Headwaters was a nonstarter for so many reasons. And the more she thought about going into politics, the more depressed she became. All that campaigning! Long days of listening to other people's troubles, followed by long evenings of listening to other people's troubles, which culminated after victory in long days trying actually to *solve* other people's troubles. Really, what was the point? To be famous and looked up to? She was already famous and looked up to!

No, perhaps the better route was to get married again. She hated, absolutely hated to admit it, but maybe her mother had been right on that score after all. Marriage, at least to the right man, would immediately solve her problems. People wouldn't wonder what she was doing. She was being married! Then she would have children, and people would wonder even less what she was doing. She was raising children! With one live-in nanny per child, which she considered the absolute minimum, most of the burden would be off her shoulders but still she would be beyond reproach. She wouldn't even have to do charity work while the children were young. They provided a built-in excuse. Really, it was quite an ingenious solution, which was probably why so many women she knew picked it.

Joan stared at the city splayed out before her. All she needed was the right man. He had to be successful and he had to be wealthy. Best if he was famous, too. She did enjoy a touch of celebrity in a man: it enhanced her own.

Milo fit the bill in so many ways, and in addition he was quite solicitous of her. At least usually, though his performance in the five days since New Year's had been abysmal. He had made zero attempt to contact her. Had he phoned? No. Had he sent roses? Not a stem. A piece of jewelry, perhaps? Nary a stone. He hadn't even sent an e-mail. And this after she had given herself to him in the only way a woman could truly give herself to a man.

Of course, she knew his behavior was a direct result of that Maldonado woman showing up at the suite to lob accusations. Nor could Joan forget how truly pissed off he had been to discover that she'd turned off his cell phone. But he'd heard her perfectly plausible explanation of why she'd gone back to Carmel. And as she had predicted, the cell phone snafu hadn't cost him his job. She'd seen him on the air.

As far as she was concerned, he was out of line to keep holding a grudge. And he was seriously misinformed if he thought he could sleep with her and then go radio-silent. She would clarify that misconception but quick. And in the meantime, she would show him she had a life of her own by spending a few nights at the Ritz while conducting her Headwaters business.

Though it was a difficult trick playing hard-to-get with a man who hadn't even noticed she was missing ...

Joan heard a bustle behind her at the half-open door of the conference room. She turned to see it push open and a phalanx of bankers troop inside, dressed in all the colors of the rainbow from blue to gray. At their head was senior partner Frederick Whipple, a close friend of her father's and a onetime assistant secretary of the Treasury Department.

"Joan." Frederick grasped both her hands while his minions fanned out around the conference table, positioning themselves behind seats as if Musical Chairs were about to begin. "I am so very sorry about Daniel. Such a needless tragedy."

"Thank you, Frederick." She bowed her head, as had become her habit when the condolences rolled in.

"Please allow me to make the introductions." Frederick proceeded to give names to the half dozen suits who would aid him in the proceedings. Joan made no attempt to keep track of who was who. She would deal only with Frederick, as her father had done.

Everyone sat down. Frederick assumed his position at the head of the conference table, as befitted his five-star-general role, and Joan sat at his right hand. Fresh coffee was served, and after some chitchat Joan was asked the reason for her appointment. She addressed herself to Frederick.

"As you know, Daniel loved Headwaters Resources," she told him. "He loved the day-to-day running of the company, he loved building its team, he loved facing its challenges. But Daniel is gone now." She paused and looked down at her lap, as though she needed to collect herself. No one said a word. No one rushed a new widow, not even the most impatient bankers on the planet. "I want to carry on my husband's vision for Headwaters," she raised her head to say. "And I believe the best way to ensure his legacy is to sell the company."

Frederick Whipple nodded sagely. "I understand what you're saying, Joan, but I caution you against making such a decision hastily. You have undergone an enormous trauma very recently."

"I appreciate your concern, Frederick, but you can rest assured that I have considered this from every angle. With the advice of my family counsel," she added, guessing that Frederick Whipple deeply approved of Henry Gossett. Of course, she hadn't actually said word one to Henry. "And upon prudent reflection, I wish to proceed."

Joan knew that Frederick Whipple would not object again. He had no desire to rile up a valuable client who was clearly committed to a course of action. She knew from her own I-banking experience that Whipple didn't really care whether her decision was ill-advised or not. If she was so bullheaded she was going ahead anyway, he simply wanted his firm to be the one to collect the fees from the transaction.

A throat-clearing sounded from the man directly at Joan's right. She turned her head to look into the bespectacled eyes of a gray-suited thirty-something male. "Are you certain you want to sell the whole company?" he asked.

She frowned and tried to appear slightly confused. "I think so," she managed, then fell silent.

As she had hoped, a sort of charge ran through the assembled troops. Out of the corner of her eye she could see the suit direct his earnest gaze at Frederick Whipple. A wordless communication passed between them.

"Joan," Whipple then said, "have you considered bringing the company to the market?"

She widened her eyes, pretending to appear all innocence. "What are you suggesting, Frederick?"

"An IPO, Joan. An initial public offering."

"Selling shares in Headwaters for the first time," the suit added.

Joan had to stop herself from screaming out what popped into her head: *I know what it means, you idiots! Who around this table thought of it first?* But she tried to appear as if the idea had never crossed her mind. She let her hand fly to her throat in that classic feminine gesture of surprise. "Oh, my."

The suit spoke again. "Bringing the company to the market may well maximize its value."

Whipple took up where the suit left off. "An IPO of, let's say, twenty percent of the company would provide a steady stream of cash flow even as it offers you a slow exit from the company. We may be able to generate considerable enthusiasm for shares of Headwaters Resources." He paused. "Particularly with circumstances as they are."

Joan's heart leaped at that magic phrase *cash flow*. And though Frederick Whipple left much unsaid, Joan knew exactly what he meant. "Considerable enthusiasm" meant top dollar. "Circumstances as they are" referred to Daniel's gruesome murder, the tie-in to her famous family, her own role as the lovely young widow eager to continue her husband's legacy. It all added up to one dramatic possibility: If Whipple Canaday took Headwaters public, Joan Gaines might make a killing.

So to speak.

The suit started talking again. "Of course, the IPO market is the weakest it's been in years. And we'll need to assess Headwaters closely to see if an IPO is even feasible. Check into the books, analyze the assets, and find out if any of our institutional clients would be interested in participating."

Yes, Joan was worried about that, too. She could only hope these bankers would find enough to like when they probed Headwaters' books, which were not exactly a cheery read these days. But surely they would try to put the best possible spin on things, as they, too, would enjoy big fees from an IPO.

Which she had known all along.

The widow Joan produced a brave smile for all the parties assembled around Whipple Canaday's vast conference table. "Let us proceed swiftly," she urged them, "so that I can best do justice to the company that was so dear to my husband's heart."

CHAPTER SEVENTEEN

Kip Penrose couldn't remember when he'd last felt so good. Nervous, too, but that was to be expected. He raised his chin and nudged the knot on his best yellow paisley tie just a tad higher, using as a mirror the glass panes of his office armoire, which housed his TV, VCR, and personal videotape collection. No doubt he would have fresh material to add to the stash later that day. Behind the glass the VCR read out the time in little blue numerals: 12:54 PM. Six minutes to his next newscon, and boy, would this one be a doozy.

He chuckled and moved away from the armoire. He was far too excited to sit, so he loped agitatedly around his office, rotating his shoulders and trying to keep loose as though he were a quarterback waiting on the sidelines to go for the fourth-quarter game-winning drive. Was the one-o'clock hour for the newscon not perfect? Also the fact that this was a Friday afternoon? Kip believed most people got the ax Friday afternoon so they'd have the weekend to lick their wounds and their first jobless workday wouldn't roll around till Monday.

Kip marched to his desk to make sure his prop for the newscon was in order. Sure enough, inside a folder lay the FBI report on Theodore Owens III. Kip had requested the report days earlier, knowing what it would contain. It had arrived just that morning, ready to be displayed to the media at the appropriate dramatic moment.

Kip congratulated himself on his understanding of drama.

That was one of the things that made him a good politician. His favorite politician of all time, Ronald Reagan, was a master of drama, and so was Kip Penrose.

"Kip, did I hear you have a news conference scheduled for one o'clock?"

Kip's ears perked up at the puzzled voice of Alicia Maldonado coming at him from his office doorway. How perfect was that? He looked up from the folder to smile at her. "As a matter of fact I do."

She shook her head. He loved how befuddled she seemed. "I'm surprised you didn't tell me about it. Or"—a sort of understanding lit up her eyes—"maybe it doesn't have to do with Treebeard?"

"Oh, it has to do with Treebeard." Then Rocco appeared behind Alicia at the doorway, with his overcoat already on. He raised his brows in a *Ready to go?* expression. Kip hoisted his own overcoat from the stand behind his desk, pausing to admire its navy wool. So much more flattering to his coloring than black. Then he gifted Alicia with another smile.

"I don't need you to be at this newscon," he told her, "but you might want to, anyway. I'm sure you'd find it interesting." He grabbed his folder prop and brushed past her out the door, relishing her confusion as he followed Rocco outside to the courthouse steps.

Quite a crowd of reporters and camera crews was waiting. Kip took a few deep breaths, getting that edgy feeling he always got before doing something big. But he had to do this, right? Joan Gaines had put her foot down. And even though Alicia Maldonado could be useful, she'd been annoying him for years. Plus she'd already done most of the heavy lifting on the Treebeard case, and now Rocco could do the rest.

Kip set up himself up behind the TV microphones,

grouped on their metal stands like skinny soldiers, while Rocco took the position behind his left shoulder, where Alicia used to stand. Not anymore. Kip felt another shiver run through him. Was this a bad idea? He couldn't worry about that now. He was out on the playing field with the ball in his hand.

"I have a serious matter to bring to your attention," he said, "one I hoped I would never face. And it comes when this office is fast approaching one of the most important trials in its history, that of John David Stennis, who calls himself Treebeard."

Man, the excitement of those reporters radiated toward Kip like heat waves on a desert highway. *Drama! Drama!* Kip could almost feel the Gipper at his back, urging him on.

"The case at issue," he continued, "centers on a defendant by the name of Theodore Owens the Third. Two weeks ago, Mr. Owens brandished a gun in a crowded bar in Pacific Grove. He was irate at a woman with whom he had briefly been involved." Kip scowled for the cameras, showing himself to be a man who profoundly disapproved of such behavior. "Mr. Owens was reckless. He posed a threat to innocent people trying to unwind after a long week of earning their livelihood."

Kip then raised his voice in righteous anger, like a preacher. "I am a district attorney who takes such a transgression very seriously. Regrettably, I must inform you that the deputy district attorney who handled Mr. Owens' case, the very prosecutor working at my side to bring the accused killer Treebeard to justice, is not of the same mind."

Kip shook his head and struggled to appear sorely disappointed. "That prosecutor dispensed swiftly with this matter, recommending a plea bargain to Mr. Owens' defense counsel. A plea bargain," he repeated, as if he found those two words exceedingly vile. Then he made himself sound amazed, as if the unbelievable, the truly astonishing, had happened. "That prosecutor recommended a charge of misdemeanor brandishing! And then agreed to the minimum sentence so that the defendant would face only three months in county jail!"

It was time. Kip raised the folder high in the air, where it glinted in the sun like a beacon. Flashbulbs popped. TV camera lenses refocused. "I have here a report from the Federal Bureau of Investigation outlining Mr. Owens' criminal history. Given the plea bargain, naturally you would assume that the defendant had no serious blemishes on his record. But no." Kip dropped his arm to his side. "For Mr. Owens is a felon, convicted in the state of Massachusetts, someone for whom it is illegal even to possess a firearm. California law requires that Mr. Owens be charged with a felony for this latest transgression. And if convicted he would receive not only a second felony strike on his record but a lengthy sentence in state prison."

Kip raised his voice dramatically. "Mr. Owens came frighteningly close to flouting the law. And how did he manage that, you ask?" Kip paused and for the first time understood what "bated breath" meant. "Because of the lackadaisical, incompetent performance of Deputy District Attorney Alicia Maldonado, who was more interested in moving a case off her desk than in seeking justice for the law-abiding citizens of Monterey County!"

The reporters were stunned, Kip could tell. They were raising their eyebrows at each other and writing furiously in their little notebooks.

Time to deliver the final blow. Kip lifted his chin, thinking of the one very important woman who would approve mightily of what he was doing and how he was doing it.

"Therefore I terminate Deputy District Attorney Alicia Maldonado for gross incompetence, effective immediately. Deputy District Attorney Rocco Messina will assume her duties on the Treebeard prosecution. Questions?"

Those came thick and fast, but Kip had answers for all of them. He told himself that was because this was his lucky day. Somewhere in all the back-and-forth, he turned around and spied a dark-haired woman standing at the courthouse door, far enough away not to be easily visible but close enough to have heard every word.

Kip turned back to face the journalists massed before him, a smile lighting his features, a bead of sweat slinking down his back. He'd done exactly what Joan Gaines had asked him to, and he'd done it in such a way that Alicia Maldonado's reputation would never recover.

***

Milo had to hand it to Joan. She'd gotten him to agree to meet her, in a restaurant no less. It was as though eight days of post-*flagrante delicto* silence simply hadn't happened. She'd called him and amidst all her chatter managed to say the one thing that could make him agree to meet her, the one thing that fit with his new Joan Gaines agenda.

Maybe I can tempt you with a little inside information on the case. Doesn't that get your reporter juices flowing?

Yes, that most certainly did. His primary goal was to do bang-up reporting on the Gaines case, meaning he definitely wanted inside dirt. If she was willing to dish it, fine. Ironic, but fine.

Yet he was hardly at ease. Joan was at best a schemer; at worst she was dangerous. Of course she had refused to talk over the phone. In desperation he had sent Mac and Tran to collect beauty shots of the peninsula, which would keep them occupied for a few hours at least. He could not risk having them see him in the company of the lovely widow.

A waiter glided over, his dress shirt and half apron as blindingly white as a naval officer's. "May I get you a glass of wine while you're waiting?"

"Thank you, no, I'm fine." Milo's new spartan regimen, which he'd adopted immediately upon exiting Richard Lovegrove's office, did not allow for lunchtime tippling. It barely allowed for evening tippling. It certainly didn't allow for women who led him down paths he could ill afford to travel.

He sipped his carbonated water and chuckled softly to himself. How fitting that he should be contemplating his new abstemiousness in Pacific Grove, a community founded a century before as a Christian seaside resort. That puritanical sensibility continued to hold sway at the nearby Asilomar conference site, though it had been modernized in recent years with New Age overtones.

Joan, of course, would be oblivious to the irony. No doubt she had proposed Joe Rombi's restaurant for their rendezvous because it removed her from the Carmel/Pebble Beach axis, where she was highly recognizable and hence forced to maintain the fiction that she was in deep mourning. Luncheon excursions to chic Italian eateries with former boyfriends did not exactly jibe with that image.

Milo's anger with Joan was boundless, but still it did not compare to his anger with himself. What an idiot he had been. How totally he had let his little brain do the thinking. How thoroughly he had allowed himself to be taken in yet again. Joan Hudson Gaines was no more than a whiny, self-absorbed rich girl with the moral code of a piranha. He had known it, yet he had ignored it. He was detestable. But it was no more.

The scales at long last had fallen from Pretty-boy Pappas's eyes.

He downed his fizzy water, rattled an ice cube into his mouth, and was admiring Joe Rombi's selection of vintage French Art Deco posters when Joan sailed into the restaurant. She wafted expensive perfume and looked as if she'd spent the entire morning in a salon. Being Joan, she probably had.

"Hello." She sat opposite him, removed her dark-lensed Chanel glasses, and smiled—a broad, welcoming smile that said, *Surely nothing could be seriously wrong between us?*

"Hello, Joan."

"I know you're still mad at me but I'm determined to jolly you out of it."

He said nothing. The bright-white waiter came by. "What may I get you?" he asked Joan.

"I'll have a glass of pinot grigio, please."

The waiter's gaze skipped to Milo. "And for you, sir?"

Milo hoisted his fizzy-water glass. "A refill, if I may."

Joan arched her brow. "Won't you share a glass of wine with me?"

"I'm working this afternoon."

She leaned across the table and lowered her voice, her tone conspiratorial. "Surely we can think of a better way to celebrate our reunion than you working all afternoon?"

"I have a story to write."

She rolled her eyes and lolled back in her chair, producing an impressive pout. "You really want to make me suffer, don't you, Milo?"

Her self-absorption was gigantic. Milo was amazed there was room for it at their table. He was even more astonished that it hadn't suffocated him before now.

Their drinks came. She clinked her glass against his without comment.

He broke the silence. "So what did you want to tell me about the case?"

Her eyes over her wineglass grew more disapproving, before she remembered herself. She put a smile on her lips, then picked up her menu. "Let's order first, shall we?"

That was achieved fairly quickly, though Joan as usual made numerous off-menu requests. Milo already knew what he wanted, since he'd had so much time before her arrival to ponder the question. Once the waiter glided away, Joan straightened in her chair and squared her body toward him as if she were about to deliver a prepared speech. It ran through his mind that indeed she was a politician's daughter.

"I want you to know," she said, "that I have thought long and hard about what I did New Year's Eve. Milo, I recognize that it was irresponsible of me to turn off your phone, and childish, and I am very, very sorry. I truly apologize."

Neither her tone nor her gaze could be more earnest. A less knowledgeable man would have been fooled. But it served Milo's purposes to warm her up and get what he needed out of her. So ...

"I accept your apology," he told her.

She laughed and laid her hand over his. "I'm so relieved!" Then she leaned closer and batted those baby blues at him again. "Though I didn't think you could stay mad at me for long."

There was no point disputing her. There was no point reminding her that apart from turning off his phone—which, bad as it was, might be explained away—she had committed another, more serious transgression. She had lied to him. Repeatedly. And about a very serious matter—where she was and what she was doing the night her husband was murdered. Either Joan had forgotten that little prevarication, or she figured it didn't much matter, or she wanted to kick it under the table in hopes that over time it would just slink away. She saw the world, and him, through the prism of her own delusion. He understood that failing, because he was just recovering from a bad case of it himself.

"Where are you staying?" she asked him.

"The Monterey Plaza Hotel." He was doing everything by the book these days. No more quirky inns or out-of-the-way B-and-Bs.

"There's always room for you at the Lodge," she murmured.

There was no need to disabuse her of that notion because of the timely arrival of their entrees. Joan refused parmesan on her tomato and basil pasta; Milo accepted it on his pesto. He thought for a moment that he would do almost anything at this point to set himself apart from Joan Gaines.

They were about a third of the way through a silent inhalation of their lunches when the floodgates opened. Cynic that he had become, Milo saw the display as no more than another trick in Joan's arsenal. She could see that Coquette hadn't worked its usual magic. Earnest Joan had fallen flat. Perhaps Waterworks might enjoy more success?

"Milo"—much sniffling and nose-wiping—"I would just hate for one stupid mistake to drive us apart. We are so good together. We have so much potential. I will just never forgive myself—"

Milo stopped eating, despite the powerful lure of his pesto fettuccine. It seemed just too rude to eat pasta during a woman's tears. The waiter approached, then suddenly veered left through the swinging doors to the kitchen, clearly judging this not the best moment to inquire whether everything was satisfactory.

"Can't we get past this, Milo?" she was asking. Her face by now was nearly as red as her tomato sauce. "Can't you find it in your heart to forgive me? Is what I've done so very wrong?"

He pondered that last question. Then he found himself saying something he knew he shouldn't but somehow couldn't resist. "I don't know, Joan. You tell me."

Something in the depths of her eyes shifted, hardened. "What are you asking me?"

"I'm asking you if you've done something very wrong."

She said nothing for a long time. When she did speak, her voice had a new edge to it. "Surely you don't think it's possible that I killed Daniel."

"It's possible, certainly." He decided to hedge that. "Anything's possible."

The restaurant seemed very still. It being such an odd hour—too late for lunch, too early for dinner—there was only one other group dining, a threesome several tables away. Milo was vaguely aware of the ebb and flow of their conversation, the occasional tinkle of their laughter. They were finishing dessert and coffee. They were getting ready to leave.

They were clattering out of their chairs when Joan spoke again. "You're attracted to her, aren't you, Milo?" Her voice was venomous. "You're attracted to that cheap Latin spitfire."

He almost laughed. *Attracted* was way too weak a word for the pull he felt toward Alicia Maldonado. "What I'm asking has nothing to do with her," he said.

"It has everything to do with her, because apparently, unlike me, everything she says you believe. Well, you might be interested to hear that what I was going to tell you today actually has to do with your little Spanish rose."

He frowned. "What are you talking about?"

"She's been fired!" Joan's tone was exultant. "Not just from my case but from the entire district attorney's office. For gross incompetence, no less! Oh, yes, I see the shock on your face that Senorita Maldonado could be anything less than perfect. But let me assure you that she is." Joan leaned forward. "She is positively demented, Milo. She is a psycho."

Then Joan proceeded to tell him a story he could hardly believe was true. And as she told it, he could clearly see the triumph in her eyes, hear the glee in her voice, and he knew as surely as he knew his own name that somehow Joan had orchestrated Alicia's downfall.

He felt a rage gather itself inside his chest, almost painful in its intensity. This powerful woman, the daughter of a governor, the heir to a fortune, who lived a life of ease but still found it difficult—that such a woman would wreak havoc on the life of someone so much more honorable and hardworking than she ...

"So now she's out of a job, which is what she deserves," Joan was saying. "For what she's done to me, I hope she dies soon. She's not fit to do my gardening, let alone prosecute my husband's case."

He had risen to his feet, he realized. His napkin had dropped to the floor. He was actually tempted to overturn the table onto Joan's pampered lap.

"—two of a kind," she was saying. "Your family is as pathetic as hers. Both of you are poseurs, and I hope you suffer the same fate she did. You are an ill-bred, social-climbing—"

He stopped listening to Joan but could still see her. Her face was twisted in anger. Her words were vile flying things he had no time for.

This woman deserved no words from him, nothing, nevermore. He turned and walked out of the restaurant, leaving the bill unpaid, though that was the sort of nicety Joan would attend to. Kill her husband, that she might well do. But fail to adhere to a social convention? Not possible.

CHAPTER EIGHTEEN

"How did I not see it coming?" Alicia paced her living room like a woman possessed, Louella exhorting her to slow down, sit down, calm down. It was just after five on Friday afternoon. The sun was making its last stand of the day. The Lopez boys next door were playing stickball in her driveway, while the smell of their mother's greasy cooking invaded her bungalow like a pestilence. Cars buzzed past the front windows, courthouse commuters using Capitol Street as a shortcut to Route 183.

Commuters. People who still had jobs.

"Who could have seen it coming?" Louella sat cross-legged on the couch in front of the window, sipping a diet ginger ale. The sun made a frizzy halo of her bleached-blond hair. "Stop beating yourself up, Alicia. How many cases do we plea-bargain? Four out of five? This one fit the bill. What you did made sense at the time."

"Penrose set me up."

"We don't know that."

Alicia knew it. She didn't know how he had done it but she knew that he had. Her pacing accelerated. "He knew I wouldn't check on Owens with the FBI." That was the only national database to check, but no prosecutor did for a misdemeanor charge. For a felony, sure. As it was, Alicia had taken the extra precaution of making sure Owens had no outstanding warrants from other states, which most prosecutors didn't bother with for lesser crimes.

"Penrose wants to plea-bargain everything, remember?" Louella was saying. "That's his modus operandi."

"There's more going on here than that." Alicia sagged onto the couch next to Louella and let her head drop against the back cushion. "I feel so unbelievably stupid to let that buffoon get the better of me."

It was too weird to be real. All afternoon, since that godawful press conference, Alicia had felt as if she were watching her life with someone else's eyes, as if what was happening to her surely must be happening to some other poor sap. Yet it was *she* who had to clean out her desk, *she* who had to carry her cardboard box out of the district attorney's office into the chilly January air. People she'd worked with for years darted back into their offices when she walked past, as if she were suffering a disease they could catch if they got too close.

Alicia shook her head. "When Veronica Hodges immediately settled on misdemeanor brandishing for Owens, without arguing with me for a second, that should have been an enormous red flag. That woman would dispute whether the sun rises in the east." The phone rang again, for the umpteenth time. Alicia let the machine pick up. "Hodges knew what exposure she had. She knew she was getting away with something huge."

For once Louella had no comeback.

Alicia went on. "What I don't get is how Penrose could have known what Owens' history was."

"I don't see how he could have. That's the point."

"The timing is just too suspicious." Alicia stood up and resumed pacing, as though the couch were a jury box and she a prosecutor lining up arguments to persuade Louella to convict. "On New Year's Day I show Joan Gaines proof positive that she lied to me about being back in Carmel the night her husband was murdered. The very next afternoon Kip insists on assigning me Owens, which turns out like this. Am I crazy or did Kip use Owens to get me off the Gaines case?"

Louella met her eyes, her face somber. "You're not crazy but I just don't see how Penrose could have known."

"And nobody else heard him badger me to do a deal. 'No reason to go balls-out on this one,' he tells me. 'Guy's from a good family—it's a first offense,' he says. He actually told me that!"

"There's no evidence he didn't believe it."

Not yet. But she knew—she'd always known—that Penrose would get her if he had the chance. Or if he could create the chance.

"You know, Alicia," Louella went on, "maybe you should focus on how to fight this. There are steps you can take."

"I could sue for wrongful termination. And you can be damn sure I will." Her case would go before the County Board of Supervisors. If she could find a way to prove how Kip had manipulated her, she could get her job back. "But that'll take forever. You know how slow the Board of Sups is."

"I could loan you a little—"

"No." Alicia held up her hands as if to stop the flow of Louella's words. Jorge had offered money, too, but she wouldn't take it from him, either. "I appreciate it, Louella, really I do, but I can't take your money. I know you're not exactly rolling in cash."

Nobody who worked at the courthouse was, with the exception of Penrose, and that was because after his own stint as a prosecutor he'd done years in private practice. Alicia figured some of the judges were pretty well-off, too, but most everybody else lived paycheck to paycheck. She wouldn't admit to Louella just how close to the edge she was herself.

Her checking account was down to a hundred and twenty-three bucks. She'd confirmed the balance at an ATM on the way home from the courthouse. Now she had one more paycheck coming in, for the week she'd just worked; then that was it. That wouldn't last long, not with the money she gave her mother every month to help with her mortgage and the cash her sister Carla kept needing.

The phone rang again. "I'll get it this time," she said, then headed for the kitchen.

It was Jerome Brown, Treebeard's defense lawyer. "I don't know what to say, Alicia, except I can't believe this."

"Then you're in the same boat I am."

"What happened?"

How to explain? "I didn't know Owens' history. Nothing showed up on the CLETS. And even though this was a misdemeanor charge I checked for outstanding warrants. But nothing showed up. I never would have plea-bargained if I'd known about the felony."

"That's what I heard you say on the news."

She closed her eyes. She'd fed Jerome the same line she'd been feeding reporters all afternoon. It was true, but it hardly erased the allegation of incompetence. "Is this getting a lot of coverage?"

"Hard to say. We just saw you on the local news at five, and my wife said she heard it on the radio."

Great. Her reputation was trashed. Even if she got reinstated it was this firing that people would remember. If she got rehired, that would run on page sixteen of the newspaper when this story had headlined page one. Goodbye, any chance at elective office.

"I suppose I should be happy about it," Jerome was saying, "because it'll help me defend Treebeard." He paused. "After all, it's one thing to go up against Rocco Messina and quite another to face Alicia Maldonado."

For a second or two she couldn't say anything. Then, "Thanks, Jerome."

"If there's anything I can do, I mean it, you let me know."

"I will." She lay down the receiver, then returned to the living room. Louella was rising from the couch in a series of awkward motions. "Damn." She started kicking her feet, like a halfhearted Rockette. "My legs fell asleep. Have you noticed how that happens more often the older you get?"

Alicia halted in the middle of her living room and stared out her front window. In the asphalt parking lot of the ratty apartment building across the street, two men had their heads bent over some kind of business. It looked like a drug deal but for once Alicia didn't much care. "You know what's the craziest thing of all?"

Louella stopped kicking. "What?"

"That a few weeks ago all I was worried about was not getting the big case that would jump-start my career. Now I don't even have a career to jump-start."

"Yes, you do. Don't say that."

"Joan Gaines will get away with it now. Who's going to stop her?"

"Alicia, it's not even clear she did anything. And second of all, now is not the time to be worrying about Joan Gaines. You should be worrying about yourself." Louella grabbed her backpack, dumped at the side of the couch, and slung it over her shoulder. "I hate to say this but I gotta go. Can you believe I've got a date tonight? Talk about timing. With Tom in Water Resources."

"The one you turned down for New Year's?"

"Yeah, but now it's January tenth. So he's looking more palatable." Louella headed for the front door, then stopped and turned around. "Hey, you want to join us? Or should I cancel and you and me do something? We could—"

"No. Really." Alicia pushed Louella out the door. "Go. I'm fine."

A few more pushes, a few more lies about how really okay she was, and Alicia convinced Louella to go. She shut the door and leaned her forehead against it. The truth was, she wanted to be by herself. She wanted to wallow, and plan, and curse Penrose. And while those were activities that could be accomplished with a companion, there was a bitter consolation in doing them alone.

She was about to relatch the chain when the doorbell rang. She pulled the door open. On her stoop stood Milo Pappas.

***

"May I come in?" As a precaution Milo lifted his right foot off the WELCOME doormat and inserted it into Alicia's tiny shadowy foyer. She looked like she might slam the door in his face at any moment.

"What are you doing here? And how in hell did you get my address?"

"May I come in?" he repeated.

She didn't answer, but after a moment she stepped back and allowed him to brush past her into the house. He turned to face her in the small front room, though she remained in the foyer, as if she expected to be ushering him out again very soon.

He had the same reaction he always did to Alicia Maldonado: she was a drop-dead beauty. Even in her decidedly unglamorous faded jeans and peasant blouse, she was stunning. Then he remembered he was taking a hiatus from such observations.

"People at the WBS station here know where you live," he told her. Right after he'd left Joan, he'd hightailed it there and quizzed the reporter covering the Treebeard trial on why Deputy D.A. Maldonado had gotten fired. He'd used every bit of yank a star network correspondent had with a local reporter to pry Alicia's address out of him. "Is the story true?"

"Do you mean did I do the plea bargain? Yes. Did I know the guy's history? No, or I never would've done a deal."

That was basically what she'd said on the sound bite the reporter showed him. That seemed to be her only excuse and it struck him as a weak one. He knew what that was like. "Did Penrose rig this to get rid of you?" he asked her.

Bingo. He could tell from her startled intake of breath that he'd hit pay dirt. Ever since he eavesdropped on her argument with Penrose, he'd known there was serious antipathy between the D.A. and his deputy. Then in the videotape of that afternoon's press conference, he watched Penrose do a piss-poor job of masking his glee at being "forced" to fire her. Being the target of a so-called superior's ire was a phenomenon Milo well understood. And sympathized with.

She said nothing, so he pressed on. "Is there anything you can do about it?"

"Plenty."

"Like what?"

She advanced a few paces into the front room and put her hands on her hips. Her eyes were defiant. "That's none of your business."

"I'm trying to help." Though even as he said it he knew he was hardly in a position to offer career advice.

"I don't need your help. And as I recall we haven't exactly been on the same side lately."

We could be now, he wanted to tell her. Instead he pointed to the couch. "Do you mind if I sit down?"

"Go ahead."

But she remained standing and offered no refreshment, which made him feel about as welcome as a door-to-door salesman hawking undesirable wares. He looked around the room, full of the sort of furniture he'd thrown out after college. The rust-colored Navajo throw rugs were pretty, though, as were the posters. "You're a big Kahlo fan," he said.

There was a flicker of surprise in her eyes, probably that he even knew who Frida Kahlo was. Maybe he should mention that his parents had an original in their home on Thessaloniki.

"She was a real fighter," Alicia said.

"I always preferred her to Rivera." But that didn't warm her up, either, though he suspected she shared his opinion. They stared at each other for a few seconds longer, then Milo again broke the silence. "I'm not your enemy."

She shook her head. "I don't know what you are. The last time I saw you ..." She stopped.

"I was sleeping with the enemy? Well, I'm not anymore."

He dropped his eyes and concentrated on the rug, which covered scarred, uneven hardwood flooring. It had taken him a while to cool down from his run-in with Joan. He still couldn't believe the bile that had fallen from her lips. It was as if the mask had come off and he'd seen that what lay beneath was rotten and corrupt.

"For the record," he said, "Joan and I dated years ago. She broke it off. It was tabloid fodder at the time, pretty unpleasant stuff."

He raised his eyes. Alicia's expression was unreadable. Maybe she was one of those rare Americans who didn't pore over the gossip columns. Good for her.

"I certainly didn't intend for anything to happen between

us," he went on.

Her voice was cool. "Funny. It seemed to anyway."

"It sure as hell did. And I was a total idiot, I can tell you that."

Alicia looked away. Milo had the idea she'd become one iota less suspicious. He watched her walk to a side table and wipe nonexistent dust off the broad striped leaf of a potted ficus. Funny. Joan was supposed to be the thoroughbred, yet Alicia Maldonado seemed made of nobler stuff. Here she stood in her very small, very plain house—in a neighborhood Joan wouldn't be caught dead in—and still she had a certain regalness about her.

"I have a proposition for you," he told her.

She looked away from the plant and arched her brow. "Why do I feel like I've heard that one from you before?"

"A business partnership. It's strictly on the up-and-up."

"That'd be a real change."

"I never once lied to you, Alicia. I may have withheld a thing or two but I never told you anything but the truth."

"What are you withholding now?"

What, indeed? Nothing he could think of. In fact, at the moment he was playing it unusually straight. Maybe this was the new and improved Milo Pappas in action.

He rose from the couch and approached her. She retreated a step and crossed her arms over her chest, as if to put another barrier between them. He met her eyes. "I think Joan knows more about Daniel's death than she's letting on. A lot more."

Clearly that took her by surprise. Her mouth dropped open and she drew an unsteady breath. Then her eyes narrowed. "So one night you sleep with her and the next you think she had something to do with her husband's murder? Some lover you are."

"Let's just say that I've seen a different side to Joan."

Alicia shook her head. "Boy, you are some kind of quick-change artist. And even if I did believe you, why are you telling me this now? What am I supposed to do about it? I'm off the case, remember? I'm out of the D.A.'s office. This is somebody else's problem."

"You don't really believe that."

"How many times do I have to say this, Milo? I can't be of any use to you anymore!"

"Not true. Not if you and I join forces."

"What?" She laughed. "What are you talking about?"

"I need a killer story. You need vindication. If you and I prove that Joan had something to do with killing Daniel, we'll both get what we want."

She laughed again, though it was more of a scoffing sound. "The last thing I need is a man I can't trust trying to get me to ... how did you put it?" She made big quotation marks in the air, her voice laden with sarcasm. " 'Join forces with you?' What's that a euphemism for? Feed you every piece of evidence the D.A.'s office has compiled? Forget it. For all I know you could be working with Joan. You could be an accomplice to murder. I don't know what your agenda is but I know I want nothing to do with it." She stalked to her front door.

"Hold on just a minute." His voice came out harsher than he'd intended. "Now you're accusing *me* of killing Gaines?"

She said nothing. She was an unreadable presence in the shadows of the foyer.

"For your information, I found out he had been murdered when I was in New York. It came over the wires while I was anchoring the evening news. You want to see a tape of me subbing for Jack Evans on December twenty-first? I can get it for you."

Her voice was soft but icily suggestive. "You don't have to be physically present to be involved in a murder."

Cool it, he told himself, though it was a challenge. All these accusations of Milo Pappas doing wrong, ratcheting ever higher into allegations of murder. There was truth to some of them but not one whit of truth to this one, the worst of all.

"Let me tell you something, Alicia." He couldn't stop from advancing toward her. "I had nothing to do with that man's death. From the day Joan dumped me, I didn't see her again until I covered her husband's funeral. You are way off base if you think I had anything to do with it. And I've got to tell you, it pretty seriously pisses me off that you would think I did."

He forced himself to back off and return to the front room. His heart was thumping as if he were once again at Georgetown running the stadium steps. She said nothing and remained in the foyer.

He wondered if this whole thing was worth the trouble. This woman could be a real pain in the ass. He'd probably be better off just doing a pro forma job covering Treebeard's trial and trying to resuscitate his reputation with a different story altogether.

But he didn't really want to let it go. That was what separated the real journalists from the impostors, he told himself. Not letting go.

Part of him knew he didn't want to let her go, either. Not yet. He wanted a connection, however tenuous.

He turned to face her one more time. "Look, you believe Joan killed Daniel. You may or may not be right, but how are you going to prove it on your own? You have a better chance working with me."

"Oh, so now you're a PI as well as a journalist? You must

have a lot of free time on your hands, buddy." She pulled open her door. In blew a blast of frigid air, redolent of exhaust from the nonstop flow of cars. "You're leaving now."

He didn't move. "There's no conflict of interest anymore. I'm still covering the story but you're no longer in the D.A.'s office. You get total vindication if you prove Joan was the murderer."

"You're really big on this 'vindication' thing. Somehow it makes me wonder if you want it more than I do." She opened the door wider. "Out."

Fine. He'd had all he could take for the moment. He moved forward but paused at the door to stare down at her. "Think about it," he said. "You're not getting rid of me so easily."

***

Joan was finding it very, very difficult to read spreadsheets with her eyes constantly filling with tears. Very, very difficult!

She gave up. She propped her elbows on Daniel's eighteenth-century Hepplewhite writing desk, rested her forehead in her hands, and let the tears flow. She couldn't believe that on this afternoon of all afternoons she had to be at Headwaters waiting for a 6 PM conference call with Frederick Whipple. His minions were swarming all over the building, poking their noses into files and asking questions of employees and all in all making great pests of themselves. It was necessary, she knew, but it was all just too much.

She raised her head and sniffled, fumbling in her Prada handbag for yet another tissue. Not that she'd been serious about Milo, not really, but nevertheless she was astounded by his behavior. Just who did Milo Pappas think he was?

Certainly if any dumping was going to occur, it should have been her unloading him, like last time. Her initial instinct that his network-news success might lead him to misunderstand his place relative to hers had been quite on point.

She had been so deliciously angry at Joe Rombi's, so powerful giving him the plain truth about Alicia Maldonado, another presumptuous no-name who had to be taught just where in the great wide world she stood.

Joan was seriously undone. There was nothing for it but to take one of the Xanax Dr. Finch had given her. She'd been very careful how she took them, but there were moments when she just couldn't get by without their help.

She fished the amber prescription bottle out of her handbag and jiggled one out, washing it down with her now cold Darjeeling tea. It was such a shame she wasn't angry anymore. Anger had felt so much better than sadness. She hated to admit it but this could be yet another case of her mother being right all along. Right about Daniel and right about Milo. Her mother had warned her that she should stick to men who shared her background and breeding. Well, neither of these specimens had stood up under the test. Milo had revealed himself to be a lowborn cad: using a woman still reeling from grief for his own sexual pleasure, then tossing her aside. Using *her*, a Hudson! He should have been tremendously grateful she allowed him into her bed in the first place. It might be appropriate behavior among Greeks, but among Episcopalians it was appalling.

Joan took several deep breaths. She had to stop thinking about it, at least for now. She had to gather her wits. The conference call was in five minutes. And besides, one day very soon she would think of a way to give Milo Pappas his comeuppance, the way she'd given it to Alicia Maldonado.

Joan had just finished repowdering her face, though she

was still lamenting her puffy eyes, when Frederick Whipple's sidekick, the gray-suited male twenty-five years his junior knocked on Daniel's door to summon her to the call. She followed him downstairs to the first-floor conference room.

Joan assumed her rightful place at the head of the table. "Craig, good to see you."

From his post at her left, Craig Barlowe nodded back. "Hello, Joan." She noted that his demeanor had not improved. Ever since she'd told him she was selling Headwaters, he had been positively sullen. Probably he thought he'd end up out of a job. She thought he'd been lucky to hold on to this one as long as he had.

The gray suit sat at her right and one of the minions fussed with what they all insisted on calling the "squawk box," which perched like a high-tech centerpiece on the conference table's gleaming mahogany surface. Frederick Whipple, from his office in San Francisco, was soon telephonically connected.

Greetings were exchanged. Less important business was dispensed with. Frederick rapidly got to the point.

"As you know, Joan, my associates have spent the greater part of the week analyzing the viability of an initial public offering of Headwaters Resources. I must tell you there is some difficulty with that approach."

Joan's heart sank. Frederick embarked on a dissertation about debt loads and regulatory constraints and stagnating economic conditions, but it all added up to one thing: she'd have to settle for just selling the company, which would mean less money than an IPO.

Whipple paused to sip something, apparently. Outside the conference room's three small windows, set deep into the whitewashed adobe, it was already dark. Joan wanted to scream. It was Friday night and what did she have to look forward to? Nothing. No dinner date, no rendezvous, no party, no nothing. And now no IPO either.

"However," Whipple's voice intoned from the squawk box, "Headwaters Resources does possess some unique attributes that our institutional clients are finding quite attractive."

Her ears perked up.

"For example, Headwaters owns thousands of acres of old-growth forest, which are increasingly rare and hence quite valuable. In addition, in the wake of the dot com bubble, there is a renewed interest in the basic industries, which can produce solid and predictable returns."

Joan glanced at the gray suit. He caught her eye and smiled.

Could it be a go?

"Investors have renewed interest in established companies in this uncertain market," Whipple droned on. "The technology companies that were in such demand in years past are not luring investors at this point in time."

Frederick Whipple kept her in suspense for a while longer, enumerating Headwaters' good points, then said, "In short, Joan, I believe that Whipple Canaday can position Headwaters Resources in such a way that it will generate enthusiasm in the public marketplace. Therefore I recommend that we bring the company to market and give all Americans an opportunity to participate in what I'm sure will be its great future success."

Everyone broke into raucous applause—everyone except Craig Barlowe, that is—and all the minions came around the conference table to shake Joan's hand. The gray suit broke out a few bottles of Dom Perignon. Frederick Whipple sounded a cautionary note or two, as was his wont as Whipple Canaday's most senior partner, but Joan tuned out and took a token sip of champagne. She couldn't have more, not after the Xanax, which apparently was already starting to work. She felt quite serene about everything she'd have to think about next, investor presentations and S-1s and research analyst briefings. She'd think about those tomorrow. Or maybe Monday.

As she began the fifteen-minute drive back to Pebble Beach, she made the mistake of answering her cell phone.

"Mother, I thought you were still in Marblehead!" The Storrow family seat, on Boston's North Shore, where her mother had spent New Year's. Joan had hoped she'd be so overcome by the native puritanism that she'd stay till spring.

"I returned yesterday."

Small talk ensued. Joan marveled how little detail about her life she cared to share with her mother. Theirs was an arm's-length intimacy, with no sign of rapprochement on the horizon. That suited her just fine.

"What have you been occupying yourself with, dear?" her mother asked.

"Oh, this and that." What had she been doing that she could tell Libby Storrow Hudson about? She couldn't go into all her treatments at the Lodge's spa. Or her efforts to ensure that a local D.A. lost her job. Certainly she should stay mute about having sex with Milo and then getting dumped by him. "I've been spending a great deal of time at Headwaters," she offered.

Silence. Joan could imagine her mother's wrinkle-lined mouth puckering into a frown. Then, "I would have thought you'd be done with that by now."

An oblique reference to Joan's supposed flitting from project to project. She swiftly decided this was not the time to mention that Whipple Canaday was taking the company public.

Though she couldn't put it off for long. Very soon it would hit the financial pages. Her mother was no longer a shareholder in Headwaters, since Daniel had bought out her father's stake, but her interest in the company could safely be described as very high.

Her mother was speaking again. Joan detected a slight change in her tone, as if they were moving from inconsequential matters to the heart of the conversation. "I met with Henry Gossett this morning," she said.

That wasn't good. "How is Henry?"

"We reviewed some matters having to do with the trust."

That was really not good. "Was this in your new capacity as trustee?" Joan couldn't help but sound snide.

"As a matter of fact, it was. Joan, I'm afraid I must ask you to make a change in your living arrangements."

Ahead of her on Highway 1, brake lights flared bright red. "What are you talking about?"

"It has come to my attention that you are still residing at the Lodge. You have been there for nearly three weeks now. The bill, I must say, is imposing. On top of which I note that you spent three nights this week in a suite at the Ritz-Carlton in San Francisco."

She resisted saying, *So what?* "I had business in the city."

"Business." Her mother enunciated the word as if it were impossible that Joan could ever engage in such a thing. "Be that as it may, our cash-flow situation is such that we must exercise some restraint. Double-booking suites at two luxury hotels is no longer permissible, at least not at present."

Permissible? "Are you telling me to move out of the Lodge?"

"Joan, Henry and I have had your home thoroughly cleaned, from top to bottom. It is absolutely pristine. Still, if you are not comfortable returning there, you are always welcome to stay with me here on 17 Mile Drive."

Joan narrowly avoided rear-ending a black Mercedes sedan. *I would rather die than live with you!* "I don't want to move out of the Lodge," she said, but somehow it came out wrong, making her sound like a petulant child stomping her foot.

Her mother was silent but Joan got the message loud and clear through the humming airwaves: *You don't have a choice.* Libby Hudson was trustee. Joan merely received an allowance. She might as well be six years old getting her coins doled out on Saturday morning.

"Oh, dear, I'm going through a bad patch," Joan lied. "I can't hear you. 'Bye." Then she pressed the end button, opened the Jag's passenger-side window, and with all her arm's strength flung the cell phone into the foliage that lined Highway 1. That was the end of that conversation.

CHAPTER NINETEEN

Alicia couldn't believe how busy a nominally unemployed person could be.

She opened a package of ramen into boiling water, then sprinkled dried basil and oregano on top and set it on medium heat. Lunch would have to be a twenty-minute affair given her 12:30 PM telephone appointment with Franklin Houser, the scion of the Idaho family that had sold Headwaters to Daniel Gaines and Web Hudson two and a half years before.

She was starving. She'd spent the morning, in fact most of the week, at the public library, poring over microfiche news stories on the transaction. There wasn't much to be found, since the company was privately held, and the grunt work of digging up what did exist was laborious. But Alicia guessed it was a far sight better than bouncing off the walls of her house.

Besides, what else could she possibly be doing? She had filed her suit for wrongful termination. Louella was pursuing the case file from Massachusetts on Theodore Owens' felony conviction. How could she not keep trying to nail Joan Gaines?

Milo Pappas had been completely on target not to believe she'd lost interest in the case. In fact, *interest* didn't nearly describe how she felt. *Obsession* came closer. And the notion of vindication that he'd kept throwing around had begun to sound pretty good, too.

Not like any of this was easy. She was on her own now.

Gone were the D.A. office benefits of free phone and fax and photocopier. Gone were the cops and the D.A.'s investigative arm. Whatever help she could get from anybody now would come by way of favors, which she'd never been good at asking for. And she was up against a suspect who had all the world's power and money at her disposal.

Safe to call it an uphill battle.

Alicia grabbed a box of Triscuits from the cupboard and turned on her kitchen TV for the noon news. News watching was another big unemployment activity. On Tuesday she'd been forced to suffer through endless coverage of Treebeard's probable-cause hearing, complete with Kip Penrose and Rocco Messina out on the courthouse steps in full strut. Of course, with all the evidence against Treebeard, which she'd lined up so neatly, he was bound over for trial. Yet Penrose looked as if he'd just outdone Mark Spitz and won nine gold medals in the Summer Olympics.

To make matters worse she couldn't stop herself from watching Milo's reports on the story. They were good. Quite good. And you couldn't look away while he was on-screen. At least, she couldn't.

She gave the ramen one final stir, then transferred it to a bowl and carried it to the kitchen table, a Formica-topped rectangle that would fit right into Dudley's. She grabbed some crackers and started eating.

Yet however compelling she found Milo Pappas, on and off the air, his "proposition" remained as baffling as it had been when he'd first offered it. Apparently his reporter crony spilled her phone number as well as her address, because Milo Pappas called her at least once a day. His frequency was right up there with Jorge's. It was, she had to admit, fun. He kept insisting they work together on the Gaines murder; she kept insisting she couldn't trust him. It bothered her that at some point he'd give up trying to convince her. Probably some point soon. She didn't like the idea that he'd stop calling, that she'd no longer have something he wanted. It also made her feel like she was still in some sort of cosmic professional loop to know where he was jetting off to to cover his stories. He was in San Francisco now, after getting a break on a banking story he'd been pursuing. Before that he'd been in Seoul, and before that San Diego.

She poured the last of the ramen down her throat and set the dirty bowl in the sink. Unfortunately, the Triscuits box was now empty, as her cupboards would soon be. She would be forced to go grocery shopping and spend money she didn't have. The only good news was that on sale, ramen went for only a dime a package.

Time for the call. On went her telephone headset, one of the few items she'd taken from her office. Lots of things she'd left, as it felt too much like surrender to empty her desk entirely. She scanned her list of questions, made sure her pen worked, then punched in the Boise area code and number.

A woman answered, presumably a housekeeper. "Houser residence."

"This is Alicia Maldonado with the Monterey County district attorney's office. Mr. Houser is expecting my call."

"Just a moment, please."

Alicia didn't mention that at the moment she was persona non grata in the D.A.'s office. Or, for that matter, that she was no longer prosecuting Daniel Gaines' accused killer. She "withheld" that change in status, as Milo Pappas himself might have done. When she booked the call, she'd wrapped herself in the cloak of the law—which she still felt justified wearing—and spewed forth a litany of arguments that persuaded old man Houser to speak to her.

Of course, it helped that no one else from the Monterey

County district attorney's office had gotten to him first. Not Kip Penrose, certainly; not Rocco Messina; no one. Nor had Milo Pappas. Alicia told herself that no one else was investigating as thoroughly as she was. She preferred that interpretation to the other likely possibility: that it was patently obvious there was nothing to be gained from this line of inquiry.

But who knew? She'd heard of more than one family business that had provided a motive for murder. And while she had found an opportunity for Joan Gaines to have killed her husband, she hadn't found means or motive. Not yet.

"Ms. Maldonado?" Mr. Houser's voice was a strong, vital sound, despite his nearly eighty years. Alicia had gathered from their earlier conversation that he was an impressive man. He'd founded Headwaters Resources in the fifties and put his lifeblood into it, intending to pass it on as a family business. But his only child was killed in a skiing accident, leaving Houser no heir to take over. Hence the desire, as he neared the end of his life, to sell.

"I appreciate your taking my call, Mr. Houser."

"My pleasure. I enjoy speaking about my business successes from the deep, dark past."

Alicia began with routine questions about how Daniel Gaines had approached him. There was some discussion of the bankers from Whipple Canaday, who were heavily involved in the transaction. Houser took her back to the summer day when Daniel Gaines and Web Hudson had flown up to Boise to finalize the deal.

"What was your reaction to Daniel Gaines when you first met him?" Alicia asked.

"Oh, he was nice enough. Tall, good-looking man, had a kind of movie-star charisma. But it was because the governor was involved that I was interested."

"Governor Hudson? Why is that?"

"Now, he was one of a kind. Quite a record he had, as governor of California, then US senator. Smart, too, smart as a whip about business, even though he'd spent his whole life in politics. Him I wanted to do business with."

"So you were much more taken with Mr. Hudson than with Mr. Gaines?"

"No question. Don't get me wrong, Daniel Gaines seemed pleasant enough. But not really sharp, not in the way Web Hudson was. In fact, I don't think I would have done the deal if the governor hadn't been involved."

Interesting. She arched her brow, scribbling on her legal notepad. This jibed with her own low opinion of Daniel Gaines, whom she'd always suspected of riding his father-in-law's coattails. Maybe this explained why Web Hudson had been involved in the Headwaters purchase in the first place. It had perplexed her why the former governor would be brought in if he had no business experience and Daniel Gaines was such a high-flying Manhattan financier. But clearly Franklin Houser, and perhaps other people in business, didn't think Daniel Gaines was such hot shit on his own.

Houser continued speaking. "I have to say I was disappointed to find out that the governor would play only a figurehead role in the company. Once the transaction was completed, that is."

"What do you mean?"

"Well, the governor would be chairman of the board. And Gaines CEO."

She was confused. "But was the governor's role bigger while they were actually buying the company?"

At that Houser started laughing. "Ms. Maldonado, Daniel Gaines would never have been able to buy my company without his father-in-law."

She frowned. "Why is that?"

"Because the governor put up the money!" Houser laughed again. "Look, I sold them Headwaters for a hundred million dollars. This was a leveraged buyout, so they financed a great deal of the necessary capital. Two thirds. But they needed to come up with one third in cash, roughly thirty-four million. Do you know how much Daniel Gaines put up?"

"No."

"Four million!" Surprise was evident in Houser's voice, even after all this time. "And I found out later that even *that* he had to finance."

She was scribbling furiously. "Are you saying that Web Hudson put up thirty million dollars of his own money and Daniel Gaines put up four million he had to borrow?"

"That's correct. And the governor gave Gaines quite a sweet deal even on top of that."

"How so?"

"It was in how they divvied up ownership of the company. Heads up, Gaines' four million translated to an equity stake of a little less than twelve percent. But he ended up with twenty-five percent, thanks to the governor. Granted, it was Gaines who paved the way for the transaction, but nevertheless I was very surprised by the governor's generosity."

Houser fell silent. Alicia's pen flew across her legal pad. So Daniel Gaines put up almost none of his own money and ended up owning twenty-five percent of Headwaters Resources? She wished she had a father-in-law like that. "Mr. Houser," she said a few seconds later, "how do you account for it?"

The old man emitted a drawn-out sigh. Through the phone line Alicia imagined him deep in thought, choosing words, trying to explain. Finally he spoke. "Ms. Maldonado, I believe it comes down to simple human emotion. The governor didn't have a son. I believe Daniel Gaines took the place of the boy he never had." He paused. "I lost my own son. I can understand the feeling. But frankly, what saddens me is that I'm not convinced Gaines appreciated what the governor did for him. He didn't exhibit the gratitude that personally I would have liked to see."

Alicia ended the call soon after. Left in her mind was a highly unflattering picture of Daniel Gaines.

***

Milo sat in a stiff-backed Federal chair, a reporter's notebook in his hand, his knees inches away from the shapely legs of one Molly Bracewell. Mac was posed just behind Milo's right shoulder, his broadcast camera mounted on a tripod and pointed directly at Ms. Bracewell's perfectly made-up face and stylishly short blond hair. Tran buzzed around setting up lighting. Their own gear was much more likely to create a positive effect than her office's overhead fluorescents.

"I appreciate your taking the time to allow me to interview you this morning," he told her. How true that was.

"My pleasure." She smiled.

He guessed she spoke the truth, too. For Ms. Bracewell was giving him a look Milo recognized only too well. In this case, he was grateful that he'd morphed into the new, monkish Milo. For if he were still the old, rakish Milo, he might have been tempted to get to know her a little better, if only to ascertain exactly where she hadn't had plastic surgery.

For Molly Bracewell was a "done" woman. All America had witnessed the transformation. It wasn't quite as dramatic as the metamorphosis Linda Tripp, Monica Lewinsky's fair-weather friend, had undergone, but it was impressive. Shortly after she masterminded the winning campaign of Nevada's current governor, she went under one of Beverly Hills' most skilled knives and emerged a new woman. True, the rejuvenated Molly Bracewell wasn't a natural beauty, but surgery had transformed her from moderately attractive to damned good-looking. She had an easy femininity about her as well, and was exceedingly well-groomed.

"What is your official position with Governor Steele's campaign?" Milo asked.

"I function as the strategist." She rose to allow Tran to string a lavalier microphone up her sleek, teal-colored jacket. "Brandon and I worked together before, you know, when he ran for mayor of San Diego."

"Of course." And of course Steele had won.

Molly Bracewell had let no moss grow beneath her stilettos. Milo's sources told him that Gaines couldn't have been dead more than forty-eight hours before she lined up her next gig. And that was with the incumbent governor, Gaines' most serious competition. She'd kept mum on her new job until a seemly two weeks passed, but then made sure Steele held a splashy news conference to announce that he'd brought her on board. Different parties, rival candidates, opposing platforms meant nothing to her. All she cared about was riding a horse that would win. Milo both admired her ambition and found its nakedness off-putting.

She resumed her seat, her mike wired. "So *Newsline* had been planning to profile Daniel?"

"It was under discussion before he was killed, yes."

She arched her brow. "But you still want to do the story?"

"It's no longer a profile of Daniel Gaines but a broader look at the governor's races in the western states."

Tran interrupted. "I need to check volume levels. Ms.

Bracewell, would you please count to ten?"

Tran fussed with the knobs on his audio box until he was satisfied with the result, then put Milo through the same exercise. There was some strain between correspondent and crew since the showdown at WBS headquarters, but Milo trusted that with time and exemplary behavior on his part, that would pass.

Molly Bracewell pulled out a compact to do one last pre-taping check of her already flawless face, then looked past the metallic sphere to meet Milo's eyes. "I hope you'll come back to Sacramento to interview Brandon." She smiled.

"I would love the opportunity." Milo smiled back. He was walking a thin line here—exercising professional charm without raising other, more personal expectations—but knew he'd be much more likely to get what he wanted out of Molly Bracewell if she were predisposed toward him. That would be true both when the camera was running and when it had stopped. Now was not the time to rob her of any illusions.

Mac spoke up, the soft whir of his camera audible in the silent office. "We've got speed."

Milo nodded. "Let's get started."

An hour later Milo regarded Molly Bracewell across the booth they'd secured at Il Fornaio restaurant, a few blocks from Steele's campaign headquarters near the state capitol building. The restaurant was housed in a grand, high-ceilinged space, and attractively outfitted with tufted chocolate-brown banquettes and big Italian ceramic pots holding gargantuan sprays of exotic flowers. Yet his companion was no less impressive than the decor.

Molly Bracewell had proven herself a fabulous interview. She was better than most of her candidates at generating perfect sound bites. Ask her a hard question and she concocted a response that managed to sound both believable and sincere, all while keeping her cool as the lens zoomed in on her features.

They were past the first course and into their entrees. Pasta with Maine lobster and brandy sauce for her; garlic sauteed prawns and roasted potatoes for him. Pellegrino for both, this being lunch and a workday.

Milo judged that by now, Molly Bracewell was sufficiently comfortable with him to delve into the tawdrier gossip. "So," he said, "tell me what it was really like to work with Daniel Gaines."

She arched her tweezed brow. "Off the record?"

"Of course."

"Even off the record," she said, a teasing glint in her eye, which clearly had been enhanced with an aqua-tinted contact lens, "I'm reluctant to tell you what I really think. It's terrible form to malign the dead."

"Was he that bad?"

"Oh"—she made a dismissive wave of her hand—"he was hopeless. If he weren't Web Hudson's son-in-law, he wouldn't have had a chance in hell of getting elected dog-catcher."

Milo sipped his Pellegrino. "What was his problem?"

She began ticking off on her manicured fingers. "A, he wasn't that smart. B, he thought he was. C, he was bad at taking direction. And D, he had absolutely no discipline."

"Why did you work for him then?"

"Because he was going to win." She leaned across the white linen, her manner conspiratorial. "He had movie-star looks, connections to die for, no pun intended, and an enormous amount of money backing him up." She fell back against the banquette. "I never have that much to work with."

Molly Bracewell was silent for a moment, dabbing the white linen napkin at the edges of her very pink lips, then spoke again. "Of course, those connections were a double-edged sword."

"What do you mean?"

"Well." She leaned forward again. "His wife was a disaster. She was a total wild card. We were constantly worried she'd derail Daniel somehow." Then her features contorted and she slammed backward into the banquette, hiding her face under her right hand. "Oh, my God, Milo, I am so sorry. I forgot you two were involved once."

Apparently Ms. Bracewell was a tabloid reader. Well, she did need to keep her finger on the pulse of the nation. "That was a long time ago," he said mildly.

She peeked at him coyly from under her hand. "No hard feelings?"

He spread his hands as if in innocence, then laughed. "I'd love to hear more."

"Hm." She lowered her hand and shrugged. Molly Bracewell clearly enjoyed the gossip game, which at that moment was good news for Milo. "Well, I would say that Joan Gaines had a loose grip on reality. I remember Daniel telling me that she'd asked him if he married her only because she was Web Hudson's daughter." She shook her head. "He laughed and laughed, then said to me, 'What other reason could I have had?' I felt sorry for her that day, which believe me was a rare sensation."

Milo, too, felt a pang for Joan, but it was fleeting. At this point he was more inclined to wonder whether that painful exchange had given Joan a motive for murder. He eyed Molly Bracewell, who clearly was primed to share confidences. "Were you and Daniel close?" he asked.

She laughed. "Do you mean were we having an affair?"

Blunt little vixen, wasn't she? "Not to put too fine a point on it."

"No, we weren't, though he was certainly more than willing."

"And you?"

She leaned forward. "Milo, if I slept with every"—she paused—"*politician* who asked me, I'd never get out of bed."

Again she smiled. Milo smiled back, though he found it an odd and uncomfortable sensation. The old Milo invariably fulfilled this sort of promise; the new one would back off.

He topped off her Pellegrino from their shared bottle. "What about his father-in-law? What did you think of him?"

"Oh, he was marvelous. Brilliant. Totally out of Daniel's league. But I have to tell you"—and her voice took on a note of genuine surprise—"he had a blind spot where Daniel was concerned."

"Why do you say that?"

"Do you know he named Daniel trustee of his living trust?"

"You're kidding." Milo frowned. "I would've thought he would have named his wife."

"He should have." Molly Bracewell shook her head. "Because I got the distinct impression that Daniel went wild with that money. I know he did something with the trust that really pissed Joan off. They had an enormous argument. She even moved into a hotel for a few days."

"Do you know what it was about?"

"I wish I did."

"When was it?"

Molly Bracewell narrowed her eyes. "I did specify off the record, Milo."

"I realize that, Molly. Don' t worry." He gave her his most convincing smile. "I'm just curious." This time he did the leaning forward. "Didn't you want to know what it was about?"

"Of course I did." She kept her gaze level. "But Daniel died before I could pry it out of him."

Milo caught his breath. "So this happened—"

"Not long before he was murdered." She paused. "About two weeks before."

They were silent for a time, eyeing each other. The lunchtime crowd buzzed around them, claiming tables, exiting tables, eating, laughing, chatting. Oblivious to the life-and-death questions that hovered like a shadow over the third booth by the east window.

It was Molly Bracewell who spoke first. "I thought the same thing that you are, for about thirty seconds. But it's got to be Treebeard. The evidence against him is overwhelming. You know, his lawyer came to see me."

"Jerome Brown?"

"Nice guy. But he's clutching at straws." She laughed. "He was trying to find out if I was pissed at Daniel. Me! Why would I want Daniel dead? I was planning to ride that horse all the way to the White House."

Milo kept his tone mild. "Since there's all that DNA evidence against Treebeard, maybe Brown is thinking Treebeard might have been framed."

"Well, maybe he was. But you have to be smart to set somebody up for murder." Molly Bracewell raised her index finger in the air. "And knowing Joan Gaines the way I do? That woman is not capable of pulling something like this off." She shook her head in a vigorous motion that brooked no argument. "If Treebeard didn't do it, I applaud whoever set him up. They were brilliant. And believe me, that doesn't describe Joan Gaines."

Milo nodded. He wouldn't think so, either. But so much lately was different from what it had appeared to be.

***

Joan paced the cream-colored carpet of her master bedroom, very surprised at the e-mails she'd been reading on Daniel's desktop computer. They actually made her think more highly of him. Who would have thought Daniel was clever enough to devise a way to give Headwaters a cash infusion that required only some surreptitious tree cutting? A bit of work on the side that several Humboldt County lumbermen apparently were quite willing to perform? Then a quiet shipment or two overseas, the details of which Daniel had already ironed out?

Yet here was this clever plan, "all teed up" as Daniel liked to say. True, it was risky. It was dangerous. But it had one characteristic Joan believed true of the best schemes and the most convincing lies: supreme boldness.

Ideas began to percolate in her head as she gazed about her master bedroom. She was back in her home again, thanks to her mother forcing her out of the Lodge. If only her father had named her trustee after Daniel! Then she would have much more control over her financial fate. At least this bedroom was a joy. She'd allowed Daniel to have the first floor done in the contemporary style he so admired—all metal and glass, the only colors neutral taupes, grays, and whites—but her taste reigned supreme in the bedrooms, where she'd gone wild with Italian Provincial furnishings and yellow, blue, and green Florentine prints. At the moment she was clashing wildly, dressed in her red silk peignoir, but she was sick to death of wearing black.

She shivered and drew the thin fabric closer around her body. It was disconcerting how she felt Daniel all around her in this house. They had never been together at the Lodge; there it was almost as if he had never existed. But here ... She could imagine him at any moment emerging from the master bathroom, his powerful body wrapped in a white towel, his pectoral muscles flexing as he towel dried his thick blond hair. Or she could hear him striding across the oak hardwood of the first floor, talking loudly into the cordless phone, conducting a meeting with campaign aides grouped in the living room. In the last weeks of his life, this house had been a cauldron of activity. Now it was silent. And empty.

Outside the bay window, the sun was gone from the sky, though a residual orange glow rose from the surface of the Pacific. The usual assortment of joggers, gawkers, and dog walkers made their way along Scenic's curving path, high on the bluff.

Joan forced herself to walk out of the master bedroom and back down the long corridor to Daniel's home office. Again she sat down in front of his computer, set up just as it had been when he was alive. It gave her the creeps. Piles of campaign stationery were still stacked on the desk, the "Gaines for Governor!" letterhead cheering at her in red, white, and blue. This afternoon was the first time since he'd died that she'd bothered to boot up the computer. Some mix of boredom and curiosity had prompted her to probe what secrets it might contain. And led her to ... this.

The basics were simple. She'd learned them from Daniel. The Forest Service prohibited logging companies from cutting trees more than thirty inches in diameter—the so-called ancient trees—to protect the irreplaceable old-growth forest. The loggers didn't like that because it meant that the biggest and most valuable trees were off limits. Tensions ran high on both sides because so few of those trees were even left. But everyone understood the regulations, and flouting them meant both stiff penalties and a public outcry, neither of which wanna-be politician Daniel Gaines would tolerate.

What Joan hadn't known was that however valuable those trees were in the US, they were worth scads more in Asia. She laughed out loud. There were a few suggestive emails from a Mr. Fukugawa in Tokyo to prove it. Of course, she had to read between the lines, because this Fukugawa fellow was smart enough not to spell everything out. Thank God! Otherwise the cops might have gotten a whiff of what was about to begin.

And Daniel had figured out how to spin it if he ever got caught. He would claim either that the trees were dead or that he was conducting "fire-risk reduction," which gave him leeway to chop them. And make a killing! Hundreds of thousands of dollars per tree. After the lumbermen got their take, that certainly would have helped Headwaters' bottom line.

Daniel must have been seriously worried about the red ink, she thought, because this was a risky proposition. He'd always made a big show of claiming that Headwaters was environmentally responsible. But what if one of the lumbermen squealed? Or got greedy and said he would squeal if he didn't get more money?

Joan looked up from the computer, overcome by a rare wave of admiration for her husband. This was a ballsy scheme. It saddened her to think he had concocted it without breathing a word to her. True, he never talked to her about the business, which she always resented. After all, she almost had her MBA! Her eyes teared with renewed anger. They might have been a team, like her parents, if only Daniel had let her in.

She wanted a glass of wine. She geared herself up to walk downstairs to the kitchen, which unfortunately was right next to the library. These days she spent virtually all her time on the second floor. She hated being downstairs, where everything had happened. She left Daniel's office and padded downstairs on her bare feet, clutching her peignoir around her. Her pace accelerated as she neared the library.

It was hellacious even being close to that room, though she had to admit there was no longer any evidence of what had happened there. Her mother had been true to her word and made sure of that. Still Joan shuddered. The crimson pool on that Bokhara rug she would never forget. But the Kashan that replaced it was unmarred, and gorgeous against the built-in oak bookcases that rose floor-to-ceiling on three of the four walls.

Into the kitchen, where the chardonnay was chilling in the Sub-Zero. Joan poured herself a glass, then began her return trip. Just as she rocketed past the front door, the doorbell rang.

Damn. She halted, then stood on tiptoe and raised her eye to the peephole. *Double damn.* It was her mother.

"Joan?"

Her mother either had heard her footsteps or seen her swish past the front window, dressed, unfortunately, in a bright red peignoir. *Triple damn.*

"Joan, open the door, please."

Disapproval was writ large on Libby Hudson's patrician face when Joan reluctantly pulled open her front door. "You're in your negligee," her mother announced, sweeping past her into the foyer. "Did you even bother to get dressed today?"

No, she replied silently. "What do you care whether I did or not?"

The older woman's brow arched, even as her eye dropped to the wineglass in her daughter's hand. "And you're drinking."

"It's not exactly ten o'clock in the morning." Joan raised

the glass as if in toast. "Care to join me?"

"I think not." Libby Hudson clasped her hands in front of her as if she were about to address a panel of committeewomen. "But I did want to tell you that I have learned what you are up to with Headwaters."

Here it comes. Joan set down her wineglass and crossed her arms over her chest. "You're referring to the fact that I'm selling the company? Who did you hear that from?"

"It hardly matters. The point is that I am astounded you made this decision without discussing it with me beforehand."

"You're no longer a shareholder."

"I can only suppose that you tired of the company as swiftly as you have tired of every other enterprise you have ever undertaken."

"And you wonder why I don't discuss things with you?" Joan was horrified to feel tears not far behind her anger. "Why should I when I know you'll disapprove?"

A light flush suffused her mother's cheeks, which surprised Joan. The older woman trained her gaze on the hardwood floor. "I am very sorry if I give you that impression." She sounded distinctly awkward, even stiffer than usual. "And I do not care to fight with you, Joan. Despite what you may think, I wish only the best for you, and always have."

That left Joan at a loss for words. She watched her mother turn to go, then halt at the front door, still with her eyes averted. Again her tone assumed the harsh edge Joan was used to, which actually came as a relief. They were back on familiar ground.

"But I must register my disapproval of this surreptitious behavior," her mother said. "I would appreciate that you not blindside me in the future."

Out she strode, leaving Joan frustrated and restless. With nothing better to do, Joan retrieved her wineglass and climbed the stairs, returning to the master suite's bay window. One of California's most spectacular vistas spread out grandly before her.

She was at her mother's mercy. Her mother, who treated her as a recalcitrant child. Her mother, who had forced her to move out of the Lodge against her will. Her mother, whose arthritic hand was wrapped so tight around the living trust's purse strings, it might as well be a death grip.

Wouldn't extra cash help get Joan out from under her mother's thumb? Surely independence required risk. If Daniel could manage such risk, she could.

Joan decided quickly. She would call this Fukugawa fellow, then go to Humboldt County to meet with the lumberman Daniel had lined up to lead the cutting team. Perhaps en route she'd spend a night at the Ritz in San Francisco. That was always nice.

Joan sipped her chardonnay, relishing both the buttery taste and her mother's disapproval. She would book a suite at the Ritz for sure. There wasn't the least question about that.

CHAPTER TWENTY

Part of Alicia couldn't believe she was doing what she was doing. A greater part couldn't stop herself.

Her silver VW was one of hundreds of vehicles inching north along the S curves that signaled 101's final approach to the city of San Francisco. To her right across four lanes of freeway hulked Potrero Hill, a residential district where property values waxed, then waned, with the Bay Area's roller-coaster Internet fortunes. A mile and a half ahead the tightly grouped skyscrapers of the financial district poked into the twilit sky, the towers aglow with rectangular squares of light for those office workers still at their labors as the six-o'clock hour neared. Behind downtown a bank of fog huddled over the cityscape like a cottonball giant, obscuring everything from Russian Hill west to the Pacific.

Over the phone Milo had instructed her to take the Fourth Street off-ramp, then make her way through the financial district to the eastern slope of Nob Hill and the Ritz-Carlton Hotel. He had been in the city for a shoot, he'd told her, and though his crew had already flown south to Los Angeles, where he would follow the next morning, he had that evening free. He had a room at the Ritz and had booked a second one for her, his treat. It was both to prove his goodwill and to give them an opportunity to trade information on the case. He had learned a great deal from interviewing Molly Bracewell, he said, and had made dinner reservations at a restaurant called Hawthorne Lane, which he liked very much and hoped she would enjoy as well.

A sign ahead directed Alicia to stay on the right as the off-ramps to downtown approached. Her VW crept forward, surrounded on all sides by vehicles battling for every suddenly freed inch of asphalt. She made her way past the Seventh Street exit, her heart pumping a nervous rhythm.

Of course she'd been skeptical of Milo's invitation, and of course she'd resisted it strenuously, though even as she'd concocted one reason after another why acceptance was impossible, she knew pretty quickly she desperately wanted to go.

She was thirty-five years old and had never received such an offer in her life. And as her mother routinely reminded her, she was not getting any younger.

Besides, she told herself, what did she have to lose? Milo had already divulged several tidbits of information that she hadn't known; maybe he'd spill more. And despite his stated desire to "trade," she didn't have to reveal a damn thing she didn't want to. Already he had told her that just weeks before the murder, Daniel had done something to anger Joan so intensely that she'd moved into a hotel for a few days.

Could it be true? Alicia had consulted the MasterCard bill she already had on hand for Joan Gaines, and sure enough, there in black and white was a charge from the Lodge in Pebble Beach, dated December third. Alicia hadn't noticed it before, being so focused on Joan's charges for the night of the murder. But here was apparent confirmation of what Milo had learned, and what could be the beginning of a trail leading to a motive for murder.

Next Alicia had called the reservations desk at the Ritz-Carlton to confirm that there was a room booked under her name. Indeed there was. That had sealed the deal. One hour of painful packing later—her wardrobe too pathetic by far for what she imagined the Ritz-Carlton and Hawthorne Lane to require—she was on the road.

All along the route, she told herself this excursion would aid her investigation into Daniel Gaines' murder. All along she told herself that was the only reason she was making it, to pursue justice and restart her prosecutorial career. And all along she knew she was doing a poor job of fooling herself.

By now she was off the freeway and zooming along city streets past Moscone Center, the Museum of Modern Art, and the Yerba Buena Center for the Arts. Office workers spilled out of bars drawing Thursday night happy-hour crowds. Commuters bundled against the fog huddled at bus stops and hurried along wide sidewalks. Alicia supposed the goal for many of them was a quiet evening at home, maybe a little homework with the kids, maybe a little TV.

She winced. In fact, a quiet evening alone was what she had told Jorge she needed, when he'd called asking her to dinner. She didn't care to probe why she hadn't told him the truth, that she had a business meeting in San Francisco relating to the Gaines murder. Jorge knew she hadn't abandoned investigating it, and he was such a dear man he even encouraged her in the pursuit. Yet she had lied to him, throwing his goodwill back in his face.

At the crest of Nob Hill, Alicia turned right from Pine onto Stockton and then onto the gentle sweep of drive that fronted the Ritz-Carlton. Almost before she'd stopped the car, a uniformed valet opened the driver's-side door and offered a hand to help her exit. "Welcome to the Ritz-Carlton, ma'am. Will you be staying with us this evening?"

"Yes, thank you." She surrendered her key, accepted a stub in trade, and tried not to grimace as yet another valet hefted her battered fifteen-year-old Samsonite out of the trunk. Then she turned to face the hotel's imposing stone facade.

No wonder Milo likes this place, she thought. *It looks like a Greek temple.* In fact it bore an astonishing resemblance to pictures she'd seen of the Parthenon. It even had columns, which she'd seen before only on the courthouse. But this enormous, grand, floodlit structure put that building to shame.

To Alicia's eyes, the inside was no less spectacular. It was like an extraordinarily gracious home, with ornate crown molding and marble floors partially covered by Oriental rugs. On the walls hung oil paintings of women in white dresses. Crystal chandeliers twinkled, a jazz pianist entertained cocktail drinkers, and exotic flowers sprang from enormous ceramic pots. It was as though the cares of the real world were a million miles away.

Her reservation was in order, and she had a message, a note scrawled in Milo's hand.

Alicia, my shoot will run till after seven. Relax and enjoy. Let's meet in the lobby at ten to eight to go to the restaurant. Cheers, M.

Alicia stuffed the note in her handbag and followed a bellman as he guided her to the elevators. The enjoying she'd be able to manage. The relaxing wouldn't happen.

***

Shortly before eight o'clock, Milo entered a wood-paneled elevator on the Ritz-Carlton's eighth floor and pushed the button for the lobby. He was excited. All day he'd thought about Alicia. Interviewing bankers, he'd thought about Alicia. Shooting his stand-ups—one in front of the Bank of America building and another on the Embarcadero—he'd thought about her. She'd danced in and out of his head: infuriating, stubborn, unbendable Alicia. He wondered if he'd like her any other way.

Clearly she'd thawed toward him in the nearly two weeks since he'd shown up unannounced at her home. The fact that he'd gotten her to join him in the city proved that. How much she'd warmed up he couldn't gauge. Was this just a business trip for her, a chance to further her investigation of the Gaines murder by finding out what he had learned? Or was it possible that she, too, harbored a more personal ulterior motive?

He found her standing in the lobby next to a marble column. He smiled at the sight of her and saw that he wasn't the only man to do so. For though she hailed from dowdy, prosaic Salinas, that night Alicia Maldonado pulled off a good imitation of a sophisticated San Franciscan. On top of the huge advantage of natural beauty, she had the good sense to keep the adornment minimal. Her clothes were understated and black, her hair loose and long, and her makeup so sheer as to be almost transparent.

"Hello." He strode toward her and extended his hand.

She took it, a slight reserve in her demeanor. "Hello."

"I hope I haven't kept you waiting."

"I just came down myself."

He extended his arm toward the doors. "Shall we?"

She walked ahead of him without comment. They joined the short queue for taxis. "Are you enjoying the hotel?" he asked.

"It's lovely. Thanks for arranging it." She raised her eyes to his. "I'm going to reimburse you."

"No"—he waved a dismissive hand—"I won't hear of it."

"But it's too much."

An extra room at the Ritz wasn't a stretch for him, but he didn't want to seem so cavalier as to dismiss it as nothing, either. "It really is my pleasure. And it gives us a chance to catch up on the case."

At that the dark depths of her eyes lit with interest. "I take it you got a lot out of Molly Bracewell."

"I did." The next cab was theirs. Milo tipped the bellman and slid next to Alicia onto the battered Naugahyde seat. "Hawthorne Lane," he directed the driver, who promptly sped down Nob Hill and cut across Market Street into the South of Market area. "But let me tell you about it over dinner."

Minutes later he regretted not telling her about it straightaway, because he was having trouble thinking up other topics of conversation. He kept getting distracted by the sweet scents of rosemary and mint wafting from her hair every time it was ruffled by the wind sneaking through the cab's slightly open windows. "Our restaurant is in a building that used to house a newspaper," he said finally.

"Really?" She sounded interested, which encouraged him.

"In the twenties it was the home of the *San Francisco News*, which eventually merged with the *Call Bulletin*. These days there's a fine-art printer upstairs." The cab turned in to narrow Hawthorne Street, then made a right into the even more constricted alley called Hawthorne Lane. Milo paid the driver and they exited the cab. "It's a landmark building, one of the best examples of the period's industrial-style architecture." They stared up at the redbrick, warehouse-style structure.

"You sound like a guidebook." Alicia's tone was wry. "Do you always know so much about the restaurants you go to?"

"It's the reporter in me. Besides, after coming here so often I finally asked." He put a guiding hand on her back to lead her up the few stairs to the entry. "Please."

The interior was sleek and contemporary, softly lit and paneled in cherry wood. They were led to a booth in a large, high-ceilinged room with an open kitchen at one end, complete with chefs wearing toques, a wood-burning oven, and gleaming smoke hoods.

"It smells fantastic," Alicia murmured.

Milo noted that the waiter smiled at the comment, or perhaps at her. He seemed to lavish undue care to draping the linen napkin over her lap. Once he bustled away, Milo eyed the wine list. "They have Opus One."

She shook her head, clearly uncomprehending.

"It's a cabernet. Not much is produced so it's hard for restaurants to get." And at nearly two hundred dollars a bottle, not for the slim of wallet. "Will you share it with me?"

"Sure." She set aside her menu. "So, Milo Pappas, you know all about this building. You know all about the wines on the list." Gently she tipped toward him the porcelain charger at her place setting. "What can you tell me about this?"

"Designed by the owner. Continuing the autumn theme you'll find throughout the restaurant, in both color and pattern."

She laughed. "Are you making that up?"

He tapped his index finger against his head. "Like Sherlock Holmes, I don't just see. I observe."

"Hey!" Her tone was fake indignant. "I'm the detective here."

"Really?" He leaned forward. "So what have you discovered about Joan Gaines and her nefarious deeds?"

"We only suspect they're nefarious."

"I'm gratified to hear you say 'we.' "

"For the moment you're on my good side."

"It's a nice place to be."

They stared at each other, before the waiter interceded to take their wine and dinner orders. He returned quickly to make a proceeding of uncorking and serving the Opus One.

Milo raised his glass in toast. "To cooperation rather than competition."

She clinked her glass against his. "Like the Americans and the Russians."

He held off from sipping. "They have rather an uneasy truce, Alicia."

Her eyes narrowed, though teasingly. "So do we, Milo."

They sipped, still staring at each other, until Alicia looked away. Somehow Milo felt he had gained still more ground. He leaned forward and lowered his voice, giving her a smile that had warmed many a female heart. "You know, I'm not such a bad guy."

She shrugged. "I've decided you're probably not an accomplice to murder."

"That's as far as I've gotten?"

"Believe me, that's progress."

She was a tough one. He made his voice challenging. "All right, Ms. Brilliant Detective, what have you learned about Joan?"

"You first."

"You're going to get cagey on me?"

"Listen, buddy." This time she leaned forward. "You got me to San Francisco promising information. Now spill it."

He leaned back. "All right, in honor of our shaky detente, I'll start. Joan told me she and Daniel had an unhappy marriage."

"That's not exactly a news flash. It's obvious Joan wasn't happy." She made a *Come on, come on* motion with her fingers. "Give me something else."

He didn't want to go too far with this but didn't want to clam up too quickly, either. "Molly Bracewell told me that Daniel Gaines propositioned her but that she refused him. So Joan may have been telling the truth when she said she went back to Carmel the night of the murder to see if Daniel was with Bracewell."

"What did you think of Molly Bracewell?"

He thought for a moment. "Smart. Capable. Extremely ambitious. Bit of a snake."

"What does she think of Joan?"

"Her opinion isn't high. She thinks Joan is too stupid to have framed Treebeard for Daniel's murder." He sipped his wine. He wasn't sure he agreed with Bracewell on that one. "Your turn."

Alicia seemed to weigh her words carefully. Then, "Bracewell's alibi is watertight. She couldn't have been physically present at the murder." She paused. "I don't think she had anything to do with it."

"I never thought she did." He narrowed his eyes. "What aren't you telling me?"

Alicia's gaze slid away. Their appetizer, a cheese souffle, arrived. Milo directed the waiter to set it in the center of the table, then urged Alicia to try it.

Her eyes closed as she chewed. "It's fabulous. It tastes like cheesy air."

They ate for a while, then he repeated his question. "What aren't you telling me about Bracewell?"

They were getting down to brass tacks. Clearly she was mulling over whether to confide in him or not. Then, finally, she told him something he didn't know.

"Treebeard said that the day before the murder he received a letter on Gaines campaign stationery asking him to the Gaines house the next night to try to hash out their differences."

That was interesting. "If that letter really exists, obviously it was sent by the person who framed Treebeard for Gaines' murder."

Alicia nodded.

"Where is it now?"

"Treebeard says he lost it. But he described the letterhead perfectly."

"Who does he say signed it?"

"Molly Bracewell."

Milo watched her. "You believe him."

She said nothing.

"But you don't believe Bracewell had anything to do with it." Could Joan have sent such a letter? Clearly Alicia thought there was a good chance she had.

Alicia was silent for some time. The souffle was cleared; salads were placed before them. Both left them untouched.

"There's a lot that's very ugly about Treebeard," she said eventually. "It's easy to believe he's guilty of this murder, given not only the evidence but his character. But it's people like Treebeard who made me become a prosecutor."

"What do you mean?"

She shook her head. "Where I grew up, I saw a lot of people get victimized and not know how to do anything about it. They got robbed or they got assaulted and they just ate it. They didn't know how to file charges, or they didn't speak English, and the cops didn't always explain things. I don't only blame the cops, though, because they had way more than they could handle." She paused. "It was just a lot of unfair stuff. People got screwed every day. They got screwed by life."

"You think that's what's happening to Treebeard?"

"He's an easy mark." She shrugged. "All I can say is, I hear his story and something in me believes him." She raised her eyes to Milo's. "And I'm not exactly easy to convince."

His mind was working. He had to be careful here. "So you see that as part of your job? Trying to make sure people don't get screwed by the system?"

"You make me sound like an idealistic fool."

"Not a fool. But—"

She cut in. "Idealistic? I probably am. Given all the shit I see I'm amazed I can be." Abruptly she picked up her fork and dug into her salad. He took her cue and for a time they ate in silence. Just as abruptly she started speaking again. "I probably lost my elections for that reason."

"You ran for office?" This was another revelation. "What did you run for?"

"Judge. Twice."

So she'd lost twice. Somehow that didn't surprise him. She could be unyielding and politics was a dance of compromise. She also had that enormous chip on her shoulder when it came to the wealthy and powerful, who often had a lot to say about who won elections. "Why did you lose?"

"Because I don't suck up. I get in people's faces. I think it's more important to do the work than to network."

He smiled at her. "You're not very cooperative, either."

The look she gave him was far less withering than it might have been a few weeks before. "You're suggesting I'd go farther if I were?"

He spread his hands as if in innocence. "Hey, you can practice on me."

Then her eyes turned playful. "I already am."

By the time they finished their entrees—grilled lamb chops for him and a tenderloin of beef for her—their truce had solidified into a straightforward give and take. Milo had divulged everything he learned from Molly Bracewell and in turn been rewarded with several tidbits from Alicia's conversation with Franklin Houser and more details on her jail-house interview of Treebeard.

It was win-win, as he had known it would be. He was invigorated, as he had expected.

Their vanilla bean brulee arrived. Like the souffle it was set in the center of the table for them to share. Milo laughed watching Alicia dig into its hard caramelized surface. "You're a beer drinker, a meat eater, and a dessert lover."

"What can I tell you? I believe in real food."

This was one refreshing woman. *Where was the hard-boiled prosecutor?* he wondered. *Where was the closed-faced attorney?*

She looked up from the brulee. "So why did you tell me before that you need a killer story?" She set down her spoon and leaned her elbows on the table, her eyes curious. "Aren't you way too big a star to have to be a good reporter?"

This was not a subject he cared to delve into. "Let's just say my star isn't quite as high as it used to be."

Her brows arched in clear surprise. "You're having trouble with your higher-ups? I would think you'd be a master schmoozer."

"Thanks a lot."

"I mean it as a compliment. I was even thinking you could, I don't know ..." Her voice trailed off. She retrieved her spoon and took another bite of the dessert. He had the sense she was deliberately avoiding his eyes. "Maybe give me a little advice."

He was immensely flattered. *"You're* asking *me* for advice?"

She raised her eyes then. "Don't make this harder for me than it already is, Milo."

"All right." He thought for a moment. It occurred to him that he couldn't even remember the last time he'd been asked for his counsel. "I would say there's a difference between being true to yourself and being stupid. Pardon the choice of word," he added, as she opened her mouth to object. "What I mean is, you can make strategic compromises. It doesn't mean you're selling out. That's what I believe the most effective politicians do."

She nodded. Clearly she was listening intently, which he found very satisfying. He realized that few people paid him this much attention.

"There's something else," he said. "Life is a series of small steps forward. It's trite but it's true. Success works the same way. Take it one small step, one small challenge at a time."

"Now this I'm having trouble buying." The spoon went back down beside the nearly empty brulee. She leaned her elbows on the table. "You're not exactly an expert in the slow rise, Milo. You had a huge boost by being born your father's son."

"Maybe less of one than you think."

"What do you mean?"

"True, my father was in the diplomatic corps, and at the end of his career he held a prime post, ambassador to Washington. But he was not a wealthy man."

She clearly had trouble buying that. "But don't you pretty much have to be wealthy to be an ambassador? I mean, that's the way it works in this country."

"My family has a distinguished history, that's true. We're aristocrats, I guess you'd say. But the bulk of the family money was gone before my father's time. He had to work for a living. Because of the family, he had a lot of friends who created opportunities for him, which he made the most of."

She was very still. "What about you?"

He leaned forward. "You and I have that in common, Alicia. I have to work for a living, too."

She spoke softly. "I'll be damned."

He raised his hands. "Hey, don't get too comfortable. I'm still a member of the despised ruling class."

She tossed her napkin at him across the table. He caught it. "Shall we order a nightcap? Maybe a glass of port?" They'd been dining for over three hours but he didn't want the evening to end. It was a weeknight and he had an early flight the next day, but at the moment he didn't care.

"Sure." So she didn't, either. He ordered; their glasses arrived; again they raised them to toast. "My turn," she said, then clinked her glass against his. "To strategic compromises."

He smiled, and sipped. Around them the restaurant was emptying. It was late. It was time for rock-bottom truths. "So, Alicia."

She gazed at him over her port, a wary look in her eyes. "What?"

"Why'd you always give me such a hard time?"

She arched her brow. "Milo Pappas, you don't know what a hard time is."

"No, seriously." He kept his tone light but he really wanted to know. "From the first day I met you, you were always a little distrustful of me, a little suspicious. Why is that?"

She eyed him. He could tell she was deciding whether this was a time for truth or for fiction. Finally she spoke. "You were a little too slick. A little too good-looking. A little too sure of yourself."

"That works for most people."

She said nothing.

"Not for you, apparently."

She shook her head. "No, not for me."

"And now?"

Their eyes met. The couple at the table nearest theirs rose and headed out. Their section of the restaurant was empty.

"I guess," she said, "I know now there's someone real

under all that gloss."

He had to laugh. "There sure is."

"It's funny." She cocked her head, swilling the port in her glass, rich and crimson. "My father would be thrilled I was having dinner with someone like you. A big TV news star. An ambassador's son." She shook her head and raised her eyes to his. "He'd think he'd done his job well."

Milo watched her. Clearly her father had. "He would have so many reasons to be proud of you, Alicia."

She said nothing. Milo had the sudden impression that she was struggling not to cry. "He died at age thirty-six." Her voice was so soft he had to lean in close to hear her, even in the empty room. "He didn't live long enough to see me become a lawyer."

"Somehow I bet he knows you did."

"Sometimes I feel like I failed him. By losing those two elections."

"You didn't fail him, Alicia."

"He always wanted me to be a politician, a big Latina politician." She kept speaking, almost as if to herself. "He had a shitty life. And he was only one year older than I am now when he died."

"He couldn't have had a shitty life." Milo had no knowledge of Alicia's father yet felt perfectly confident making this pronouncement. "He had you for a daughter."

She raised her eyes to his then, and they were brimming. Milo felt a jolt pierce his own soul. "That's what he said to me once. He said I was the great joy of his life."

That was so easy to imagine. To his astonishment, Milo felt his own eyes tear, partly for Alicia, partly for the father he wasn't so sure was proud of him. Wordlessly Alicia grasped his hand across the small table. For a time they both just held on. Their waiter moved past, not stopping.

A second later Milo squeezed her hand. "I hope he doesn't think we're crying over the food."

She smiled, a weak but dazzling smile he could look at for a long, long time. "I should go fix my makeup."

"There's no need. You're beautiful." That wasn't a line, he realized, not an exercise of his easy charm. That was truth.

She squeezed his hand back. There was truth in that, too. And promise.

***

Alicia thought later how odd it was that she and Milo behaved like strangers in the cab back to the hotel. They maintained a public decorum, even an indifference, never talking, never touching, erecting a facade of placid companionability that belied what surged beneath.

When they arrived back at the hotel, she followed him wordlessly. He did not ask; she did not answer. She was beyond such mundane arrangements. If he was using her, then she was using him. It was a trade she was willing to make. Choosing his room gave her the power to retreat, should she feel the need. Escape she could well imagine, a midnight flight down the carpeted corridors back to her own room, if the abandonment of her good sense suddenly became too much for her. Or if he did.

Once alone, they faced each other. His kiss was a marvelous thing, delicate and learned, excruciating in its subtlety. Demanding, too, and ultimately frustrating, like an overlong first act to a play so ripe with promise. There was greater reward when more than mouths were involved, when her sweater was pulled over her head and her bra unclasped and tossed aside, when his fingers found her breasts, then guided his tongue there, to wreak havoc with her memories of what past men had done to her, as if they were mere amateurs and here she had found a master player.

They were standing, though unsteady on their feet. Perhaps the unreliable tectonic plates beneath Nob Hill were choosing that reckless hour to shift and resettle. They collapsed onto the bed, feathery beneath them. She would not allow only her own skin to be exposed to the night air; she was curious, too; his clothing was a hindrance she had no interest in accommodating. Off it came, exposing a body she had pictured in her mind's eye yet whose details captivated her. He was as beautiful as she had imagined, his rampant desire for her more than enticing.

He was hard to control, though. He was not satisfied with a half-dressed woman; that he quickly made clear. He wanted her naked; this was not a man satisfied with half measures. She could not hide her distension, the moisture he had called up in her. It was his to play with and heighten. His tongue was a wanton invader in her private places, a teaser that lapped and lunged and titillated all while she both urged him on and tried to corral him, her hands clenched in his dark curly hair.

That game had to stop, too. Neither wanted to play it to its obvious conclusion. There was too tempting an alternative.

She forced him onto his back, which startled him at first. Yet judging from the glint in his dark eyes, she knew he would play the game her way, at least for a time. Their need was so great, or perhaps it was because they fit so well, that they forged together with exquisite ease. She rode him teasingly at first, then with more purpose, her head thrown back, his hands on her breasts, then on her hips, forcing her to pummel him with greater urgency.

She had guessed right; he would not let her finish what they'd started. He claimed that as a man's right. He toppled her onto her back. She responded by twisting her legs around his torso. He answered that move by pinning her arms against the pillows.

Maybe they would have reached even greater heights had they been able to control themselves. Such a delirious game sometimes ended too soon, especially the first time it was played. But they were spent when it was over, and entwined, and soon asleep, damp and comfortable. Until the next wave assaulted them, just before the dawn.

CHAPTER TWENTY-ONE

"More coffee?"

Milo poised the silver pot over Alicia's cup, as empty as the Ritz's Terrace restaurant. It was so early it was still dark outside the windows, which overlooked a sizable redbrick courtyard. He could hear the hiss of the sprinkler system dampening the shrubbery that rimmed the perimeter, and farther away the clang of a cable car as it climbed California Street.

"Please." She smiled, and nudged her cup and saucer closer.

He refreshed his own. "Thanks for getting up so early."

"What time's your flight?"

"Nine." Down to LAX, for a follow-up piece in Pasadena on the New Year's Eve terrorist bombing four weeks before.

Alicia rose from her chair. "I'm going to get more eggs from the buffet. Do you want something else?"

He was still hungry. "I'll take another blueberry muffin."

"You're going to single-handedly clean the place out."

He patted his abdomen, as flat as it had been at age twenty. "I'm trying for a gut like Aristotle Onassis."

She rolled her eyes. "That'll help your TV career."

His TV career was the last thing on his mind at the moment. His far greater worry, as Alicia strolled toward the buffet, was what in the world was he going to do about this woman.

So much for his hiatus from those of the female

persuasion. It had been as short-lived as one of Joan's "projects." Yet he knew this was much more than a dalliance. He was well beyond intrigued when it came to Alicia Maldonado. In fact, he was loath to leave her to fly to LA for his story. He'd begun to plot and plan when he might see her again. He was stunned to find himself trying to concoct a way around their bicoastal lives, and tossed around the idea of suggesting she apply for a job in D.C.'s district attorney's office.

This was not Milo-like behavior, particularly for a woman who blew to smithereens his usual ideal of blond, willowy, and pampered. Moreover, he had no idea how she felt about him, which put him at a highly unusual disadvantage. She made no declarations of love, asked no questions about the future.

She returned to the table bearing his muffin and cocked her head at the window as she sat back down. "Too bad it's too cold and dark to eat outside."

"It's sort of like a garden in here." The restaurant was a riot of prints and stripes, all green and yellow, every inch of surface covered with fabric or wallpaper or carpeting. "You should stick around the hotel this morning. Get some more sleep. Checkout's not till noon." He had an irrational desire for her to return to the bed they had shared, as if somehow that would keep her close for a while longer.

"I might." Then she raised her head and squinted at something behind him. "My God," she murmured, "look what it says in that man's newspaper."

He swiveled in his chair. The headline on the far right column screamed at him: "Headwaters Resources to IPO."

"Isn't that the *Chronicle*?" Alicia said. "Don't we have a copy?"

Milo was already reaching to extract it from the briefcase

at his feet. He quickly found the business section, and the Headwaters story on the third page.

Alicia rose to read the piece over his shoulder. "Whipple Canaday's doing the transaction," she said. "That's the same bank Daniel and Web Hudson used when they bought Headwaters from Franklin Houser."

Milo scanned the article. "There's a quote from Joan. 'My husband ran Headwaters with the same vigor and vision he applied to all his pursuits. I believe a public offering of the company he loved is the best way to continue his legacy. It also has the great advantage of allowing all Americans the opportunity to participate in its future success.' " He shook his head. "She can really shovel it when she wants to."

Alicia sat back down. "Isn't this awfully fast?"

"It's amazingly fast. Gaines has been dead only a little more than a month."

"She never said anything about this to you?"

He tried to remember. "One time she said something about Headwaters. But never anything about going public." It had been a gorgeous December morning, the morning of Treebeard's arraignment. He and Joan had been eating breakfast on the terrace at the Lodge. Those were details he would not share with Alicia. "She said she was going into Headwaters that day, and something about the way she said it made me wonder if everything was all right there. I remember her telling me she wasn't sure if it was or not."

"It can't be in too bad shape if it's going public." Alicia was frowning. "I wonder if this is connected to the big fight Joan and Daniel had in early December. Because her taking the company public so soon after he died seems very odd to me."

"I agree. But Molly Bracewell told me that what pissed Joan off had to do with the trust, not Headwaters." Milo set aside the newspaper, his mind working. "You know, this helps us."

"How?"

"Because companies preparing to IPO have to release scads of information to the public. There's something called an S-1 filing, I remember my brother Ari telling me. He's an investment banker in London."

"Then this will help." Alicia pushed back her plate, a light growing in her dark eyes. "It's been so damn hard to get information on that company."

He glanced at his watch and grimaced. It was already past seven. "I'll call Ari and ask if he can find out anything about it. Or put me in touch with someone who would know something."

She was chewing on her lip. "Maybe I should be the one to talk to your brother. Your shoot's all day, right?"

It was. And it would be a tough one. And the new and improved Milo Pappas must not allow himself to be distracted. "Would you mind?"

"Of course not. Would you call him first to tell him who I am?"

He smiled and leaned closer. "And who exactly would that be?"

Clearly he'd caught her off-guard with that one. She looked away, her brow furrowed.

He grasped her hand. "How about I describe you as 'a very good friend'?"

She raised her eyes to his. "What's that a euphemism for?"

"It's for 'fabulous woman I can't wait to see again.'"

Her features relaxed. "That doesn't sound too bad to me."

He made a dramatic clutch at his chest. "'Doesn't sound too bad'? Alicia, you're killing me here."

"You'll live." Her smile widened. "Now write down Ari's number. You've got to get out of here or you're going to miss your plane."

He jotted the number on the back of a business card, then had the presence of mind to record another series of digits as well. "I'm giving you my calling-card number," he said. He didn't want her saddled with the long-distance charges for a London call. Then he had another brainstorm, which he was both hesitant to mention yet reluctant to abandon. He lowered his voice. "Alicia, do you need a little something to tide you over?"

Her response was instant. "No."

"Are you sure? Because I am completely happy to help. I know you have obligations to your family on top of everything else. Honestly, I'd be glad to help."

This time she was silent. He took that as an opening and reached back down into his briefcase for his checkbook.

She shook her head. "I feel very weird about this."

"Don't." How much? He didn't want to insult her, yet wanted to be genuinely helpful. He settled on two thousand dollars and began to make out the check.

Then he heard a female voice, not Alicia's, from very nearby. His hand froze.

"Well, doesn't this beat all."

No. It couldn't be. It wasn't possible. But then he heard it again. Disdainful. Snide. Unmistakable.

"Isn't one of you going to say you're surprised to see me?"

Slowly he raised his head to see Joan standing beside the table, wearing an expression of such triumph, such contempt, such utter superiority he was rendered speechless.

She raised her hand as if to forestall him. "Please don't let me interrupt you. I can see you're conducting business." She glanced down at Alicia. "Payment for services rendered?"

He found himself on his feet. If Joan hadn't moved so quickly, he thought he might have punched her. But she had already skittered away, deeper into the restaurant, smiling as if to maintain the public fiction that all was right in her world.

Smiling with her mouth, that is. Because her eyes held a cold, malevolent promise.

Joan turned her back on them then. Milo's heart thudded against his rib cage. Vaguely he was aware of Alicia speaking to him in a soothing voice that failed to have anything close to the desired effect.

"It's all right, Milo," she was saying. "It's all right. It doesn't matter."

But it did matter. For sure it mattered. Because Joan would come after him. Somehow.

***

As Joan exited the Ritz-Carlton's circular drive onto Stockton Street, her Jag's tires screeching on the asphalt, she tried to convince herself that all she felt was anger. Anger was an emotion she could manage these days. Anger didn't require a Xanax or a glass of wine or a massage. Anger fueled her. It made her bolder and more active. Anger was far superior to hurt, or bewilderment, or fear, all of which lurked beneath her rage like a festering malignancy, threatening to burst forth and destroy her if she didn't maintain control.

Well, she would be active now. She made a left onto California Street and climbed Nob Hill. She gathered speed despite the steep ascent and hurtled past a cable car offloading tourists bound for Chinatown, their heads swiveling to watch her as she careened past. Her own goal was 101 North and her tete-a-tete in Humboldt County with the Headwaters lumberman primed to perform the extra tree felling she wanted done. She had a second goal as well, devised the instant she had left Milo Pappas staring after her in the Ritz-Carlton restaurant.

Joan abruptly pulled over to the curb at the crest of the hill, oblivious to the outraged drivers forced to maneuver around her in the heavy flow of traffic around the Fairmont Hotel and Grace Cathedral. She had no choice but to stop driving. She was too enraged to do more than one thing at a time, and one task above all others had become paramount. Her anger made her fingers tremble so uncontrollably it took her several seconds to gather herself sufficiently to punch the correct buttons on the car phone.

Though she wasn't master of her body, Joan was in complete possession of her wits. She knew exactly what she wanted to achieve, and she knew exactly how to do it. She would have done it before, but lacked the ammunition.

No longer. Milo Pappas had not only handed her the gun, he had loaded its chambers.

"Operator," she said once she had a line, "connect me to the WBS television headquarters in Manhattan. To the news division," she specified.

Milo had been worried about losing his job before? Well, she'd make sure he really had a reason to worry now.

***

Alicia cleared quickly out of her room in the Ritz-Carlton, too much a bundle of nerves even to consider going back to bed. Before she left she spoke to Milo's brother Ari, whom she caught in his London office. He told her that for some years companies had been required to file their IPO documents electronically and that he'd already confirmed that

Headwaters' information was on-line. She jotted down what she needed to know to find the Web site herself, then thanked him and called down for her car. In minutes she was on city streets headed for 101 South.

But no amount of dodging and weaving would get her home quickly. She'd forgotten she was driving straight into the morning rush hour, as fearsome an opponent as the prior day's evening commute had been. And stop-and-go traffic did nothing to aid her personal equilibrium.

She'd been on this freeway a mere fourteen hours earlier but it might as well have been a lifetime. On this, the morning after, she ricocheted between elation and panic. Had she reached new heights of idiocy to sleep with Milo Pappas? Had she reached a new moral low by cheating on Jorge? Was she streamlining or sabotaging her investigation into Joan Gaines by cooperating with Milo? Was he the most wonderful man in the world or the worst scoundrel imaginable? She had different answers by the mile, all of which rang alternately true and false. On some level she thought it was pointless even to ask those questions. She'd done what she'd done. Whether it was stupid or smart she'd have to live with the repercussions.

Traffic eased fifty miles or so south of San Francisco, past San Jose. She was able to do the second half of the trip in half the time it had taken her to do the first.

As she screeched to a stop on her own driveway, she spied a delivery on her stoop. She climbed out of the VW and approached it cautiously, like it might detonate. She was amazed it hadn't been stolen or broken or somehow otherwise destroyed.

Two dozen roses, long-stemmed, bloodred, in a vase sporting a huge white bow. Her fingers were cold as she opened the tiny parchment card, attached to the bow with an old-fashioned hairpin. *I miss you already, M.*

She let out a shaky breath, admonishing herself for a brief surge of disappointment. *He didn't tell me he loves me.*

A second, more combative inner voice had a ready answer. *Why should he? You don't know how you feel.*

That wasn't entirely true. She knew something of how she felt: alert, giddy, terrified, deliriously happy, fretful. In other words, a goner where Milo Pappas was concerned.

She carried the roses inside and set them on the coffee table, staring at them for some time before she forced herself to step away. Then she booted up her computer and within minutes was on-line and had located the Web site where Headwaters Resources was cut open and dissected for prying eyes to see.

Given what she didn't know about business, much of what she read made little sense. Yet a good bit of it was fairly easy to understand. The company was described, along with its business strategy and competitive strengths and market position. What jumped out at Alicia came under organization and ownership.

She read through that section, then read through it again. There it was, in black and white. At the end of November, Daniel Gaines bought Web Hudson's stake in Headwaters Resources and became the company's only shareholder.

Alicia raised her head, trying to take that in. Less than a month before he was murdered, Daniel Gaines came to be the sole owner of Headwaters. Good-bye, Web Hudson, without whom Gaines never would have been able to buy the company in the first place.

And how much did Gaines pay for his father-in-law's stake? Thirty million dollars. Alicia knew from Franklin Houser that thirty million was exactly what Web Hudson had paid for it two and a half years before. So thanks to Daniel

Gaines, Web Hudson's estate got zero return on that investment. Zero return for Web Hudson's making it possible for Daniel to buy the company in the first place. Zero return for being so generous as to double Daniel's stake from twelve to twenty-five percent. Zero return for treating his son-in-law like the son he never had.

You didn't need an MBA to know that Web Hudson's estate got screwed.

For a time Alicia was baffled. If the estate of Joan's late father owned the stake, how did Gaines even have the authority to sell it? It took her a while to remember what she had learned the night before, what Molly Bracewell had told Milo: that Gaines was trustee of Web Hudson's living trust. That meant he controlled Web Hudson's assets, one of which was the stake.

That realization made Alicia's mind work so quickly she had to bound out of her seat to pace her front room. On the face of it, it certainly looked like Gaines had violated his fiduciary responsibility to his father-in-law's estate. He feathered his own nest to the detriment of the living trust. And what else had Bracewell told Milo? That Gaines did something with the trust that made Joan so angry she moved out of their house into the Lodge. Now Alicia knew that happened mere days after this transaction. Probably Joan found out and went ballistic.

It wasn't hard to imagine that this might make Joan pretty damn mad. What a slap in her father's face. What bald greediness on her husband's part. What contempt for the older man's memory. Not even to mention the negative effect on the trust's bottom line, and thus on its two beneficiaries: Joan and her mother.

The phone was ringing. Again. It had been ringing a lot, and whoever was calling wasn't leaving a message. This time

Alicia ran to the kitchen to answer. It was Louella.

"Where the hell have you been?" A very het up Louella, not so much mad as excited. "I've been calling all morning!"

"I've been out." That was a lame excuse but Alicia knew Louella would highly disapprove of her little assignation in the big city. "Why? What's up?"

"Can I come over?"

"Sure, but—"

"I'm coming over." She hung up. Alicia rolled her eyes and went back to the computer. There was one piece of the puzzle she was missing. Where had Gaines come up with the thirty million to buy his father-in-law's stake? Because when he and Web Hudson acquired the company, Gaines couldn't even come up with four million.

After ten minutes of trying to make sense of five years' worth of spreadsheets, Alicia found an entry that pulsated in front of her eyes.

She stared at it. In late November, Headwaters took on additional debt. How much? Thirty million dollars. And what was the purpose? To repurchase Web Hudson's shares. Making Daniel Gaines the company's sole shareholder.

The pieces clicked into place in her mind. Daniel Gaines was both buyer and seller of his father-in-law's stake in Headwaters. He could set the price, and he could accept it.

It could not be more obvious. It added up. It was appalling, yet made sense. Daniel Gaines certainly had been a hotshot financier here. He'd parlayed four million dollars of borrowed money into sole ownership of a company valued at more than a hundred million dollars.

Yet it might have cost him his life.

Alicia could just imagine Joan's reaction. Joan could well think that Daniel had stolen Headwaters from her family. She would be furious. Yet what could she do about it?

She couldn't get far by divorcing him. Given California's community-property laws she'd get only half the assets from the marriage. And Daniel would walk away with a huge windfall, at her family's expense.

But if Daniel died? She'd get it all. Most spouses without children left everything to the surviving spouse. And even if by chance Daniel Gaines had no will, California law required that everything go to his widow.

The doorbell rang. Alicia ran to her foyer and flung the door open. Louella stood on the stoop. "You will never believe what I've found out about Daniel Gaines," Alicia said.

But Louella just pushed past her into the house. "And you will never believe what I've found out about Kip Penrose."

Alicia shut the door. "What?"

Louella turned around in the front room and held out a manila folder. "It finally came in. The file on Theodore Owens' felony conviction. From Massachusetts, twelve years ago. Guess who prosecuted the case?"

Alicia raised her hands to her face, reading the truth in Louella's eyes. "Oh ... my ... God."

"You got it, kiddo. One of the up-and-coming assistant district attorneys in Worcester County at the time. Who later moved to California." Louella slapped the file. "Kip Penrose."

CHAPTER TWENTY-TWO

As Joan sped the Jag north along 101 deep into the heart of Humboldt County, she was reminded that this part of Northern California did not possess the charms she typically sought in her destinations. True, the highway was lined with coastal redwood, which she found herself appreciating more than usual, but there wasn't a single five-star hotel or restaurant for hundreds of miles. People here enjoyed natural beauty, apparently, which was all well and good, but Joan rather preferred man-made attractions. The big draw in these parts seemed to be the rumored appearances of Bigfoot, a.k.a. Sasquatch, a manlike beast that topped nine feet, weighed over seven hundred pounds, and reportedly suffered from fairly severe body odor.

Joan feared the lumberman she was driving to meet would match much the same description.

She careened along the narrow curving highway in an uneasy silence. She'd long since turned off the radio, frustrated that all she could find on the dial were preachers and country-music stations. Every once in a while the fog billowed so thickly she was forced to slow down, which both relieved and irked her. At one and the same time, she wanted to get this meeting over with and yet didn't want it to begin. It was nerve-racking. What was the protocol in such a situation? Thanks to Daniel's earlier efforts, the lumberman had already agreed to involve himself in this enterprise, so she didn't have to convince him. In fact, over the phone he'd told her with obvious pride that he'd long ago assembled "a team o' good hardworkin' men," which she supposed he thought would reassure her. What she wanted to hear was that they were men who knew how to keep their mouths shut. Of course, that was in part what the cash was for.

Ten thousand dollars, in neat bills newly extracted from Wells Fargo Bank and now conveniently tucked into a business-size envelope in her handbag. The money had come from one of her personal accounts, where Mr. Fukugawa already had wired his promised down payment of twenty-five thousand dollars. And there were several multiples of that to follow when the first shipments arrived in the port of Tokyo. This afternoon she would do her own cash handoff to lumberman Hank Cassidy, make the final arrangements, and get this operation going.

It was really happening. Her mother couldn't stop it, even if she knew about it. Nobody could. Joan supposed it was juvenile to derive such satisfaction from doing things Libby Hudson would disapprove of, but there it was. This was Joan's small way of declaring independence, which she'd thought she'd done numerous times before but which somehow never seemed to take.

Joan saw from a white-on-green highway sign that she was fast approaching the town of Redcrest. She had to focus so as not to miss it; sometimes these towns went past before she even knew she'd hit them. It was quickly obvious as she slowed the Jag that Redcrest was a major stop for tourists out to see the Avenue of the Giants, a thirty-mile scenic drive boasting some of the biggest, oldest redwoods in the state. Given her own intentions in Headwaters' forests, it gave Joan the creeps.

It was easy to spot the Burlwood Cafe at Redcrest's main crossing; Hank Cassidy had given her directions from there.

She headed north and took the first right onto a dirt road that led straight into the woods. About sixty yards in she found the promised clearing, a black pickup truck, and Hank Cassidy. He was leaning against the truck chewing a weed, which he tossed aside when he saw her. Joan knew lumbering was a highly dangerous profession, and she regarded its practitioners as he-men of the first order. Tall, broad-shouldered Hank Cassidy fit the bill. She was surprised to find him fairly attractive, in a jeans, cowboy hat, and work boot sort of way.

He tipped the brim of his hat at her when she emerged from her car, an Old West gesture she rather liked, too. "Ma'am."

"Mr. Cassidy." She held out her hand, which he shook, briefly. He seemed to have his features permanently arranged in a half scowl, with frown lines deeply etched into his skin. Then he cocked his head to indicate the woods behind him. "Let's mosey on a little further back there."

So he wanted to be even more hidden. That showed caution, a trait she was happy to find in Hank Cassidy. Never having "moseyed" before, Joan tiptoed along the dirt, which she rapidly could tell would not be kind to her Cole Haan calfskin mules.

When they were twenty yards or so into the woods, Cassidy turned to face her. "Thought you'd be wearin' black."

She was puzzled. "You mean because I came from the city?"

"Because your husband's newly dead." The scowl deepened.

She had no idea how to respond to that.

But Hank Cassidy spoke into her silence. "Your husband understood the lumberin' business." Admiration was evident in his voice. "None of this fool worryin' about habitat or too much silt flowin' into the river, killin' off the chinook salmon or the steelhead trout. Not that I don't fish the Mattole River," he added, as if to forestall that horrifying suggestion. "But a man's gotta make a livin'. And sensible loggin' and sensible nature preservation can coexist side by side—that's what I say."

"I quite agree, Mr. Cassidy."

"Let's do our business. You got what we talked about?"

"Yes." She reached into her handbag, but Cassidy held up a restraining hand, his eyes looking past her at the clearing. "Wait—I hear somethin'." Seconds passed, while Joan struggled to hear anything other than the natural sounds of the forest. "Now," he said.

Joan found herself quite impressed at the speed and agility with which Hank Cassidy claimed the chunky envelope and slid it into the interior pocket of his well-worn sheepskin jacket. "You're not going to count it?" she asked.

His eyes got even narrower. "Doin' this kinda business, Mrs. Gaines, we best trust one another."

"Of course. I didn't mean to suggest otherwise."

He nodded. "That's that, then. My men 'n' I'll start this evenin'." He began to walk away.

"What? That's it?"

He stopped to look at her. Somehow she knew the phrase *fool woman* was lumbering across his brain.

"I mean," she hissed across the few yards that separated them, "you know what to do?"

"I went over all that with your husband, ma'am."

"Don't you need a way to contact me if you need to?"

For just an instant the scowl became something like a smile, though it was less of comradeship than derision. "Ma'am, I'll find you if I need you." Then Hank Cassidy tipped his hat at her again and went off on his way.

Well, apparently that was that. Joan began the return trip to her Jag, oddly reassured despite the brevity of their interaction.

Hank Cassidy seemed to know what he was doing. She watched him drive away, the tires of his black truck kicking up dust. In his own way, he struck her as a powerful man. And as Joan Gaines well knew, powerful men could handle their own business.

***

Kip Penrose sat at his desk, his manicurist at his side for his regular Friday 3 PM appointment, when his intercom sounded. He pulled back his right hand, whose nails the tiny Korean woman had been buffing, to press the intercom's little red button. "What is it, Colleen?"

"Mr. Penrose," she said, sounding unusually tentative, "people are telling me there's a press conference about to start on the courthouse steps."

She sounded perplexed, and so, he had to admit, was he. "A press conference? Called by whom?"

"That's the strange thing, sir." She paused. "It sounds like by Alicia Maldonado."

"How could *she* be calling a press conference?" he boomed. "She doesn't even work here anymore!"

A few beats of silence. "It is her, sir," Colleen then came back on to say. "It's been confirmed."

Kip fell back against the hard spine of his desk chair. Alicia Maldonado called a press conference? He didn't like the sound of that, not one bit.

His manicurist cocked her chin at his right hand. "Start again?" He barely understood a word she said, but she charged only eight dollars a visit and came to his office. You couldn't beat that.

"Not yet," he told her. Why in the world was Alicia Maldonado staging a press conference right under his nose? Possibilities sprang to mind, all of them highly disconcerting. Then he had an idea.

He pressed his intercom button. "Colleen, is Alicia actually on the courthouse steps?" Because if she was, he could throw a wrench into this whole thing. She had no right to be actually on the county property, using it as if she were a government employee. She wasn't anymore. He'd seen to that.

"No, sir," Colleen said. "Actually she's on the sidewalk. Quite a group of media she's drawn, too, sir."

Kip frowned. The sidewalk was public property. In other words, fair game. "Any sheriff's deputies out there?"

"Yes, sir. I'm told a few are keeping an eye on things."

Damn! Maldonado wasn't doing anything actually wrong, so he couldn't just stop her press conference from happening. So what was he going to do?

Terrifying ideas crashed through his brain. Had she figured out the truth behind Owens' felony conviction? Was that what she had assembled the media to announce? Kip had known that was a risk, but it was one he'd been forced to take to keep Joan Gaines happy.

Kip slammed his hand down on his desk. *Damn that Alicia Maldonado!* She was too smart for her own good.

His manicurist's voice piped up. "Start again? Start again?"

"No! That's it for today." He'd just have to live with five buffed nails and five unbuffed. That was the least of his troubles. He pulled a ten out of his wallet, demanded a dollar back, and sent her on her way.

After she was gone, he began pacing his office. How was

he going to find out what Maldonado was saying before it hit the news? He didn't want to stand out there and listen, like some fool who had no idea what was going on. It was highly upsetting how close to the truth that was.

Maybe the best thing to do was go home. He could slip out through the back door, drive home, and watch the news. Then he'd hear what Alicia Maldonado had said and how the reporters assessed it. After that he could craft his own response.

Kip stopped pacing, suddenly calmer. He'd always been good at putting a positive spin on events. Really, when it came down to it, that was how he'd gotten as far as he had. And who was he up against? A woman. A Hispanic woman. Lost two elections she should've won. Token all the way. He'd gotten the better of her once, and he could do it again.

Kip ran to his desk, pressed the button on his intercom, and tried to sound casual. "Colleen, I have a late-afternoon dental appointment. Please send all my calls to voice mail. I'll see you Monday."

Somehow he had a feeling she didn't believe him, but he couldn't worry about that. He grabbed his trench coat and briefcase, turned off his lights, and left, giving Colleen a businesslike nod.

Kip kept up a fast pace. The real challenge was not to get caught by a reporter between the D.A.'s office and his Mercedes in the lot across Alisal Street. He'd already decided that his best bet was to use the walkway from the west to the north wing, then exit onto Church Street. From there he could hightail it to the lot and hope to high heaven that no reporter noticed him, though he did have to get dangerously close to them at one point.

Out the D.A. office door. Across the red tile. Upstairs and through a few corridors to the walkway. Through the walkway. Downstairs, and to an exit.

Ah, fresh air. Kip crossed Church Street, his pace never flagging. He felt dampness in his armpits and under his suit and trench coat. By now his dress shirt was clinging to his back. Thank God it wasn't too far to the lot. The last danger spot was crossing Alisal. He arrived at the corner of Church and Alisal and glanced to his right. What he saw fifty yards away, right in front of the courthouse as Colleen had described, made his heart thump even more than his fast-paced escape: Alicia Maldonado in front of a pretty big crowd of reporters. She seemed to have their full attention. That was both good and bad.

Kip was forced to wait for the light to change. The flow of cars was too heavy for him to dash across the street, plus he might catch somebody's eye if he tried. As he waited he heard Alicia Maldonado's words wafting his way, as if carried by the wind.

His heart plummeted through his rib cage like a bowling ball through thin air. It was as bad as he had feared.

"—incontrovertible proof that D.A. Kip Penrose knowingly withheld information about a felony conviction that he himself won years ago in Massachusetts. This is a clear attempt on the part of the district attorney to thwart the course of justice, and to derail me, one of his own deputies, from its pursuit."

Finally the light in Kip's direction turned green. He leaped into the crosswalk, made it across Alisal quickly, and stepped onto the opposite curb. At that moment something, something perverse, made him glance behind him, and what a mistake that was. Because wouldn't you know it? He caught Alicia Maldonado's eye. She raised her eyebrows, clearly amazed to see him. Then damn happy. She pointed in his direction, and all of a sudden the reporters were turning their heads and staring at him, too.

One of them, Jerry Rosenblum from the WBS station, raised his hand in the air. "Hey!" he called. "Mr. District Attorney! Please wait up!"

But Kip had no intention of waiting up. He pointed at his watch, contorted his face into an expression of *Sorry, too busy to talk now!* and made for his Mercedes.

Oh, if only his Mercedes were close. Or if only life were simple. For some of the reporters were running, and some were already across Alisal—why did the light change for them right on cue?—then some of them were across Church, and before he knew it they were surrounding him, shouting questions at his face, their cameras shooting videotape of his fleeing form, as if he were a fugitive on the run.

"Why did you tell Deputy D.A. Maldonado to plea-bargain the Owens case when you knew Theodore Owens had a felony conviction?"

"Did you set Deputy D.A. Maldonado up for a firing she didn't deserve?"

"Do you have a bias against women prosecutors in your office?"

"How will you explain firing Ms. Maldonado to the Mexican-American Bar Association?"

He had answers to none of those questions. He simply unlocked his Mercedes, got in, and drove away, knowing that he had handed Alicia Maldonado one of her biggest victories ever.

***

Milo stood six feet in front of Mac's camera in Old Town Pasadena, ready to go live. A lavalier microphone was attached to his lapel, Southern California's midafternoon sun baked his shoulders, and his earpiece fed him the audio to the *WBS Evening News*, emanating that very moment from the network's Manhattan studios. Tran stood a foot behind Mac, shoulder strap holding up the audio box that rode on his hip, his eyes never straying from the little knobs and dials that adjusted his correspondent's sound quality.

A small crowd of gawkers eyed the proceedings, which were taking place in a town square where earlier that day California Governor Brandon Steele had held a press conference. As usual Milo enjoyed the onlookers' attention, though he couldn't shake the unease he'd felt ever since the run-in with Joan at the Ritz-Carlton in San Francisco.

In his earpiece he heard the director from the control booth back in Manhattan. "Forty-five seconds back." The newscast was more than halfway through its first two-minute commercial break. Milo would lead the "B" segment with his live package on Governor Steele's new antiterrorism program, which sought massive federal reimbursement. It was a big story, partly because California was an important state with lots of electoral votes and partly because Steele was positioning himself as the governor most willing to challenge the president on this issue.

Milo smiled to himself, guessing that Steele's campaign strategist, Ms. Molly Bracewell, was pushing her candidate in this direction. She was one woman who would relish facing down the current resident of the Oval Office if she thought it would gain her man any ground with the voters.

But Molly Bracewell made Milo think of Joan, and thinking of Joan made his smile fade.

She would seek revenge on him, he knew. For not only had he dumped her, he had committed the even greater sin of replacing her with a woman Joan regarded as beneath contempt. But what would she do? What *could* she do?

Bracewell's words raced across his brain, leaving dread in their wake. *She was a total wild card. We were constantly worried she'd derail Daniel somehow.*

And maybe she had, in the worst way possible. For a time Joan had loved Daniel; then she had stopped; then he had died. Where did that leave Milo? He didn't think Joan would try to kill him, but that morning her eyes had held a vow that she would hurt him if she could.

"Fifteen seconds back," came in his ear.

Focus. Milo nodded, raised his chin, and stared into the lens. His heartbeat accelerated, as it always did before going live. It wasn't nervousness so much as high alertness, the same adrenaline rush that fueled an athlete in the seconds before a competition, or an actor about to step onto a stage.

He was ready.

That is, until he saw Robert O'Malley stride into his field of vision and halt a few steps behind and to the right of Mac and Tran. Though Milo never looked away from the lens, out of the corner of his eye he could see O'Malley cross his arms over his chest. He could feel the heat of O'Malley's stare. O'Malley was in California. And he was going to watch the live shot from that challenging, in-your-face position.

Milo heard Jack Evans's voice in his earpiece. "Today in California, Governor Brandon Steele—" In seconds, Milo would be on. Through the thunder in his ears he listened for his cue, though part of his frazzled brain asked questions he couldn't begin to answer. *What in hell is O'Malley doing here? What does he want?*

For it had to be enormous to draw O'Malley across the country. O'Malley liked to stay put in New York, like a king in his realm, the better to protect his territory and massage the network relationships that kept him on his throne.

But Milo had to push all thoughts of O'Malley aside, for

soon he would be live and would not give that bastard the satisfaction of seeing him stumble. He focused on Evans' voice, now intro'ing Milo's segment. "—*Newsline* correspondent Milo Pappas joins us live from Pasadena with this report. Milo?"

He made his own delivery strong and sure. "Jack, Governor Brandon Steele tossed down a gauntlet today, one his campaign hopes the president soon will pick up."

In his earpiece Milo heard his package roll. He forced himself to practice his tag. He did not acknowledge O'Malley in any way. Seventy seconds crawled past. Milo waited for his own recorded voice to deliver his cue.

At which point he spoke. "Governor Steele has a tough campaign year ahead of him. He enjoys the advantage of incumbency, but along with that benefit comes the burden of a record his many challengers can attack. Milo Pappas, WBS News, Pasadena, California."

For a few beats he didn't move. He heard Jack Evans thank him, which he acknowledged with a nod. Then he heard the director again in his ear. "Thanks, Milo. Great job. See you next time."

Again Milo nodded, unable to find words to respond to that good-bye. He pulled out his earpiece and removed the mike from his lapel, handing both to Tran. Neither Mac nor Tran would meet his eyes. There was nothing for it now but to face O'Malley.

O'Malley cocked his head behind him, away from Mac and Tran, away from the jostling crowd. "Come with me," he said.

It's done, Milo thought, walking silently alongside his nemesis. *It's over.* It was like being led to execution, or slaughter. Man or beast, it was the same result.

They stopped beside an oak tree. Pedestrians sidestepped

around them, going into and out of the small stores and restaurants that lined the street.

"You've been fired," O'Malley said. "Effective immediately. That live shot was the last time you'll ever be on WBS air." He pulled a business-size envelope out of an interior pocket of his black leather jacket and handed it to Milo.

It was a termination letter, replete with what looked like all the requisite legalese. Moral turpitude was mentioned somewhere, along with unheeded warnings and failure to satisfy contractual obligations. It was signed by both Richard Lovegrove and a senior counsel with WBS's legal department.

"I've spoken with your agent," O'Malley was saying. "The contents of your office will be boxed and shipped to your home. I'll need your press pass and your WBS ID."

Milo didn't hand them over. Not that fast. "What's this all about?"

O'Malley looked surprised that he even asked. "You want the short answer? Joan Gaines called Lovegrove this morning. She told him you were diddling her and using her as a source. What, Pappas, did you forget the difference between pillow talk and off-the-record information?"

"What off-the-record information? She never said a damn thing to me that I used in my pieces!"

"Save it." O'Malley shook his head, a look of disgust twisting his features. "Lovegrove's warning had no effect on you, did it? If you had one brain cell in that pretty head of yours, you would've kept yourself zipped at least until the Gaines story was finished."

Milo clenched his fists to keep himself from punching O'Malley's smug, superior face. "You set me up, O'Malley. You were the one who forced me into covering Gaines' murder in the first place because you knew my history with

Joan would be a ratings grabber."

O'Malley just laughed, a wicked, triumphant sound. "I make no apologies for wanting to spike the numbers, Pappas. But I sure as hell didn't tell you to hump the widow. You came up with that idea all on your own." Then he leaned closer and dropped his voice to a confidential tone. "You know what's really rich? The widow said you were screwing not only her but some prosecutor on her husband's case. You never learn, Pappas, do you."

That last wasn't a question but a statement of fact. At the moment Milo couldn't dispute it.

"Come on, hand over your press pass and ID."

This time Milo relinquished them, mouthing words he wasn't sure he believed. "You can expect me to challenge this legally," he heard himself say.

O'Malley laughed again. "It's airtight. We have given you so many warnings and documented every one. Your ass is cooked. All you'll get out of filing suit are legal fees."

For once Milo thought O'Malley had spoken the truth.

"If you ever get another network job, which I doubt," O'Malley went on, "I suggest you leave your cock at home."

"You're an asshole, O'Malley."

"Maybe so." He leaned closer. "But I'm an asshole who's the executive producer of *Newsline*. Who are you?" Then he turned and walked away, slowly, casually. Milo watched him go.

He'd lost. He'd proved all his detractors right. Everybody who'd ever called him Pretty-boy Pappas had hit the target. Now they would crow and he would cry, and it was his own damn fault.

His. And Joan's.

CHAPTER TWENTY-THREE

It was almost ten Saturday morning when Alicia's doorbell rang. The five hours she'd already been awake had been an eternity of waiting. She flung the door open to find Louella and Department of Justice criminalist Andy Shikegawa on her stoop. She waved both of them into her front room.

"You got it?" she asked—needlessly, because Shikegawa's presence told her they had.

Louella turned around and brandished a white envelope in her hand. "Hot off the press."

"Can I see it?" Alicia took the search warrant with cold fingers. There it was, in legalistic black and white: permission to search Joan Gaines' house on Scenic for evidence relating to the murder of Daniel Gaines.

Not that the property hadn't been searched before. It had been, thoroughly, when Gaines' body was discovered. But perhaps some clue had been missed? Or was present now but hadn't been before? Those were long shots but all Alicia could hope for.

This search warrant was her last chance. For while she could argue that Joan Gaines had killed her husband, all that backed her up was circumstantial evidence. She needed something real, something tangible, something undeniable, to link the lovely widow to her husband's murder. Otherwise Treebeard would go down.

She handed the search warrant back to Louella. "Did

Frankel put up much of a fight?"

Shikegawa laughed. "Let's just say the good judge proved the old adage wrong."

They'd all heard it—and repeated it—a million times. *What do you call an attorney with an IQ of fifty? Your Honor.*

"Not that Frankel's convinced beyond a reasonable doubt," Louella added, "but she found all the new information about Headwaters and Web Hudson's living trust pretty compelling."

"And you convinced her to let me go with you?"

Shikegawa piped up. "That took a little more doing." Alicia was fired, after all, which made it highly unorthodox for her to be able to participate in the search. "But we made it clear that you were the one who came up with everything new."

"And, of course, she's known you for years," Louella added. "I also told her that Penrose had been discouraging you from pursuing Joan Gaines as a suspect. What came out in your press conference yesterday sure didn't hurt."

Shikegawa clapped Alicia on the arm. "You looked good on the news."

She rolled her eyes, though privately she agreed she'd done well. She was embarrassed that in the evening she'd pulled a Penrose herself: surfing among the local newscasts to find her own appearances, and taping a few for posterity.

Not that her own interlude of Penrose-like behavior made her any more sympathetic toward old Kip. As far as she was concerned he deserved whatever he got, and from the early noises people were making, that might be quite a comedown.

"I got to hand it to you, Alicia," Louella said. "Now you've even got me thinking Joan Gaines might have offed her husband." She turned and spied the roses, still in their position of honor on the coffee table, then bent to sniff them.

"These are gorgeous. That is really sweet of Jorge." She stood back up, her expression puzzled. "Did I miss your birthday?"

"No." Alicia did not want to get into this.

Louella gave Alicia a penetrating stare, then turned to Shikegawa. "Andy, why don't you go on ahead? Alicia and I will meet you there."

"Fine." Shikegawa moved toward the front door. "You called Carmel PD and the sheriff's department, right?"

Louella nodded. "Bucky Sheridan's on his way, and we'll get two squad cars from the sheriff's department to set up a cordon if we need it."

"Good." Shikegawa left.

Alicia ran to her bedroom to get her purse and overcoat, then headed for the door. "Ready?"

"Not so fast." Louella grabbed Alicia's arm. "You have such a guilty look on your face." She cocked her chin at the roses. "Those aren't from Jorge, are they?"

"I don't want to talk about it." Especially since she hadn't heard word one from Milo since he'd left her at the Ritz-Carlton the prior morning. Though she'd called his cell. Twice. And left a message both times.

"Who are they from?"

"Forget it, Louella." Though Alicia couldn't. She was back to feeling like a fool. A genuine, certifiable idiot. With an arrow piercing her own heart.

Louella shook her head. She looked, and sounded, highly dubious. "I hope you know what you're doing."

Alicia was silent. She hoped exactly the same thing.

***

"Is it me or is it hot in here?" Kip Penrose crammed his index finger between his Adam's apple and the collar of his dress shirt, then craned his neck, trying to give his windpipe some breathing room. Goddamn Saturday morning and he was dressed in a suit and tie and sitting in his office. Under TV lights that had to be making the ambient temperature ninety degrees.

"I'm fine," reporter Jerry Rosenblum declared, and Kip could've kicked him. Sure, *he* was fine. He was asking the questions, not answering them, and he was behind the lights, not under them.

It hadn't taken Kip long to decide he couldn't go through another news cycle without presenting his side of the Alicia Maldonado firing story, weak though that might be. Nothing could be worse than seeing himself portrayed either as an incompetent buffoon who couldn't remember whom he'd prosecuted in years past, or as a malicious bigot who would stop at nothing to get rid of a Latina on his staff. So this morning Kip was spinning the story his way, giving one-on-one interviews in his office with local reporters, a format he hoped would afford him more control than a press conference.

So far, that wasn't the case.

"Let me ask you that question again," Rosenblum said.

Kip stumbled a lot, which didn't exactly build his confidence. Thank God he wasn't doing this live.

Rosenblum consulted his reporter's notebook. "How do you explain instructing Deputy D.A. Maldonado to do a plea bargain in the Owens case when you knew from prosecuting Owens yourself that he had a felony conviction?"

"Jerry"—Kip forced himself to smile pleasantly at the reporter—"here's where the misinformation I was telling you about earlier comes in. I did not instruct Ms. Maldonado to do a plea bargain in the Owens case. She made that determination on her own."

That was his story and he was sticking to it. He was following the politician's creed: If the truth doesn't work, lie. Even if the lie doesn't work, repeat it. Because eventually everyone will get bored and move on.

Besides, he had plausible deniability. He had made sure to assign Alicia the case at Dudley's. He'd also made sure that no one who mattered overheard him argue for a plea bargain.

Unfortunately Rosenblum's face wore an expression of disbelief. "But Deputy D.A. Maldonado takes more cases to trial than any other prosecutor in this office. Every defense attorney I've talked to says she hates to bargain."

"First of all," Kip said, "she is no longer Deputy D.A. Maldonado. She has been fired from that position. And second," he added, raising his voice above Rosenblum's attempt to interrupt him, "there is no dispute whatsoever about whether Ms. Maldonado sought a plea bargain in this case. She did."

"At your urging," Rosenblum repeated.

"No!" Then Kip remembered himself, or rather remembered the camera, inches from his face, recording his every twitch. He took a deep breath. "I did not urge her to do so," he declared.

Rosenblum again consulted his notebook. "When the Owens case crossed your desk, before you assigned it to Deputy D.A. Maldonado, didn't you remember that you had won a felony conviction against him years before?"

Kip smiled. "Jerry, do you know how many cases cross my desk?" He made an expansive gesture, indicating, *Many! Many!* "I don't take note of the defendant's name, rank, and serial number. Moreover, do you know how many felony convictions I've won?"

Rosenblum shook his head.

"Too many to count," Kip lied. Truth be told, about a

dozen over the years he himself had been a prosecutor. He hadn't exactly been a star in court. "And, I admit it, I couldn't rattle off to you the names of all those felons." Kip laughed. "Come on, Jerry! Could you tell me the names of everyone you've ever reported on?"

The guy didn't even crack a smile. "No. But when I see one I recognize it." Then he blindsided Kip with a question he wasn't in the least prepared for. "What is your reaction to news that citizens are banding together to mount a recall initiative against you?"

Kip felt his jaw drop. "What? Well, I'll sure as hell put a stop to that!"

Then he remembered himself. And the camera. But it was too late. Because by then he had a pretty good idea which sound bite would make the news that night.

***

Joan drove the dust-caked Jag up the driveway of her home and braked right there, not bothering to park it in the garage. Even pushing the automatic door opener seemed like too much trouble. It felt like all she'd done in the last forty-eight hours was drive, drive, drive: two hours up to San Francisco, then five hours each way back and forth between the Ritz-Carlton and Redcrest, and back again this morning to Carmel.

It better have been worth it.

When she walked into the house she was astounded to find her housekeeper sitting in front of the kitchen TV, eating a vile burrito-like concoction and watching a cartoon. Joan stalked over to the set and jabbed the power button. "Elvia, I don't pay you to watch television!"

The woman's face fell. "But it helps me learn English,

missus."

"Learn English on your own time." Joan slammed her purse down on the granite counter. "Make me some coffee. I'm going to take a shower." She headed upstairs.

"You've been getting calls, missus," Elvia called after her, but Joan ignored her. She would shower first and deal with calls later.

She made the water scalding, as if heat could purge the frustrations of the last days. She showered quickly and didn't linger over dressing, wondering as she selected an outfit where she might go to lunch that wouldn't be crawling with weekend tourists.

She was at her dressing table finishing a light makeup when she heard a sudden commotion downstairs, near the front door. She frowned, her mascara wand suspended in midair, trying to make out what was going on.

She heard a man's voice. It was raised, arguing with Elvia. Then she recognized who it belonged to.

Oh, my God.

Footsteps on the stairs, then in the hallway outside the master suite. Joan sprang up from her dressing table just as Milo slammed open the door of her bedroom and burst inside, Elvia frantic at his heels.

"Missus, I tried to stop him!" Her face was twisted. "He pushed past me! He's the man calling you all morning!"

"It's all right, Elvia." Joan was amazed how calm she sounded.

"It's *all right?*" Milo laughed, an odd, forced sound. He couldn't stand still, it seemed. He was moving constantly, pacing her creamy white carpet like a beast in a luxurious padded cage. "All right for who, Joan? Not for me!"

Elvia was wringing her hands. "Should I call the police?"

"Not yet, Elvia." Joan realized her mascara was still

clutched in her hand. She tried to appear casual as she set it back on the dressing table, though it was sticky from the sudden dampness on her palms.

Milo shook his head. "There's no need for the police. You have nothing to fear from me, Joan, though apparently I have a great deal to fear from you."

Her hand froze above the dressing table. Oh, Milo could claim benign intent all he wanted, but at this moment she feared him. And while there was every indication that Lovegrove had done what she wanted and fired Milo, the satisfaction she expected to feel was tinged with dread, as if her behavior might have repercussions she hadn't predicted.

Now Elvia was wringing her hands. "What should I do, missus?"

"You may go downstairs, Elvia. In fact, we all will."

She didn't like Milo in her bedroom. Not this time. He was all coiled muscles, like a big cat stalking his prey. No longer did the power he seemed barely able to contain excite her. What might he do if it suddenly got away from him? She followed Elvia downstairs, Milo so close behind she swore she could feel his hot breath on her neck.

Elvia hurried into the kitchen, looking behind her furtively just before she disappeared behind the swinging door. But Joan felt buoyed in the living room, splashed with sunshine streaming in through the huge windows overlooking the Pacific. She turned to face Milo. She would take the offensive, the best way to protect herself. "I'm assuming you've come to apologize?"

His eyes widened with obvious amazement. "*Me* apologize? Haven't you got that wrong, Joan? Aren't *you* the one who should be begging for forgiveness?"

"Whatever for?"

His voice shook the room from hardwood to ceiling. "For

calling Richard Lovegrove and getting me fired!"

She laughed, proud that she could produce the sound. "You're giving me an awful lot of credit. If you got fired, just look in the mirror to see who caused it."

"I know exactly what you did, Joan." His voice had transformed into a low growl. He advanced toward her. "Don't play me for a fool."

"Weeks ago you were worried you would lose your job. Remember that?" She retreated a step, his belligerence poking at the bubble of her confidence. Her voice was coming out shrieky now, but she couldn't seem to control it. "You had problems at WBS long before you and I got back together."

"We never got back together. We had one night, the biggest mistake of my life." He was up close to her then, his eyes pinpoints of anger. His finger, raised in accusation, trembled menacingly close to her face. "Just tell me the truth and I'll go. For once in your goddamn life, tell the truth, Joan."

The doorbell rang.

"I had nothing to do with it," she said, though her denial sounded pathetically unconvincing even to her own ears. Much more compelling was the pounding of her heart, which beat at such a swift betraying pace she was sure Milo too could hear it.

And who was at the door? Someone who could help her? Where was Elvia? Joan tried to step backward again, to get away from him, but found herself backed up against an armchair, unable to do anything but topple onto its cushions as he leaned over her.

"Admit it," he said. She cringed from the threat in his voice. "Tell me the truth, Joan." Now he had his hands on the naked flesh of her upper arms and was shaking her. The doorbell rang again. Who could it be? Maybe whoever it was would save her. Through her fear she was getting confused, wondering what truth he was talking about. Was he talking about himself? Was he talking about Daniel? "What really happened, Joan?" he was saying, over and over. She squeezed her eyes shut, tried to block him out, but he wouldn't move, he wouldn't step back, he wouldn't let go.

Then the doorbell rang again. This time she heard Elvia scamper past. Milo released her and reared backward. She had a chance to hoist herself out of the armchair and squeeze past him, but he reacted fast, so fast, and spun around to grab her again, his grip unyielding.

Then Elvia pulled open the door. Into Joan's home walked Alicia Maldonado, her black eyes flaring with a terrible light. Though they looked past her, straight at Milo.

***

"What in the world are you doing here?" Alicia said the first thing that came into her head, foolish though it was. It was obvious what Milo was doing, standing with a flushed face and guilty eyes clutching Joan in his arms.

Immediately Milo released Joan and stepped toward Alicia. "Joan got me fired," he said. "She did the same thing to me she did to you."

Is that why you've got your arms around her? she wanted to scream. *Is that why you haven't called since we slept together?* "Stop." She raised her hand against him, steeling herself against whatever clever explanation he might concoct for the scene she'd just witnessed. "Stop right there. I don't want to hear it."

He stepped closer, incredulity stamped on his face. "You're not even going to hear me out?"

"No. I've done too much of that already." She didn't

know what to believe anymore. First Milo was a reporter, then he was Joan's lover, then he was her lover, now Joan's again ... who could believe a word that came out of that man's mouth? Pain shot through her, pain brewed of heartache and disappointment and dreams dashed. And right at the edge of it, tantalizingly close but out of reach, was crazy, crazy hope that this time—maybe this time—he was telling the whole truth and nothing but.

Joan stepped forward. "There's no reason for any of you to be in my house." She glared at Alicia. "You're not even employed by the district attorney anymore. I want all of you to leave. Right now."

Louella flashed her ID badge from the D.A.'s investigations department. "We're not leaving, Mrs. Gaines. We'd like you to consent to a search of this property."

"What? I will not! Why should I? It was searched before!" Joan put her hands on her hips and shook her blond head vigorously. "I will not be put through that again." Again she glowered at Alicia. "And that woman has no right to be here."

"Actually, I have a judge's permission," Alicia said.

"So do we." Louella handed Joan the search warrant.

Alicia watched Joan carefully. She gave a good imitation of control, though as she read the warrant her skin paled a shade and the hands holding the document betrayed a tremor. It was better, easier, to focus on Joan than on Milo, who hovered between Joan and herself, probably trying to decide where to align his forces.

He edged closer to Alicia then, apparently making his choice. "Listen to me." His eyes bored into hers. "I'm telling you the truth."

Maybe, maybe not. She stared back at him, refusing to flinch, refusing even to blink. "I don't know what to believe anymore."

"Believe this. I never lied to you. I'm not lying now. Joan got me fired and I came here to confront her." Briefly he shut his eyes and Alicia watched frustration contort his features. She wanted to believe him. She wanted so much to believe him. But while she wondered whether she could or not, Louella stepped forward.

"Mr. Pappas, we will have to detain you while this property is being searched."

"What? Detain me?" He shook his head, then pulled a cell phone from his pocket. "No. I'm calling my lawyer."

Shikegawa walked in past the housekeeper, who stood at the front door wringing her hands. "What's going on here?" he said.

"Everything is fine," Alicia said, then she turned to Milo. "Would you just cooperate? Please?" She hadn't meant for it to sound like a naked plea but somehow it had. He looked at her and for a second she felt thrust back in time, to that unforgettable interlude when it was just him and her and their bed in the Ritz-Carlton Hotel.

He seemed to remember that too, because he said, "All right, Alicia," and then without another word turned to follow Bucky Sheridan through the swinging door into the kitchen.

She didn't know whether she felt better or worse when he'd done what she asked. The Gaines' living room was full of people yet still felt oddly bereft. But he was gone and there was nothing for it but to go on with the search. *That's why I'm here*, she reminded herself. *Not for Milo but for the case.*

Louella turned to Joan. "Mrs. Gaines, we'd like you to wait in the library."

Alicia watched horror spread over the new widow's face. "In the library?" she repeated, her hand flying to her throat.

Alicia knew the choice of location was no accident.

Mentally she applauded Louella, her excitement at what she was about to do beginning to gain the upper hand over her confusion.

A female sheriff's deputy led Joan away, the widow's blond head bent and her hands clutched over her face.

Louella then turned to Alicia, in her eyes a question.

"I'm fine," Alicia said. And she was. She was the prosecutor again, fighting for her job, fighting for her reputation, fighting for her life. "Let's do it."

CHAPTER TWENTY-FOUR

I'll go crazy if I have to stay here much longer. Joan could find no position in the library where she was comfortable. She couldn't sit for longer than seconds in the leather armchair. She couldn't even think of trying to pass the time by pulling a book off the shelves. She resorted to pacing the Kashan rug, even crouching on it and rocking back and forth. It had to be seventy degrees inside but still she wanted to wrap her arms around herself and warm her body, which was so very, very cold.

What are they doing here? Why are they making me a prisoner in this horrible room? Treebeard is the one going to trial! And how did that Maldonado creature, who doesn't even have a job anymore, convince a judge to give her a warrant?

That woman was the source of all her problems. That was the only thing that was clear in the midst of this insanity.

Joan walked to the library's sole window, which offered a north-facing view along the bluff, and became even more agitated. Two police cars were in front of her property. And people were gathering around them with curious looks on their faces, as if there would be something entertaining to see, a spectacle about to begin.

She had a paralyzing thought. Maybe *she* would be the spectacle, the clown in the biggest of the circus's three rings.

But how could that be? It was Treebeard going to trial! And did she see a TV camera out there? God, she saw two.

Why? Why were they hounding her? She shuddered,

remembering the last time the press had mobbed outside her home.

Behind her she could swear she heard laughter, more of a cackle really, and spun on her heels. "Who's there?"

No one responded. There was no one to respond. She was alone in the library. But then she thought she heard it again, by the window this time, as though the laugher were darting and weaving about the room. She twirled around to face in the other direction. No one was there, either.

"Who is it?" That cry was her own voice, she realized, calling out shrilly into the empty space.

The door to the library opened. Joan let out a yelp before she saw it was the female sheriff's deputy.

Who was frowning. "Are you all right, Mrs. Gaines?"

Joan ran up to her. "No, I'm not all right! I don't want to be here. I want to go upstairs to my bedroom."

The deputy shook her head no. "I've been asked to keep you here, ma'am."

"That's crazy!" Then she heard the phone ring. "I want to answer the phone," Joan declared, though she never answered it unless she was alone in the house. Elvia always did. Then, as if by psychic command, Elvia appeared in the hallway behind the deputy. For once Joan was delighted to see her face, which at least was familiar and didn't hold any surprises.

"Mr. Whipple called before, missus, and now it's Mr. Barlowe from Headwaters." Elvia held out the cordless phone. Joan snatched it and turned away. The library door clicked shut behind her.

Now *this* was the right idea! She should've called somebody herself. Why hadn't she thought of that? Ever since Milo had burst in, her mind hadn't been working right. But now she'd call Gossett to get these people out of her home.

Maybe he could bring over that defense lawyer he'd put on retainer and scare them out. Make them see that two could play at this game.

She put the receiver to her mouth. "Craig?" At this point she was happy even to talk to Barlowe.

He didn't say hello. "What do you know about Hank Cassidy?"

"The lumberman?"

"You *do* know him. Fuck!"

She heard a crashing sound, like glass breaking, and pulled the receiver away from her ear. *Damn!* She should have thought first and spoken second.

Because now Barlowe was back on the line, raving like a madman. "I'm getting calls from everybody, you name it. The California Forestry Association, the EPA, Department of Forestry, Frederick Whipple, even the governor's office. And the media, Joan, the media! We are in serious shit thanks to you. I knew you'd do something asinine but I never could've predicted this."

She was having trouble keeping the receiver at her ear, her hand was trembling so badly. "What are you talking about?"

"Lumbermen are singing like canaries! About you paying them cash to cut down old-growth trees and planning to ship the timber overseas! Are you denying it, Joan? Are you?"

"Of course I'm—" she began, but Barlowe cut her off.

"Don't lie to me! Because if you tell me the truth, me at least, maybe we can control this thing. But not if you lie!"

Joan heard Barlowe gulp for breath on the other end of the line, but all she could do was clutch the receiver, hardly able to breathe herself. What should she say? What should she do? She needed advice, from Gossett or Whipple, even her mother, someone older who knew how to manage things.

Because she had no idea.

"What happened?" she asked timidly, lamely, which set Barlowe off on another tear.

"What happened?" he shouted. "You really want to know, Joan? We had a major accident last night, that's what happened! Turns out some of our men did a little extra cutting on the side on one of our biggest, oldest trees. And believe me, it wasn't one we had officially earmarked. That baby was nearly two hundred years old and about as off-limits as you can get. And guess who went down with it?"

No. Oh, no.

"Yes. Your friend Hank Cassidy. Who, thanks to you and this insane scheme of yours, is dead."

***

Alicia mounted the stairs to the second floor of the Gaines home, criminalist Andy Shikegawa approaching her on his way down. He carried his small crimson leather journal, his crime-scene bible, in which all his notes were jotted in a careful hand.

"Find anything?" she asked—stupidly, because surely she would have heard if he had.

He shook his head. "No."

"You've gone through the master suite? And the other bedrooms?"

"Also Gaines' home office," he said, then pinched the bridge of his nose, pushing down his wire-frame glasses. "Got any aspirin?"

"No, but I'm sure Louella does."

"She's downstairs with Lucy?" Lucy Johnson, the second DOJ criminalist, who'd also been present at the initial search of the crime scene.

"Yes," then, casually, "Mind if I look around upstairs?"

He stepped aside to get out of her way. "Be my guest."

Alicia climbed the last of the stairs, hope fading fast. So far they'd found nothing. Who did when revisiting a crime scene over a month after the fact? Still, she'd had to push for the search, her last chance to trap Joan. But all too easily she could imagine an ignominious retreat, tail between her legs, Shikegawa and Johnson and Louella too kind to deliver a single *I told you so*.

And what would Milo say? Milo who sat downstairs, detained by this last-ditch search she had made happen. When all of this was over, would he think her a fool or a hero? She didn't know which she would choose herself. Merely pondering the future beyond this search sent a rogue wave of doubt crashing through her. If this ended with her finding nothing, Joan would win. She would lose. And what of her and Milo? *Was* there a her and Milo?

I can't think about him now. By force of will she pushed Milo out of her mind as she arrived at the second-floor landing, where the hardwood gave way to creamy white carpeting, thick and luxurious. To her right was the door to the master suite, all the way open. The interior was flooded with sun, thanks to a huge bay window giving on to a stunning view of Carmel Point and the bay. Along the corridor were half-open doors to bedrooms, three of them, and at the end of the hall to her left was what had been Daniel Gaines' home office. Her legs led her in that direction.

She stopped on the threshold. It was a small room, clearly a working office. It was obvious from its simplicity, from the bulging dog-eared files to the rolling swivel chair on a scarred rectangle of Plexiglas, that its owner had been Daniel and not Joan. Alicia guessed that the library downstairs, where Gaines had died, was where he'd held meetings. This was where he'd done actual work.

She stepped farther into the room and approached the desk, set opposite the door beneath the room's only window, over which a shade was half-pulled to block the sun. Deeper inside she noticed a faint lingering scent of men's cologne, as if Daniel Gaines had just been present, sitting at the desk, working on his computer. Here, where no doubt he had spent many hours, Alicia felt the man as she did nowhere else in his house. It was unnerving.

On a small side table left of the desk hunched a copier/fax; beneath it on the floor was a bulky laser printer. The desk's surface was completely covered by a phone, the desktop computer, stacks of files, and, she then noticed, an open box of Gaines campaign stationery. There was the red-white-and-blue logo that Treebeard had described and which she herself had seen on New Year's Eve when Louella had given her a sample.

She stared at it. From downstairs she could make out the murmur of conversation; in that silent room she heard only her own breathing.

Of course Gaines would have the stationery here. This was his home office. Another thought prompted her to kneel in front of the laser printer, which was linked by thick, dusty cords to the computer. She latched her fingers beneath its paper tray and tugged. The tray pulled open. Loaded into it, again, was the stationery.

Shikegawa and Johnson went through the computer when they were collecting evidence from the house, on the Saturday when Gaines' body was discovered. If the letter Treebeard described had been here, they would have found it, right?

Then again, they hadn't been looking for it, for the simple reason that they didn't know it existed. The only reason she knew was because of what Treebeard had told her when she interviewed him at the jail, and that was a week after the Gaines home was searched. The only other person who'd heard Treebeard's account of the letter was his defense attorney, Jerome Brown.

Alicia had told only Louella about it. She hadn't said a word to Penrose or Shikegawa or Johnson. Before this second search of the Gaines home, only Louella had helped her investigate the possibility that someone other than Treebeard had murdered Daniel Gaines.

Alicia stood up, then pulled out the desk's rolling chair and sat down. It creaked at her weight and slid sideways a few inches on the Plexiglas sheet, as slippery as ice. The computer was booted up, its screen saver a black background with stars shooting toward her as if she were hurtling through space. One touch of the keyboard brought up Windows Desktop, which displayed all the usual icons: My Computer, Internet Explorer, Recycle Bin.

She launched Windows Explorer, then opened the My Documents folder. Beneath it were a dozen subsidiary folders, which broke down further into personal, Headwaters, campaign, and trust categories.

It can't be here, she told herself, but trolled through the folders anyway. *This is a waste of time*, her brain said, but her fingers pecked away on the keyboard regardless, rebellious agents going about their own business. *Why would the letter be on Daniel Gaines' computer anyway? He wouldn't have framed Treebeard for his own murder!*

After a few minutes it occurred to her to use the Find function. What word should she search for? She typed in *Treebeard* then clicked on Find Now. No files appeared. Maybe *Bracewell*. That was one name Treebeard had said had appeared on the letter.

Bracewell's name brought up a huge number of files. Alicia was partway through them when another thought struck her. Wouldn't whoever had written the letter have avoided saving it on the hard disk? Wouldn't they have written it, printed it, and deleted it, never saving it? They might have thought that would make it as if the letter had never existed.

But Alicia knew the letter wouldn't just disappear. Even if it had never been saved it would remain among the Temp files unless those files had been purged from the hard disk. She knew from her own habits that she very rarely did that kind of computer housekeeping.

Alicia minimized the files she'd been scanning, then brought up the Temp files. There were tons of them, but it was possible to search for files created on a specific date. She typed in December seventeenth through nineteenth, the nineteenth being the day before Daniel Gaines was murdered, the day on which Treebeard said he received the letter.

She clicked on Find Now. The number of Temp files was reduced to about a dozen. Listed alongside them were their size and the date and time on which they had been last modified. One was a small file bearing the date *12/19, 11:08 AM*.

Alicia held her breath and clicked on it. It opened.

A shiver ran up her spine, into the hairs at the back of her neck. She stared at it for a long time, unable to believe what she was seeing. Yet there it was, undeniable, and just as Treebeard had described. His name appeared nowhere on the letter but other phrases leaped out at her. *Please join us at Daniel Gaines' home Friday evening at nine o'clock ... Perhaps some private conversation would allow us to find common ground ... Best regards, Molly Bracewell.*

***

Milo drummed his fingers on the round glass table in the kitchen nook of Joan's home. The nook really was more like a greenhouse, with paned windows on three sides affording a view of the road above the bluff.

He was puzzled. For on that road not only were gawkers beginning to gather, so were newspeople, so many that the sheriff's department had cordoned off the area with yellow crime tape. Two camera crews already had set up behind the tape, in addition to a still photographer. Reporters were arriving on the scene in news vans and ENG trucks, which signaled that live shots would be happening for the noon news.

All this for a search warrant? Implausible. But what else could it be? Milo had no idea, which depressed him. He was out of the loop, fired, no longer of import in the news business. For all he knew Mac and Tran were out there among the mob, taping a stand-up with his replacement. Weeks before his ego had chafed at the assignment. Now he wished it were his.

As it was, he felt as if it were wartime and he was battling on all fronts. Yet he was too drained to be upset. Perhaps the life force had seeped out of him while he was throttling Joan, leaving him a shell of a man, with a ruined past and an uncertain future. No job. No reputation. No Alicia.

He'd had her for a time and then he'd lost her. Why? Because his anger at Joan had gotten the better of him. He'd run back to her house like a man possessed, or a man obsessed. Who could blame Alicia for wanting to wash her hands of him?

The cop sitting to Milo's left cleared his throat. BUCKY SHERIDAN, his badge said. Somehow he didn't look like one of the department's top performers.

"Officer Sheridan," Milo asked, "do you know why there

are so many reporters outside?"

"Beats me." Then the cop raised his brows. "You don't know? Aren't you one of 'em?"

Milo let that pass. "Is it the search warrant?"

"Beats me."

Not exactly a font of information, was he? Milo resumed watching the housekeeper, who was doing a lousy job mopping the floor. She did some areas repeatedly and totally missed others. But he had to assume she was scared to death. One month ago her employer was murdered in the house. Today for the second time cops were crawling all over the property and reporters were massing like jackals on the street outside.

As he watched, she stepped backward without looking and knocked over her pail of sudsy water. "*Dios mio,*" she muttered, then just stood still, as if it were all too much, holding her mop with one hand and massaging her forehead with the other.

Milo rose to his feet. "Here, let me help."

She raised tired eyes to his face. "*Gracias, senor.* Thank you."

Between the two of them they made quick work of cleaning up, while Officer Sheridan did his bit by observing their progress from the table. Toting the pail and mop, Milo trailed the woman to a mudroom off the kitchen. She pulled open a utility closet stuffed to the gills with foul-weather paraphernalia, from Gore-Tex parkas to slickers and mud boots and garden clogs.

"These both go in there?" he asked. It was hard to believe.

"Mop only, please. I take pail." She relieved him of the latter as he pushed the mop back inside, then apparently had another thought. "Get me broom, please?"

"No problem," he said, but it wasn't true. Not only did he

have to shove past all the gear, he then had to root around against the back wall among the collection of brooms. His hands closed on one and he pulled it out, then stared down at it, frowning.

This is no broom.

It was a long, slim piece of highly buffed wood, about five feet in length, with one small notch carved into the top and another carved into the bottom.

This is no broom. It's a bow.

An unstrung bow, which made it hard to recognize.

Milo stared at it, awestruck. It fit right in with the brooms and mops. It was the same size, made of the same material. But with a totally different purpose. Its aim was to kill.

***

Alicia stood in the library with Joan, the sheriff's deputy, Shikegawa, Johnson, and Louella. They were gathered around Joan like a posse, or a lynch mob. It was deliberate, cruel but deliberate. Alicia handed Joan the letter to Treebeard, which she had printed out on Gaines campaign stationery, and watched her carefully. She was trying to shock an admission out of her, as she had New Year's Day. That time it had worked. She needed it to work again.

For while the letter lent Treebeard's story credibility, it didn't convict Joan. It was damning, but circumstantially so. Alicia still needed more.

"Explain this to me," Alicia demanded. She made her voice harsh and accusing. "You wrote this, didn't you?"

Joan just shook her head, though she looked ready to crack. Her eyes were puffy from crying, and her skin was mottled. Chips of mascara littered her cheeks. The sheriff's deputy who'd been watching her said the phone calls she was getting, one after another, were upsetting her. Something about Headwaters, and a lumberman dying in an accident.

Alicia thought that must explain the reporters and TV crews and photographers massed outside, and the news chopper circling overhead. No one in the media, except Milo, of course, even knew about the search warrant. That couldn't be what had drawn the press to the Gaines property in such numbers.

Joan handed the letter back, her eyes defiant. "I've never seen this before in my life."

"Don't lie to me." Alicia raised her voice. "You lied to me before and the truth still came out, didn't it? This letter came off the computer upstairs. Your prints are all over that keyboard," she said, though she had no idea if that was true. "Who else had access to that computer but you? Come on, Joan. Admit it!"

But again Joan shook her head, and backed away a few steps. "I'm not saying another word until I speak to my attorney. He's on his way. Leland Jennings."

"You think a big-name defense lawyer is going to get you out of this?" Alicia advanced on Joan, holding the letter out to her. "Come on. Take credit for your handiwork. It's pretty clever, I have to admit. More clever than I thought you were capable of."

"Shut up! You just shut up!"

The veneer was cracking. Alicia stepped closer still. "You wrote this to Treebeard, didn't you? Then you signed Molly Bracewell's name. You wanted to set him up for Daniel's murder and implicate her at the same time."

"Shut up!" Now her arms were flailing, her voice spiraling upward like a helium balloon.

"It's driving you crazy, isn't it? Knowing you killed Daniel? Knowing how cleverly you did it? But having to keep it all to yourself for the rest of your life?"

One of those arms suddenly jutted straight out and pointed at Alicia. "*You're* the crazy one! *You* are! For trying to pin my husband's murder on me!"

Before Alicia could respond, a commotion behind her at the library's door made her turn around. It was Bucky Sheridan, his face even more flushed than usual. Next to him stood Milo, who somehow looked different than he had before. Calmer, more relaxed.

A word popped into Alicia's head. *Vindicated.*

Bucky hoisted something long and thin in the air. He gripped one end of it in his right hand, which was encased in a protective plastic glove. "Look what we found. In the mudroom off the kitchen."

There was amazement in Bucky's voice.

No wonder.

"It's a bow," Alicia heard herself murmur. *The murder weapon? Here in Joan's house?* Slowly she pivoted to face Joan, who stood wide-eyed and openmouthed across the library. "That's the bow you used to kill your husband, isn't it?"

"I did not kill my husband!" Joan screamed, though she was panting, and her eyes were wild, which gave the lie to her denial. "I haven't seen that in ages. I didn't even know it was in the house. My parents gave it to me when I was, I don't know, thirteen."

"You really are something, aren't you?" Alicia stepped closer to Joan. Now she was only a foot away. It must have been her proximity that sent Joan scuttling sideways, like a crab, close to Milo and Bucky. "Stealing one of Treebeard's arrows," Alicia went on, "writing a letter to get him here to the house, arranging all of this for a night when you knew you would have an alibi in Santa Cruz—"

"Shut up!" Again out stretched the arm, though this time

it trembled violently. The index finger jabbed at Alicia's face. Joan's own skin was a bright, angry red, as if she'd been slapped. "You are the reason all this is happening, you bitch!"

Alicia watched, oddly calm. *What a vile creature*, she thought, *like something that slinks along the bottom of the sea*. She arched a brow. "In some ways I don't blame you for killing Daniel, Joan. I know how he stole Headwaters from your family. It was like he spit on your father's grave after your father did so much to help him."

"Shut up!" Joan's hands were clutched over her ears, while she shook her head violently. Then her arms fell and her voice reached a shrill, ear-piercing note. "Shut up!"

It happened mesmerizingly fast. Alicia watched as Joan grabbed the bow from Bucky's unsuspecting grip and raised it high above her head. Then she pounced on Alicia, her eyes crazed blue spheres, like those of a madwoman, or perhaps a sane woman who'd just been pushed too far.

It's like when I was in a car accident, Alicia thought, watching Joan's arms go up, up, up. *I knew the other car was coming but I couldn't do a single thing about it ...*

Then the arms were coming down, the bow was arcing in one swift, relentless motion, and all at once Alicia felt herself thrust aside. She watched Milo step between her and Joan, saw his body twist away from the bow, his arms raised protectively over his head.

The silent library was rent with a mighty crack.

CHAPTER TWENTY-FIVE

Joan perched on the edge of the narrow metal cot in her jail cell, her hands folded in her lap. She was trying very hard not to touch anything, not to smell anything, not to hear anything. The more she kept herself aloof from her surroundings, the less real they became. The more she could dismiss the urine odor from the toilet so close to the cot; the more she could banish all the banging and buzzing sounds, and the endless muffled sobbing of some woman several cells to her left. The more she sat silently, within herself, not moving, not thinking, the more easily she could believe that her imprisonment was a gigantic error that soon would be corrected.

For it was an error. Despite that treacherous letter, despite the unearthing of that bow, despite the endless accusations of that vampirish Maldonado creature who would not stay dead, she had not killed Daniel. *I did not kill him*, Joan repeated to herself. *I didn't.*

Close by, she heard a clanging of metal upon metal. A buzzer sounded. A door opened, then closed. Heavy steps came nearer, each footfall accompanied by the jangling of many keys.

A female warden, an enormous black woman sporting a pair of equally outsize wire-frame glasses, appeared beyond the bars of her cell. "You got a visitor."

Joan scurried toward the tall, silver-haired, impeccably dressed man who then stepped into view beside the warden.

There was no one in the world she wanted more to see. "Leland."

Her cell door swung open. Attorney Leland Jennings strode inside and clasped Joan's small hands in his own. The door slammed shut behind him, the entire cell shuddering with the force, but at least this time she wasn't imprisoned all alone.

"Leland," she repeated, helpless to think of anything else to say. She wanted to weep. At this moment Leland Jennings reminded her of her father. He was strong, knowledgeable, someone who would take what was wrong and make it right again. Her father might not always have given her her due, but he never, ever betrayed her the way Daniel had.

"You poor dear," Leland Jennings said, which did make the tears flow. "Come sit down," he added, and with him at her side Joan was more willing to sit on the cot.

For a time he let her weep, making consoling noises and handing her tissue after tissue as the need arose. It surprised her that such a distinguished gentleman could secrete such an enormous supply of tissues on his person.

Finally she produced a last sniffle. "I apologize, Leland. I am not myself."

"Of course not." He smiled, which made little crinkly lines appear at the outer edges of his bright blue eyes. He did so remind her of her father!

It took her some time to regain control. "They'll never be able to make this stick," she said. She rose from the cot and listened to her declaration hang in the cell's heavy air, trying to gauge whether it had the ring of truth. It didn't quite, so she tried again. "They have no case against me whatsoever."

Leland Jennings pursed his lips and looked into the distance, as if some justice-system truth were out there that only he could see.

"Isn't that right, Leland?" she demanded.

It took forever for him to say anything. Finally, "From what I have seen of the evidence, it is no more than circumstantial."

"Well, that's hardly enough!" *Particularly when it comes to me*, she wanted to add, but stopped herself. "The case against that Treebeard man is far more convincing. What about all the DNA evidence they've got against him? Has that prosecutor woman conveniently forgotten about that?"

"Joan," he said, and her back stiffened at the patronizing note she suddenly detected in his voice, "it is clear they plan to argue that you framed Treebeard for your husband's murder. They will not try to claim Treebeard was not at the scene."

Something about the phrase *plan to argue* made Joan feel positively faint. "You could defend me against a circumstantial case if it came to that, couldn't you, Leland?" That last bit came out more desperate-sounding than she had intended. Again she felt tears threateningly close to the surface.

"Of course, Joan. If it came to that." Leland Jennings smiled the sort of smile that made juries believe every single word he told them about his unfairly maligned client. It had the same reassuring effect on Joan. She reclaimed her position next to him on the cot. Then her curiosity got the better of her. "How is Milo Pappas, by the way?"

"He has a broken forearm and some lacerations about the head and neck. From the splintering of the wood," Leland Jennings added.

She found herself again upset, this time at the limited extent of Milo's injuries. For everything that man did to her he deserved far worse than a broken bone and some cuts. It was also a real shame that she hadn't hit her mark. She would have dearly loved to have cracked the bow on that Maldonado woman's head. Then a terrifying thought occurred to her. "They can't charge me with murder for Hank Cassidy, can they?"

"No." Leland Jennings patted her knee. "No one disputes that was an accident."

But according to both Craig Barlowe and Frederick Whipple, it was an accident that killed not only Hank Cassidy but the chance of a successful IPO. Whipple claimed the revelation that Headwaters was flouting environmental regulations would tarnish the company beyond repair.

Joan shut her eyes. She couldn't think about that now. All she could focus on was her own survival. She turned to her attorney. "When are they going to let me out of here?"

Leland Jennings sighed, the sort of drawn-out, pained sigh that signaled bad news was about to be imparted. Joan steeled herself. "Joan," he said finally, "I don't anticipate you'll be released anytime soon. This is a capital case, after all."

She rose to her feet, though the movement was unsteady. "I don't care what kind of case it is. I want you to get me out of here. Do it or I shall retain an attorney who can!"

He remained mute, just staring at her. All of a sudden she found his behavior infuriating.

She set her hands on her hips. "Are you forgetting who I am?" she demanded. "I am Joan Hudson Gaines, the daughter of former governor and US senator Web Hudson. I am not someone who should be incarcerated, not for several hours, let alone for some indeterminate period!" She walked to the door of her cell, as if she were dismissing Leland Jennings. Which she was, for the moment. "I suggest you find a judge and clarify the situation."

He seemed to consider her words, then rose and

approached the door of her cell. "Warden," he called, then turned to face her. She was astonished to see not one iota of warmth in his expression. Rather he regarded her with the look of a man at a rather distasteful piece of business.

The warden appeared behind the bars. Leland Jennings seemed to weigh his words carefully before he spoke.

"Joan, I suggest either that you purge that sort of thinking from your head or keep it to yourself. For if we do find ourselves in trial, I can promise it won't win you any points with a judge or jury."

Then he walked out, leaving Joan alone, petrified, and incarcerated. And wondering if perhaps the Hudson name wasn't worth so very much after all.

***

Alicia sat in the ratty chair beside Louella's desk in the D.A.'s office and asked a question neither woman could answer. "Why would Libby Hudson want to see *me*?"

Louella frowned, sipping overheated coffee from a Styrofoam cup. "What time did she say she's coming by?"

"Six."

Both women raised their heads toward the loudly ticking round white-faced clock above Louella's cubicle window, whose hands pointed to 5:51 PM. Louella shook her head. "I can't believe she thinks she can get us to drop the charges."

Alicia found everything on that Saturday evening hard to believe. It was hard to believe that Joan Hudson Gaines was sitting in the Adult Detention Center charged with her husband's murder. It was even more mind-boggling that Alicia had put her there, resuscitating her own prosecutorial career by refusing to abandon a murder investigation she believed was seriously offtrack. Judge Dede Frankel was planning action against Kip Penrose with the California Bar Association for impeding the investigation. And Treebeard would soon be a free man.

Not only that, but Milo Pappas had landed in the emergency room for protecting Alicia from Joan Gaines. Alicia found that about as unfathomable as everything else.

Outside Louella's window Alicia watched a couple stroll past, arm in arm, heads bent against the January wind. They had the look of being on a Saturday date, not their first and certainly not their last. They laughed and chattered and walked quickly, their steps in easy unison.

"I'm going to break up with Jorge," Alicia said.

Louella arched her brows. "Come again?"

"I should've done it before."

"You mean you should've done it before you got those roses."

Alicia said nothing. She was increasingly convinced she had treated two men unfairly. She might be able to go only part of the way toward making amends, but it was time to do it.

Louella lolled back in her chair and trained her eyes on the ceiling. "Mind if I ask you something?"

"Shoot."

"Mind if I go after Jorge?"

"You want to? Really?" Alicia laughed, then thought about it. "No, I don't mind."

"Mind if I ask you something else? Did you get those roses from Milo Pappas?"

She felt Louella's laser stare. "Yes."

Louella said nothing for some time. Then, "You know, I have to say I was impressed watching him jump in front of you like that today. That was pretty heroic stuff."

That notion bounced off the gray padded walls of

Louella's cubicle. In the chaos of Joan's attack, Milo's injury, and Joan's arrest, Alicia had had no time to talk to Milo. He'd been sped off in an ambulance without even a backward glance to her. *Even if he was "heroic," what am I supposed to do about it? By now I'm sure he wants nothing to do with me.*

The early noises from the Board of Sups were that she'd get her job back. Though it was too soon to say for sure, it certainly looked as if she would take Penrose's place in prosecuting Joan Gaines for Daniel Gaines' murder, with Rocco Messina at her side. Reporters had already begun to ask if she planned to challenge the badly weakened Kip Penrose for D.A. in November. If he were the target of an official investigation, he might be pretty easy to beat, despite all the fund-raising money he had socked away. She'd have to mount an instant campaign, but for the first time in years she'd have enormous name recognition. Not to mention major momentum, if indeed she were appointed the lead prosecutor in the Gaines case. Her name would be in the news constantly without her having to spend a single ad dollar.

All of a sudden Alicia Maldonado was a hometown hero again. Overnight she'd gone from a miscreant prosecutor to a never-say-die D.A. who protected the little guy from the rich and powerful. It was a second chance in a world that didn't hand out a lot of those.

She wondered if she'd be pressing her luck to try for a second chance somewhere else, too.

Louella's phone rang. She answered, said yes twice, then hung up and turned to Alicia. "Libby Hudson's here, with her lawyer." She rose from her chair. "They're waiting in the conference room."

***

Milo arrived at San Francisco airport three hours early for

his red-eye flight home to D.C. He paid the driver who'd ferried him north from Salinas, then paused on the pavement in front of the terminal.

Saturday evening was a strange, in-between time at airports. It was the midpoint for the weekend-travel crowd, so none of them were in evidence. Businesspeople wouldn't be flying until the following afternoon and evening. Only travelers with odd itineraries were around, like him.

He set his briefcase atop his rolling bag. Wide glass doors slid back to admit him into the cavernous terminal. In a departure from his usual habit, and in deference to his broken ulna, he decided not to carry his bag onto the plane but to check it through.

The redhead working business-class check-in recognized him before he'd handed over his driver's license. Her eyes widened in obvious surprise at his appearance. "Mr. Pappas, how are you?"

His face was more than a little banged up. "It looks worse than it feels," he told her. Actually, he felt like hell. Physically and every other way.

"I've been hearing on TV about what you did," she said, then flushed. Milo knew why. News of his abrupt firing from WBS was a widely reported sidebar to the tale of his battering at the hands of his former lover, Joan Gaines. At least he was getting credit for protecting prosecutor Maldonado from the accused husband killer, which burnished to an even higher sheen his reputation as a stud.

He was enough of a cynic to believe that was the reason that WBS executives were spinning his termination the way they were. The network's official line was that WBS and its star correspondent had "arrived at a mutual decision to part ways." Milo guessed that WBS brass knew the public would not applaud their firing a reporter who protected women despite harm to himself. He was equally certain that O'Malley was spreading a more insidious explanation of Milo's termination to anybody who would listen.

"You're all set," the ticket agent said a minute later, and handed Milo his ticket with a smile. He thanked her and proceeded to security. This was the last time he'd fly on WBS's dime, he realized. After how many thousands of flights over his dozen years of employment? Still, the network was dotting every I and crossing every T, returning him to his home base before washing their hands of him.

He emerged at the other side of security at a loss. Now he had two and a half hours till his flight. Where to go, what to do? Always-on-the-go Milo Pappas wasn't used to such a surfeit of time. Or pleased with it, either. Time was hardly a joy when it felt empty and useless.

For lack of a better alternative, he set himself up in the airline's red-carpet lounge. A beer and a few handfuls of nuts later he felt better, but not by much.

Would he get another TV job? Certainly. With a network? Possibly. With the prestige of *Newsline*? No way. Unless he was named a rival network's main anchor, which was about as likely as O'Malley suddenly morphing into his biggest fan, whatever post next came his way would be a comedown.

Then again, the unlikely had been happening lately. Amazing as it was, Alicia had found enough evidence to charge Joan with Daniel's murder. She'd bulldozed her way from a gut feeling to an arrest, despite getting fired in the process. It was impressive. She'd get her job back, he knew. Or a better job. He wasn't worried how Alicia would fare. She was made of strong stuff.

How ironic that Alicia thought he was involved with Joan when he wasn't. It was the only time he could remember when he'd been wrongly accused of cheating. He was blameless, but guilty by reputation. And it had cost him the first woman in years he cared about losing. It left him feeling hollowed out, as if for a long time to come his life would consist of nothing more than going through the motions.

A waitress came by and Milo ordered a second beer. In a corner of the lounge a television was tuned to MSNBC, which was doing a roundtable on women who committed murder. Joan Gaines would be an enormous story, Milo knew. Her transgressions against Daniel, and against nature—given the tree-felling scheme that had just been exposed—would make her one of the most notorious figures of her day. "Governor's Daughter Turns Husband and Tree Killer!" The tabloid potential was mind-boggling.

Joan Gaines would be a huge story and Milo Pappas would be sidelined. *How ironic*, he thought; *how sad*. How in keeping with everything else in his life at that painful juncture in time.

***

Alicia preceded Louella through the wide-open door of the D.A. office's main conference room. It was as unprepossessing a space as could be found in any county office building, with turn-your-skin-green fluorescent lighting, grime-streaked windows, and furnishings so timeworn the Salvation Army would refuse to accept them for donation. It looked like the sort of room where people who worked too hard made what they could of bad situations.

At the table's head sat a woman as unsuited to her surroundings as the queen of England would be to a trailer park. She was a tiny but powerful presence, white-haired and bird-thin, in a severe navy suit softened by the largest, most outrageously perfect pearls Alicia had ever seen. Behind her right shoulder, like a loyal vassal, stood an older man in a conservative suit.

Alicia was mildly irritated that Libby Storrow Hudson had claimed the conference table's most powerful position, but supposed that a woman of her ilk would do no less. Alicia offered her hand. "I'm Deputy D.A. Maldonado," she said, earning such a keenly appraising stare she immediately felt compelled neither to blink nor look away.

It took Libby Hudson some time to speak, but when she did her voice was as cold as the wind that lashed her native Massachusetts. "Have you been reinstated as a prosecutor, Ms. Maldonado?"

"Not officially, though I expect to be shortly."

"And you have that expectation because you've arrested my daughter for her husband's murder." Libby Hudson's voice was oddly matter-of-fact, given the enormous emotional underpinning of her statement.

Alicia regarded her for a moment. "Your daughter was arrested for Daniel Gaines' murder because of very compelling evidence, Mrs. Hudson."

The older woman arched her brow. "Compelling, is it? Well, we shall see about that."

So that is why she's here. Alicia stepped aside to allow Louella to introduce herself, and made the acquaintance of Henry Gossett, who she learned was the Hudson family counsel. Then, in her own strategic positioning, she claimed the opposite head of the conference table.

This visit wasn't so surprising, really. More than once family members had appealed to her to drop charges against their loved ones. Occasionally they made a persuasive case. In this instance Alicia would refuse to be swayed. For what arguments could Libby Hudson make? The evidence against her daughter might be circumstantial but together the pieces created a perfect mosaic of guilt. All Libby Hudson could do was fall back on the usual bullying tactics of the rich and powerful: subtle though undeniable threats that the Hudson family would make Alicia's life difficult, derail her career, besmirch her reputation. All of which had already happened, and over all of which Alicia had already triumphed.

No, she wouldn't budge, though the prospect of tangling with the Hudsons was more than a little fearsome. *Get used to it*, she told herself. *This is practice for the face-off you'll get in court.*

Louella took the seat to Alicia's left, while Henry Gossett claimed its mirror opposite. The two opposing pairs were perfectly balanced, though empty space yawned between them.

Through the conference room's dirty windows came the muffled noises of a Salinas Saturday night, the revelry just getting under way. People walked past en route to early dinners at Spado's a few blocks down Alisal Street. Car horns blared as traffic began to clog the street, and rap music pounded so loudly from a passing radio that Alicia felt the floor shudder beneath her shoes.

Libby Hudson spoke. "You claim the evidence you have against my daughter makes a compelling case for her guilt. Yet this office claimed the same thing against Treebeard just days ago."

Louella spoke up. "New evidence has come to light that indicates your daughter framed Treebeard for her husband's murder."

"Are you referring to the bow found on the property?" Gossett asked. His tone was disdainful.

"In part," Alicia said. "Joan's fingerprints are all over it."

"Of course they are. She was forced to use it to protect herself from Milo Pappas."

Alicia and Louella glanced at each other. That was quite a twist Joan and her attorney were putting on that episode.

"What other evidence do you have?" Henry Gossett demanded.

Alicia kept her tone measured. "Mr. Gossett, we have no intention of arguing our case before you and your client. It will be presented before a judge and jury and not before."

"Long before you go to court," he insisted, "you will be required to share your supposed evidence with defense counsel."

"And I will do so, as the law requires."

Again Alicia felt herself under Libby Hudson's laser stare. Clearly she and her attorney were trying to ascertain just how much Alicia and Louella actually knew versus how much they were bluffing. Alicia didn't want to tip her hand yet at the same time had no desire to prolong a pointless conversation.

Libby Hudson spoke. "My daughter was in Santa Cruz the night Daniel was murdered. She didn't return to her home until the following morning."

Louella answered. "Actually, your daughter did return to her home that night, Mrs. Hudson. We have an eyewitness who places her there, and in addition a credit-card receipt proving she was in the area."

Alicia stared across the expanse of conference-room table and saw the first chink in the older woman's armor. Beneath the discreet cover of foundation her skin paled, just a shade, and her mouth revealed the slightest tremor. Gossett was about to speak when Libby Hudson laid a silencing hand on his arm.

"Ms. Maldonado," she said, "you claim to have means and opportunity for my daughter to have committed this crime. But what motive could you possibly imagine she possessed for murdering her own husband?"

Alicia spoke carefully. "I know that over the course of his marriage to your daughter, Daniel Gaines became a very powerful member of your family. I also know that he did not always exercise that power well, either when it came to your husband's living trust or to Headwaters. Believe me, Mrs. Hudson, I will be able to convince a jury that your daughter had a motive for murder."

Alicia fell silent and the two women regarded each other. For a moment Alicia was thrown back to that evening in the Lodge, when she and Kip Penrose had gone to brief Joan Gaines on the investigation into her husband's murder. On that night Alicia had stared into the imperious eyes of this woman's daughter. Superficially the eyes of mother and daughter were the same, blue and ice-cold. Alicia sensed, though, that the will they revealed was much more powerful in the older woman than in the younger.

"You are determined to press murder charges against my daughter?" Libby Hudson asked.

"Yes," Alicia answered.

For a time, no one said a word. Then Libby Hudson looked at her counselor and nodded, as if she were delivering a signal. He dropped his eyes and shook his head, only once, the picture of a man who had argued vigorously but here, now, was forced to accept defeat.

Alicia watched the interaction between attorney and client and something clicked into place in her mind. *Wait. Joan wasn't the only Hudson to have a motive for murdering Daniel Gaines.*

Alicia stared across the conference table at Libby Storrow Hudson, so proper, so aristocratic, so strong-willed. *She had the same motive for killing Daniel that her daughter did. Arguably an even stronger one. As Web Hudson's widow she was the other major beneficiary of his living trust. She, too, would have been outraged at how Daniel had abused the trust and stolen the Headwaters stake from the family. She was directly hurt by it, even more than her daughter. And she would feel Daniel's insult to Web Hudson even more keenly.*

Fragments of memory crowded into Alicia's brain, bits and pieces of legend and lore that people chewed on when they were in the mood to gossip. She spoke into the silent room. "Mrs. Hudson, you competed in the Olympic trials some years back, is that correct?"

The older woman smiled. For the first time, the look she gave Alicia was tinged with respect. "Yes, I did."

Somewhere far away in the D.A.'s office a phone rang. Alicia was far more conscious of the thunder in her own ears. "In what sport?"

Libby Hudson hesitated only briefly. Then, "Archery."

There it was, the final piece.

"You killed Daniel Gaines, didn't you?" Alicia asked.

"Yes," she said, "I did." The confession was delivered in the same matter-of-fact tone Alicia had heard earlier. No regret, no emotion, just a woman saying what she must.

"He was never worthy of my daughter," she went on. It was a confident declaration, made by a woman who had a very clear notion where she stood in the world. "He was never worthy of association with the Hudson name. He was a detestable, lowborn man who used my family in whatever vile, scheming ways he could concoct." She paused, and shuddered visibly. "I killed him because I could not allow him to destroy my daughter's life, which, as you apparently discovered as well, he was in the process of doing. And now I have the identical motive for telling you the truth. I will not destroy Joan's life by allowing her to pay for a crime she did not commit."

Alicia had some difficulty focusing her thoughts, which were batting around in her brain like crazed birds desperate to escape their cage. *Could this be another lie? Is this woman saying what she must to protect her daughter?* If so, it was the most astonishing display of maternal loyalty Alicia had ever seen. Yet somehow she believed Libby Hudson capable of such a feat of courage. Much more than she could believe her daughter capable of it.

"You see," Libby Hudson went on, "it doesn't really matter what happens to me. I will fight to be exonerated, you may be sure. Yet whatever the outcome, I will already have lived a bountiful life. Joan is young and has many years ahead of her. I have protected her inheritance. I have ensured her future." She turned her piercing blue eyes on Alicia. "A mother knows when a child needs a guiding hand. I know that Joan does, and I have provided it."

Louella was shaking her head. "This doesn't add up. We confirmed your whereabouts and you were in Santa Barbara when Daniel was killed."

Alicia spoke before Libby Hudson did. "But she may well have driven up to Carmel from Santa Barbara with no one knowing. And gone back the same way." *Much as her daughter went back and forth from Santa Cruz.*

The older woman nodded. "Yes, I made certain to appear to be out of town. I was at San Ysidro Ranch. I knew that on December twentieth Joan planned to stay overnight at Courtney Holt's home. I knew Daniel would be alone. I made the drive north and arrived at Joan and Daniel's home at about eight-thirty in the evening.

"It was I who summoned Treebeard to the house. It was I who wrote the letter that I gather you have now found. It was I who posted the letter at Treebeard's campsite, and stole an arrow from the quiver he left there. I knew I could not carry a bow in and out of the house, for the risk of being seen with it, so I used one I gave Joan years ago and hid it where I believed it would not be discovered."

It all made a sort of crazy sense. Joan might well have been telling the truth when she said she went back to her home that night to see if Daniel was having an assignation with Molly Bracewell. Then another thought occurred to Alicia. *Could Joan be as much a perpetrator of this crime as her mother was? Were mother and daughter in league together?*

Libby Hudson turned her head as if to gaze out the dirt-streaked windows. "I've always been athletically inclined, from when I was a young girl. Horseback riding, tennis, golf, sailing. Diving, a bit. But my greatest passion was archery." Her eyes took on a faraway gleam. "It's a magnificent sport," she murmured, almost as if to herself. "Such artistry. Such beauty and grace."

Alicia had the fleeting thought that Libby Hudson no longer was speaking of archery but of the murder of her son-in-law. For there had been a gruesome beauty to that as well. The perpetrator very nearly had escaped justice. She had left almost no trace of evidence and betrayed no guilt. Perhaps because she had felt none.

Even now she was getting what she most wanted. Her daughter was safe. Ironically, it might have been the perfect crime were it not for the very person Libby Storrow Hudson had committed it to protect.

For it is Joan who lacks character, Alicia thought, *Joan who both benefits from this extraordinary sacrifice and is undeserving of it. And who most likely will never fully grasp its extent.*

EPILOGUE

Three days after Libby Hudson's confession, Alicia woke at dawn, drove two hours to San Francisco Airport, left the VW in an economy parking lot, and boarded the third transcontinental flight of her life. She disembarked at Dulles International Airport and took an express train to Washington, D.C. Without pausing at any of the city's tourist attractions, all of which she longed to see, she splurged on a cab that delivered her and her battered Samsonite directly to the redbrick town house owned by Milo Pappas.

It was shortly after seven in the evening, dark and cold, with snowflakes blowing. Some collected on the street lamps that threw golden bowls of light on the browned lawns of a winter city. Some dusted the peaked roofs of the stately homes and embassies that lined Milo's street. And some settled on Alicia's hair and eyelashes as she stood at Milo's door and wondered whether, after coming all this way and spending all this money she didn't have, she should ring his bell.

Ring it. Because if you don't it'll be the biggest mistake of your life.

She had a way of blowing opportunities, she knew. Her failures plagued her even more than her successes buoyed her. What a failure it would be to let Milo Pappas get away. And for what? Pride?

Her hand reached out and rang his bell.

It didn't take him long to answer. When he did, he stood

in his foyer simply staring at her, amazement lighting his eyes and causing an uncharacteristic lapse in his manners.

"May I come in?" she asked.

"Of course! I'm sorry." He stepped aside quickly, then reached out his unbroken arm to hoist her luggage over the threshold into his entryway.

Once inside, she felt very awkward. "I'm sorry I didn't call first."

He scoffed at that. "You don't need to call first, Alicia." Somehow it made her feel better to hear him say her name. "Let me take your coat," he offered then, and that made her feel better still. Maybe he wouldn't try to get rid of her quickly.

He led her down a few stairs into a living room. It had art on the walls, towering ceilings, and a brick fireplace in which a log fire blazed. It looked like something that would show up in a decorating magazine.

From the indentation in a sofa, and the glass of red wine next to an open paperback, she could guess what he'd been doing when she showed up unannounced at his door. Maybe he didn't have plans for the evening? Or maybe they were late plans? It was hard for her to imagine how Milo might fill his hours, but reading alone in front of a fire was what she could see herself doing, not him.

He invited her to sit, and offered her wine. He returned and handed a glass to her with a smile. "It's no Opus One."

She sipped. "It's delicious, though." To her it didn't taste all that different from Opus One. She wouldn't confess that just yet.

He sat across from her and took his own wineglass in his hands. In the fire a log broke, then crackled in a cloud of sparks. "How'd you find me?"

"I have friends who are investigators."

"Ah." He smiled. "Louella has access to some kind of database."

Louella was heavily in favor of Alicia making this trip. Though there was no reason for it, clearly Louella felt guilty for planning to pounce on Jorge as soon as a decent interval passed. The last Alicia had spoken to her, the interval had shrunk from three weeks to five days.

"You've been watching the news?" Alicia asked, then instantly felt a pang at the question's stupidity.

Milo simply shook his head. "Libby Hudson's confession? I'm astonished by it."

"It makes sense, though."

"I always had trouble believing Joan could pull something like this off."

"But I believe her mother could." She paused. "I'm embarrassed I didn't suspect her earlier. Once I knew about Daniel's control of the living trust, and that he had bought Web Hudson's stake in Headwaters, it should have occurred to me. I was just so focused on Joan." Again she hesitated. "Once I get an idea in my head, sometimes I can't see past it."

He met her eyes, saying nothing. It was time. This was what she had flown across the country for.

"I did that to you, too, Milo. I'm really sorry. You were right. Somehow I always expected the worst of you. It was totally unfair of me and I really regret it. I'm sorry."

He nodded, then swirled the wine in his glass and watched it as if with fascination. "I've got something to do with how people judge me, Alicia. Don't worry about it." He raised his eyes, and she was startled to see sadness there, and a sort of wisdom. "But I accept your apology, and I appreciate it."

They fell silent. Then he smiled, and she caught a glimpse of the jaunty Milo she was used to. "So I guess this means you'll get your old job back?"

His tone was light, but she had the idea this wasn't a casual question. "I will. And I've been getting calls from people in my party wanting me to run against Penrose for D.A."

Milo's brows rose. "This November? Are you going to do it?"

"I'm thinking about it." She paused. "Actually, I'm pretty ready to do it."

"Will you do me a favor?"

She was curious. "What?"

"Will you call Molly Bracewell and ask for advice?"

"Oh ..." She didn't like that idea. "She's such a slick one, I don't know ...."

"Alicia." Milo raised his index finger in the air. "Does she win or not?"

There was only one answer to that question. Alicia was silent.

"Then talk to her. She'll put you in touch with people who can help you."

"You're telling me to play the game."

"Do you want to win this time?"

She'd better. It was her third try. It was really now or never. Milo leaned back as if satisfied. "What about you?" she asked. Another noncasual question.

He didn't quite smile, but almost. "My agent's getting some calls."

"Really?"

"Don't sound so surprised."

"I'm not surprised! Calls from whom?"

"Well, one is a correspondent position with ABC. Back in London, where I started in TV. Not a prime-time magazine, though. Loads of travel. And far from the brass in New York, which isn't a good thing."

He didn't seem to like that one. Somehow that pleased her. "What about the others?"

"One's a local anchor job, here in D.C." He shrugged. "I'm not so sure I want to go local, though. I've never done it, so maybe I'd like it. I just don't know."

"Are there any more?"

"There's one more." Again he stared into his wineglass. She got the funny feeling he was avoiding her eyes. "This one's in LA, with Fox. They're launching a new prime-time magazine this summer." He paused. "I'd be the anchor and also do stories."

She liked the sound of that one. "Wouldn't that be good? It's national and you'd be the anchor?"

"True," he allowed. "But it's a little less prestigious than *Newsline*."

"But it's in the US," she pointed out.

He smiled at her, and there was the old Milo glint in his eye. "Actually, it's in California."

"Yeah, I think you mentioned that." But she couldn't help smiling back.

Then he left his place across from her and came to sit at her side. They looked at each other. "Hi," he said.

"Hi."

He raised his hand and brushed her cheek. Lightly, so lightly. She closed her eyes. His touch lingered, the way she remembered, the way that tied a knot in her heart that somehow hurt so good.

Then his doorbell rang. Alicia's eyes fluttered open. She tried hard not to feel a crashing disappointment. *Was this a friend coming over? A date, maybe?*

"Hold on." Milo rose and headed for the door. "I'll be right back."

She waited, trying to make out what was going on. Then Milo came back bearing red plastic bags clearly loaded with takeout. He raised them in the air. "You like Chinese?"

Her heart soared, like a kite released in a happy wind. "I love it."

He walked out of the room, she guessed into a kitchen. "I always order more than I can eat. Come help." Then he appeared again, bereft of the takeout. "But not until you move that suitcase of yours into my bedroom. I've got a broken arm, you know."

She smiled. Maybe the bad part was over. Maybe they could be comfortable again. Maybe they could be more than comfortable.

He disappeared back into the kitchen, calling over his shoulder. "Would you mind watching *Newsline* later? It's on tonight."

She set down her wineglass and rose from the couch. "Is it any good?"

"Not as good as it used to be." He paused, and when he spoke again his voice had a different note in it, a hopeful note she recognized in her own heart. "Though I think a lot of things are changing for the better."

She walked toward his voice, smiling. Imagine that. For once she agreed with him.

Diana loves to hear from readers! E-mail her at ***www.DianaDempsey.com*** *and sign up for her mailing list while you're there to hear first about her new releases. Join her on* **Facebook** *at* **Diana Dempsey Books** *and follow her on* **Twitter** *at* **Diana_Dempsey**.

Acknowledgments

Writing *To Catch the Moon* allowed me to live vicariously on the gorgeous Monterey Peninsula. It also introduced me to an arena I previously knew little about: criminal prosecution and the inside workings of a district attorney's office. Two women proved fantastic guides: Monterey County Deputy District Attorney Ann Hill and Los Angeles County Deputy District Attorney Marlene Sanchez. Both were tremendously generous with their time and expertise, and I thank them.

I am grateful also to Audrey LaFehr, Jen Jahner, Francesca Farr, Martha Caskey, Ann Shannon, Dr. Paul Robiolio, Aixa Martinez, Christina Papoulias Barton, Mona ElNaggar, Donna Edmondson, Yu-Jin Kim, Burt Levitch, and Robert Scott.

I run out of superlatives when it comes to my critique partners: Bill Fuller, Tracie Donnell, Danielle Girard, Sarah Manyika, and Ciji Ware.

Rhonda Freshwater of Freshwater Design again delivered terrific cover art, and I thank her.

Writer though I may be, I lack the words to thank my husband, Jed. He is excellent in his editorial advice, tireless in his encouragement, and unstinting in his praise. Not only that, he's willing to fetch nightly takeout when I get close to deadline. This book is for you, Jed, though it's paltry reward.

Diana Dempsey traded in an Emmy-winning career in TV news to write fast, fun romantic fiction. Her debut novel, *Falling Star*, was nominated for a RITA award for Best First Book by the members of Romance Writers of America. Other of her novels have been Top Picks of *Romantic Times* or selections of the Doubleday Book Club.

In her dozen years in television news, the former Diana Koricke played every on-air role from network correspondent to local news anchor. She reported for NBC News from New York, Tokyo, and Burbank, and substitute anchored such broadcasts as *Sunrise*, *Today*, and *NBC Nightly News*. In addition, she was a morning anchor for KTTV 11 Fox News in Los Angeles. She started her broadcast career with the Financial News Network.

Born and raised in Buffalo, New York—Go, Bills!—Diana is a graduate of Harvard University and the winner of a Rotary International Foundation Scholarship. She enjoyed stints overseas in Belgium, the U.K., and Japan, and now resides in Los Angeles with her husband and a West Highland White Terrier, not necessarily in that order.

Diana loves to hear from readers. Visit **www.DianaDempsey.com** to email Diana and sign up to her mailing list to hear first about her new releases. Also join her on **Facebook** at **Diana Dempsey Books** and follow her on **Twitter** at **Diana_Dempsey**.

TOO CLOSE TO THE SUN

A once-in-a-lifetime romance that blossoms beneath Napa Valley's sizzling sun ...

Winemaker Gabby DeLuca is back from Italy, nursing a broken heart and doing her best to create wonderful vintages she can be proud of. Then hotshot financier Will Henley appears on the scene, prowling for an acquisition. Will could be big trouble—for Gabby's heart as well as her winery. Or his ingenious proposition might just prove to be the best deal of both their lives ...

"This is one of those books that you don't want to put down."
Romantic Times

Chapter One

Gabriella DeLuca stood alone at dawn among the grapevines. To her east, beyond a stand of towering oak and eucalyptus, the sun poked above Napa's Howell Mountains, struggling to banish the fog that on this June morning hung heavy on the valley floor. Within hours the sun would win the battle, bathing the earth in hot light and pushing the grapes, olives, and walnuts toward harvest.

She stared at the small blaze she'd carefully set beside the steepest hillside vineyard owned by her employer, Suncrest Vineyards. In one hand she clutched a photo, in the other a bouquet of long-stemmed red roses Vittorio had given her, in another country, in another life. The roses were dry now with age, and brittle to the touch. Without allowing herself another thought—for already she had given this thought enough—she tossed the desiccated blooms into the fire.

Whoosh! The flames shot high into the air as they greedily consumed their prize. Gabby watched the last petals fall into ash.

"Vittorio Mantucci," she whispered, "*arrivederci* ..." She closed her eyes, mentally saying good-bye to the only man she had ever loved. Whom she'd also lost, unfortunately, meaning she had a grim record of oh-for-one in the *amore* department. But this morning—one year to the day after Vittorio had pulled the heart out of her chest and stomped on it with his Gucci loafer—wasn't about heartache or fury or regret. The last 364 had been about those. This morning was about ending it, for now and forever.

Gabby lowered her gaze to the glossy five-by-seven Kodachrome in her left hand. It showed her and the former love of her life in brilliant Chianti sunshine, grinning idiotically, him dark and gorgeous, her blond and unbelievably happy, vineyards and olive trees and promise all around them.

She remembered that day clearly. They had had a picnic. They had sparred over the relative merits of Tuscany versus Lombardy, never agreeing whether his family province won out over her ancestral home. They had made hasty but wonderful love on a gingham blanket, then thrown on their clothes so Vittorio could snap a photo, setting his self-timed camera on a tree stump before scampering back toward her to get in place on time.

It took great force of will for Gabby to toss the photo on the conflagration. But toss it she did—then she watched it disappear, edges first, till finally Vittorio's face caved in on itself and melted away. She stared at the space where it had been for some time, then threw in a whole packet of photos. Those took longer to be annihilated but eventually they were. That seemed to prove something.

"How's that for an Italian exorcism?" she murmured, then had to laugh, choking on her tears, both regretting the past and not regretting it, wondering if ever again she could think the name Vittorio Mantucci without a fresh gash in her heart.

So she'd traded Italy's wine country for California's. Tuscany for Napa Valley. Not such a bad deal, really. It was home, she loved it, her whole family was nearby. What did she have to complain about? And she'd traded Vittorio for— who? *Someone wonderful*, she told herself. Someone American like her, who she'd understand through and through. Someone who'd stick by her even if everybody in his family howled objections.

Or—and this poked a hole rather quickly in her romantic bravado—maybe she'd traded Vittorio for nobody.

Oh, and don't forget. She hadn't traded Vittorio. He'd traded *her*.

Gabby flopped down onto the vineyard dirt and eyed what remained of her exorcism stash. All of it reminded her in one way or another of her three years interning for the Mantucci family winery. There was the one-pound box of fettuccine, Vittorio's most admired noodle, and a box of wine. Yes, a box of wine, because Gabby knew there was no greater insult to her former lover's memory than wine so cheap it was packaged like fruit punch.

She was just feeding a fistful of fettuccine into the fire when she heard a shocked male voice call out behind her.

"Gabby, what in God's name are you doing?"

It was Felix Rodriguez. He walked toward her, a heavyset mustachioed man who'd been vineyard manager at Suncrest as long as her father had been winemaker, meaning ever since Gabby was five years old. Like her, Felix wore jeans and work boots. Unlike her, he sported a helmet similar to the kind coal miners wear, with a sort of flashlight mounted on the forehead. Perfect for keeping one's hands free while traipsing around vineyards. To put out rogue fires, for example.

"It's not in God's name, Felix," Gabby told him. "It's in Vittorio Mantucci's."

Felix's eyes flew open at the accursed name, which all DeLucas, and Felix by extension, were banned from uttering. Then he looked at her stash, and his eyes widened further. "You're barbecuing spaghetti?"

"It's pasta, Felix, pasta. And I'm not barbecuing it. I'm just burning it." She sighed. This was a hard ritual to explain.

No doubt Felix would lump in this lunacy with her other

inexplicable behavior. Like renting a house far up-valley and a difficult half-mile drive up an unlit, unpaved road. It screamed isolation, and she knew what everybody thought about that. *She wants to be alone because of that Italian boy who broke her heart.* The heads shook; the tongues clucked. Sometimes it seemed that the old families like hers majored in grapes and minored in gossip. *She should have known he'd marry one of his own.*

She sort of had known, but had ignored it. And she rented the house not only because nobody lived nearby but also because it allowed her to live right next to vineyards. Which unlike Italian lovers had a certain predictable, soothing rhythm to them.

Felix harrumphed. "You shouldn't have come in so early today. You should be home sleeping so you're not tired for Mrs. Winsted's party tonight."

"God, Felix, don't remind me." She tossed in the rest of the fettuccine, box and all. "Why anyone would celebrate Max Winsted coming back to Napa Valley is beyond me."

"She's his mother."

"All I can say is, Ava Winsted proves that a mother's love is blind." It wasn't often that Mrs. W drove Gabby crazy, but she was doing so now. Hand over Suncrest to that nincompoop son of hers? "What is she thinking, Felix? He's going to kill this place. He's going to come in here and run it in whatever asinine way he wants to and he's going to kill it."

Felix wouldn't respond to that. He would keep his mouth shut and his head down and not risk his job, which was probably what Gabby should do, too.

She shook her head. That was the problem with working for a family-owned winery. If the family ran out of sensible people to run the place, the winery got screwed. And all the employees along with it.

"Maybe Max learned something in France," Felix offered.

"All Max Winsted learned in France is how to say *'Voulez-vous coucher avec moi ce soir?'* in three different levels of politeness," she shot back. But Felix didn't seem to get the reference.

Gabby poked a stick at her fire. It was all so frustrating. And scary. She'd come back to California to pick up the threads of her life, grow into the winemaker she knew she could be, maybe even recover enough to love again. After losing Vittorio, all she wanted was the bulwark stability of her family and of Suncrest, both steady, unchanging, the Rocks of Gibraltar of her emotional landscape. The DeLucas were fine, thank God, but the winery? With Max Winsted taking over, all bets were off.

She'd known him since she was five years old and he was a newborn, and pretty much from the day he was out of diapers he was a jerk. He got more smug and self-satisfied every year. And the biggest irony of all was that even though he was born to Suncrest and the employees only worked there, sometimes she wondered if he loved it as much as they did.

He sure didn't act like it.

Gabby felt Felix's eyes on her, and she forced a smile. "I'm sorry, Felix, I shouldn't be so negative." She knew she shouldn't, since as assistant winemaker she was fairly high up the management ranks and should be rallying the other employees around their new boss. "It's just hard for me to imagine working for that . . . buffoon."

He stifled a smile, then his face turned somber. "I know you love this place, Gabby."

She stared at him. "You do, too, Felix."

He sighed, his eyes skidding to the fire. "We all do."

A wind came through, riffling the flames. Gabby

shivered, half wishing the sun would halt its rise, the day would never dawn, the homecoming party would never happen. But she'd learned the hard way that wishing didn't always make things so.

***

Will Henley Jr. was proud of himself. He'd positively blasted through his morning ritual. Once the alarm at his San Francisco bedside blared at the usual 4:30 AM, he did a killer half hour on the rowing machine—a holdover from his years as stroke for Dartmouth's lightweight crew—then noted the workout's intensity and duration on a chart. He scarfed a few bowls of whole-grain cereal, showered, shaved, and selected a pin-striped suit and lightly starched French-cuff dress shirt from his custom collection. Then he sped his silver BMW Z8 the two fog-bound miles from his Pacific Heights Victorian to his corner office in a refurbished redbrick warehouse on the Embarcadero.

That put him at his mahogany desk at 5:45 AM, a ball-busting early arrival even by the type A standards of Will's employer, the private-equity firm General Pacific Group, known among the business and financial cognoscenti as GPG.

Will settled in to sip the low-fat latte he'd had sent over from the building's dining room. Strewn across his desk and file cabinets and handcrafted bookshelves were dozens of Lucite cubes, each representing a GPG deal he'd helped transact. On the north wall hung a flat-panel screen flashing real-time stock quotes from Europe and the closing numbers from Asia. Wall Street wouldn't begin trading for nearly another hour.

But Will's first task that morning had nothing to do with financial markets or private-equity transactions. He lifted his phone and punched in a Denver number he knew by heart. And even though a voice-mail announcement came on saying Rocky Mountain Flowers wasn't yet open for business, Will began speaking at the tone.

"Hey, Benny, pick up." He waited a beat. "Pick up, Benny. I know you're there. It's Will Henley in San—"

"Hello." The voice was slightly out of breath.

"Hey! Thanks, guy. Did I catch you sweeping?"

"First thing every a.m."

"Sorry to interrupt."

"No problem." Benny clattered around a bit. "So what is it this time, Will? Anniversary? Birthday?"

"Birthday. Beth's."

"Roses or tulips? Or I could do some sort of combo for you—"

"Do a combo." Will squinted, thinking. "Pink and yellow—she'd like that. And send it to the office, not the house."

Benny laughed. "So everybody can ooh and aah over it. The usual message?"

"Please." Will smiled. It was a good message. It made her happy every year.

"You got it, sir."

"Put 'em in a vase rather than a box, please, Benny, and try to deliver them early in the day, okay?" Will glanced up to see Simon LaRue, one of GPG's general partners and hence a truly big dog, hovering at his door. He waved him in. "Very good," he said into the phone. "Thanks, my man."

Will hung up while LaRue halted in front of his desk, six feet two inches of perfectly groomed American male in a three-thousand-dollar handmade suit. Simon LaRue might be dark-haired, but he was a golden boy, just like Will, just like all the partners at GPG.

He arched a brow. "Sending some lucky lady flowers, Henley? Anybody we should know about?"

Will laughed and tried to look enigmatic. Given his perennial bachelor status, which at age thirty-four was rapidly becoming a point of fascination not only within his family but also among his conservative colleagues, he didn't want to admit the bouquet was for his sister.

Nor did he want to admit, even to himself, one tiny part of his motivation for the gift-giving. It was residual guilt, even after all these years, for leaving Beth in Denver to run Henley Sand and Gravel while he traipsed off to chase his dreams. As the elder child and only male, custom demanded that he follow his father at the helm of the family business. But Will had wanted a bigger stage. And by God, had he gotten it.

LaRue smiled. "Ah, those were the days. Bachelorhood with all its infinite pleasures and variety." His slim, manicured fingers lifted a Lucite cube from Will's desk. "So you gonna make lots of money for us in Napa Valley?"

Will settled back in his chair and linked his hands behind his head in a deliberate gesture of confidence, though that was hardly what he felt in this regard. "Don't I always?"

"There's no such thing as always." LaRue toyed with the cube, has dark eyes focused on it as if mesmerized. "There's only your last deal."

That was one of the machismo-laden truisms GPG partners bandied about. There were others, even less clever, all of which basically boiled down to *What have you done for me lately?*

Will laughed again. "Hey, my last deal made us ten times our money!"

"And is still in business. These days that's a stunning success. But from you we'd expect no less." LaRue replaced the cube, next fingering a framed photo of Beth, posed in

Aspen alongside her husband and twin sons and an assortment of skis and poles. All four sported matching sweaters, Will's own Scandinavian coloring, and the goggle-eyed sunburn produced by a Rocky Mountain ski vacation. LaRue's brow arched. "You ever heli-skied, Henley?"

That was the sort of testosterone-driven extreme sport of which LaRue—and all right-minded GPG partners—would approve. "Do you mean was I ever dropped from a chopper in a remote location to ski solo down a kick-ass pristine mountain with no one around to save me if I screw up?"

LaRue nodded.

"Nope. But it sounds like good old-fashioned fun."

LaRue laughed out loud this time, the desired response. He set down the photo, focused briefly on its mate—a fortieth-anniversary shot of Will's parents—then sauntered back toward Will's door. "Give my regards to the lovely Ava," he threw over his shoulder, and then he walked out.

Will sighed and unlinked his hands, then leaned forward to rest his elbows on his desk and sip his cooling latte. The last thing Ava Winsted wanted from Will Henley—or from anybody else at GPG—was regards. She'd much rather the entire firm disappear from her life and that Will Henley in particular stop making offers to buy her winery. She'd told him no, and apparently she'd meant it.

But that didn't mean Will Henley would give up. He hadn't gotten where he was by caving.

He grimaced, imagining the look on Ava Winsted's Hollywood-perfect features when he crashed her son's homecoming party. Not crash, *exactly*—he had finagled his way in as an invitee's date—but barging in where he wasn't wanted was not among Will's favorite activities.

Still, he had to go. As far as he could make out, Suncrest was his key to making money in Napa Valley. And he had to make as much money as possible to satisfy GPG's general partners and investors, whose lust for huge returns was unquenchable.

Will drained the last of his latte. Yup, he'd gotten that bigger stage, all right.

***

Ever the actress, Ava Winsted forced herself to laugh—to sound positively gay—as she turned from the French doors in her casually elegant, light-filled living room to face Jean-Luc Boursault, the Paris-based screenwriter she hoped would pen a new, post-Suncrest chapter for her already storied life.

"I'm just thrilled to see Max take over," she lied. "He learned so much in France, he'll bring an entirely new perspective to Suncrest. Who knows? He might even end up a better vintner than his father."

Ava watched Jean-Luc decide—wisely, she thought—not to challenge that fantastic pronouncement. From his perch on a cheerful blue-and-yellow Cottage Victorian armchair, he merely took another sip of his Suncrest sauvignon blanc, which Ava considered a delightful late-morning libation. Slight of build, with thick graying hair and eyebrows that threatened to run one into the other, Jean-Luc looked bohemian, affluent, and intellectual, much as he had when she'd met him fifteen years before. "Porter Winsted," he offered mildly, "is a difficult act to follow."

Who knew that better than Ava? Her late husband had been a man among men, the scion of a Newport, Rhode Island, family who'd built two stunning careers—in commercial real estate and winemaking—yet remained to the end hardworking, self-effacing, and kindhearted.

Ava's eyes misted. She turned her back on Jean-Luc to

gaze out the French doors, the familiar panorama of vineyards and olive and eucalyptus trees blurring into indistinct masses of green and gold under the valley's unremitting midday sun.

She felt Jean-Luc's hand soft on the small of her back. "You miss him still."

Still. Two years only he'd been gone. Two years already he'd been gone. Sometimes when she awoke, Ava forgot Porter was dead, and reached out across the cold, cold sheets only to remember. The stab of pain that followed was astonishingly raw, every time. But it happened less and less often now, which in its own way saddened her. She was growing used to him being gone.

"I will always miss him," she told Jean-Luc. *But I'm only fifty-five and I still feel alive, most days anyway.* She turned her head to meet her friend's eyes. They crinkled with a smile, and she was reminded again that Jean-Luc was in love with her, and had been for some time, and would wait however long it took for her to be ready for him.

Which might not be that long anymore.

"Will you miss running the winery when Max takes over?" he asked her.

At that, Ava had to laugh, but didn't have to lie. "Not in the least. You know me, Jean-Luc. I am many things, but a businesswoman is not among them." She turned from the view to wipe nonexistent dust from a round glass-topped table crowded with art books and photo frames. "I had to run Suncrest after Porter died. And I think I managed it reasonably well."

"Better than that, Ava."

She shook her head. "My heart was never really in it, not the way Porter's was." She cast her mind back to those long-ago years when she'd resented Porter's passion for Suncrest.

Perhaps *obsession* was a better word. No woman could be as demanding a mistress as a fledgling winery, and it had caused their young marriage real distress. But they had emerged intact, and the winery prospered beyond anything they'd imagined. "Porter loved Suncrest, Jean-Luc. It is his legacy."

But it is not mine. Hers was as an actress.

Hollywood would have no room for her, Ava knew. She might have assiduously protected her blond, Breck-girl looks, and no one could deny that she had some impressive credits to her name, but she was still a fifty-something has-been. Fortunately Europe was more willing to embrace women *d'un certain age* who still knew how to light up a screen. Screenwriters like Jean-Luc Boursault even wrote parts for them.

Ava's mouth pursed in wry humor. Imagine that.

Jean-Luc returned to his armchair, his wineglass refreshed. "And you are certain Max can manage as well as you?"

"Oh, of course." On went Ava's megawatt smile, for even with a friend as dear as Jean-Luc she felt compelled to maintain the fiction that she had complete confidence in her son. What she'd learned in Hollywood was equally true in Napa Valley: Image was everything. She would not derail what chance of success Max had by appearing to doubt him from the start. "He grew up in the wine business. And now he's had this apprenticeship in France. He's far more knowledgeable than I ever was."

And far more reckless. And far less disciplined. And so stunningly oblivious of his own limitations.

Ava sipped from her wineglass, thinking back to those painful weeks before Max had decamped to France. The whole episode was so unseemly and embarrassing and she hated even to think of it. Such a classic tale: a young lady, the daughter of a small Sonoma vintner, who, the morning after, regretted what she had done. Started to think it hadn't been her choice at all. Ugly accusations flew from her father, and veiled threats, and Ava hastily cobbled together a face-saving solution. She wrote a massive check to charity in the family's name and packed Max off to the Haut-Medoc, claiming a long-planned apprenticeship.

She shut her eyes. Why was there so little of the father in the son? Where was Porter's caution, his thoughtfulness, his good sense? True, Max had many natural gifts. He was intelligent and nice-looking and didn't lack for confidence or charm. But there was a wildness to him that frightened Ava and made her worry for the future.

And now of course there was the problem of Suncrest. She knew that the most prudent course would be for her to continue to run the winery. Yet, though it made her feel horribly guilty to admit it, she was done with it—*done*. She'd had enough of marketing strategies and distribution agreements and P&L statements. She could play the vintner no longer. It was a role she was handed against her will and she'd hated it from the moment she walked onstage.

Of course, the other option was to sell it to Will Henley and GPG. Suncrest would survive if she did, though probably not in a form of which Porter would have approved. Those buyout firms changed businesses—she was a savvy enough businesswoman to understand that. But sometimes it was hard to believe Suncrest would fare any better in Max's hands.

Ava abruptly set down her glass. "Shall we have lunch?" she asked, and swept toward the sun-drenched terrace beyond the French doors without waiting for Jean-Luc's answer. "I've asked Mrs. Finchley to lay a table for us in the pergola."

Jean-Luc looked confused. "Didn't Max's flight land two hours ago? Shouldn't we wait for him to get here to eat?"

"Oh no, let's not." Ava knew her son well enough to know it was unwise to wait for him for anything.

***

Ninety miles south of his mother's intimate lunch with Jean-Luc Boursault, Maximilian Winsted was doing some entertaining of his own. He stood at the foot of a San Francisco Airport Marriott queen-size bed, puffing on a Gauloises cigarette and eyeing Ariane, Air France flight attendant, First Class. Her bodacious Parisian self was draped across the bed, the top half of her uniform strewn all over the industrial-strength blue carpet alongside her bra and pumps and pantyhose. She was giggling so much, she kept spilling her champagne on her breasts, where it ran across her nipples and only made her laugh harder. At this rate, Max didn't think it'd be a huge challenge getting off the bottom half of her uniform, too.

Vive la France!

He chuckled, took a last gulp of his own bubbly and stubbed out his cigarette. Bet Rory never got a stewardess into bed, or Bucky either, that tool. They didn't have anywhere near his charm. Sure, he'd had to spend most of the ten-hour flight from Paris standing at the rear of the cabin flirting and telling stories, but now he was going to get his reward: Ariane's full roster of private First Class favors.

I can still top them, he told himself. So what if Rory was graduating from Yale Law and Bucky was in med school? Max Winsted was still the biggest stud from Napa High, class of '97, and he was about to get even bigger.

"Viens!" The arm holding the champagne glass motioned

him to come closer. Her bright red lipsticked mouth smiled, her big dark eyes teased. *"Viens jouer, Max!"*

"Let me just shut the drapes." After eighteen months of French food and French pastries and French wine, Max suspected he'd look better in the dark.

Since his shirt was already off, he sucked in his stomach before he walked to the windows, double-thick to keep out the roar of the 101 freeway six stories below. He was surprised to see how much traffic there was even at noon. He had plenty of time, though, since the party didn't start till seven and from here the drive home took only an hour and a half.

Besides, he'd get there when he got there. The party was more for his mother than for him, anyway. The important business started the next day, when he got down to running Suncrest.

He tugged on the drape cord to shut out the view. "Your winery is how big?" Ariane was behind him all of a sudden, pushing her boobs into his back and reaching around his belly.

"Big." Max turned to face her. "More than a hundred thousand cases a year." At least that would be true once he was in charge.

Ariane grabbed him lower, holding his gaze. Her eyes sparkled. *"C'est très, très grand."*

He harrumphed. "No kidding."

"You're very rich?" She pronounced it *reech* but he got the point.

"Très," he told her. *And just wait to see how much richer I'll be this time next year.*

Oh, he had plans. Big plans. Suncrest would really be on the map once Max Winsted was at the helm. No more treading water like it had been under his mother's management. Of course, what else could you expect from her? She didn't have a practical bone in her body. And while his father had been an excellent businessman in his day, he'd been old-school. Too cautious. Too plodding.

"What types of wine"—Ariane was kissing his neck now, her left hand still working its magic south of the equator—"do you make?"

"You know what?" He wasn't interested in wine talk at the moment. "Let's go over there."

He pushed her back toward the bed, where she didn't need one single *s'il vous plaît, mademoiselle* to whip off her skirt and lean back giggling against the pillows, five feet six inches of living, breathing, willing French female. Who, thanks to Max Winsted, was about to have the best time of her entire life.

Made in the USA
Las Vegas, NV
14 May 2021